Series by Julie Johnstone

Scottish Medieval Romance Books:

Highlanders Through Time Series
Sinful Scot, Book 1
Sexy Scot, Book 2
Seductive Scot, Book 3
Scandalous Scot, Book 4

Highlander Vows: Entangled Hearts Series
When a Laird Loves a Lady, Book 1
Wicked Highland Wishes, Book 2
Christmas in the Scot's Arms, Book 3
When a Highlander Loses His Heart, Book 4
How a Scot Surrenders to a Lady, Book 5
When a Warrior Woos a Lass, Book 6
When a Scot Gives His Heart, Book 7
When a Highlander Weds a Hellion, Book 8
How to Heal a Highland Heart, Book 9
The Heart of a Highlander, Book 10

Renegade Scots Series
Outlaw King, Book 1
Highland Defender, Book 2
Highland Avenger, Book 3

Regency Romance Books:

A Whisper of Scandal Series
Bargaining with a Rake, Book 1
Conspiring with a Rogue, Book 2
Dancing with a Devil, Book 3

After Forever, Book 4
The Dangerous Duke of Dinnisfree, Book 5

A Once Upon A Rogue Series
My Fair Duchess, Book 1
My Seductive Innocent, Book 2
My Enchanting Hoyden, Book 3
My Daring Duchess, Book 4

Lords of Deception Series
What a Rogue Wants, Book 1

Danby Regency Christmas Novellas
The Redemption of a Dissolute Earl, Book 1
Season For Surrender, Book 2
It's in the Duke's Kiss, Book 3

Regency Anthologies
A Summons from the Duke of Danby (Regency Christmas
Summons, Book 2)
Thwarting the Duke (When the Duke Comes to Town, Book 2)

Regency Romance Box Sets
A Very Regency Christmas
Three Wicked Rogues

Paranormal Books:

The Siren Saga
Echoes in the Silence, Book 1

What a Rogue Wants

Lords of Deception, Book One

by
Julie Johnstone

What a Rogue Wants
Copyright © 2013 Julie Johnstone
Cover Design by Heather Boyd
Editing by Sandra Sookoo
Proofreading by Jennifer Barker

The best way to stay in touch is to subscribe to my newsletter. Go to www.juliejohnstoneauthor.com and subscribe in the box at the top of the page that says Newsletter. If you don't hear from me once a month, please check your spam filter and set up your email to allow my messages through to you so you don't miss the opportunity to win great prizes or hear about appearances.

Dedication

For my father who has been my loyalist and most support-ive fan from the start. I love you.

For my critique partners Samantha Grace and Aileen Fish. Words cannot express how thankful I am to have such wonderful critique partners and friends like the two of you. Thank you for all your many readings and all the support you both have always shown me.

For my editor Sandra Sookoo who showed me how to really work a scene and helped me to dig deeper into my characters to make this a better book.

~Julie

If you're interested in when my books go on sale, or want to be one of the first to know about my new releases, please follow me on BookBub! You'll get quick book notifications every time there's a new pre-order, book on sale, or new release with an easy click of your mouse to follow me. You can follow me on BookBub here:

www.bookbub.com/authors/julie-johnstone

One

London, England
1804

*L*ord Grey Adlard entered White's gentlemen's club, intent on one purpose—to find and wring the neck of Gravenhurst, his former best friend as of roughly twenty minutes ago. Before Grey got two steps into the entrance-way, Henry, White's stuffiest and Grey's favorite footman, appeared.

"Milord, may I take your hat and coat?" As usual, Henry's droopy eyelids made it hard to gauge his reaction, but Grey bet his soggy state shocked the proper footman. Hell, it shocked *him*, and he was far from proper.

He held out his dripping coat and hat, trying to ignore the water pattering against the floor from his garments. He looked like a damn fool. At Henry's annoyed inhalation, Grey narrowed his eyes, daring Henry to say a word. After being forced to traverse down a thorny rose trellis and take an unplanned midnight swim in a freezing lake to escape the sudden appearance of Lady Julia's irate father, Grey was in no mood for Henry's reproach. "Is Gravenhurst here?"

"Of course." Henry took Grey's coat with the tips of his fingers and eyed it distastefully. "Lord Grey, you are dripping on my floor."

Grey glanced at the puddle at his feet, his neck warming

in irritation. His favorite shoes were ruined, not to mention his trousers. Tiny rips covered the front of the fine, black material. Gravenhurst would pay to replace these, *if* he decided to let the man live. "Sorry, Henry. Might I have a towel?"

"You might. But first, you must promise no fisticuffs. I'd hate to have you and Lord Gravenhurst thrown out again."

Grey scanned White's for Gravenhurst. He found the man positioned diagonally from the entranceway, one blond eyebrow raised, left foot propped leisurely on his right knee, coat off, cravat loose, drink in hand, and perfectly dry. The man deserved to be dumped in the lake. "Might I have that towel before I catch my death?"

"Milord, your promise?"

Henry's brazenness made Grey smile. He preferred audacity over timidity any day. "You're impertinent." He said it to goad Henry. The man's sharp-witted responses never disappointed.

"Yes, milord."

"That's it?"

Henry's mouth twitched upward in a faint smile. "I'm afraid so, milord. We're very busy, and short-staffed."

Bollocks. There was no fun to be found anywhere tonight. "Fine. I promise no fisticuffs." He dried himself with the towel Henry handed him. When he was as dry as he could manage, he handed the towel to Henry. "I'd like to remind you that my fight with Gravenhurst was years ago."

"All I remember are the broken chairs and tables, milord."

Grey eyed Henry. "Gravenhurst and I are now far too old and wise to engage in fisticuffs inside White's." *Outside* was implied, of course.

"I agree with too old." Henry's eyebrows rose in challenge.

Entertainment at last. "You know—" Grey ran a hand through his disheveled, wet, hair. "—I'm not sure why I put up with your insolence."

"I believe, milord, it's because you know I'm right, and our verbal sparring amuses you."

"I'll never admit such a thing," Grey tossed over his shoulder as he strode away. He nodded to Lords Peter and Perkins, who gaped in return. He could count on those two dimwits to gossip all over Town about his appearance, which if nothing else, would cause his father a moment of discomfort. Grey smiled. The night wasn't a total loss after all.

He pulled out a chair and sat, his trousers smacking wetly against the wood. The candlelight from the center of the table glowed on Gravenhurst's tan skin and light hair and made him look wicked. Fitting. No telling what the man was up to now. "Do not," he said as Gravenhurst started to snicker, "laugh or say a word to me until I've had a drink or I'll rearrange your nose for you, which might be an improvement to the crooked thing."

Grey grabbed the full glass Gravenhurst put in front of him and downed the liquor. A slow warmth started in his mouth and spread to his chest, pushing away a little of the iciness clinging to his damp skin. He would need a least two more drinks to warm himself and cool his irritation, but now he could talk civilly. Setting his glass down, he leaned back and allowed himself to relax for the first time in over an hour. "Your information was incorrect."

"You don't say?" Gravenhurst replied, a smile pulling at his lips. "I thought as much when I saw you enter. So her father's back in Town?"

"He is indeed."

"Bollocks. I'm sorry, Grey."

"Think nothing of it. I almost broke my neck climbing down a rickety trellis and nearly froze to death swimming in their lake escaping, but don't hold yourself accountable for giving me incorrect information."

"Seems to me being caught by Lord Blackborn in his daughter's bedroom would've been the perfect opportunity to finally get your father's notice."

"I stopped wanting my father's notice ten years ago. I'm perfectly happy being the invisible second son of the mighty Duke of Ashdon." He ignored the inner twitch that always occurred when he lied. Someday, he'd master that reaction.

"So your constant exploits are for—?"

"Irritating him." He wasn't about to begin exploring why he acted as he did. He had an agreement with himself to never examine his actions toward his father. So far, the agreement had worked out perfectly. He raised his hand and signaled the server for another glass of whiskey. "It's a perverse but enjoyable pastime. One I'll not see ended by being snagged in marriage with a lady like Julia who beds all who take her fancy. That would irritate me, not my father."

Gravenhurst regarded Grey over the rim of his glass. "If you really want to shock and irritate your father, I have a way."

Grey leaned his elbows on the table. The sympathetic look on Gravenhurst's face bothered Grey more than his wet state. Pity, even from his best friend, made him uncomfortable. "I want nothing more than to be the exact opposite sort of man than my stick-up-the-arse father. What's this way you speak of?"

"Marie Vallendri is now living in Golden Square. I propose we go there tomorrow, you meet her and invite her to your parent's country party."

"That's brilliant." Grey slid his chair back and stood. "Father hates anyone French, and he'll despise a former rumored courtesan of Napoleon's, famous opera singer or not, dining across from him at dinner."

"You'll really do it?" Gravenhurst's face had gone pale.

Grey chuckled. He hadn't been sure, but now he was. Passing up a chance to shock Gravenhurst was out of the question. "Were you trying to call my bluff? Really Grave, you should know better. Pick me up at ten and we'll make our way to Golden Square. By dinner tomorrow night, I expect Miss Vallendri to be my newest mistress and sitting at my parents' table eating turtle soup." Never mind he didn't particularly want a new mistress. That wasn't what this was really about. "If this doesn't make my father want to secure me a commission and send me far from him, I don't know what will."

"You're sure this is wise?"

"I'm sure it's not, and that's what makes it perfect," Grey said and strode toward the door with as much dignity as he could muster over the squishing of his shoes.

Lady Madelaine Aldrige scrambled out of the hired hackney and tugged on her dearest friend Abigail Langley's hand. "Do hurry."

Madelaine nearly careened down the steps when Abigail jerked her hand away. She whirled around to face her friend. "Why'd you do that?"

The bright morning sun in her eyes made it hard to see Abigail's expression, but her frown was apparent in her tone. "Look at these people." Abby cast her voice low, though only God above knew why she bothered.

"No one can hear you, Abby." Madelaine raised her voice above the merry music drifting from Golden Square and scanned the perimeter of London's art district. Vendors lined the streets with their wares and mulled about in small clusters while laughing and joking. The sight was glorious. Ladies strolled along the paths without chaperones or companions, couples sprawled in the grassy banks on blankets with picnics and art canvases clustered around them, jugglers performed by the spouting fountains and in the distance Madelaine could swear she saw a woman shooting an arrow at a target. Her heart nearly exploded with excitement. There *was* more to life than following societal dictates! It felt grand to be right about something for once.

She rummaged in her reticule, fumbling in her impatience to find the coins she needed for the hackney driver. Once secured, she paid the man and sent him on his way before Abby changed her mind and forced them both to leave. Abby was a worrier that way. Her friend chewed on her nail, a sure sign she was having serious doubts.

Madelaine linked her arm through Abby's and led them toward the sound of a trumpet, or was that a saxophone? Who really cared? It was beautiful music filling the air. "Abby, do quit looking as if someone's going to point at us and shout 'frauds!' Artists don't give a whit about two women from Lancashire coming to explore a little." At least she didn't think they did. "We're safe here. Free to roam around and do exactly as we wish. Artists live as they want without the restrictions of Society."

"How do you know?"

"I read it in the gossip sheets, so it's at least half true."

"I suppose." Abby did not look convinced with her creased brow. "We cannot stay long. An hour at most."

Madelaine sighed. "I know." Why couldn't her one voyage into freedom and the glorious unknown be longer? "Now stop worrying. We'll be back at the townhouse long before my father. He'll never know we were anywhere but Bond Street shopping for ribbon and all the other ridiculous things girls are supposed to love."

"I do love ribbon." Abby twirled a strand of her brown, curly hair around her finger.

Madelaine patted her friend. "I know, darling. I can't for the life of me figure out why. You're so sensible in every other way. But because I love you so, I left you all my best ribbons in your room." The fact that it had been an utter relief to leave the ribbon behind didn't matter. Abby had a gift for twining ribbon in her hair while Madelaine had a knack for somehow getting it knotted in her hair. "You won't forget me, will you?" Madelaine's throat suddenly ached with emotion.

Abby clutched Madelaine's arm tighter as they strolled toward the first row of vendors. "I would never forget you, Maddie, with or without the ribbons. But next time I see you, I daresay you'll be a proper lady, likely betrothed to a handsome man you meet at Court, and you'll probably not wish to talk to the housekeeper's daughter any longer."

Since she'd never been very good at being a proper lady, Abby's prediction wasn't likely to come true. She held in a sigh. She wanted a husband, but she didn't want to pretend to be someone she wasn't to get one. Yet, she knew she was odd, and her father wanted her married, no matter the pretense she employed.

"I'd never forget you," Madelaine swore as she stopped under a pretty tree blooming with pink flowers. Perching on the ledge of the stone wall that surrounded Golden Square, she inhaled the unfamiliar sweet scent. "Let's sit for a moment and take it all in, shall we?"

Abby nodded and sat beside Madelaine. The sadness that had pressed against Madelaine's chest since her mother's death felt lighter here in the square. The lightness was short lived. Tomorrow Father would deposit her at Court where he demanded she find a proper husband to marry. Not even her usual stalling tactics had talked him out of it. "No dallying," he said. No pressure there. It was only her mother's dying wish that Father had zealously embraced. She pressed her fingertips to her throbbing temples.

Tomorrow she would be a lady-in-waiting to the queen, manipulated like a puppet by the queen's dictates. Even if by some miracle Madelaine found a man who suited her, that wanted her in return, the queen's opinion could sway any match to be denied or accepted. She prayed the queen liked her. If not, life could be intolerable. She couldn't botch it this time. She'd failed her mother in life, but she would not fail her in her death, nor would she cause her father any more pain and sorrow than she already had. Failing to find a husband, after he'd used his friendship with the king to secure her a position with the queen would mortify her father.

Somehow, she would become a proper lady, though the idea of spending the rest of her life only concerned with sketching, embroidering, and the pianoforte made her clench her teeth. Thank God she had today to do as she pleased. It might be her last ever.

"Come on." She stood and brushed her skirts off. "I want to eat sticky treats, look at scandalous art, and wander over to that group shooting arrows."

"The gypsies?" Abby's voice hitched.

"They're not going to rob us. It's broad daylight for

goodness sake."

Abby stood and shielded her eyes. "We can do as you wish for *one hour*. I won't have us coming in after your father. There'd be the devil to pay if he found out we disobeyed him." That was an understatement. "You might be leaving for Court tomorrow," Abby continued. "But I have to go back to your father's house and live as his servant. I can't afford his wrath."

"Neither can I," Madelaine muttered. The last fight she'd had with her mother was ever present in her mind. Fresh regret pierced her heart and made her rub at her chest as they walked toward the smell of gooey rolls.

"This trip has been a bloody waste," Grey growled as they made their way out of Marie Vallendri's townhome and into the bright sunshine of Golden Square. "Who am I going to shock my father with at dinner tonight since Miss Vallendri already has a lover?"

"How about that chit right there." Gravenhurst pointed toward a band of gypsies who'd set up a shooting booth.

"I said I wanted to shock my father, not give him a death fit."

Gravenhurst chuckled at Grey's side. "Look closer. See the tall, pretty brunette? From my experience women with curly hair have rousing personalities to match, and the chit may be dressed as a proper lady, but she wouldn't be in the art district if she was. She's ripe for adventure. I say go pluck her."

"I like your thinking." Grey studied the woman. "She's pretty enough but see how her mouth is puckered in disapproval. She's not here of her choosing. Likely she'd faint if I propositioned her."

"You may be right. Perhaps you should select a new mistress from Madame Landry's women."

"I think not," Grey said, distracted by the sudden shouting from the group of gypsies. As he moved across the square and closer to the group he could hear wagers being bantered back and forth between the men and women alike. The excited buzz of the crowd was like a drug. He stopped by a sleek-haired gypsy with keen black eyes who struggled to take the money shoved at him while scribbling wagers in a little book.

"What's the wager?"

The gypsy acknowledged Grey with an upward flick of his eyebrows and a sardonic smile. Grey instantly liked him. "The lady claims she can split the arrow lodged in the target over there." The man pointed to a target so far away Grey had to squint to see it.

"Impossible. Unless the lady is built like a man. Which lady?" He glanced at the women gathered around the group. A few of them were thick in arm and might be able to do it if they'd been shooting all their lives.

"There. That fair *ghel* with the sun on her head."

"The fair what with what on her head?" Grey reached into his coat and brought out a bag of coin.

"Come, I'll show you." The gypsy eyed Grey's coin and then wound through the throng of people. "You going to wager?"

Was he ever. No need to go showing his excitement and get taken advantage of. "Yes, but I'll see the lady before I decide for or against."

"And your friend?"

Gravenhurst shook his head. "I'll keep my funds in my pocket where they belong."

Leave it to Gravenhurst to try to spoil the fun. Nothing could spoil this novelty though. Grey shrugged. "Sorry—?"

"Romany." The gypsy stuck out his hand. Grey shook the man's hand with enthusiasm. His wasted trip was just about to become profitable and entertaining. Toward the inner circle the man stopped behind a woman whose waves of flaxen hair tumbled invitingly down her back and marked her as the woman with the sun on her head. He chortled at the description. What a preposterous idea to imagine the petite creature standing in front of him had the strength to wield the bow and shoot the arrow true enough to split the one already lodged in the target.

She had a right lovely round backside, he'd give her that, but he'd not give her his confidence. He jingled the bag of money with a grin and held it toward Romany who'd begun taking bets again from the people around him. "I'll put the whole lot on the lady's failure."

With a gasp, the woman whirled around and speared him with a dark look as well as nearly stabbing him with her arrow. "You're mistaken to wager against me, sir."

There was something invitingly erotic about the pale-skinned, bronze-eyed beauty wrapped in delicate, lilac silk. She looked dainty and helpless yet she wielded a weapon that could kill and boasted of skills no proper lady would dream of admitting. His lust awoke in a heartbeat. This was the woman he needed to prickle his father and push him toward agreeing to secure a commission. "I'll be happy if you prove me wrong, yet your stature does make me question your abilities, Lady…?"

"Miss Prattle," she responded with a conspiratorial look at the curly-headed brunette.

"What an unusual name." He winked to prod her and was rewarded when her eyes rounded.

"Yes, well, Lord...?"

"Drivel." He could barely contain his amusement.

She burst out laughing, the merry sound making him smile. "Your laugh is lovely," he said. Instantly, she sobered, eyed him warily and turned her attention downward on her arrow. She was right to be guarded. His blood hummed in his ears with his desire. Forget his parent's boring dinner. By tonight he'd have this chit in his bed. The contradiction she presented was irresistible. "I'll put my money on you *and* give you all my winnings to make up for offending you, but if you lose, you must accompany me to my townhouse."

"She'll not!" her friend exclaimed before the lady herself could reply. When the lady gave her friend a cool look, Grey had to work not to show his satisfaction. She was just as interested in him as he was in her. Today was turning out to be splendid, indeed.

"I'll take your offer."

"Excellent." He ignored her friend's outraged huff and Gravenhurst's indiscreet snickering into his hands. "There's much I want to show you." Grey imagined her excited expression when she saw his collection of archery sets. Her mouth dropped open. By God, the chit thought he was referring to something sexual. Her expression of barely contained outrage was priceless and intrigued him all the more.

"What precisely do you think to show me? Are you a collector of art?"

Her tone was brittle as glass. The challenge of making her pliable in his hands was going to be quite enjoyable. For now, it might do her good to wonder what he was about. "I only have one piece of art that's worth your seeing."

At that, Gravenhurst started guffawing but stopped promptly when the brunette lady glared him into ashes.

The woman's obvious protective instinct over her friend was admirable, even if he didn't like her interference.

"I won't be seeing your art, but I will take your money," the blond-haired chit replied before turning away, raising her arrow and saying in a loud, confident voice, "I'm ready."

Romany and his cronies immediately called for last wagers, collected the money, and then a hush fell over the crowd.

Grey moved so he could see the woman's face. He was rewarded for his effort. An adorable crease appeared on her forehead as she pulled the bow back with a creak. Her teeth bit down on her lower lip in concentration, and he could see her doing all the same small calculations he did every time he practiced his archery. She tested the tautness of her bow, the weight of her arrow, and the direction of the wind. Her knowledge impressed him. Her weight subtly shifted, but her skirt swished around her ankles and alerted him to her change in stance.

Fascination stilled him. He might lose, but the loss of his money didn't worry him. Her fingers lifted off the bow and the arrow buzzed through the air true and straight. He'd underestimated her. Her arrow sliced down the middle of the other arrow and a collective gasp, followed by cheers and groans filled the air. He wanted to cheer too, but jaded lords didn't cheer.

She whooped, her arms flying above her head in victory and her feet leaving the ground with her enthusiasm. He grinned as he watched her. She had real spirit. He no longer gave a damn about needling his father. He wanted to get to know this chit for her sake alone.

She faced him with a grin that lit her whole face. The sight was breathtaking. "I thank you kindly for your money," she said. He grabbed her arm before she disappeared into the swell of people wanting to congratulate her and those who wanted a chance to earn their money back.

"I'd still love for you to come to my town home."

"To see your one piece of art?" She tilted her head challengingly to the side.

"No. To see my archery collection."

"Oh!" The smile on her face filled her eyes and made them shine like polished bronze.

"By God, you're lovely." He'd not been so taken with a woman's beauty since he'd been old enough to understand women used their appearance to scheme and manipulate.

Her light eyebrows tilted into two twin arches as she gently pulled her arm from his grasp. "Thank you."

"Miss Prattle," her friend said through clenched teeth. "Our hour is over."

"Tell me your name," Grey insisted as his intriguing, blonde beauty started backing away from him. He didn't want her to go. Not yet.

"You already know it."

"Your real name," he amended, advancing toward her so she couldn't simply vanish into the thickening crowd. "I could call on you. Take you to the theatre. Show you things you've probably only imagined."

A lovely pink blush stained her cheeks. "I've a great imagination."

"Then let's explore it together." He didn't give a damn how forward he sounded.

"Enough!" her annoying companion said. "We must go now. It's been two hours."

"Two hours!" his beauty gasped. "Dear me. I really must go, but thank you for the offer."

He sidestepped in front of her and looked down into her

upturned face. "Meet me here tomorrow," he said, desperate to ensure he would see her again. Her indecisiveness showed as she bit on her lip. "I won't let you leave unless you agree."

"That's coercion."

"Whatever it takes." He loved the word "whatever". It left so many intriguing possibilities open to explore.

"Please remember that tomorrow." She sidestepped around him.

A sense of satisfaction filled him. "I'll see you at the fountain at ten."

Already a few steps away, she looked over her shoulder. A frown marred her beautiful face. "Goodbye, Lord Drivel."

He loved that she was willing to play the game. "Fair well, Miss Prattle."

He watched her depart, her hips rocking enticingly with each step, until he could see her no more. If he was any other sort of man, he would have followed her all the way to her carriage just for a few more minutes in her company. Gravenhurst nudged him in the side. "Do you really think that piece will meet you here?"

"Of course I do. I'd not have let her leave, otherwise."

Two

One Year Later
Windsor Castle
1805

"*L*ady Madelaine, your stitch is off again." Queen Charlotte jabbed her needle into her material and set her embroidery hoop on her lap. "Hand it to me."

With a quick glance at the queen's disapproving stare, Madelaine dismissed the idea of summoning tears. The notion had been ridiculous anyway. After a year at Court she knew better. The queen disliked her and no amount of crying would ever change that.

"Are you defying me, Lady Madelaine?" Polite iciness, and perhaps a tad of hopefulness, underlay the queen's words.

Was she? Her fingers curled around her wood hoop. Did she dare disobey the queen? Her heartbeat banged in her ears. She could do it. Then she'd be ousted from Court and back home where she actually had a friend, instead of here surrounded by a hateful queen and equally cold ladies-in-waiting.

Life would be grand. The fantasy disappeared, as always. Home was no escape. The worry she saw on her father's face the few times he'd visited her at Court would become worse if she was sent home. She'd rather endure the lectures and the loneliness than further sadden him.

The thumping in her ears lessened as her fingers loosened and she handed her embroidery hoop to the queen.

"What's this?" the queen demanded.

She swallowed her pride, huge, bitter pill that it was. "A disgrace, Your Majesty."

The queen's eyebrows raised high. "Yours, to be sure."

A spattering of nasty giggles erupted around Madelaine. She should pretend not to notice, really she should. But she just couldn't do it. Her pride was definitely going to be her downfall. Or perhaps her temper. It was an ongoing debate in her head. She shot an icy glare to each lady who dared to meet her narrowed gaze. Only three ladies out of four today? My, the odds were improving. If she dismissed support as a requirement in a friend she could now count Lady Elizabeth Adlard, whose gaze was focused on her lap, as a friend. Madelaine nearly laughed. Ah, well, at least Lady Elizabeth didn't join in mocking her.

Queen Charlotte stood, her silk skirts falling in a swish at her ankles as she did. She handed Madelaine's now bare embroidery hoop to her. "Redo this and then you may join us in the library and play the pianoforte for me."

Madelaine gnashed her teeth. The queen truly had it in for her today. She was worse at the pianoforte than she was at embroidery. Yet there was a bit of hope. By the time she redid her stitches the queen could well be tired of listening to music and might want to go for a walk through the gardens or a leisurely ride. Madelaine brightened considerably. She could walk and sit with the best of them. "I'll come to the library as soon as I'm finished."

"One hour," the queen commanded and exited the room with the rest of the ladies on her heel.

Well, all the ladies save one, but Grace, with her venomous personality, was hardly a lady in Madelaine's mind.

"Did you forget your pitchfork, Grace?" Madelaine had learned the hard way to strike first. She'd been the brunt of too many of Grace's hurtful comments to sit and wait like a fool for Grace's razor-sharp tongue to lash her.

"Lady Grace." Lady Grace Frost enunciated each word like only someone who truly wasn't a lady would do.

"So you keep saying," Madelaine murmured, "yet it seems to me true ladies have kind hearts."

"Be sure to work slowly, Madge. I've a bit of a headache and don't think I can tolerate your pounding on the keys today."

In swirl of skirts and blonde hair, Grace was gone. Madelaine snatched up her needle and spool of thread and furiously pushed the pin into the fabric while indulging the fantasy that Grace was the fabric. It was stupid to let Grace upset her. That's exactly what she wanted. Yet Madelaine was upset, foolish or not.

When the clock struck the hour, Madelaine stuffed her hoop into her embroidery box and trudged down the hall. Lost in her own thoughts, it wasn't until she was at the library door that she realized how quiet it was. She entered the library and could not help but gape at the empty room. Finally, she'd hit on a bit of luck in a year of providence drought.

She gazed at the rows of thousands of books, and a sliver of anticipation raced through her. She hurried toward the bookcase, but as her fingertips touched the first spine, the distinct creak of the door being opened filled the room. Her shoulders slumped. How ridiculously silly of her to hope for five whole minutes alone. "I'm coming." It was hard to make her tone falsely pleasant.

"Is that disappointment I hear?"

Madelaine whirled toward the door and blinked. Lady Elizabeth, with her head of curly black hair and light blue eyes, smiled at her. "I'm not disappointed," Madelaine lied.

"Really? I'd be if I'd thought I was going to be alone for a bit and then my hopes were dashed."

That was exactly how Madelaine felt, and this was the first time in a year anyone had made an effort to have an actual friendly conversation with her. She could protect herself from further hurt and ignore Lady Elizabeth or she could take a chance and reach for the olive-branch. She was always one for taking a chance. "Did the queen send you to retrieve me?"

Lady Elizabeth grew serious. "Worse. I'm to take you to the tower where you're to be whipped for insubordination."

"What?" Madelaine's stomach plummeted.

Lady Elizabeth moved further into the room and took Madelaine's free hand in her own. She studied Madelaine. "Yes. Didn't you know? A lady who cannot properly embroider must be banished from polite society until she can master the skill."

Madelaine gripped her embroidery box tighter to her side with her left arm and swallowed the catch that had suddenly come up in her throat. "It's just embroidery."

Lady Elizabeth shrugged. "Yes, but you messed up the precious pink peony. No more chances for you." The corners of Lady Elizabeth's mouth tugged into a smile.

Madelaine slowly released her breath, too happy that Lady Elizabeth had been teasing her to be angry. "I didn't know you had a sense of humor."

"I'm terribly funny, once you get to know me. You should have seen your face."

"I can imagine." Madelaine pressed her hand to her chest. "For a moment, my heart stopped."

"Oh dear. I'm sorry. I was only teasing. Come, we better go. Oh, and Her Majesty says to leave your embroidery."

"Does she now? You expect me to believe the queen means to be kind to me? I may be gullible but I'm not a fool." She hated how prickly she sounded, but her nerves were already on edge.

"No more foolery. I promise. We're to take an invigorating walk in the gardens since the weather's unusually warm. The queen is beside herself at the prospect of pointing out new plants to us."

"A punishment worse than the tower." The minute the words left Madelaine's mouth she froze. Had she gone too far?

"I know!" Lady Elizabeth burst out laughing. Madelaine's immense relief made her laugh almost hysterically.

"The queen will be most displeased to hear what I just have," a voice said from the doorway.

Madelaine abruptly stopped laughing and met Grace's hostile stare. If she pleaded, it would only give Grace satisfaction and make matters worse. She watched as Lady Elizabeth flew across the room.

"Lady Grace, please. She'll throw us from Court."

"I imagine she will." Grace untangled her arm from Lady Elizabeth's desperate clutch.

"Please, you mustn't say a word." Lady Elizabeth glanced over her shoulder at Madelaine. "We meant no harm."

Madelaine fought the urge to intervene, clenching her teeth on her need to speak.

"It sounded harmful to me," Grace said.

Unable to stand the helplessness and Lady Elizabeth's groveling a moment longer, Madelaine blurted, "I'll buy your silence with my quarterly allowance."

"How much?" Grace demanded.

"Ten pounds."

"Not enough."

"I'll recommend you to my brother," Lady Elizabeth pleaded.

Lady Grace's eyes narrowed. "Which brother?"

"Whichever you prefer." Lady Elizabeth turned deathly pale.

"Well, Lord Foxhaven is the heir, but Lord Grey does thrill me to the bone every time with just one look."

Madelaine wanted to silence Grace's viperous tongue, but the way she had in mind wouldn't garner her in any better favor with the queen. Proper ladies did not resort to violence. Oh, how she wished she didn't have to be a proper lady.

Lady Elizabeth sighed. "Fine. I'll post a letter to Grey tonight.

"That'll do nicely. Yet I require one more thing."

"What is it?" Lady Elizabeth's shoulders slumped and her voice shook.

Grace gave Madelaine a narrow-eyed look. "No more speaking to her, unless it's to insult her, of course."

Madelaine's pulse shot from a simmer to a boil, but she struggled to keep her face relaxed. She ignored Grace's stare and instead looked at Lady Elizabeth and tried to convey with a quick smile that it was all right. It wasn't at all, but she'd never let Lady Elizabeth know that. A tear trickled down Lady Elizabeth's cheek which she quickly dashed away. "I understand," she whispered, dropped her arms and walked out the door.

Grace stared at Madelaine from across the room. "I'll expect your allowance in my hands by nightfall."

"I'd expect no less from the likes of you," Madelaine replied. A small sense of satisfaction filled her as Grace opened and closed her mouth. No doubt the ninny struggled to find some nasty words to say. Too bad she wasn't quick-witted. Grace settled on a glare, turned and departed the room.

Madelaine stood for a moment with nothing but the crackle of the fire as her company. It seemed worse somehow to have found a possible friend and then lost her so suddenly than to have never had a friend at all. At least before, she had become numb to the cruelty of the other ladies-in-waiting.

She hated this place. But she couldn't begrudge her father. He'd done what he thought best for his odd daughter. He wanted her married and had judged she needed all the help she could get to finally learn to be a proper lady since she'd failed miserably to become one when her mother was alive. If only she had tried harder, not caused her mother so much heartache. Her heart twisted with memories.

A commotion at the door drew her attention back to the area. The chambermaid with the red hair swept in. "I need to draw the curtains."

Madelaine glanced at the windows and frowned. The curtains were all drawn wide.

The chambermaid laughed. "Sorry, my lady. I meant I need to straighten the pillows."

To Madelaine's eye not a single pillow in the room was out of place, but she waved the woman into the room. "Constance, correct?"

"Yes, my lady."

"Were you lingering outside the room this entire time?" She hated to be accusatory, but she needed to be pragmatic.

Silence may need to be bought. Her skin crawled at her thoughts. She was becoming a true member of this wretched Court.

"Certainly not, my lady." The woman's voice held indignation, but her eyes darted with her lies. It was on the tip of Madelaine's tongue to offer Constance coin, but then Madelaine remembered she now had no coin to offer. It was all due to Lady Grace. This was awful.

She pasted a sweet smile on her face, though she felt like screaming. "If you did happen to overhear anything, I hope you know how *grateful* I'd be, how willing to help you it would make me, if you kept your silence."

Constance cleared her throat. "I didn't hear a thing, my lady."

Madelaine clenched her fist. Falsehoods. This entire Court was filled with people who had been raised to lie.

The all too familiar sting of hurt pierced Madelaine's heart. She had to get out of here before she became someone she did not recognize in an effort to simply defend herself from those around her. The problem was she had to have an offer of marriage before her father would allow her to leave the Court, and as far as she could tell the men at Court with their freely roaming hands and whispered innuendos wanted a whore—not a wife.

Three

After a week of being locked up in the castle because of constant rain and bitter cold, Madelaine was giddy when she awoke on the seventh day to sun and warmer temperatures. Neither the queen's glare nor Grace's continuing campaign to make Madelaine look foolish in front of the queen could dampen Madelaine's spirits today. They were to spend time outside and the promise of riding her horse, though it would not be as fast as she liked, lightened her heart and added a bounce to her step.

As she raced down the stairs to meet the queen and the other ladies-in-waiting she found Grace at the bottom of the steps.

"You're dressed rather oddly for sketching," Grace said.

Madelaine's spirits plummeted. "Are we no longer riding?"

"Did I forget to tell you of the queen's change of mind?" A wicked smile flittered across Grace's face. "You better hurry if you don't want to anger the queen by being tardy."

Madelaine wanted to throttle Grace, but unfortunately that would have to wait. She raced up the stairs and quickly changed while categorizing the different ways she'd like to take her revenge on Grace. By the time she returned to the courtyard, she had ten solid retaliation methods in mind, and she would have gladly employed method one, pushing

Grace into the fountain when no one was watching, but the queen and all the ladies had already gone outside.

Fuming, she trudged in the direction the guard pointed her, kicking stray pebbles as she walked. Why had she fought her mother so? If only she'd paid attention and learned how to do at least *one* thing normal ladies did. Her mother had been right—Madelaine was willful and her father was too soft. A reluctant smile tugged at her mouth. How easy it had always been to get Father to take her side. A few well-placed tears and she would be practicing archery with him instead of inside with her mother trying to master embroidery. A gentle reminder about how long he had been gone to see the king, and she could easily escape practicing pianoforte for the much more pleasurable experience of racing him on horseback across their wide expanse of land or having a dagger-throwing contest.

None of the things she knew how to do did her any good, just as her mother had always predicted. If only she had listened, her parents would not have fought over her behavior and then her mother would be alive. The familiar sting of tears tickled her nose, but as the queen and the other ladies-in-waiting came into sight, Madelaine sniffed back the tears. She'd sooner be stuck with a hot poker than cry in front of any of them.

"How nice of you to join us, Lady Madelaine," the queen said.

"I'm sorry, Your Majesty. I had to change out of my riding habit."

"As did everyone else who was here when I said to be."

Madelaine gritted her teeth on her response while sitting and carefully situating her skirts over her ankles. Small blades of brittle grass pricked her skin through her stockings. She ignored the desire to lean down and rub her ankles—a lady did not rub her ankle in public no matter what. Even if her ankle was twisted. One public smack of her hands by the queen had ingrained that particular lesson into Madelaine's mind for good. The queen didn't hit near as hard as Madelaine's mother used to, but then again her mother had not had an audience to force her temper under control.

Inhaling a breath of the mildly cool air, the familiar calm she always got when she was outside descended on her. The emerging wintery beauty of Windsor Great Park pushed away the weariness Grace had caused. Madelaine pulled out her supplies and picked up her easel. At least if she had to be humiliated it would be under a tree that still somehow stood lushly green amongst the other trees whose leaves had already begun to turn to a dull brown.

Madelaine chanced a look at Lady Elizabeth, who had not spoken to her once in the last seven days but had offered the occasional friendly smile when Grace had not been present. It would be lovely to have one lady to count as a friend but that was probably too much to hope for. As Madelaine finished situating herself, the queen let out an irritated sigh.

"I've forgotten my favorite sketching instrument."

"I'll get it, Your Majesty." Grace jumped up and pushed back her chair.

Queen Charlotte bestowed a doting smile on Grace that made Madelaine want to roll her eyes. Instead, she kept her gaze trained on the paper before her and imagined Grace falling, face first, straight into the mud. How Madelaine would love to sketch that. The minute Grace disappeared from view, Lady Elizabeth leaned toward Madelaine. "I'm so sorry," she said under her breath.

"Don't be," Madelaine whispered back.

Lady Elizabeth gazed around them, but the queen was sitting with her eyes closed and her face raised slightly to the sun. The other ladies-in-waiting were all busily sketching. "I cannot be thrown from Court," Lady Elizabeth said.

"Please, don't worry about me." Madelaine understood Lady Elizabeth's concern, but all the same, it made her sad the woman wouldn't chance being her friend.

"I've someone I want you to meet," Lady Elizabeth said out of the side of her mouth. "Meet me in the chapel before dinner."

The invitation was an unexpected and pleasant surprise. Rather than risk any more whispering, Madelaine nodded. Perhaps she and Lady Elizabeth would be friends after all, even if only secretly. Relaxing, she studied the landscape while trying to decide what would be the easiest thing to try to sketch. In the distance, two riders appeared out of the woods, black capes billowing behind them starkly contrasted by the bright blue sky. By the way the horses raced hellbent toward them they had to be two men riding the beasts. No woman would dare to ride with such speed unless perhaps fleeing for her life.

As the horses drew nearer, the ground vibrated from the pounding hooves into the soles of Madelaine's delicately slippered feet. The bevy of whispers that erupted as all the women forgot their sketching to gaze curiously at the approaching riders made Madelaine want to laugh. Not one of these ladies would dare defy the queen's order in normal circumstances, but put two men in their paths and the queen's command to draw was promptly abandoned. And the queen did not seem to mind one bit, if her smile was any indication. Madelaine quirked her mouth. She didn't need a friend in one of the ladies-in-waiting to help her soften the queen, she needed a man. Two men from the queen's guard materialized from the stone wall they had been lounging against to stand just behind the queen on either side of her.

Madelaine shielded her eyes from the glaring sun, but she could not get a good view of the approaching riders.

"Now who could this be?" The queen's bejeweled, wrinkled hand hovered just above her eyes.

As the riders came closer, a golden lion became visible on one of their capes. Lady Elizabeth gasped, jerked up from her seat and then dipped into a deep curtsey toward the queen. "Beg pardon, Your Majesty. I believe that's my youngest brother, Lord Grey."

"Splendid," the queen said with such a genuine smile Madelaine had to cough to cover her snort. Of course the queen's good grace would extend to a man. And then remembrance flooded through Madelaine. Was this Lord Grey—the unsuspecting brother who had been called here to be delivered as a sacrifice to Grace in return for the woman's silence?

Poor man. She prayed he was a strong sort and would resist the temptation of Grace's outer beauty long enough to learn her insides were ugly. The chance was bleak though if Lord Grey was like all other men. Still, one could hope.

From the corner of her eye, Grace's yellow hair caught Madelaine's attention as the woman fairly skipped toward them. She arrived at the circle at the same moment the horses drew to a stop. No doubt she had planned her appearance once she had seen the men approaching. The men descended and led their horses toward the women.

"Lady Elizabeth, your brother has the looks of a knight of old," the queen said.

Madelaine gaped at the queen. Had she delivered a

breathless compliment? It couldn't be possible. Yet, her Majesty's eyes shined as she stared at the approaching men. Rosy color stained her normally pale complexion, and her posture was just a bit straighter, wasn't it? Yes. Yes, it was! The queen was smitten with one of the men and based on earlier comments, it had to be Lord Grey. You could have knocked Madelaine over with her sketching utensil.

Under lowered lashes Madelaine studied the men. The one on the right had hair the color of wheat and a face that could have been described as a work of art with his high cheekbones, full lips, and golden shadow of stubble. Thick, light eyebrows framed his green, friendly eyes. He stopped in front of the queen, bowed and spoke in a rich voice. "Your Majesty, it's a pleasure to see you again."

"And you as well, Lord Gravenhurst." Queen Charlotte smiled up at him before waving a hand in dismissal.

As Lord Gravenhurst stepped aside, Madelaine leaned forward in her chair eager to get a good look at the man that Grace wanted and the queen became human over. In her haste to see him, she knocked her easel with her knee. What an oaf she was! She reached for the easel, but missed, and the dratted thing slid off its perch to land in the grass. Maybe no one had noticed? Snickers rose around her, and her heart fell. Now, not only was she odd, she was a klutz. Surely things couldn't get worse.

"Really, Lady Madelaine, do try to have a modicum of decorum," the queen said. Heat enveloped Madelaine's face. It had to be impossible to be more embarrassed than she was at this moment. Keeping her gaze downward, she bent to retrieve the easel. Blast! It was out of her reach. Maybe if she shifted her weight. Her chair creaked as she did so. She held her breath and reached. Almost there. If she could just reach a little bit further. There! Her fingertips brushed the easel, and she stretched a bit more to grasp the thing. Underneath her, the ground shifted. Or was that her chair? Egads, she was falling. She tried to throw her weight backward, but the weight of the heavy hoops the queen insisted they wear pulled her forward.

Strong hands with a gentle touch pushed her back into her seat. When she glanced up, her gaze locked with wintery blue eyes and a wave of shock sent a shiver through her body. Dear God. Lord Grey was her Lord Drivel. How many times had she dreamed of him and wondered if he'd gone the next day to Golden Square to meet her?

The hairs on the back of her neck stood on end at the icy beauty of the aware gaze holding hers. He recognized her too! And if she had any doubt his thick black eyebrows arching questioningly then coming down into a furrow over narrowing eyes, quashed her uncertainty. Leave it to her to break into an anxious sweat on a cool day.

Lord Grey's haughty aristocratic expression hadn't changed a whit from last year. Yet, he *had* changed. Clearly he was not the preening peacock she'd thought he was when they'd first met. His skin was unfashionably bronze. His hair—inky black and touching his shoulders—was in disarray. But what a beautiful mess it was. He needed a shave, and that scar above his lip...The man looked like a virile knight of old. The queen had, for once, been perfectly correct. Madelaine sighed and Lord Grey blinked. She blinked back. Dear God, had she been staring? The unusual quietness told her she had.

"Here you are." Lord Grey held out her easel.

"Thank you," she automatically replied and took the easel while praying he was smart enough to keep their prior meeting secret.

"No, thank you." Lord Grey's voice washed over her

with its warmth.

"For what?" Blast. She should have let the conversation die. The queen was frowning at her.

Lord Grey leaned forward on bent knee, the fine tan cambric of his coat stretched tight over his broad shoulders.

"It's not every day that I get to come to the rescue of a beautiful lady-in-waiting." He plucked her sketching utensil from the ground and handed it to her.

As she reached to take her instrument from him, his fingers brushed hers and her skin tingled in the wake of his touch. She rubbed her tickling fingertips together and racked her mind for a coy, yet proper reply, to his flattery. Before she could speak, Grace did. "I, for one, am not the least surprised you had to help Lady Madelaine. She's a terrible lout. Why just last night, she tripped Lord Carlisle whilst they were dancing."

It was entirely too bad the opportunity to take revenge on Grace hadn't presented itself earlier. An angry blush singed Madelaine's cheeks. It was true she *had* tripped Lord Carlisle on the dance floor, but it had been purposely. His hands had kept "accidentally" brushing her bottom though she had quite sternly told him to quit. But she couldn't very well explain herself with the truth. She ground her teeth at the futility of her situation.

Lord Grey stood, his powerful frame extending in one fluid motion. He glanced down at her. Was that a conspiratorial smile stretching his lips? "I find it hard to believe someone who looks as graceful as Lady Madelaine could cause anyone to trip, yet I find I hope it's true."

"And why is that, Lord Grey?" asked the queen.

"If I might be bold, Your Majesty?"

"Of course you may."

Madelaine gawked at the queen. How amazing she

looked with a genuine smile on her face. She was almost pretty.

Grey moved to the side of Madelaine's chair, his thigh brushing her arm. "I've an affinity for awkward people, being one myself."

She would have grinned up at him for his kindness, but the queen was studying her with an inscrutable look. Whatever was Queen Charlotte thinking? Before Madelaine could ponder the likely dire possibilities, the queen stood and Madelaine scrambled to stand along with all the other ladies-in-waiting. The queen smiled and addressed Lord Grey. "You're too kind, Lord Grey. I happen to know from watching you ride and joust you have the grace of a prowling panther."

"Your Majesty—" He took the queen's proffered elbow. "—you flatter me."

"I flatter no one," the queen replied with a laugh. "Just ask Lady Madelaine."

Good gracious. If she answered truthfully it would make the queen look bad, yet if she lied, the queen would know it. The stubborn part of Madelaine that had gotten her into so much trouble was leading her there again. She didn't want to look weak.

"Lady Madelaine?" Lord Grey's gaze met hers.

She inclined her head toward Queen Charlotte. "You are my queen, therefore you are correct."

"And if she wasn't your queen?" Lord Grey asked. Blast the man. He had no idea the precarious situation he was putting her in.

"Then I would say her words carry the sting of a bee and not the sweetness of their honey. From my experience, of course," she hastened to add at Lord Grey's lifted eyebrows.

Why was he studying her as if she were some unknown species?

"Interesting. A woman not afraid to speak the truth."

She most certainly was afraid, but she'd been presented little choice.

"Perhaps," the queen agreed, though her voice held an underlying tone of doubt. "Lord Grey, tell me, are you here to see your sister or just to beguile us with your company?"

"Both. Unofficially. But officially, I'm here in service to Lord Pearson."

"As?"

"His newest equerry."

"I was not aware Lord Pearson needed a new equerry. What happened to Lord Sutton?"

"Lord Sutton has gone missing."

Madelaine waited with baited breath for the queen to demand further explanation. Instead, she nodded and gazed toward the dairy farm in the distance where the king had earlier gone with Lord Fox. Well, that figured. The one time Madelaine wouldn't mind the queen's demanding nature, Her Majesty was preoccupied. Or maybe she simply wasn't demanding with Lord Grey. After a moment, the queen focused on Lord Grey again. "Then we shall thoroughly enjoy your time here. Perhaps you can even teach Lady Madelaine how to dance."

"It would be my pleasure." Warmth infused Madelaine. Lord Grey sounded very much like a man who knew a great deal about his pleasure.

Giggles broke out amongst the ladies which ceased when the queen waved a hand toward Lady Elizabeth who scurried toward her brother.

Lord Grey enfolded her in his arms. "Poppet," he whispered into Lady Elizabeth's ear before releasing her and ruffling her hair as if she were a child. The siblings' likeness in coloring of hair and eyes struck Madelaine. "We've much to discuss."

Madelaine's heart leapt into her throat. Did Lord Grey mean to tell his sister about Golden Square? Her heartbeat raced as she discarded ridiculous scenarios of how to corner him and plead her case. Whatever was she going to do? Was he really so cruel? She studied him, and he winked at her. He understood! Her breath released with a rush, yet her nerves still tingled. He may appear willing to keep her secret, but at what price? Everyone at this blasted Court had a price.

But those questions would have to wait until she had the opportunity to speak privately with him. His fingers strayed to his jacket, and he touched a piece of parchment. The letter! Lord Grey had been speaking of the letter his sister had written him. Lady Elizabeth clearly saw the letter as well. Her eyes were rounded in surprise. Some of Madelaine's tension released, slowing her heartbeat. How silly she'd been. Of course the letter would be forefront on his mind and not his distant meeting in Golden Square with her.

An odd sort of jealousy overcame Madelaine. Lady Elizabeth was lucky. Lord Grey seemed a man more than capable of handling a malicious witch like Grace. Fleetingly, Madelaine wished she had a sibling. But that was impossible. She turned and found Grace glaring at her. Did Grace think to cow her? Madelaine wasn't the least bit intimidated, but she refused to play such ridiculously childish games. She raised her eyebrows at Grace to let her know she was a fool, and then dismissed her.

"The breeze is turning chilly," the queen said. "You are all young, so you don't notice it as I do." Everyone nodded dutifully in agreement. The queen let out a long sigh as if being constantly agreed with was tedious. "I'm off to read." She pointed at Lady Juliette and Lady Annabelle. "Come keep me company." To everyone else she waved a negligent hand. "Be inside by the time the sun hits noon, or sooner if Lord Grey and Lord Gravenhurst no longer wish to keep you company."

Murmurs of agreement scattered amongst the remaining ladies. Once the queen had walked out of earshot, Grace addressed Lord Grey. "Perhaps Lady Madelaine will sing for you."

"Or play the pianoforte," Lady Cecelia chimed in a nasty tone that matched Grace's.

Madelaine lifted her chin and forced a smile as she looked at the two men before her. She wouldn't let Grace make her appear embarrassed when she certainly wasn't. The only reason she now wished for a single feminine talent was so the queen might not find fault with her at every turn. "I'm afraid I was a beastly daughter and never paid heed to the things a proper lady is required to know." Useless as those things were.

"Such as nonsensical conversation and not appearing too educated?" Lord Gravenhurst speared Grace with a slanted-eyed look that dared her to say a word.

Finally, a sensible man. "Exactly," Madelaine replied, enjoying Grace's gasp and her splotchy cheeks.

"I'm curious, Lady Madelaine..." Lord Grey said.

"About what?" Her pulse skittered unnaturally in her chest.

"If you didn't master your lessons of pianoforte, singing and...?"

"Embroidery," his sister supplied with a small smile tugging at her lips.

"Ah, yes, the all-important skill of embroidery," he exclaimed. She wanted to laugh at his dramatics, but she somehow managed to hold it in.

"Pray tell, *what did* you master?"

She nearly gasped at his question. Was he challenging her to lie? She didn't want her secret to be revealed but she refused to be ashamed of the things she knew. "Archery, riding, and how to use a dagger." Her eyebrows lifted in defiance.

"I'm impressed and intrigued. I, too, am interested in archery." Lord Grey's friend coughed and sputtered beside him. She glared at him for trying to goad her. He smiled, and her pulse skittered oddly. Whatever was the matter with her to respond to him like all the other silly dimwits at Court probably did. She should ignore him. He proffered his elbow. "Will you walk in the gardens with my sister and me? I confess I'd love to learn if you have any special techniques you use with your bow and arrow."

Madelaine understood exactly what Grace had meant when she'd said Lord Grey thrilled her to the bone with just one look. His face had haunted her dreams many nights since she had met him, possible preening peacock or not. Court life had been a lonely, cruel surprise and fantasizing that Lord Grey was good and gallant had helped her keep hope she'd meet someone eventually. Her stomach swirled with butterflies. The way he stared at her made her believe there could possibly be something special about her.

She felt charming. The notion was silly. She was an oddity, but he *was* looking at her as if he liked that. Wasn't he? Maybe she'd been wrong to think there was no one who'd accept her for who she really was. Perhaps she *would* meet a man who she really did want to marry for love. Maybe, that man could be Lord Grey. How ridiculous she was. She didn't really know him. He probably bestowed that mesmerizing expression on every new lady he met. Yet she wanted to take a chance. She slipped her arm through his and refused to care one bit that Grace would make her life holy hell if the murderous look on the lady's face was a good indicator.

As Lord Grey tucked Madelaine's hand into the crook of his elbow and reached for his sister's arm, Grace said, "I'll come too. I'm positively dying to hear what sorts of accomplishments intrigue the notorious Lord Grey."

"Notorious?" A sense of foreboding weighed down upon Madelaine's newly light mood.

"But of course," Grace murmured. "You're well known for wooing the ladies but never committing to them. Aren't you, Lord Grey?"

His arm tensed under Madelaine's light grasp. She fully expected an annoyed denial, instead he looked supremely bored. After a moment, an amused smile played at his lips. "I suppose I am, Lady Grace."

Madelaine tugged her arm for Lord Grey to release her. Heavens she was a fool for falling so quickly under his spell. Bewitching eyes didn't mean a man was a good candidate for a husband. A fact she needed to remember. A walk with a scoundrel would do her no good. Avoiding him would be her wisest course, and she fully intended to take it, once she spoke with him about keeping their meeting secret. But now, surrounded by others, was not the time.

Four

$\mathcal{G}$rey didn't want to release Lady Madelaine's hand, but when she tugged on it for a second time, he relinquished it. His mysterious Miss Prattle was quite the lovely blusher. Was the blush out of anger or embarrassment? He could assure her he had no intentions of seducing her, but that would be a lie and could, in all fairness to himself, make her discomfort worse.

Fate had delivered this lady back into his life and he had every intention of unwrapping fate's gift. Especially after being awoken in a state of frustrated arousal many times since meeting her. Add to that excellent reason the ribbing he'd taken for weeks from Gravenhurst when the lady had failed to reappear in Golden Square and seemingly disappeared into thin air, and Grey was not about to just let her walk away from him again. Now he knew where she was and why. Far be it for him not to use the knowledge.

What the devil had a proper lady been doing in Golden Square shooting a bow and arrow? Unlocking that secret, and whatever else Lady Madelaine was hiding behind her dark eyes and deceptively delicate appearance, would be a pleasure. A lady who claimed an affinity for riding, archery and daggers was a lady with mettle. Strong women were so much better in bed than weak, simpering misses who refused to tell you what she craved and exactly how she wanted it.

The fact that she had never met him as promised no longer bothered him. No doubt she'd only been in Golden Square by trickery. He smiled. If the chit sought more than the constraints life offered her, he'd gladly introduce her to other, more exotic constraints. Lady Madelaine studied him with her slumberous gaze the color of a chestnut flecked with black. She pulled her cape tighter around her, her fine-boned hands white as cotton clutching the dark material, and her honey-colored hair bunched up under the cloth. Right now, she looked more like a trapped fox than a potential bed partner who was assessing him.

He had the unusual desire to assure her he'd never led a woman to his bed by force or trickery. Yet, now in others' company was not the time to say such a thing. There'd be time enough later to tell her he may be known as a seducer, but he'd never seduced a single lady who didn't wish the seduction and willingly participated in the game. No doubt she was probably worried about his keeping her secret and would seek him out. He could practically see her worry in her lovely eyes. Maybe she was even considering how they could rendezvous or if it would be too dangerous.

Her tongue darted from her mouth and she nervously licked her plump lips. She definitely recognized the perils of a private meeting. His muscles tightened in awareness of the invisible gauntlet that had just been thrown. Of course, he would pick it up and show her there were ways to meet privately even at Court.

"It's gotten cold suddenly, hasn't it," she said.

It hadn't at all, but he nodded. "If you want to go inside we can postpone our walk."

The relief that made her body relax amused him. He didn't wait for her answer, he already knew it. "Gravenhurst, will you see Lady Madelaine and Lady Cecelia inside? I don't want to deprive Elizabeth of our walk, and I know how much Lady Grace likes exercise." From what he had been told, the woman had a voracious appetite for vigorous bed sport.

Lady Madelaine slipped her arm through Gravenhurst's but focused her dark eyes on Grace. "I wasn't aware you enjoyed anything that required you to breathe heavily."

Grey bit back a laugh. Lady Madelaine did indeed have some steel in her spine and perhaps a bit of gossip regarding Lady Grace stashed.

"As usual, you know nothing," Lady Grace snapped, before schooling her features into a syrupy smile.

"I know more than you think," Lady Madelaine said. "Shall we go, Lord Gravenhurst?"

"By all means." Gravenhurst rested his gaze on Grey. "I'll see you in a bit."

Grey nodded and as the three walked toward the castle, he wished he were Gravenhurst. Then he would be leading the beguiling Lady Madelaine inside instead of dealing with a jealous harpy. Since he had to see the king soon, he couldn't afford to delay his duties, and setting Lady Grace straight was a must to protect his sister. Pursuing Lady Madelaine would wait, and if it didn't then the seduction wasn't meant to be or was meant to be accomplished by someone else. He hoped not Gravenhurst. The thought didn't sit well.

"I'm so glad you wanted me to stay and walk with the two of you," Lady Grace said.

He studied her. He'd never liked the woman, suspecting she had a viperous streak hidden behind the angelic façade she presented. His sister's letter and Lady Grace's nasty treatment of Lady Madelaine confirmed his suspicion. What was surprising was the queen's open dislike of Lady Madelaine.

There was an interesting mystery. Queen Charlotte was usually kind to all. Grey stared off into the distance as an idea formed. He would uncover what tension lay between Lady Madelaine and the queen, and he would disarm the hostility and earn Lady Madelaine's trust and favor. He smiled, pleased with the possibilities his idea would bring and with the fact that he had once again proved his father wrong. Father thought him uninterested in politics. It wasn't that at all. It was that his father had never bothered to discuss a damned thing with him, only Grey's older brother.

He was perfectly happy to discuss politics. He did so quite frequently in bed with a beautiful lady in his arms. If soothing the queen's anger without her even realizing what was occurring wasn't a perfect example of the political savvy his father loved to point out that Grey's brother possessed, Grey didn't know what was.

A discreet cough brought him back to the present, unpleasant task. "I did not want you to walk with my sister and me."

"I beg your pardon?" Lady Grace stammered.

"You force me to speak plainly, Lady Grace. A situation I've learned most women dislike."

"Grey!" Elizabeth hissed and clutched at his arm. "You said you received my letter. I assume you read it since you're here."

He squeezed his sister's cold hand. He'd die to protect Liz, but he did wish she were more like him than just the looks they shared as twins. While he was a devil, she was an angel. It didn't serve to be an angel, especially at Court. People turned other's kindness to weakness. "I read your letter, poppet, don't worry."

"Then you know I've recommended Lady Grace to you."

Lady Grace smiled. "Did you forget the contents of your sister's letter, Lord Grey?"

"I never forget anything. Ever. You'd be wise to remember that. Let me explain something to you. Men talk amongst themselves a great deal."

Lady Grace's eyes widened.

"I see you understand. Or I think you do. Yet I find the need to be perfectly clear since you threatened my sister, who is the one person in this world I hold dearer than myself."

"I didn't threaten her."

"You don't call telling her you'd see her thrown from Court a threat?"

She pressed her lips together. "I suppose you could see it that way."

"I do. Things, I find, are easy to see if one simply looks. You threatened my sister to gain a recommendation from her to me. Consider yourself recommended and dismissed." He ran a finger down her cheek. "I am flattered. You're beautiful. But I'm not in the market to marry, as you so kindly pointed out to Lady Madelaine. But if I were, I would choose a lady who hadn't already given herself willingly to half the men at Court."

"You're a devil."

He shrugged. "You're correct, of course. So don't think for a moment you can threaten my sister. If you so much as peep a word of her harmless girl talk with Lady Madelaine, I'll go straight to your father and make sure he knows you lay with Lord Barrington not a week ago."

"You've no proof."

He didn't have it at this moment, but he knew how to get it. "You may take that chance if you wish. Some have, but I'll warn you they regretted it. I do not bluff, Lady Grace."

The woman blanched at his words. "Lord Barrington is an imbecile. He'll never rise far at Court."

"Yes. It makes me wonder why someone as scheming as you wasted your favors on him."

Color heightened her cheeks as her eyes narrowed. "I've my reasons. My silence for yours?"

Grey nodded. "I do so love a deal."

"A devil's bargain," she hissed and stomped away.

Something nagged at Grey as he watched her depart. His sister tugged on his arm. "Grey, you were brilliant. She'll never bother me again. But poor Lady Madelaine, Lady Grace will—"

That was it! Lady Madelaine! "Hold that thought, Liz." He ran ahead until he reached Lady Grace. "One more thing," he said.

"What is it?" She folded her hands across her chest.

"You will cease harassing Lady Madelaine as well or I will forget our bargain and tell your father."

"Why do you care about her? The little fool wouldn't know how to please you *if* you managed to get her into your bed."

Lady Madelaine's discretion pleased him. He much preferred to pursue a lady who chose her lovers with care and managed to keep her bed sport secret. "It doesn't matter why I care, only that I do. So bite your pretty little tongue or find yourself married to a man who will never rise to the heights you hope to reach."

"Very well." Her nostrils flared, but she didn't say more. He had to give her some credit. She appeared smart enough to understand when she was beaten. She swiveled on her heel and walked away.

Grey went quickly back to his sister and took her arm. "I don't have long. The king is expecting me, so I have to hurry. But I'll be here for at least the next week, so we can visit. No more talk of the queen, even if you think you are alone."

"I promise. But Grey, it was harmless."

"To you. But the wrong word could get you named traitor. You should know that, and so should your new friend. Tell me about Lady Madelaine."

Elizabeth's eyes narrowed. "Why? She is not some doxy for you to play with, Grey."

"You too?" He ran a hand through his hair. "I coerce no lady into accepting my favors. They do so of their own choosing."

"I imagine it's hard to make a rational decision when someone as handsome as you has turned all his attention upon a lady."

Wistfulness laced his sister's words. "Liz, you will meet the perfect man someday, have ten children, and be utterly content just as Mother and Father are."

"And what of you?" She touched her fingertips to his arm. "Will you take a wife someday?"

"We're not talking about me," he said, neatly avoiding his sister's question. She wouldn't like that he wanted no part of marriage or love, and he didn't want to fight about it. "We're talking of you and your lovely friend. Tell me of her."

Liz shrugged. "There's little to tell. I'm ashamed to admit I've been too afraid of Grace to openly befriend Lady Madelaine."

"*Only* because of Lady Grace?" he prodded.

Liz's eyebrows shot up. "You're very observant. If only Father understood this."

"Liz," he warned, not wanting to hear a word of how sorry she felt for him because of their father.

"Fine. Fine. Yes, the queen too. She seems to have a virulent dislike of Lady Madelaine."

"Is Aunt Helen here?"

Liz smirked at him. "I already thought of her."

"Really? Then why don't you know more of Lady Madelaine?"

"Well, I only just thought of Aunt Helen. And she only just returned to Court."

"Excellent. Seek her out. Alone though. Aunt Helen will know what nettles the queen. She knows all the Court secrets."

"I'm ahead of you for once. I requested to see Aunt Helen after she refreshes from her travels. I asked Lady Madelaine to meet me later in the hope I could impart some information that might help her or at least enlighten her."

"You've a kind heart, poppet."

She shook her head. "Not kind enough." Her voice trembled. "Or I wouldn't have been too afraid to befriend her. I feel so ashamed I've allowed her to be treated cruelly. How lonely she must be, friendless here at Court."

That would probably make Grey's intention of getting the lady into his bed easier, but somehow that seemed like little accomplishment to win a woman because she was desperate not to feel alone. Instead of feeling any lust, his blood stirred toward anger. "There's no shame having been scared, but now you need to learn to be brave. It will serve you better."

"As it serves you?"

She didn't say their father's name, and Grey was grateful for that. "Yes. As it serves me. Let's go in now, so you can see Aunt Helen. She won't mind you arriving early."

"Do you want to come?"

"I have to see the king. But I'll find you later and demand a full recounting."

"Perhaps I'll tell you."

He grinned at his sister's unusual show of backbone. "Name your price."

"You must promise not to hurt Lady Madelaine. She's been hurt enough by her treatment here at Court already."

"You wound me, Liz. I swear to you, I have never hurt a single lady I give my attentions to." He went to great pains to make sure his bed partners understood neither commitment nor love were part of what he offered.

His sister pursed her lips, but said nothing.

"Come on." Grey tugged on Liz's hand. "I need to go before I earn the king's displeasure."

Five

Madelaine couldn't afford to be a fool. And if the tales she'd been listening to for the last two hours were true, Lord Grey was a man who wanted a willing wench in his bed and most definitely not a wife—therefore he was a man for fools. None of the ladies embroidering in the circle appeared to see the situation that way, but Madelaine did. The ladies giggled, whispered and placed wagers on who would win Lord Grey's heart. Madelaine doubted any of them would.

Madelaine glanced at Lady Elizabeth. She was red-faced and tight-lipped, as she had been for the last hour. But she had not denied a single word about her brother. Finally the queen chimed in with a "tsk." All grew blessedly silent as the queen stood and glanced around her ladies-in-waiting. "Young men have great appetites."

As if that was an excuse for blatantly using women!

The queen's gaze rested on Madelaine, and Madelaine forced herself to unclench her hands. "Lord Grey is a man of honor," the queen said.

Madelaine quickly pretended to study her embroidery in case her thoughts showed on her face. She hardly saw how bedding hordes of women was honorable. Lord Grey sounded more like a depraved rake. Which made it all the more infuriating that she kept picturing his wintery eyes and radiant smile. She needed to forget him—not daydream about him. She already had Lord Thorton trying to lead her to ruin. She certainly didn't need to add another rake to her troubles.

"Come, Lady Elizabeth. Help me prepare for dinner," the queen commanded. The moment her bedchamber door shut, the chatter erupted again. Madelaine forced herself to sit through two more stories. That should be long enough no one would comment that she was rushing away the minute the queen departed.

She stuffed her embroidery into her bag, longing for the chance to be alone for a moment before dinner. She needed to clear her thoughts and raise her defenses for another tedious meal where she spent more time blocking Lord Thorton's wandering hands than eating. At the rate she was going her clothes would all be falling off her by Christmas.

She bent to gather the rest of her embroidery thread and when she straightened Lady Elizabeth stood before her. "Come with me," Lady Elizabeth urged with a quick glance at the other ladies.

She needn't have bothered. They were all still far too busy giggling over Lord Grey and which of them would be the one to ensnare his heart and make him reform his ways. Madelaine dismissed them and focused on Lady Elizabeth. A pink flush still covered her skin and her eyes gleamed. "What are you up to?"

Lady Elizabeth tilted her head toward the hall and pressed her lips together as she grasped Madelaine's hand.

It took Madelaine a breath to decide this was too intriguing to pass up. Excitement filled her. Lady Elizabeth wanted to share a secret with her and treat her as a friend. She followed Lady Elizabeth out of the queen's drawing room and down the hall.

"Those women infuriate me," Lady Elizabeth said as she stopped.

A spark of hope filled Madelaine. Lord Grey had been the first man at Court to truly capture her attention. If the women had been wrong about him... "So Lord Grey is not a rake?"

"Oh, he is. Most definitely. But they know nothing of him. They think the prettiest face will win his heart and change his ways. But they're wrong."

Madelaine was intrigued despite knowing she should not be. "What do you think?"

"I *know* what Grey needs is to feel loved. Then he'll change."

Madelaine snorted. She couldn't help it. "Don't you think your brother feels plenty of love from the bosom of your family and the bosoms of all the women he has apparently seduced?"

"No." Lady Elizabeth smiled but then her mouth drew into a frown. "It's a story for another time, but Grey is an outsider with my father and our older brother."

"I don't understand." How did being an outsider make one a notorious rake? Feeling excluded usually meant someone would feel little confidence. She ought to know. Lord Grey exuded confidence.

"Neither do I. But I vow he's like he is because he never had Father's attention. He wants to feel loved." Lady Elizabeth's words held a ringing note of wistfulness. Madelaine's heart fluttered with pity for the man, even though her head was not sure he deserved it.

"I find it hard to believe your brother doesn't feel loved when so many women apparently want him."

"I'm told on very good authority that there's a marked difference between love and lust."

"Whose authority?" Madelaine scarcely believed she was having this conversation or that it appeared she now had a definite friend. Whatever Lord Grey might be, he seemed to be a good influence on his sister. The man could not be *all* bad if he had indeed convinced his sister to be Madelaine's friend.

"Madame Marmont's pamphlet on courting and marriage."

"I've never heard of that."

"You wouldn't have." Lady Elizabeth smirked. "It's scandalous and men make sure we ladies don't know about it. But last time I was home, I came across it quite by accident in my father's library."

"Truly?"

Lady Elizabeth nodded.

"How very nosy of you." She loved that Lady Elizabeth was so bold.

"It was by accident, I said."

"I know all about accidentally finding things," Madelaine replied.

Lady Elizabeth's face turned red. "Do hush. And you must go to the grave keeping my secret."

"Of course I will. What do you think your father wants with those pamphlets?"

"Actually, I think they're my mother's. They're written *for women* on how to avoid and catch certain types of men. Come, let's keep walking. If we're to reach my Aunt Helen's chambers before the dinner hour, we must hurry."

"You've an aunt at Court?" Madelaine couldn't keep the surprise from her voice.

"Of course! My family is everywhere."

Once again, Madelaine felt the tug of jealousy. Since her parents had both been only children, she had no aunts or uncles. "Why are we going to see your aunt?"

"I believe she can help you." Lady Elizabeth rested a hand on Madelaine's arm as they walked through the large chambers toward the stairs that led to the rooms occupied by the king and queen's most important guest. As a longtime friend of the queen's, Lady Elizabeth's aunt clearly held great social importance.

As they strolled through the corridor, the hum of voices mingled with the pounding notes of music to fill the passageway. "Do we have time?"

"Just. If we hurry," Lady Elizabeth whispered as a group of courtiers passed. They chattered as they moved down the corridor toward St. George's hall. The women and men were dressed in their finest clothing, each undoubtedly looking forward to a feast.

Madelaine's stomach twisted into knots. No doubt her night would be long. If she thought there was the slightest chance the queen would not notice her missing, she would skip dinner tonight just to gain a reprieve from Lord Thorton.

The women scurried up the stairs, turning right at the top and making their way down a narrow, candlelit passageway. At the third door, Lady Elizabeth paused. "I'm sorry for before. I've liked you from the start." She squeezed Madelaine's hand.

"And I you," Madelaine said, her throat thick with emotion. After so long without friends at Court, she almost wanted to cry now that she had one. Silly and pathetic, but true.

"My brother says I must learn to be brave. And I know he's right." Lady Elizabeth raised her fist and knocked on the door.

Madelaine stood with her thoughts buzzing in her head

like bees around a honey hive. So Lord Grey had really convinced his sister to be Madelaine's friend. A man who was simply a rake and nothing more wouldn't do that. Rakes only cared for themselves. As the door opened, Madelaine pushed the thoughts of Lord Grey away and focused on the lady's maid who stood facing them.

"Louisa!" Lady Elizabeth exclaimed and wrapped the older woman in a hug. Wisps of silver hair loosened from the servant's severe bun and fell to touch her hunched shoulders. "I'd no idea you were accompanying Aunt Helen."

"My lady insists. She claims nary a servant in the castle can dress her hair as I can."

"It's true," replied a husky voice from within.

Lady Elizabeth released the servant and tugged on Madelaine's hand. "Louisa, we shall visit tomorrow. Tonight, I'm on a mission."

As Madelaine was fairly dragged into the bedchambers, she struggled to enter gracefully, but her slipper caught on the edge of a rug and she tripped into the room. She quickly smoothed her skirts and then frantically tried to pin back the locks of her hair that now swung in her face. She must look ridiculous. Before she could pin the last bit of hair, Lady Elizabeth's aunt stepped from behind a dressing screen and stared at Madelaine with her large, almond-shaped eyes.

This was Lady Elizabeth and Lord Grey's aunt? Dark chestnut hair piled artfully atop her head and laced liberally with sparkling diamonds made the woman look more fitted as an idol than an aunt. Her creamy skin and perfect hair made Madelaine uncomfortably aware her own face had not been washed since that morning nor had her hair been brushed.

And her gown! She wore purple silk ordained with

glittering gems placed alluringly around her bodice. Madelaine reached to fidget with her mussed gown, but at the smile of amusement that touched Lady Elizabeth's aunt's mouth, Madelaine forced herself to draw her hands in front of her and clasp them together as if she had not a care in the world.

"Hard, isn't it, dear?"

"Pardon?"

"To hold perfectly still even though you want to fix your appearance."

A dratted flush heated Madelaine's cheeks. Well, she certainly couldn't feign bafflement now that her skin had given her away. "Yes. It's difficult but has become easier with practice."

"Brava, dear. I like a woman who is honest."

"Well, my flush left me little choice."

"Still, you could have lied."

"I suppose I could have." Madelaine could tell already she was going to like Lady Elizabeth's aunt.

"Niece, does this young lady have anything to do with your mission?"

Lady Elizabeth nodded. "Aunt, this is my friend Lady Madelaine Aldridge. Helping her is my mission."

"Aldridge, you said?"

The older woman was staring at Madelaine with the oddest expression. Madelaine began to fidget under her scrutiny. "Yes, Lady...?"

"Oh, gracious. I'm sorry, Lady Madelaine," Lady Elizabeth rushed out. "This is my aunt, Lady Denton."

Lady Denton smiled warmly at Madelaine. "You may call me Helen *in private*. All my friends do."

Madelaine blinked in surprise. "Are we to be friends?" Her cheeks immediately flamed again at the bluntness of her words.

Helen chuckled. "What's the matter, dear? Are you not used to having friends?"

"Not at Court," Madelaine answered truthfully.

"But we are now friends!" Lady Elizabeth exclaimed as she clutched Madelaine's hand. "If you are to call my aunt 'Helen,' I insist you call me 'Elizabeth'. I know I didn't show myself to be worthy of friendship before, but I swear I can be a good friend."

"What's this about not being a worthy friend?" Helen fixed Elizabeth with a narrow-eyed look. "Your mother and I taught you better."

Lady Elizabeth blushed. "Yes, I remember. However belatedly."

"You two had better spit out what's afoot. I'm to sit by the queen at dinner tonight, so I mustn't be late."

"The problem *is* the queen."

Helen's eyes rounded and she waved a hand at her lady's maid. "Make sure the door is shut tightly."

"Yes, my lady." The servant scurried to the door and a soft click filled the air.

"Niece, you must learn to make sure no one can overhear you before you ever speak negatively of the queen or king."

"I know, Aunt. Grey already reminded me earlier."

"Then do try to actually remember. Now, is Her Majesty causing you problems?"

"Not me." Elizabeth glanced at Madelaine. "It's her. The queen dislikes Madelaine for some reason and she takes every opportunity to belittle her. I thought if Madelaine knew why, she could work to earn the queen's favor."

Helen regarded Madelaine with probing eyes. "Do you want the queen's favor?"

Madelaine shifted her feet. Why was she constantly being put in a position to either tell a truth that could hurt her or lie? A fool would speak plainly to someone she had just met, and she may not be accomplished at feminine pursuits, but that did not mean she was a fool. "I don't want to be miserable at Court."

"Take a lesson, Elizabeth," Helen said. "This young lady has mastered the art of answering a question without really doing so. I predict you will rise to glorious heights in this Court."

"I do not want to rise to glorious heights here," Madelaine said.

"I'm pleased to hear that," Helen said, surprising her. "I find women who want to rise to great heights often are the very ones who should not. So you don't want to ascend to the top of the social heap, but what do you want?"

All she wanted was to find a husband she could love or learn to love, who if she was very lucky would be pleased, and not horrified, by a wife who enjoyed the same things he did. Then she would become betrothed and leave this wretched place of cattiness, debauchery and lying behind. Her mother would smile in her grave, her father would rest easier, and then she would feel as if she had somehow made amends for putting a rift between her parents.

Here she was again stuck in a position of truth or lies. Instinct told her only the truth might persuade this woman to help her. And she needed all the help she could get. "I want to find a good man to marry, so I can fulfill my mother's dying wish to see me properly wed. I was not an easy daughter."

Helen's eyebrows raised high. "How so?"

Madelaine quickly told Helen about her affinity for all things her father loved and nothing her mother did. When she was finished, that same niggling guilt that had plagued her since her mother's death coiled in her stomach.

Helen sighed. "You remind me of my much younger self. I was gloriously willful and my husband appreciated and adored it." Helen patted Madelaine's hand. "Take heart. There's a man lurking beyond this door for you. One who will appreciate who you truly are."

"Do you think you can do anything to help me?"

"Dearie, I can *more* than help you." Helen linked her arm through Madelaine's and moved toward the door.

"Aunt Helen is the keeper of the castle secrets," Elizabeth said with a giggle. "She was one of Queen Charlotte's very first confidants."

Madelaine pulled back a bit. "I don't want to put you in a position to betray a trust."

"Nonsense." Helen fairly shoved Madelaine into the hall and motioned for them to proceed. She took Madelaine's arm and leaned close as they walked so their heads were side by side. "No one places me in any position. If I do something, it's because I want to."

That was exactly how Madelaine had lived her life thus far and a fat lot of good it had done her. But she refrained from sharing those specific thoughts. "Do you have any idea why the queen dislikes me?"

"It's not you." Helen paused in her step. "Well, actually by default of your bloodline it is. Her Majesty considered your mother an enemy from day one."

"My mother? But she never even came to Court!" Madelaine clenched her hands together, outrage for her mother stirring in her blood.

"Calm yourself," Helen hissed, but took Madelaine's hand in hers and gently tugged. They started walking again, the tap of their slippered feet echoing in the deserted corridor. "Did you never wonder why your Father often came to Court but not your mother?"

Madelaine shook her head. She had assumed her mother stayed behind with her because she was an especially doting mother.

Helen sighed. "I knew your mother and liked her very much. She was childhood friends with Lady Napier, who was once Lady Sara Lennox. Sara is the heart of the trouble between your mother and the queen."

When they reached the top of the steps that led to the dining hall, Helen paused. "King George was smitten with Sara. When her family learned of it they made her abandon her plans to marry a man I think she truly did love. But then our king changed his mind or rather it was changed for him. He married Queen Charlotte instead and Sara—let us just say it took her a long time to find happiness and at great cost to her good name."

"What's my mother have to do with this?" Madelaine asked as she descended the stairs.

"Privately, Sara blamed her misfortunes on the king and therefore the queen. Your mother staunchly stood by Sara and never did take to the queen. Your mother was very beautiful. Beauty has power and the queen did not like coming newly to our Court only to have a beautiful woman who did not trip over herself to serve her. And your mother was clever. She never said an outright unkind word. Yet daily she pointed out to Her Majesty the little things of our culture she had not properly mastered."

"As the queen does to me!" Madelaine stopped before the dining room hall. Everything she had just learned vied for attention inside her head. Ordering her thoughts was difficult, but she forced herself to the task. "Yet my mother was not thrown from Court? How could it be if she openly needled the queen?"

"Because the queen knew better than to demand such a thing from the king. His Majesty and your father were close even then."

"So the king didn't know of the trouble between my mother and the queen?"

"No. Never."

That explained why Madelaine's father insisted she come to Court to find a proper husband even if it didn't necessarily explain why her father seemed to want to have her married off so quickly. She had thought to have a Season when their mourning was over, but he had been steadfast that Court was where she should be. He'd said she would not be one of many debutantes here, but one of a few honored ladies-in-waiting, therefore she should be betrothed right away. He had no inkling the men at Court would rather seduce than propose nor did he know the queen had hated his wife.

If he only knew. Madelaine pushed the errant thought away. She could never tell her father. It would devastate him to think the queen had hated Mother and Mother had deceived him by never telling him. It didn't matter anyway. She had a debt to pay to her parents and a duty to fulfill. "My mother's lack of punishment must have eaten at the queen all these years."

"Now you see. The queen never got retribution as she wished, so now she punishes you."

"It's hopeless."

"You give up too easily," Helen chided.

"What must she do?" Lady Elizabeth asked.

The dining room door opened suddenly and the noise from within rolled into the corridor like the hum of a thousand birds' wings flapping in unison. Lady Helen faced

Madelaine. "Prove your loyalty to the queen above everyone else, and then you will have her forgiveness and her loyalty."

"How am I supposed to do that?" Madelaine called to Helen's departing figure.

Helen paused and turned back to her. "I don't have all the answers. Bide your time. It will come. It always does if one is patient enough."

Madelaine trudged behind Elizabeth to their appointed table. As Elizabeth took a seat across from Lord Thorton, he grinned lecherously at Madelaine and patted the seat beside him. She sat and his hand immediately found her knee under the table. She retaliated by swatting him away as discreetly as she could.

She didn't have a single moment to bide. She needed the queen's favor. Without it, she dare not whisper a word of Lord Thorton's attempts to take advantage of her. If the queen disliked her, that bit of information could easily be manipulated to make her look like she lacked morals.

When Lord Thorton's hand found her leg again and massaged her knee, she picked up her fork, discreetly slid it under the bench and pressed the prongs into his flesh as hard as she could. His hand ceased moving. She raised her gaze to meet his—sure he would be glaring at her, but the man stared as if she were the choicest piece of meat he'd ever seen. Disgust rolled through her. Immediately, she released the fork and the pressure of his hand lifted from her leg. If only she had her dagger then maybe he would see her as a danger instead of a conquest. Tomorrow, she would secure it under her dress in case she encountered him again.

As she took a large sip of wine from her goblet, he pressed his lips by her ear. She darted a quick gaze around. Thank God everyone was busily engaged in their own conversation. "I like feisty women," he said in a slur of already consumed wine.

"You'll find me deadly, not feisty," she hissed, meaning every word. She quickly stuffed a chunk of bread in her mouth to avoid more conversation with him. But as she chewed, he slid closer. The sticky heat of his body enveloped her. Her stomach turned and she could not swallow the hunk of bread in her mouth.

She couldn't wait any longer. Time was her enemy. If things stayed as they were, she would be forced to drastic measures. She had excellent aim and had no doubt she could hit Lord Thorton if he tried to corner her alone and ravish her. But it would be deuced hard to fulfill her mother's wish and not disappoint her father if she was hung for murder. And blast hell with ice, her life may not be all she had hoped so far, but living was far more preferable than death.

Six

Grey awoke the next morning in a sour mood. Who wouldn't be in a sour mood if they had been forced to go to bed hungry because they'd waited until near midnight to see the king. Grey rubbed his aching back. Someone needed to purchase more comfortable chairs in the king's receiving chamber. Of course, comfortable chairs wouldn't be necessary if the king actually granted audiences to those he'd commanded to appear on specific days at very specific times. The most frustrating part of his night though wasn't the dinner. Dinner he could live without. Lack of food he could quickly amend. And he intended to shortly. Missed opportunities were harder to fix. And he'd missed the opportunity to speak more with Lady Madelaine. But he'd dreamed about her.

His cock hardened in remembrance. He smiled recalling the balmy weather, blue skies and Lady Madelaine's skillful mouth and hands. The fantasy had been vivid. But when he threw off his covers cold air swept over him and chased away the remnants of his dream. Reality made him frown. The last thing he wanted to do today was return to the king's chambers to once again wait idly and uncomfortably to be granted an audience the king himself had commanded, but wait he would. Like an obedient dog.

Grey growled as he groped around for his trousers. He

stomped toward his bag, pulled out a shirt, whipped it through the air to dislodge some of the wrinkles and pulled it over his head. As he thudded back to the bed and located his boots, Gravenhurst sat up in the bed next to Grey's. And then a slighter figure with a distinctly flowery smell sat up beside Gravenhurst.

Grey chuckled to himself. At least one of them had not wasted their first night at Court. "Good morning, Gravenhurst."

"By all accounts it should be," Gravenhurst grumbled.

"Did your company keep you up too late?" Grey didn't bother to conceal the sarcasm in his voice.

A derisive, feminine snort came from the woman. The brown blanket covering her head fell to her shoulders. Grey couldn't quite make out the color of her eyes in the lingering predawn shadows of the room, but a streak of sunlight cutting through the air from the stained-glass window touched the top of her head. By damned she had the reddest hair he'd ever seen. But a pretty red, like fine burgundy.

"Lord Gravenhurst kept me up, not the other way around." Her tone held amusement. "I was begging for sleep."

"I imagine you were, Lady…?"

"It's kind of you to grant me the courtesy, but we both know I'm no lady, don't "we?" The woman rose from the bed with the blanket wrapped around her slender figure, but low enough that a good portion of her ample breasts showed. Grey didn't turn away. If she wanted to display her wares, he'd be happy to look, but that didn't mean he'd be buying. The sun now hit her full on in the face, and amusement filled her green, slanted eyes. This was a lady who enjoyed being stared at. She was not a lady in the class of someone like Lady Madelaine, but no average chit either. He had had met plenty of both kinds of women and this fiery wench was bold as brass and not a wink ashamed of waking up naked as the day she was born in front of two men, one definitely a stranger and one a semi-stranger. "Do you work in the castle?"

"I do."

"Talkative chit, aren't you?"

She shrugged. "Most men I meet don't want to talk." She dropped the blanket and stooped to pick up her gown. Her amply curved body looked like one made specifically for pleasure, but for once he wasn't filled with the rush of desire a beautiful woman usually caused. The woman pulled on her dark, threadbare gown and turned her back to Grey and Gravenhurst, who now stood fully clothed by Grey. "Lace me up?"

Gravenhurst quickly obliged. When he finished, the woman swiveled around, planted a kiss on his mouth, and then reached behind her and twined her long hair into a knot at the nape of her neck. "You were exactly what I needed last night, my lord."

"Likewise." Gravenhurst handed the woman a gleaming, gold coin.

She tucked the coin between her breasts, and then locked her gaze on Grey. "You've a reputation, you know."

"So I've been told. Am I to believe I'm so notorious now that I'm the talk of the—?"

"Ladies-in-waiting."

He instantly pictured Lady Madelaine. "If you're trying to intrigue me, miss, you've succeeded. Do tell."

"I accidentally overheard them placing wagers on who would win your heart."

That could be a boon or a curse, depending on which

side of the wager Lady Madelaine placed her blunt. "You accidentally overheard them?" He raised a questioning eyebrow. "As in you eavesdropped?"

"Nay. I was tidying the queen's drawing room when they came in. I had to hide because we chambermaids aren't supposed to be seen."

A sarcastic comment burned to be said, but he had no wish to give her anymore reason to despise the queen's ladies as her derisive tone indicated she already did. Instead he asked, "Did all the ladies place a wager?"

The woman's smirk turned to downright amusement. "Don't tell me a particular lady has caught your fancy?"

The question made Grey grind his teeth. Lady Madelaine had bewitched him a bit, but it was nothing a good romp wouldn't cure. He wasn't his father. He didn't want to get married and have children so he could ignore all but one of them. He sure as hell wasn't going to go falling in love with Lady Madelaine and pledge his life to her. That would be just like his father, and he was done trying to please the old bastard. "Not really."

"All wagered but one."

"Which lady?"

"You're quite certain one of them hasn't stirred your appetite?"

Madelaine had done more than stir his appetite. With one encounter she'd unleashed it, and it seemed his need to know her was only growing. "Quite certain." The words barely escaped his clenched teeth.

"If you say so. Goodbye, milords." The woman was out the door without waiting for a reply.

Grey grabbed his coat off the chair, shoved his arms in and glared at Gravenhurst. "I'll not have time for breakfast thanks to you allowing your guest to sleep over." He was being unaccountably surly toward Gravenhurst, but he couldn't seem to stop his growing irritable mood.

"Don't try to tell me we kept you up. We were long finished by the time you crept in."

"Yes, but she detained me just now."

Gravenhurst chuckled. "Aye. For five whole minutes. How tedious for you. What's really the matter?"

Grey shrugged. He wished he knew.

Gravenhurst grinned. "Is it because a certain lady is here at Court? Is Miss Prattle still under your skin? Have you tried to meet her again and she didn't bother showing?"

"Shut up," Grey snapped.

Gravenhurst frowned. "Kidding aside. Did things not go well with the king?"

"He was indisposed all day and night, but he refused to excuse me. I don't comprehend why the king wants to speak with me—a mere equerry to a lesser land holder. I'm of no importance."

Gravenhurst splashed water on his face before toweling it off and replying. "He honors you because of your father."

Grey nodded, his irritation deepening. Never mind that he had wanted a commission. He was to be an equerry as his father commanded. The irony of his situation set his teeth on edge. His father had never taken any interest in him until Grey had told him he wanted to be a soldier. Then he'd taken enough notice to tell Grey "no" and give him orders to come here. After which the old bastard had ridden off with Grey's older brother as usual. Resentment curdled in his belly like sour milk. "I better go. I'll have just enough time to grab a hunk of bread and head to the king's chambers by my appointed hour."

By the time he reached the main floor, he'd worked himself up into the foulest mood he could recall in years.

Not since his sixteenth birthday, when his father had promised to take him hunting, just the two of them, had Grey been so irate. And that day had been a black one, for certain. When his father had shown up near midnight with Edward, Grey had not been merely upset that his father had broken yet another promise to him without explanation and seemingly in favor of spending time with Grey's older brother. Grey had been furious and vowed that night he would get his father's attention, even if he had to do it by being the old bastard's worst nightmare.

He laughed at what a foolish notion that had been. His father would have had to care first. The bastard didn't. He didn't blink an eye when Grey was thrown from Eton, or accrued a king's ransom worth of gambling debt, or drank himself into a month-long stupor. The only time he'd batted an eye was when Grey had bedded one of the lady's maids employed to care for Liz. That's when he'd realized how to get under his father's skin.

Grey rounded the last turn to the dining hall. When had he realized his actions weren't changing a damn thing? He felt certain his little epiphany had occurred this past year. Yet he liked women. So he seduced the ones that were willing. But he would never get married. Let his father stew for the rest of his life on how he'd failed.

Grey pushed open the door to the dining hall. At this hour it would be empty, except for the servants preparing for breakfast. Good thing too. He was not in the mood for pleasant conversation, and the servants would be too busy to talk. The servants nodded toward him as he strode into the hall, but as he expected, they continued in their preparations for breakfast.

He ambled over to the far wall, where a different assortment of breads and cheeses should be laid out, but none was there yet. His stomach growled again. A servant came through the door with a large tray lifted above his head. The pleasant scent of warm bread wafted on the air. Grey smiled and was just about to call out to the man when the dining hall door swung wide again, and Lady Madelaine flew through the door, in a flurry of pale green silk which contrasted quite nicely with her honey hair that tumbled around her shoulders.

The exquisite picture she presented would have stirred his lust, but her dark eyes were round with fear and her hands grasped spasmodically in front of her.

From across the room, he raised his hand to get her notice, but the door swung wide again and hard footsteps rang in the otherwise quiet room. Grey narrowed his eyes as Thorton strode toward Madelaine. What the hell was that man doing up so early? Thorton was a liar, a cheat, and a lazy ass.

Lady Madelaine shot a glance behind her, and then swung toward Thorton, her gaze darting all over the room. What was this? If the lady was secretly meeting with Thorton, Grey would toss up his breakfast. Oh hell, he'd not eaten breakfast.

Lady Madelaine backed behind a table, and lifted her skirt. Bile filled Grey's mouth. He'd not watch the woman he'd fantasized about being plundered by another. He turned on his heel to go, but a long flash of metal caught his eye. His jaw dropped at the gleaming dagger Lady Madelaine held in front of her. He'd seen stranger games between a man and a woman, but this had to be the strangest.

"Lady Madelaine, you wound me," Lord Thorton said, coming to stand on the opposite side of the table from her. Grey stood still and silent, not sure whether to excuse himself or hide and save her the embarrassment of knowing he'd witnessed her and Thorton.

She squared her shoulders. "I've not wounded you yet, you swine, but I swear if you grab me again, I'll use my dagger." Now that was definitely an interesting choice of words to elicit a man's desire. Maybe they played at prey and hunter.

"Come, Lady Madelaine. Don't make me use force. This could be pleasant for both of us."

Grey's heartbeat sped up a notch. Something wasn't right.

Lady Madelaine raised the dagger higher. "If your hands are on me, I vow it will not be pleasant."

Thorton lunged across the table, and true to her word, Lady Madelaine plunged the dagger straight down toward the man's leg. "You bitch," Thorton cursed loudly, causing the only servant remaining in the room to flee.

Red covered Grey's vision. He kicked the chair blocking his path out of the way. The wood splintered as it hit the table with the force of his anger. He was beside Lady Madelaine in four long strides. Her eyes smoldered, but her body shook. Grey pushed her gently behind him and faced Thorton.

Thorton jerked the dagger out of the wood and material of his trousers. The material ripped as the dagger let loose. "You saw it, Adlard. The bloody bitch tried to stab me. You're my witness."

"I did not *try* to stab you," Lady Madelaine spat. "I gave you a reprieve with my generous warning. If I intended to stab you, believe me, the dagger would have pierced flesh."

Grey snatched the dagger from Thorton while studying Lady Madelaine's grim face. Her words as well as her aim impressed him. "I saw you try to accost her."

"The hell you say. She wants me."

Grey glanced back at Lady Madelaine. "Do you want this man?"

She shook her head. "Unless you count wanting him dead."

He smothered his laugh as he turned back to Thorton. "It's too bad she decided to be generous, Thorton. In my opinion, you deserved a dagger in your leg, at the least." Grey wanted to kill the man for trying to force himself on her. Grey curled his fingers into fists. "If you ever touch her again, I'll not be near as generous as the lady. But take heart, I know just where to strike with a dagger to make your death quick." He touched the pulsing vein on Thorton's neck. "My father considered teaching his sons all means of self-defense of the utmost importance."

Thorton shoved Grey's hand away. "I won't forget this," the man snarled.

"Neither will I," Grey promised.

Thorton opened his mouth as if to say something else, and Grey raised the dagger challengingly. "Shall we test my lessons?"

Thorton spat on the floor and slammed out of the room. Grey gripped the dagger, trying to calm himself and slow the blood roaring in his ears and his painful heartbeat.

Lady Madelaine rested a hand on his arm. "You can release my dagger now, Lord Grey. He's gone."

Grey relaxed his hold and handed the dagger over. A witty reply laced with sexual innuendo was on the tip of his tongue, but when he looked into her warm, anxious eyes his witty reply was gone. "Were you afraid?"

"Yes. Were you?"

The honest admission and question surprised him. Honesty at Court was so novel. "I wasn't afraid for myself."

"For me?"

"Yes." With a start he realized he was telling the truth not merely trying to seduce her. "What if I hadn't been in the dining hall? What if Thorton had ravished you? I'd hate to think anyone had you against your will."

Her cheeks redden. "I do try to avoid him."

"You need to tell the queen."

She shook her head.

Damnation. He understood. The queen disliked her. She could very well use the information against Lady Madelaine. And the other ladies-in-waiting definitely would. "Do you have a brother?"

"No." She seemed amused by his questions. He ran a hand through his hair, wild thoughts careening in his head.

"What of your father?"

"I cannot disappoint him." Grey nodded in understanding. She wouldn't be the first lady abandoned at Court with the silent or sometimes explicit orders to not fail in finding a husband. "You need a protector."

"Lord Grey, are you offering to protect me?" A look of disbelief crossed her delicate features.

"Certainly not." He couldn't seduce her if he vowed to protect her. But he couldn't very well leave her to the likes of Thorton. He scratched at his head, trying to bring some semblance to his thoughts, but it was a lost cause. "I must admit I was surprised and gladdened to find you at Court."

"Were you?"

The way her blush deepened like a cherry ready to be picked made him hard as stone. So deceptively innocent yet complex. He loved the puzzle she presented. "I was." He moved closer and brushed a hand across her collarbone. She jerked in response. For a seductress, that was an odd response. Maybe this was the game she played? "You made an appearance in my dreams more nights than I should admit."

Her lips parted as if his statement surprised her. Her acting abilities were superb. He ran a finger up her arm, gliding over fine silk and a gentle curve of muscle she must have developed from the sports she spoke of loving. His blood pounded thickly in his ears. "That was very naughty of you not to return to meet me in Golden Square as you promised, but I'll forgive you since I realize you must have slipped away without asking. Is that true?"

She nodded, her pulse hammering at the base of her neck. Good. She was just as excited as he was.

"Will you keep my secret?" Her tongue wet her upper then lower lip causing him to harden further. This state had to be dangerous to his health. He needed release. Where could they possibly meet. Perhaps the stables? He could pay off the stable boys to disappear for a while. They would simply have to think of an excuse for her to slip away.

"I'll keep your secret, for a price." He pressed closer and reached to grasp her, but she skittered away and went around to the other side of the table. Her hands splayed against the dark grain as she stared at him.

"How disappointing, Lord Grey. For a moment, I thought you to be different from all the tedious men I've met at Court, but I see you are exactly the same."

"Bite your tongue. I'm the same as no man. Meet me in the stable and I'll prove it."

Her eyebrows knitted together. "I'm afraid you have the wrong impression of me."

"You don't like the stables?" Blazes, he was having more fun bantering with her than he'd ever had talking to any woman. "I assumed since you loved sports you wouldn't mind a tumble in the hay."

"You assume wrong on many counts, Lord Grey."

Her words held an iciness that doused a chill over his desire. There was a critical piece to her puzzle he was missing. "I beg your pardon, Lady Madelaine, if I was crass. I was simply bantering with you."

Her eyebrows arched high. "So you didn't just invite me to a tumble in the hay?"

"Oh, I did. Rather poorly done of me. I assumed a lady such as yourself who loved sports and adventure would like the idea of a tumble in the stables. But I understand now. You prefer a bed over the stables. I can accommodate you, but you'll have to give me time to figure out where we can meet privately and how to get you there."

She slapped her palms against the wood, her frown turning beautifully thunderous. "Lord Grey, you've misunderstood every word I've said. I don't wish to be pursued or tumbled."

"You don't? But at Golden Square—"

She held up a palm. "You were correct in assuming I slipped away without permission. Which I had never done before that day. I knew I was to be deposited at Court the next day. A situation that didn't please me. I wanted one last adventure to see things I'd never seen. The adventure never included bed sport."

"That's not much of an adventure."

"I seek a husband, Lord Grey. The adventure of marriage will be quite enough for me." Her blush burned bright on her face.

Blazes. He'd misjudged her character by leaps and bounds. It was strange he didn't feel as surly as he should about his mistake, considering his state of arousal. Rather, he was glad to have finally met a woman who was a true surprise in a good way. Under the circumstances, his honor now demanded he offer his services as protector, even if his loins wanted otherwise. "I suppose, given this enlightening conversation, I've no choice but to protect you from Thorton."

Lady Madelaine walked to the side table and picked up a roll. "And here I was certain the tales about you were true." She took a bite of the roll and chewed but the corners of her mouth tugged upward into a smile.

"What tales?" He came to stand beside her and get a hunk of bread for himself.

"Well." She swallowed. "The other ladies-in-waiting likened you to Casanova, but if this is you at your most charming, I'm afraid you fall short." She grinned.

"I'm glad I can amuse you. But I vow I can be extremely charming."

"In that case, I'm happy you understand turning your immense charms on me is pointless for what you are after."

"Come." He offered his elbow. "In case Thorton is lurking, let me walk you where you are going." He had enough time to do that and still get to the king's chambers at the appointed hour. She slipped her arm through his and a jolt of awareness shot through him. He'd held many women before, during and after the heat of passion, but none had ever made his body hum with a simple chaste touch. It occurred to him as they walked, and her warmth heated his side and her floral scent filled his nostrils, he had not promised to protect her from himself, only Thorton. A small tug of conscience reared its annoying head to pose the question of which was worse—a wolf in sheep's clothing or simply a wolf.

"I'm no wolf."

She stopped and glanced at him. "What did you say?"

"I said I'm no wolf. I'm not at all like Thorton."

"Lord Grey, no one has accused you of that."

"Yes. I'm sorry." By God, he was rambling. He'd never rambled because of a woman in his life. It was almost a relief when Lady Madelaine disappeared with a quick goodbye into the queen's chambers. Now if only his conscience regarding the lady would disappear.

Seven

$\mathcal{G}$rey pushed thoughts of Madelaine aside as he entered the king's audience chamber. Yesterday there had been two guards who had asked him to identify himself, but today the guards were not at their post. That was odd. Across the room, beyond the formidable, oak door that led to the king's bedroom, angry voices erupted, followed by a strange clattering sound.

Temptation had always been a problem for Grey. Women tempted him. Danger tempted him, and now his curiosity tempted him. He needed to see what was happening. No doubt that would lead to danger, which would lead to a problem. But the thrill of excitement was too great to ignore.

With a quick glance around the candlelit chamber to ensure he was alone, he moved to the midway point between the outer door and the bedchamber. He half expected a guard to burst out from the king's chambers and yell "got you" just as Edward used to do when tormenting him by forcing him to play endless games of hide-and-seek.

He smiled at the memory. Thanks to Edward's excellent instruction on how to move through the shadows, Grey had never been caught during any of his more wicked adventures. From behind the door, shouting commenced again followed by a single, harsh command that rang with the king's noble tones. The room fell so silent that each breath Grey took hissed in his ears.

"Cease bickering," a voice commanded, as only the king could. "You there." A fervent murmuring of voices rose to fill the silence. "Bring me my favorite blanket. No need to freeze to death while I endure Sir Walter's cures."

As the oak door creaked open, Grey slipped behind the dark folds of the floor-length curtains. He should let his presence be known, but then he wouldn't have any idea what was happening. The other thing Edward had taught Grey was to know everything about any situation you are entering. The next time he saw his older brother he would have to thank him for all the advice. A pinch-faced page rushed into the room, grabbed a plush, burgundy blanket off the settee and flew back through the oak door.

Grey smiled at the cracked door. It was perfect. If he moved closer and was careful, he could see into the room without being seen. He slipped down the length of the wall until he was by the door, and then he positioned himself where he could see through the crack.

At the main entrance to the inner sanctuary, candles blazed and illuminated the pinched face of the page huddled near the wall. The sapling's eyes grew wide and Grey followed the man's gaze.

The scene froze his blood. His breath caught, and then released on a rush of disbelief. Cursing his mistake, he checked the faces, but none appeared to have heard his noisy exhalation.

The king reclined on his bed against a mound of pillows. Grey hadn't seen the king in two years, but he did not look like himself. And age wasn't to blame. His hair was cropped short, his face pale and the bones there too sharp and protruding as if a great amount of flesh had recently been lost.

Grey glanced further down the king's body and a wave of nausea washed over him. Notched bowls surrounded His Majesty's naked upper torso to catch the lines of crimson that trickled down his thin arms. The king jerked when the white-haired man standing over him pressed something silver to His Majesty's arm. One of the wooden bowls tipped and a crimson stain seeped across the ivory sheet.

The page sprang forward from the wall, but stopped as the king's eyes opened and pinned him. "Leave it. You can clean me up like a shiny coin when Sir Walter is finished."

"As you wish, Your Majesty."

The king's answer was a ragged breath that filled Grey's ears. The man beside the king had paused, his hand suspended in the air, and with his wild white hair and menacing tool he looked like a mad man. Yet the king must trust him. "Proceed, Sir Walter," His Majesty commanded.

The man bent over the king for some time and when he rose, beads of sweat dripped down his forehead. Bile filled Grey's mouth. Puckered skin littered His Majesty's arms and pulsed blood from the dozens of small punctures wounds. Grey had seen enough. He moved away from the door, along the wall and back to the audience chamber where he sat to wait for the king to admit him.

This time, Grey would wait without complaint. Any man who endured a bloodletting such as the king just had without so much as a whimper deserved more than the respect demanded by his title. The king had just won Grey's respect as a man.

Not more than an hour later, the oak door to the bedchamber flung wide open and Sir Walter shuffled out followed by the page, Peter, and the two stony-faced guards Grey had met the day before. The tallest of the two guards

stopped in front of Grey as everyone else quietly left the
room. "His Majesty says you may enter now."

Grey narrowed his eyes at the unexpected words. He
hadn't been announced. Had the king finally remembered
him or had someone seen him lurking at the door? He
didn't think it was the latter, but he'd soon find out. He rose
and followed the guard into the king's bedchambers, his
nostrils flaring as he inhaled the fetid stench of oozing
wounds. He forced deep breaths to accustom himself to the
acrid smell of blood lingering all around him.

By the time he stood in front of the king, Grey had
himself under control. He dropped to his knee by the king's
feet and bowed. "Your Majesty."

"Rise, Lord Grey."

Grey stood and had to look down to meet the king's
gaze. His Majesty sat in a high-backed wooden chair clothed
in robes of dark green, which enhanced the thinness and
paleness of his face. His faded, yellowed eyes locked on
Grey. "On second thought, sit here." He waved a hand
toward another high-backed chair that faced him. "I don't
like to look up to anyone." A slight smile spread across the
king's gaunt face, and Grey could almost recall the vibrant
man who he had last seen two years ago when the king had
stopped to lodge at their house on the way back to
Windsor.

Grey settled into the uncomfortable chair. "You bid me
to see you before I started my duties as equerry, Your
Majesty."

"I did. And I'm pleased to know you do not disappoint.
You arrived precisely when I told you to, sat all day
yesterday and waited patiently today while I was preoccupied. And you did not even blink to see me in such a state."

"You saw me at the door?"

"Only because I was watching for you. If you are to work for me you must thrive on danger. You proved you do by approaching my door uninvited."

Grey stared at the king, trying to work through his maze of words. Work for His Majesty? He supposed even though he would be directly reporting to Lord Pearson every British subject technically worked for the king. Yet still... "As your subject, of course."

"No, Grey."

Grey narrowed his eyes at the king's unexpected familiarity. What was going on? He felt as he often did when stumbling upon Edward and Father in conversation—lost as to the true nature of the talk. "I beg your pardon, Your Majesty, but I'm afraid I don't understand."

"Yes. I know. Forgive me. Let us start from the beginning. Pearson does not need an equerry."

There it was again—the king had slipped into familiarity. Unpardonable to question or comment though. "He doesn't?" Grey asked, settling on the matter which he could address.

"No. He doesn't. Pearson, your father, your brother and the others need another man to join their ranks. As do I. Pearson was a ruse I required as the offer can come from no one but me." The king leaned over and picked up a small, rectangular, gilded box off the table. On the lid a silver circle had been engraved. "Do you know what's in this box, Grey?"

Was this a trick question? Was he supposed to know? Hell, all of a sudden he wished he'd spent more time listening to all the boring tutors his father had hired to teach him and less time dreaming of his next scheme to win his father's attention. It hadn't worked, anyway. "I'm sorry, Your Majesty, I don't."

"Your future, if you so choose, is in this box. Never let it be said you had no choice. You do. This moment is your choice. Your father and your brother recommend you to me, and they both say you are more than ready. I'm told you're already trained in many of the things you'll need to know."

Grey didn't know what the hell the king was talking about. He hadn't put any stock in the whispers that the king had certain spells, but maybe the whispers were correct. But remaining silent was the wisest option.

With bony fingers, the king released the latch that secured the lid of the box. The lid opened with a creak. He withdrew a silver ring and handed it to Grey. Grey rubbed his finger over the smooth surface of the silver. Six small, red stones, only noticeable when the ring was held up close, were set evenly around the ring. "My father has a ring that has six stones in it," Grey said. He'd always wondered what the six stones had stood for, and his father's flimsy explanation had never seemed believable to him. His pulse picked up in pace once again.

"Yes. He would."

"And my brother." Grey gripped the ring in his now sweating palm. "The rings are only similar in the number of stones. Yet still, I can't help but think there's more to the similarity."

"I gave your brother his ring on his twentieth birthday. Much too young really. But we had a dire need."

"Look inside the band," His Majesty commanded.

Grey brought the ring up close and squinted to make out the engraving. "Loyalty. To who? You?"

"To me and to each other. Do you see the way the 'y' loops around to touch the 'l' then back to meet the end of the 'y'? The word was engraved to form a perfect circle that symbolizes the unending trusts between me and my spies. Each ring has a different word engraved in it. Can't have anyone linking the rings together. Your father's ring says trust. But the words are also looped to form a connection."

"Spies?" Grey clamped his mouth shut the second he realized it was hanging open.

"Of course. How do you think we stay so powerful? Kings must make luck, Grey, and always be six steps ahead of everyone else. My spies are my luck—each a step that keeps me on the throne. One of them has been killed. And now I need another."

Astonishment was too weak a word for what Grey was feeling. "And you are asking *me*?"

"Were your father and brother wrong about you? You seem surprised."

By God he *was* surprised. His father must feel something akin to warmness for him to recommend him to the king. Shame swept through him like a raging fever. He clenched his teeth together on the need to confess the ass he had been for the last fifteen years. A thirty-year-old self-indulgent bastard didn't deserve to be a spy for the king. But, by damned, he wanted this. He would become a spy. Hell, he would devote his entire life to being a spy. And then maybe he would earn his father's love and respect. He paused. It had been years since he'd admitted to himself he wanted those things.

The king smiled at him. "Your eyes give me your answer. Put on the ring and say the vow."

He quickly did as he was told, and once the words of loyalty were spoken, and he was dismissed to spend this one day as he wished, he knew exactly what he wanted to do. He wanted to find Madelaine and make a fresh start. Maybe they could take a stroll or a ride through the park.

He wanted to get to know her not as the man he had been, but as the man he wanted to be—no longer an unrepentant rake but a man of honor like his brother and father.

⋘⦓⦔⋙

It took him a good hour to find Lady Madelaine, but it was worth the effort and the coin he had to part with to get her lady's maid to reveal that Lady Madelaine had slipped out of the castle to collect some flowers as a surprise for the queen. Grey snorted at the thought. There weren't any flowers in bloom this time of year, and the maid had said Lady Madelaine was carrying something wrapped in a cape.

He suspected she'd slipped away to get in some target practice with her bow and arrow, and when he spotted her close to the woods and hidden by several tall trees from the view of anyone who chanced to look out the castle window his suspicion was confirmed. He started to make his way toward her, but stopped as she drew up her bow and arrow and aimed at a distant tree she'd placed a circular target on.

He didn't want to startle her or throw off her aim with his approach. By the look of concentration on her face, and from what he'd already seen of her archery skill, she took her practice seriously. He leaned against a tree to watch her. She pulled her bow taut, moved her face into and away from the wind, and shifted her stance.

Desire made him shift his own position. She fascinated him. He'd never seen a look of such determination on a woman's face unless she was determined to trap a man into marriage. Lady Madelaine wanted marriage, an admission by her own lips. He should be avoiding her at all cost yet he was here. What would marriage to her be like? He'd never considered marring anyone. A lady to tumble for pleasure and to annoy his father with scandal was the closest he'd ever linked himself with any woman.

He knelt down by the tree no longer wanting to approach her. What better way to learn the real her than to watch her. Her guard would be down. Every time she smiled, he smiled. Her exclaims of frustration made him laugh. But the way she threw her arms over her head in triumph when she made a good shot was the best part of watching her. She was beautiful, and his lust was stirred. Yet something else was awakened.

He'd been stirred to lust many times in his life. It was her uniqueness that he found compelling. She cared for things women were not supposed to. She loved these things so much she'd chanced sneaking away and incurring the queen's ire or worse. Lady Madelaine was going to have a deuced hard time with the marriage she was seeking if her future husband minded a wife who wasn't the typical female most men seemed to want.

Most men, except him. He smiled and frowned in turn, but a stick breaking beside him interrupted his musings. He reached for his dagger and glanced up at the shadowy figure above him.

As he shielded his eyes from the sun's glare, Gravenhurst dropped to his haunches. "Spying?" he said, looking between Madelaine and Grey.

"Something like that." Grey shifted uncomfortably at being caught, Gravenhurst's knowing smirk, and his friend's choice of words. Gravenhurst had been the one person Grey had ever confided anything in, and it seemed strange not to be able to tell his friend about becoming a spy for the king.

"Are you working out a plan of attack?" Gravenhurst asked.

"Not exactly." Grey watched Madelaine draw another arrow. He quickly told Gravenhurst of his encounter with Lady Madelaine and Thorton, and their enlightening conversation afterward.

Gravenhurst chuckled. "I'd say that's the worst misjudging of a lady you've ever done."

"I've never misjudged what a lady wants, until now."

"And misjudging her makes you smile?"

Did it? Grey quickly wiped the smile from his face once he realized Gravenhurst was correct.

"Who do you think she's imagining she's shooting?" Gravenhurst sat on the ground and crossed his legs out in front of him.

Grey ran a hand over the stubble on his face. "Could be me or Thorton. It's hard to say."

"Take heart, Grey. Your character may be tarnished in her mind, but I doubt she thinks you a bloody bastard, which is undoubtedly how she thinks of Thorton."

"You're helpful as always," Grey said, irritated his time alone to study her was being interrupted. "Why are you here anyway? Bored?"

"I came to find you."

"And you have. Spit it out and be gone."

"I'm under the king's orders." Gravenhurst swatted at a bee buzzing around his face. The sun glinted off his ring. Grey frowned, followed the path of his friend's hand and hissed low as he counted the six stones he'd never paid heed to before. He stared at the man he'd considered like another brother for as long as he could remember. He thought he knew Gravenhurst as well as he knew himself, but doubt now bombarded him. What did he really know of anyone?

What was certain and what was fabrication? Gravenhurst's parents had died when he was very young, and he'd been raised by an uncaring, distant relative who'd let Gravenhurst come and go as he pleased. His friend had spent more time at Grey's house than his own, and Grey had not even minded when Gravenhurst and Edward had become good friends as well. Grey had been glad that Gravenhurst had someone else who cared about his welfare. These were facts.

Gravenhurst was gone a good many months out of the year. Another fact. He claimed he loved to travel and he would rather do it when he was young, in good health, and unencumbered by a wife who wouldn't be able to endure the adventures he went on. This was likely fabrication. Gravenhurst had never once asked Grey to go on one of his trips with him, and now that Grey cast his mind back, he was certain his friend had been gone many of the same times Edward or Father were gone. He swallowed a knot of astonishment. "You work for the king."

Gravenhurst slapped Grey on the shoulder. "That I do, my friend. And not, mind you, as an equerry."

"You bloody bastard. Why didn't you tell me?" His words came out on an exhalation.

"I didn't tell you because I wasn't able to. Just as you will never be able to talk of what you do with anyone but the king or one of the other five spies who are part of our circle. I took a vow to keep the secret, just as you have. You cannot be angry with me for that."

"I'm not angry, just shocked at the discovery. How long have you worked for the king?"

"Since I was twenty-one."

Grey whistled. "Eleven years. They recruited you young."

"Come on. We'll talk as we walk."

"Walk?"

Gravenhurst nodded toward Lady Madelaine. "Either we move or the lady catches us here."

Grey scrambled to his feet and followed Gravenhurst back toward the castle. "There's much to accomplish in the next couple of weeks," Gravenhurst said. "The king wants me to prepare you to track down Sutton's killer with me."

"Sutton was a spy, and he was killed?"

"Yes. He was captured while on a mission in France with Stratmore several months ago. And our contact in France confirms Sutton was killed by De La Touche."

"Stratmore is a spy? Lady Madelaine's father?"

"Try to keep up, Grey."

"I'm keeping up, damn it. That doesn't mean I'm not surprised. Who is De La Touche?"

"Napoleon's most favored spy. And his deadliest one. Mostly we spies have a code. We lie, we cheat, we steal, but normally we don't kill, unless absolutely necessary."

Grey nodded, but his mind reeled. Stratmore a spy. Pearson a spy. And Grey's father had killed men. His brother? How little he really knew about his own family. The shame of all the jealousy he had felt swept through him again. He'd assumed so much about his father, and it was all wrong. "I take it this man De La Touche does not abide by the spy code of conduct."

"No. He doesn't. In the last five years, he's killed two of our spies. Sutton makes number three."

Grey walked into the courtyard of the castle and stopped. He glanced back and waited until Lady Madelaine came into view. All this talk of killing made him want to ensure she got into the castle safely, though he knew she was safe here. She trudged toward the castle, her sluggish steps making it obvious she didn't want to return to her mundane duties as a lady-in-waiting. A smile tugged at his lips. Poor dove. He understood her reluctance. He watched her for a moment, before refocusing on Gravenhurst. "How can you be certain Sutton is dead?"

"Our contact has never been wrong. Besides that, he identified Sutton's body and retrieved his ring, which you are now wearing."

Revulsion swept through Grey. He had to force himself not to yank off the dead man's ring. It was only a ring. It wasn't as if he'd killed the man for it. But damnation, he was bothered knowing his chance to be a spy had come from a man's death.

Gravenhurst clasped Grey's shoulder. "Don't dwell on it. I don't dwell on the man I replaced. Sorry I had to lie. But I couldn't very well tell you one of the king's personal spies was killed and you had been tapped to replace the fallen man."

"No, I don't suppose you could. Why did my father recommend me now? After all these years? I had thought, when the king told me the news yesterday, that Father might have been waiting for me to mature, but if you were chosen so young, why me now?"

"You'll have to ask your father to be certain. I was a perfect candidate though. Orphaned young. No living close relatives. No wish to ever marry or have children. And you? I can only speculate, but I imagine your father wanted to keep at least one son out of harm's way. But bloody fool that you are, you thrust yourself into danger daily. Might as well be doing it for a noble cause."

A sense of need swelled inside him. He would make his father proud. He'd not acknowledged the desire to want to in many years, but now he could. He was facing all sorts of buried demons today. "Why hasn't anyone tracked De La Touche down before now?"

"We have, but he got away from us. Sutton was the lead for tracking him down, but now Sutton is gone."

"Am I to be the one to hunt De La Touche?"

"No. You're to help me. Once our contacts trace De La Touche's new hiding place we'll go together. You'll be my backup."

"Excellent. I'm ready."

Gravenhurst chuckled. "You're not even close to ready, my friend. But when I'm through with you, you will be."

Eight

Retracing her steps, Madelaine plodded up the hill. Her back screamed for relief from her hunched over position, but if she stood she couldn't see the grass near as well. At the top, she straightened and rubbed her back. "It's hopeless."

"Nonsense," Elizabeth replied. "We *will* find the queen's ring."

"I don't see how." Madelaine waved a hand toward the lake. Up here it looked smaller than it really was. "Look at all the ground we covered with our morning stroll. She's set me an impossible task. That ring could have slipped off her finger anywhere. I think she wants me to fail." Madelaine slumped to the ground in defeat.

"Don't fret." Elizabeth sat down and patted Madelaine's arm. "We'll find it, and then perhaps she'll start to see how devoted you are to her."

Madelaine snorted. "It was kind of you to volunteer to help me, but you should go back to Frogmore and join the others for lunch."

Elizabeth shook her head.

Madelaine stared at her new friend. She was very grateful, but she couldn't allow her to continue to help. "I'll be fine. There are guards everywhere out here."

"I know that, silly. But the guards won't help you look.

And two pairs of eyes are better than one."

"But if she's angry with me it may filter to you."

"Her temper will cool soon enough if it does. Besides, the costume ball tonight will put her in a fine mood."

Without thought, Madelaine hugged Elizabeth. "I owe you for this."

"No." Elizabeth stood and held her hand out. "I owe you for how terrible I was."

"You were not terrible." Madelaine grasped Elizabeth's hand and stood. "You were afraid. There's a difference. Consider whatever debt you think you owe, paid. Shall we head back down the hill and around the lake once again?"

"Absolutely." Elizabeth looked past Madelaine and grinned.

"What is it?" An infectious smile pulled at her own lips, though her situation hardly warranted anything to be happy about.

"I have a feeling our luck is about to change."

"You do?"

Elizabeth nodded.

"What makes you feel that way?"

"Not what, but who."

Madelaine came to her friend's side and stared down the gentle slope of the hill they had climbed. Down, by the lake, making his way toward them was a tall, broad-shouldered man with gleaming, curly black hair. Her heart fluttered. "Whatever do you think your brother is doing out here?"

Shaking her head with a smile, Elizabeth said, "I imagine he's looking for you. After all, he is your protector now."

"Bite your tongue!" Madelaine exclaimed. "I told you he offered to protect me from Lord Thorton. That is all. Don't you dare say a word. I'd die of mortification."

Elizabeth giggled. "I doubt you'd perish, but I promise not to hint that I know Grey likes you."

"He doesn't like me," Madelaine whispered, afraid he might somehow hear. He must have jogged up the hill for he was almost at the top.

"He's my brother. I've known him all my life. And I tell you, you're special. He's offered a lot of things to a lot of women and protection was never one of them."

"Indeed she is special," Lord Grey said, cresting the hill. Damp, black curls clung to his forehead, and she had the urge to reach out and push the thick locks to the side. Her fingers tingled, as well as the rest of her body.

"What are you doing out here, Lord Grey?" She had no idea how to respond to his statement that she was special. She couldn't deny the way her heart had jerked with his words, but she needed to be careful. Wanting to seduce her was not the same as wanting to court her.

"I was looking for you."

How did every word he said manage to sound crafted for seduction? Warmth spread through her limbs. She might have stood there indefinitely staring at him if not for Elizabeth nudging her in the side. "Told you," Elizabeth whispered near Madelaine's ear.

"What did you tell Lady Madelaine, Liz?"

"I told her you liked her."

"Elizabeth," Madelaine hissed in warning. "I don't think that at all, Lord Grey."

"You should." He stepped so near her, his heat enveloped her and his scent of fresh pine surrounded her. He reached toward her, and a thousand pinpricks raced across her skin in anticipation of his touch. Then he paused and her breath hitched. Was he reconsidering touching her? He dropped his hand to his side, and her heart dropped a little with it. But then he gave her a glorious smile. The same one that yesterday had made her feel as if he'd never smiled like that for anyone but her. She trembled and prayed neither he nor his sister noticed how he affected her.

Elizabeth's eyes protruded. "Well, this is certainly something I have never seen."

"What is?" Madelaine asked, glad to have the attention off her.

"Grey playing by the strict rules of etiquette." Elizabeth stared at her brother. "I had thought perhaps you didn't know how." Her voice held a teasing note and she was grinning.

"Of course I know how." A wolfish smile spread across his face. "I just never met a woman I wanted to play by the rules for." Heavens, was he serious? Was this some new ploy of seduction he was trying? She had no idea how to respond.

"Rendered you speechless, did I?"

The pompousness was more like what she expected from a libertine. Not the previous astounding admissions that had left her ridiculously giddy. She swallowed. "Your approach surprised me, that's all."

"My approach up the hill?" A smirk graced his full lips.

"No." She glanced to Elizabeth for help.

"Grey, the queen lost one of her favorite rings and she's charged Madelaine with finding it by twilight."

Lord Greys' eyebrows furrowed together. "Is that why you two were hunched over as you made your way up the hill?"

"You were watching us?" Madelaine couldn't keep the surprise out of her voice.

"Of course. You looked lovely with your honey hair swinging around your face. But not as lovely as earlier."

"Earlier?" Had he really said "earlier?" She had the loveliest tingly sensation in her stomach.

He lifted his arm and pretended to draw back an arrow.

She gasped at his revelation. "Are you following me?"

"Worried?" He smirked at her.

"Should I be?"

"No. I'll keep all your secrets. I promise."

Her stomach fluttered but the feeling was not embarrassment. His words excited her. "I imagine you've made
many promises to many women in your life."

"I feel as if you two are having a private conversation
even though I'm standing right here," Elizabeth said,
cutting off whatever her brother had been about to say.

"You're quite right, sister dear. It was unpardonably
rude of us. Now tell me, where was the queen when last she
remembers having her ring?"

"She can't say." Madelaine swept her hand in front of
her. "We were everywhere today. Around the lake. Up the
hill. *And* back. It's too much ground to search. I'll never find
it, and she'll have one more reason to dislike me."

"I'll help you. I'm an excellent tracker."

Elizabeth nodded. "He has the uncanny ability to find
anything or anyone."

An odd frown crossed Lord Grey's face, but then it was
gone. "My father and my older brother Edward taught me
how to see clues most people ignore."

She didn't miss the change in his tone. Something bothered him. Was he thinking of his father? She understood
longing for a parent's love. She'd spent many useless hours
hoping her mother would accept her, but there was no
point dwelling on that right now. "You're certain you don't
mind wasting your time helping me?"

He took her ungloved hand and squeezed it. The

warmth of his fingers curled deliciously around her cold hands. However did he manage to smolder like fire with the cool wind now blowing? "Time spent with you, Lady Madelaine, will not be wasted."

Lord help her, she wasn't sure if he was trying to seduce her or not, but how easy it would be to fall prey to him if he was. She shouldn't take up his offer of help. The sensible thing to do would be to politely decline. But what if he *was* interested in her for more than seduction? Heavens! She was just as bad as the other ladies-in-waiting who thought they would be the one to win Lord Grey's heart. Yet if someone could win it, why not her?

"Shall we look together?" she asked, trying her hand at boldness. The cool blue of his eyes warmed instantly as a grin lit his face.

"Together sounds perfect." He offered her his arm.

Madelaine slipped her arm into the crook of his, but she couldn't quite settle on where she should rest her fingers. To clutch his upper arm would be too bold. She wouldn't mind a bit seeing if he was built as powerfully as she was imagining. She *could* link her own hands together. That would be uncomfortable. Before she could decide what to do, he placed her hand over his. More butterflies assaulted her stomach.

"You two go to the tea house where the walk started and search there again," Elizabeth said. "I'll start here, and we can meet back in the middle at the lake. And don't worry—" she continued, cutting off Madelaine voicing the impropriety of being alone with Lord Grey. "Her Majesty cannot disapprove. We are in the open, for heaven's sake. I can see the tea house from here, so it's not as if you're alone."

Madelaine nodded and held onto Lord Grey's arm as

they started down the hill. There was nothing weak about him, as far as she could tell. His arm could have been crafted of steel. He could easily be a soldier. Curiosity made her speak. "Why did you choose to be an equerry rather than a soldier?"

He paused and gave her a strange look. "I did not choose it. My father told me I was going to be an equerry and that was the end of the discussion."

"You don't seem a man to be told what to do."

He laughed. "I'm not."

"But here you are doing as your father has commanded."

"Only because I planned to be the worst equerry ever. I had every intention of bending my father to my will eventually."

"I don't understand. You speak as if you've changed your mind."

His eyebrows raised a fraction. "I've decided being an equerry may be more adventurous than I previously thought."

"Really?" Madelaine startled when he took her hand again and started back down the hill. "It's hard to imagine that watching over some preening lord's horses could be that adventurous."

"You'd be surprised."

She had no idea how to interpret his statement. It seemed to her he wasn't being truthful. Yet why would he lie? Maybe he wanted to impress her. The thought both excited and worried her.

What was she thinking? He surely could care less about impressing her. If the most beautiful and accomplished women at Court had failed to win his heart, then she certainly had no hope with her oddness. "Lord Grey—" She paused in her step. "—I—" Blast. A searing flush covered her face and neck. "I don't want to mislead you with my agreement to let you look for the queen's ring with me. I want your help, but I still don't wish to be seduced."

"That's good." He twined his fingers with hers for a second before releasing her hand and looking straight at her. "I don't wish to seduce you anymore."

"Why not?" Her blush grew hotter. "Is it because I lack feminine accomplishments?"

When he threw back his head and laughed, embarrassment swirled in her belly. Blast him! She hated being laughed at. Everyone was always laughing at odd Lady Madelaine. She straightened her shoulders and forced herself to look him in the eyes. "There is no need to laugh at me."

"I'm not laughing at you." He scrubbed a hand over his face. "I'm laughing at the absurdity of the situation."

"You find me absurd?" She barely knew the man and already he stirred her ire. Of course, she knew better than anyone that igniting her temper was no hard task.

"No." His smile vanished and his eyes became serious. "I find you refreshing, beautiful and honest. It's because you lack *normal* feminine accomplishments that I want to get to know you. I'm afraid I've been too long living a life of debauchery, but I've recently discovered I would very much like to change."

She wanted to believe him, but really did the man think her a fool? Did he think she'd forgotten his earlier attempt to get her to meet him in the stables for a rendezvous? "When did you have this epiphany? Five minutes ago?"

"No." He raised her hand to his lips and brushed a kiss across the back of her hand. The beat of her heart echoed in her ears. "I knew I wanted to change my wicked ways the moment you told me you wanted a husband and not a seduction."

His words made staying mad out of the question. A pleasant warmth settled low in her belly. "So you expect me to believe you decided to change your ways just because of meeting me and learning I don't desire to be seduced?"

"Certainly not. That would be foolish of you. I recently found myself unleashed by former self-imposed chains of stupidity. And I find I am no longer driven to do certain things."

That foolish part of her that had always hoped her mother had been wrong and someone might find a woman who was different refreshing felt flattered that he truly seemed interested in her and curious as to what exactly had altered in his life to make him want to change. "I don't understand."

He scrubbed a hand over his face. "I don't expect you would. Might I ask you to indulge me? Let me prove to you I only want honorable things from you."

"Only honorable things? You're sure?" It was hard to believe it was possible, but she wanted to believe. She wanted her mother to have been wrong.

He nodded. "I'd also like to kiss you, but I don't consider that dishonorable. And I won't ask yet."

"You won't?" Her lips tingled at the thought of his mouth pressed against hers.

"No. Not yet." He ran a finger down her cheek. She had the overwhelming desire to lean into his touch, but he pulled away. "Not until I am sure you don't think I'm merely still trying to seduce you."

With her blood roaring in her ears and her heart pounding, saying she believed him so his lips would find hers was on the tip of her tongue. But before she could speak, he took her hand. "Come on. The sun will go down in the next few hours and finding the ring will become much harder."

She nodded and followed him silently down the hill. It wasn't until they were at the very bottom that she realized she had not once glanced down to look for the queen's ring.

Nine

"Look there." Lord Grey pointed to the ground before tugging Madelaine down beside him. "Do you see that?"

"I see grass. Is that what I'm supposed to see?"

"No. Really look." He rested his hand at her nape and cradled it. She tried to study the blades, but it was hard to concentrate with Lord Grey's warm fingers against her skin and his body so close to hers. She abandoned the ground and focused on listening to the hiss of his breath. Gads. She had to do better than this. Doubling her efforts, she focused all her attention on the grass. What was different? What did he see? She sucked in a surprised breath. "Some of the blades are mashed."

"Bravo!" He lightly squeezed her neck before his hand fell away. Moving lower, so that his face almost laid against the ground, he traced an outline repeatedly. "This is a man's tracks."

Madelaine scrambled lower until she was once again side-by-side with him. "How do you know?"

"Look at your slippers."

She immediately obliged.

"There are two ways I can tell. One, women have much smaller feet than men."

"Not all women," Madelaine said. "My father's cook

hails from German stock, and her feet, like the rest of her body, are enormous."

Lord Grey chuckled. "All right. Most women have feet that are smaller than men. Satisfied?"

"Yes." But she was more than satisfied. She was happy. Being here with him made her feel carefree. The realization came as a shock. She hadn't been happy since the day she came to Court.

"Lady Madelaine, might I ask another favor of you?"

The blue of his eyes had darkened as he spoke. And his voice had become husky. She didn't think she had the power to deny him anything in this moment. So, she nodded.

"When we are alone, will you call me Grey?"

A rushing sound filled her ears, making her blink. She took a calming breath and said, "Yes. And you may call me Madelaine."

"*Madelaine.*"

The way her name rolled seductively off his tongue made gooseflesh raise on her arms. "Lord Grey—"

"Grey," he corrected.

"Grey." A strange tension was mounting within her. As if something coiled inside her body and one touch of Grey's lips to hers would make the coil release. She had to get them back on track. "What is the other way you can tell that these footprints are a man's?"

"They're deeper than a woman's would be because men are heavier." He grinned. "Except for German women, that is."

An irrepressible smile tugged at her lips. Grey was not only handsome, but he was funny and smart. No wonder he'd never had a bit of trouble finding women who wanted his attention. She could imagine the pleasure a seduction by him would bring. A dull ache, unlike anything she had ever felt before pulsed within her.

She curled her fingers into the grass. Pleasure from a seduction would be temporary. She needed to remember that fact, and the reality that Grey may say he did not want to seduce her, but she still needed to be careful. He knew no other way to woo a woman than to his bed, and she was apparently as vulnerable as every other hare-brained lady when it came to him.

She sprang to her feet and shook the wrinkles out of her dress. He stood in one fluid motion and reached toward her. Her muscles tensed. Was he going to kiss her? Pull her against his chest? Wrap his arms around her and—*good grief.* She had to get control of her imagination. He plucked something from her hair, and then held it up between them. "I was just getting the grass out of your hair."

"Yes, of course." A hot blush warmed her cheeks.

He chuckled. "You can stop worrying."

"I'm not worried."

"You looked worried. In fact, with your eyes rounded you looked much like a fox being hunted. I swear I'm not trying to seduce you."

"Perhaps claiming that is your ploy to reel me in." Gads. She couldn't believe she'd just said that. But he had her confused and unsure. He had her wanting to believe someone liked her, oddness and all.

He frowned. "What must I do to prove I'm a man of my word?"

Should she be coy? Lie? No. If they were to really know each other and have a true chance, she had to be truthful. She prayed she wasn't being utterly foolish. Her mother had always told her she'd need to hide what she liked if she truly couldn't change, and here she was still not doing what her mother had said. "We must be friends before we can be anything else."

"I want that. I vow I do."

His words were so earnest that she believed him. God help her, she did. Nothing would be worse than falling for Grey only to be humiliated if he proved himself false. The hell she had previously endured at Court would seem a dream when compared to the nightmare Grace would undoubtedly put her through if she ever learned Madelaine had been so foolishly stupid. She would take the chance though. "All right. I promise to take you for your word unless you prove that you take me for a fool."

He leaned closer, his pupils dilating. "I take you for many things, Madelaine, but a fool is not one of them." His husky voice made her melt inside.

"You're doing it again." Her voice was trembling.

"Doing what?" His tone was like a caress.

"Sounding seductive," she said with a racing heart.

He grinned. "It must be my natural sound. I'm afraid you'll just have to live with it."

She laughed. "I bet you were a handful as a child."

"I was indeed. I'll tell you some stories eventually. Come." He waved his hand toward the east side of the lake. "You ladies walked this way, correct?"

"That's very impressive." She trailed him. "Maybe you'll get to use your tracking skills when you're an equerry to find a rogue horse."

He turned and gave her the same strange look he had when they'd spoken earlier on the subject of his being an equerry. "That's odd," he said.

Was he talking about what she'd said? Her stomach twisted into knots as self-doubt flooded her. Wait a second. He wasn't even looking at her. She stared across the great park and breathed slowly. She needed to try to have more confidence, but it was so hard. "What's odd?"

"There." He pointed toward the grotto that lay across the wide expanse of grass and trees.

For a moment, she saw nothing, and then a flash of red caught her attention. "That's the upstairs chambermaid! What on earth—?"

A man emerged from the grotto. She didn't know him. And if she'd ever seen him she would have remembered. The burn scars that covered the right side of his face were visible, even from this distance. She shuddered. As if sensing her stare, he pulled a dark hood down. Grey chuckled before speaking. "Now I see what the chambermaid is up to. Do you know that man?"

Madelaine glanced behind her at Grey's face. His eyes were narrowed on the couple.

She'd grown up sheltered, but she'd learned many shocking things since coming to court. Still… Her curiosity couldn't be denied. "Grey, do you mean to say she—with him—there in the cave? She wouldn't."

"I beg to differ. I'm sure she shares a room with another servant, which means she's restricted in where she can accept *companionship*. I've met the woman. She's got a healthy appetite. And if the man she's with is also sharing a room and it is currently occupied…" He shrugged.

"*You bedded her.*" Gads. She'd not meant it to come out so irritated and accusing. She had no right to be angry. It was none of her business who Grey had slept with.

"Not me. I swear."

His blunt denial and the foolishly hopeful part of her that wanted to trust him overcame her sensible side, and she decided to believe him.

"Do you recognize the man?" Grey asked.

Madelaine squinted into the distance. "No, but they're so far. Did you see the scars on his face?"

Grey nodded. "He dresses oddly."

"Perhaps he's from the village."

"Perhaps." Grey's brow furrowed. "I wouldn't have thought her to be a woman to give herself to a commoner though. She seemed rather scheming when I met her."

Madelaine was dying to know exactly where Grey had met her, but they stood in silence as the chambermaid and her companion disappeared toward the castle. Once they were gone from sight, Grey swaggered ahead. She pressed her lips together on her curiosity. If he didn't want to offer explanations, she had no right to ask. She had to double her steps to keep up with his long strides, but falling slightly behind had definite benefits. His breeches hugged his derriere and powerful thighs and his morning coat displayed his broad shoulders rather nicely. She was so busy staring at him that she forgot to watch where she was going and stubbed her toe on a broken tree branch. She bit down on her lip to avoid crying out, but she must have made some noise because Grey stopped.

"What's the matter?"

There was no point in lying. Besides, she was a terrible liar. She tended to stammer when she lied. "I stubbed my toe."

"Weren't you watching where you walked?"

"Oh yes." Half embarrassed and half irritated, she smirked. "I was indeed. I saw a rock and thought to myself 'I'll walk right into that to see if it hurts.'"

"Beautiful and sharp-witted. I like that." He winked and continued with his swaggering.

The scoundrel! He knew she'd been staring at him. Grey stooped down at the edge of the lake under the same tree the queen had stopped to rest under. "You paused here?"

"Yes. How did you know?"

"The flattened footsteps lead here in a pattern that shows someone was walking, but here they become jumbled together and unless you were all walking into each other, you had to have stopped." He looked around and stood before walking to the tree the queen had sat under. "Did Queen Charlotte rest here?"

"Yes. We put a stool there for her. Oh! And she took her gloves off here!" Madelaine rushed over to where Grey was bent over. He reached down and came up with the queen's ring grasped in his fingers. The ruby stone shined in the sunlight. "You found it!" Overcome with gratitude, she threw herself into his arms.

The force of her collision sent their bodies swaying backwards toward the tree, and for a breath, she thought they would fall in a tangle of arms and legs. Grey's grunt rumbled in her ear as his solid arms encircled her waist and pulled her firm and tight against a wall of hard muscle. He righted them but made no move to release her.

Embarrassment heated her as she stared at his chest. "I'm sorry. I was overcome with excitement. Thank you." Too mortified by her impulsive actions to look at him, she tried to pull away, but his arms tightened like bands of steel around her waist.

She glanced up.

Amusement danced and flickered in his gaze, and pleasure tipped up the corners of his mouth. "If you don't want me to have thoughts of seducing you, then you cannot go throwing yourself into my arms. You're quite simply irresistible."

The world around her grew quiet and murky, and then

one thought crystallized. He thought her irresistible. She was the oddball. The lady who did not fit in. She had to say something and cease staring like a simpleton. "You're irresistible too." Gads! What a stupid silly thing to say.

A strange glint filled Grey's eyes. He ran a finger down her cheek. "I want to kiss you very badly."

"Go on then." Her heart hammered with her bold words. "Kiss me."

He cupped her chin causing a tremor to run through her body. Grey stroked her lips with a thumb, and deep inside a pulsing need awoke. He leaned down until his lips almost touched hers. "You're sure?"

She'd never been surer of anything in her life. "I'm certain."

"And you believe I want more than to seduce you?"

Staring at his lips, she nodded. "I believe you."

He groaned as his mouth came down on hers, hot and seeking. His thumb pressed against her chin, and she opened her mouth to allow him in. His tongue stroked, swirled and lit a fire within her that she feared could not be controlled. She pressed harder against him, wanting more of this new consuming feeling.

"Grey!" Lady Elizabeth's voice cut like a clap of thunder through the silence.

He pulled away, but held Madelaine firmly by the arm.

Her knees wobbled but that she could get under control. It was her labored breathing she was unsure she could slow down. His dark gaze bore into her as he scrubbed a hand over his face. "I shouldn't have done that, but I couldn't resist. Forgive me?"

"How could I not? I asked *you* to kiss *me*. Remember?"

He grinned. "I quite forgot. I'm not used to being the one seduced. You muddled my wits."

She'd muddled *his* wits? She'd just been kissed for the first time in her life. And what a perfect kiss. She wasn't sure she'd think properly for days. With an embarrassed laugh, she faced Elizabeth who strode toward them with a dark scowl on her face. Madelaine ought to care that Elizabeth was angry about something, but all she could do was smile. She'd never felt so wonderful in all her life.

Ten

Grey had never liked masquerade balls or any ball really. He could never seem to allow the wallflowers to remain ignored. Their sad faces pained him, and he always ended up dancing with one, which invariably led to his having to gently divert their attention to someone else who was actually interested in marriage, and besides that, taking pity on the wallflowers hadn't been good for his rake reputation.

Tonight was different. He was looking forward to the ball and the chance to speak with Madelaine. And to dance with her. Touch her. Twirl her around the floor. He didn't care if there were hoards of wallflowers, someone else would have to rescue them tonight. Now, if only the damned dinner would end, so the ball could start. He intended to begin a proper courtship of Madelaine, as he'd earlier assured his sister, but this boring dinner was dragging on.

Sandwiched between the queen and Lady Grace, Grey stared across the space at Madelaine and Thorton, while imagining the meat on his platter was Thorton's head. Grey sliced into the beef with his knife and started to chew. Thorton delved his hand under the table, and Madelaine's back went rigid. Grey almost choked.

"Are you all right, Lord Grey?" Lady Grace asked.

He nodded while gulping in a greedy breath of air. He

was going to smash Thorton's face, if the man touched Madelaine again. Grey's blood boiled the farther to the bench's edge Madelaine was forced to scoot in order to avoid Thorton's groping hands. Hell, she was in danger of tumbling to the floor any second.

Grey had to rescue her. "Your Majesty, might I be excused to go and talk to my sister. We've not had a chance to speak today." That was true enough. After Madelaine had left to deliver the ring to the queen, Liz had shouted at him for a good half-hour for kissing Madelaine.

"You may be excused after you tell me of your mother. What has she been doing this past year and why have we not seen her at Court?"

"I couldn't say." It embarrassed him that he'd been too busy cavorting throughout London and Essex with various women to bother seeing his mother much. And when he had seen her, he'd been more interested in whether his actions had ruffled his father than to ask after his mother's wellbeing.

The queen looked at him with knowing eyes. "A wife will settle you down, Lord Grey, and I imagine that will please your mother immensely. Then she will actually see you, instead of reading about you in the gossip sheets."

"You're wise as always, Your Majesty." He took a gulp of wine to avoid further conversation and to wash down the shame threatening to choke him. He had much to atone for, and as soon as he was finished with training he would go see his parents and apologize to both of them. "If it's acceptable, I would like to make a fresh start at being a more attentive son and brother by going to speak with Elizabeth now."

Queen Charlotte nodded. "Of course you may."

He started to rise, but the queen restrained him with a

hand. "After you dance the first set with Lady Grace."

"As you wish," he said through clenched teeth and a false smile.

A half hour later he was twirling Lady Grace around the dance floor at the dictate of the queen while watching Madelaine dance with Thorton. Lady Grace prattled something in Grey's ear. He could hear the annoying buzz of her words, but he dismissed them for the nonsense they undoubtedly were. Until she said Madelaine's name. He snapped his eyes away from Madelaine and Thorton, who was behaving for the most part, and looked at Lady Grace. "What did you say?"

She lifted one eyebrow. "I said it looks like you have competition."

"For what?"

"In seducing Madge."

His hand clenched involuntarily over Lady Grace's fingers.

"You're hurting me." Her words held bite.

He loosened his grip and spoke. "I'm not trying to seduce her. And her name is Madelaine."

Lady Grace smirked as they twirled until the song ended. "That's a very clever ploy you've adopted. I hope it works for you. I look forward to dancing again tomorrow night and hearing about your progress."

"I won't—"

"Shh," she interrupted his effort to tell her he would not be dancing with her again. "The queen is waving to me. Hold your thoughts until tomorrow night." She turned and slipped through the crowd. No point going after her. The damnable woman would believe what she wanted, no matter what he said.

He located Liz and Madelaine standing off to one side

by the terrace doors. When he reached them, his breath caught. Madelaine was a vision from afar, but up close, her beauty stole his senses. He wanted to devote all his attention to her, but sticking to his goal to make up for being self-absorbed for too many years to count, he smiled first at his sister. "You two are the loveliest women at this ball. Liz, you make a perfect Cleopatra, and Lady Madelaine—" He finally lowered his gaze down her green, gossamer dress. His blood thickened in appreciation at the curves barely covered by the delicate material. "Who thought of your costumes?"

Madelaine's gaze met his. "I came up with mine, and your aunt thought of Lady Elizabeth's. I daresay she thought of your costume as well."

"Do you know who I am?" He fingered the sheet wrapped around his body but then followed her gaze to the necklace he wore. Did she know it was a replica of a phallus? His aunt had a wicked sense of humor and love of Greek history, and it amused him to play along.

"You're Eros. God of lust." Some sort of sparkling powder covered Madelaine's natural skin color, but her neck splotched red with embarrassment.

"Ha!" Liz snorted. "How appropriate for you."

"It *was* appropriate," Grey corrected. It was on the tip of his tongue to ask them both if they wanted a refreshment, but Gravenhurst's fast approach distracted Grey.

His friend bowed to both ladies then nodded at Grey. "The king sent me to find you. He says your training is to begin tonight."

"Tonight? I was supposed to have the day to do as I wished."

"And you have. It is now evening. Leisure time is over. Lord Pearson has arrived and the king wishes you to learn the man's preferences for his horses. I'm to take you to the stables." In no position to argue, he grasped Madelaine's gloved hand and kissed the top of it. Confounding etiquette that required women to wear gloves. He wanted to feel her soft heated skin against his lips as he had this afternoon. But it was not to be anytime soon. Unsettled, he reluctantly released her. "I'll see you tomorrow night at dinner."

"Perhaps not," Gravenhurst interrupted Madelaine's reply. "Equerry training can be long and tedious, Lady Madelaine. Lord Grey may be too tired to come to dinner."

"I won't be," Grey corrected, trying to keep his annoyance with Gravenhurst's suddenly superior attitude in hand.

"Don't say I didn't warn you."

"*If* I'm too tired to come to dinner, which I'll *not be*, Liz you must promise to keep an eye on Lady Madelaine during dinner. Make sure to work out a signal with her in case she needs rescuing from Thorton."

Liz furrowed her brow. "Why would she need rescuing from Lord Thorton?"

Madelaine's wide gaze rested on him.

"Thorton has taken an unhealthy liking to Lady Madelaine."

Madelaine's lips parted in surprise. "However did you know?"

He loved that he'd finally surprised her in a good way. Maybe this would be the start of really gaining her trust. "It's my duty as your protector."

"We should gut the man!" Liz said.

He grinned. "That's the Adlard spirit, Liz. But let me handle Thorton. All I want you to do is work out a signal with Lady Madelaine and intervene if you must. Spill your wine. Burst into tears. Tear your dress. Whatever it takes."

"I won't fail," Liz promised.

"I know you won't." He chucked his sister on the chin then glanced at Madelaine. "I'll kill the man if he continues to fail to control his hands."

"Come on, Romeo," Gravenhurst said. "You've a job to learn, and Lady Elizabeth has assured you she won't fail your command."

As Grey was leaving, he paused and glanced back at Madelaine. "Don't go anywhere alone."

She nodded.

"Promise me."

"What a demanding protector you are." She laughed. "I promise."

Satisfied that she would be safe in his absence, he strode through the room behind Gravenhurst. It was probably a good thing he hadn't had the opportunity to get to know Madelaine very well yet. He barely knew her now, and she was already a distraction at a time when he didn't have the slightest doubt that he needed to have all his concentration focused on becoming a superb spy. She was safe, so he would simply push her from his mind, until he saw her again.

When Gravenhurst and Grey neared the stables, Grey asked, "What sort of training are we going to do?"

In the dark, Gravenhurst's expression was unreadable. Horses neighed from within the stables, and a cold wind blew Grey's hair over his eyes. He shoved it back as Gravenhurst said, "I'm going to train you to stay alive." His voice had a hard edge. "Tonight I'll start teaching you to never assume anything except that someone always wants you dead. Study your surroundings. Know your enemies."

"Sounds like useful lessons."

Gravenhurst snorted, grabbed a lit torch from a stand, and proceeded past the stables toward a dark, twisting path that led into the woods of the park. He stopped suddenly at the edge of the path. Grey nearly bowled him over.

"A little warning would have been considerate."

"The men striving to kill you will not be considerate."

"Point taken," he conceded as Gravenhurst faced him and regarded him without a word. Insects of the night chirped around them. Music drifted on the swirling wind from the castle to fill the silence between them. It would have been pleasant, but he was tense as hell. He wanted to perform well. He didn't want to disappoint his father.

"Take this," Gravenhurst said and shoved the torch at him. Grey gripped it and stared at his friend's shadowed face. Gravenhurst leaned down and came up holding two daggers. He offered one to Grey, and then headed down the path.

Grey sidestepped a gnarled tree root that rose across the ground. He pushed branches out of his way as he followed Gravenhurst deep into the woods. A branch came swinging at him, and he ducked. It hissed by his ear right before the sharp twigs slid across his cheek and left a stinging cut. "Damn it." He couldn't afford to be too slow in reacting to anything.

Up ahead, his friend chuckled as he crunched through fallen leaves and twigs to make his way into a clearing. Gravenhurst walked over to an iron post and with a clank slid the torch into a slot. He came to the center of the circle and beckoned to Grey. "We'll train with daggers and fists until the torch runs out, and then we'll train blind. Once first blood's drawn we'll make our way back to the castle."

Grey's muscles tensed in anticipation. He curled his fingers around his dagger. "You've never beat me in a fight."

Gravenhurst's robust laugh echoed in the silence. "Part

of my cover, my friend."

Grey gripped his dagger and moved toward the center of the circle.

Gravenhurst tossed his dagger from hand to hand and started circling Grey. "You're moving slow. Your mind is elsewhere."

Grey refocused his attention just as the whistle of steel sliced the air and filled his ears a second before Gravenhurst's blade cut through his coat, shirt and skin.

Pain burned a path down his arm. He dropped his dagger. It hit the dirt with a thump. His arm throbbed as he removed his coat. He touched the place where the blade had sliced and his fingers met with sticky blood. "You've cut me."

"Pitiful," Gravenhurst said. "You're going to have to be a lot more alert if you don't want to end up dead. Pick up your blade."

Grey reached down and grasped his dagger. "I assume you've decided we need to stay."

"Hell yes we need to stay. I didn't expect your training to be over in less than a minute. But now I know your Achilles' heel. Just make sure your enemies never learn it, my friend."

"I don't have an Achilles' heel." Grey lunged toward Gravenhurst and the tip of his knife snagged Gravenhurst's coat but did not meet flesh.

"You do. But I'll give you this, if you have to have a weakness, Lady Madelaine is a beautiful one to have."

Eleven

Five tedious days had passed since Madelaine last saw Grey at the costume ball, so when she walked around the sharp turn of the trail leading to the queen's country house and he was standing alone by the entrance-way, she quickened her step and nearly tripped over her skirts in her excitement.

Probably, she ought not to act so eager. She tried to slow down, but her feet didn't want to cooperate. Her half-boots padded against the hardened snow as she rushed across the grass. She'd dreamed of him every night since he'd so valiantly tried to make sure Lord Thorton couldn't bother her at dinner anymore. Dreams really hadn't done Grey justice.

Her stomach flipped. He leaned negligently against the iron gate with a booted foot propped against the dark steel for support. The buckskins he wore encased his powerful thighs in a sinful way. That tingling sensation, that only he elicited, swept over Madelaine's skin. His dark-colored coat had been left open to reveal the white cambric shirt next to his skin. When she reached him, she was panting from her efforts to hurry.

"Grey, how nice to see you."

"Only nice?" He quirked his eyebrow.

Blast. She'd tried to temper her words, but she didn't

want to. "Very nice. I've looked for you every day."

"I've dreamed of you every night," he countered in a voice as smooth as silk.

She shivered, but it had nothing to do with the falling snow. "Then what's kept you away? Surely not equerry training?"

He glanced down at his bandaged hand.

She automatically reached for him and lifted it to her. "What happened? Did a horse bite you?"

"Yes. That's right." His gaze flickered beyond her for a second toward the stables. "A horse. The ass. He has a bite as sharp as a dagger."

"Perhaps you should shoot him if he's uncontrollable." She dropped his hand in case someone chanced a look out of the window. Really, she should be going in, but she couldn't make herself just yet.

He stood and moved back as if he'd read her thoughts and understood her concern. "I can't shoot the beast. He's invaluable to the king, even if he is surly. But enough about the horse. Tell me, has Thorton bothered you at all?"

She blinked in surprise at Grey's steely tone. A tingle raced down her spine. He was truly worried for her. "He's not had the chance to bother me. I've not been alone since the moment you left me."

Grey tugged the edge of her fur-lined hat. "You're alone now. Thorton could follow you out here and try to take advantage."

"He wouldn't."

"Don't be naïve. Men are cunning when it comes to getting what they want."

She swallowed, uncertainty filling her chest. Was he speaking of himself or Lord Thorton? Seeing him now, so handsome, so smart and an obvious favorite of the king and queen it just didn't seem possible that he would want to court her out of all the women here. He could have his pick, and she was certainly not special. Well, not in a way that made her an Incomparable. She was special in a way that made other's snicker. Perhaps he really only wanted to conquer her. She'd heard the continued whispers of the other ladies-in-waiting regarding him. Her self-doubt crept back in, annoying companion that it was.

His brows had drawn together and his normally blue-gray eyes had turned dark as he stared at her. "I didn't mean to frighten you. I want to keep you safe."

He sounded so earnest that some of her uncertainly flittered out of her mind. "You didn't frighten me, and I'm not being naïve. Lord Thorton has been called home on business. So you see I'm perfectly safe. I only went to that cottage over there to fetch the queen's stole, but it's not there. Are you here to see your sister or the queen?"

He stepped closer. "I'm here to see you."

"Me?" A burst of happiness swelled inside her chest.

"Yes. You. I've been so bloody sore from my training that I've been unable to walk at the end of every day. That's why you've not seen me. But when dawn came this morning, I knew I couldn't go another day without a glimpse of your face. So I crawled out of bed—"

"You crawled?"

"Yes. My need to see you has made me undignified. I hardly know you, but you've bewitched me."

The bewitching was more the other way around if you asked her, but even *she* understood there were some things you just didn't tell a man. "So how did you know where to find me?"

"I bribed that redheaded chambermaid."

"How did you know how to find the chambermaid?"

She followed his amused expression to her hands, only realizing they were on her hips. She immediately crossed her arms in front of her chest, but the amusement in his eyes reached his mouth, so she dropped her arms and tried to appear relaxed.

"You're jealous!"

"I'm not." But she was. Her stomach plunged. "I've no right to be. We've no agreement. And as you said, you barely know me."

In a flash, his arm came around her waist, and he pulled her away from the gate and to the side of the door where there were no windows.

Her heartbeat turned erratic at his touch. "What is it?"

"Courting you will be the death of me." His lips hovered so near hers that when he spoke, the warmth of his breath washed over her cold lips. Reflexively she licked them. He groaned and dashed a hand through his hair.

"Is that supposed to be a compliment?" she teased, but heavens, she loved that she seemed to affect him as he affected her.

"It's definitely a compliment. Do you know I once scoffed during my lessons on Greek mythology when my tutor spoke of the cause of the Trojan War?"

"Did you?" Her words came out as a breathless whisper. She was sure he was telling her something important, but being so near him made clear thinking impossible. At this moment, she couldn't even recall the Trojan War. All she could think of was Grey's heat, his scent, and the way his hair curved so enticingly around his strong jaw.

"I did more than scoff. I told my tutor there was no possibility I would ever believe a man had started a bloody war over a woman. But I think I was wrong."

Her heart thundered in her ears. She recalled the Trojan

War now. Menalaus, the king of Sparta, had waged war on Troy because Paris of Troy had taken Menalaus's wife from him. "What do you think now?"

"I think I could start a war over a woman, *if* the woman was you."

His seductively sweet words elicited a rush of desire in her that left her trembling. "I vow you're trying to seduce me." Her words came out husky.

He shook his head and stepped away. "I promise I'm not. I just wanted to say hello, and ask if you could come to my aunt's apartments tonight. She's having a small gathering after dinner. Can you get away? Liz has already gained permission for herself, so the two of you could come together."

He was asking her to come to his aunt's to be with him. Spend time with him. She could hardly imagine this was true. Yet it was, and she needed to speak before he decided she was dull and rescinded the invitation. "I think I can come. The queen has said she is spending time alone with the king tonight after dinner, and I was not one of the ladies she asked to attend her, so I'll make the request."

"Excellent." Grey took one of her gloved hands and pressed a kiss to the back of it. "I look forward to after dinner then."

A thrill sent her pulse skittering more. If she could gain permission, she'd be able to sit and talk with him and get to know him better. "What if you're too tired? Will you send a note?"

"I won't be too tired. My training should be wrapping up today. There's a test, and I mean to pass it."

"I'd no idea equerry training was so difficult."

"Neither did I. I swear I'm going to tame that beastly horse today." Grey's brow furrowed, giving him such a

handsome, disgruntled look that on impulse, she pressed a
quick kiss to his cheek.

"Good luck," she whispered before dashing to the entrance and going inside. She floated through the
entranceway, but came crashing back to reality when Grace
walked into the room and glared at her.

"Where have you been? The queen's beside herself. She
was about to send one of the guards to search for you."

Madelaine brushed the snow off her dress, took off her
hat and gave it a little shake. "The stole was not where the
queen said, so I combed the cottage for it." She walked over
to the entrance table and with her back to Grace, carefully
set her hat down and slowly removed her coat. Her ears
burned with her white lie. She had searched for the stole,
but only for a second. It was Grey who had detained her,
but she wasn't about to tell Grace that. "I didn't realize how
long I searched. I'll go apologize—"

She forgot the rest of her sentence as she faced Grace.
The woman stared at her as if she knew her darkest secrets.
"I spied Lord Grey coming out of the woods on our way
here earlier, did you?"

"Certainly not." Thank God she truly had not seen him,
or she'd likely be a stammering mess right now. Grey's
equerry training certainly was odd. She'd seen her father
train an equerry before and it had never seemed difficult to
her. In fact, the training was usually over in a few hours.

"Do you know what I think?"

Madelaine pursed her lips. "I didn't realize you bothered
with contemplation."

Grace moved and stopped right in front of her. "I think
you're lying."

"Which proves to me you shouldn't bother thinking.
I'm telling the truth. I didn't see Lord Grey coming from the

woods and even if I had, what of it?"

"I think you saw him and then you met him. And that's what took you so long. I doubt you looked more than five minutes for the queen's stole."

"Lucky for me I answer to the queen and not to you." Madelaine started to breeze past Grace, but the woman grabbed her arm.

"You've a certain look about you, Madge."

She squared her shoulders. "And what look is that?"

"You've the look of a woman falling in love. Your eyes shine, your skin glows, and you've had a smile on your face since the day Lord Grey rode into Court."

Madelaine's breath caught in her throat. She'd not stopped to truly examine her feelings toward Grey. Was she falling for him? The mere question made her heart constrict. She was afraid he would hurt her or worse yet, ruin her. But she was also afraid there was no turning back.

When he was near, her oddness seemed to hardly matter. Life with him, if things proceeded as she hoped, could be all she had imagined. Grey was the knight of her dreams. The valiant warrior who'd come riding into Court to sweep her away from those who scorned her and save her from a loveless marriage that she would have to succumb to. Except Grey was no knight, but he *was* an equerry, so he was quite capable of sweeping her up onto his horse and riding away. She laughed out loud at her silly notions.

"You're a fool," Grace snapped. "Do you know how many silly women have had the same ridiculous expression on their face as you do when speaking of Lord Grey?"

Madelaine forced her smile away and stared hard at Grace. She'd disliked Grace, but now she despised her. The woman was planting seeds of doubt in her mind after she'd just managed to rid herself of the doubt that had been there.

No matter how she wanted to ignore Grace, the doubt now niggled and worried Madelaine. She'd rather die than show Grace she held any power to worry her. Madelaine lifted her chin. "A good many, I suppose."

"You suppose correct. And do you know what they all had in common?"

"A dislike of you?"

"You're gaining quite the barbed tongue, Madge. Good for you. You'll need it when the ridicule worsens. Believe me, just when you think things can't get worse, they do."

The fleeting sadness of Grace's face touched Madelaine. "You sound as if you speak from experience." Grace softened and looked human, approachable, almost friendly. Maybe they could call a truce? Perhaps Grace had painful reasons for acting as she did. Before Madelaine could decide whether it would be wise or foolish to offer a ceasefire, Grace's expression hardened. Her lips pressed together and her eyes narrowed.

"Oh, I have experience all right. And knowledge. I can't recall how many times I've seen Lord Grey change tactics when the woman he's after proves to want to be chased. He's a regular strategist."

Madelaine ground her teeth together. She'd not give Grace the satisfaction of a response.

"You're his latest prey. And I imagine *you're* proving less eager to bed him than he is used to. I daresay he's vowed he doesn't want to seduce you. And then perhaps brushed your hand or kissed you after *you* demanded it."

Madelaine's heart pounded in her ears. She swallowed and spoke. "Is this warning derived from personal experience?"

"Of course, you silly ninnyhammer. But Lord Grey wasn't the man. Don't say I didn't warn you when you find yourself used and ruined. If you're lucky, your father will promptly remove you from Court and marry you to some aged friend who will die quickly and leave you a rich widow. If you're unlucky, he'll leave you here to rot. Come, the queen awaits us both."

Grace swept out of the room before she could respond.

Madelaine made her way to the library, unsure of everything. Pity for Grace's obviously hurtful past dulled Madelaine's dislike of the woman. The pity also lent Grace's words a ring of truth that sent Madelaine's thoughts in a thousand directions.

Voices carried down the hall from the library. She paused, listening as the queen demanded to know what was detaining her. Maybe she shouldn't ask permission to go to Helen's apartments tonight. But if she didn't see Grey and allow herself the chance to get to know him, she'd never know for certain whether he had wanted to court her or to seduce her.

She could find a lord who didn't set her heart to pounding. But that would undoubtedly be a man who wanted the normal type of woman. She could spend the rest of her life pretending to be someone she wasn't, in order to make that lord happy. She could never chance true love. But if she didn't, she was afraid her heart would become impenetrable, and then what would be the value of life?

Twelve

*T*ired but eager to see Madelaine, Grey dressed quickly for dinner. He changed the bandage covering the deep gash Gravenhurst had accidentally given him the second night of training and then slipped on his boots. By God, he was sore from the long hours of dagger, sword, and one-on-one combat training and tracking. The endless romps through the pitch-black night searching first for objects and then people Gravenhurst had hidden had left Grey cut, bruised and stiff as a stick. If he tried to bend too far, he might break.

But it was over. He'd bested Gravenhurst in every test the man had thrown at him today. Tonight he would enjoy the reward of spending time with Madelaine, even if the mere act of sitting hurt his body. He'd forget the pain the minute he saw her brown eyes light for him and a lovely smile of greeting come to her beautiful face. One of the things that drew him to her was the way she looked at him. Not jaded or knowing as so many women of the Court he'd been with. Nor wary as the ones who'd been warned against him, or lustful as the women whose favors he'd declined to partake in for one reason or another.

Madelaine stared at him with an open, trustful gaze as if he was good and true, which made him want it to be so, even more than he'd already wished for since finding out about his father and brother.

As he shrugged into his dinner coat, the door swung open and Gravenhurst sauntered in pulling the door shut as he entered.

Grey straightened his jacket. "You needn't have shut the door. I'm leaving for dinner."

"Change of plans." Gravenhurst stripped off his soiled shirt and strode to the wash stand to clean himself. He tossed his shirt to the ground exposing his back and the red, angry cuts Grey had given his friend.

"Sorry about the cuts."

Gravenhurst waved a negligent hand before he dipped both of them into the water. "Don't apologize. Your training was necessary."

"And finished."

"Not quite," Gravenhurst replied while donning a clean shirt.

Grey crossed his arms over his chest and glared. "I should've gutted you."

"Careful." Gravenhurst straightened his jacket. "That volatile temper could get you killed where we're going tonight."

"I'm not going anywhere with you. My only plan is to see Madelaine." Grey strode past Gravenhurst and through the door.

He had one foot in the hall when Gravenhurst said, "That's a noteworthy plan. And I like it. I really do. Yet the king has just taken me to task for not training you in the art of subterfuge."

"I'm plenty deceptive," Grey retorted. "Just tell the king to ask around."

Now fully clothed, Gravenhurst sauntered from the room and held Grey's overcoat toward him. Grey shook his head. "I won't be needing that coat. I'm going to dinner and then I'm going to spend a lovely evening indoors in the warmth of my aunt's apartments with Madelaine. I'm going to drink wine and get to know the woman who has intrigued me."

"A fine plan, as I said. Off with you then." Gravenhurst pressed his face near Grey's. "I'll tell the king you don't wish to be one of us." He tapped discreetly on his ring.

Grey's thumb went immediately to the king's ring. He recalled his vow to protect and serve above all personal wants, above all personal needs, above all else. "Damn it to hell." He snatched his overcoat from Gravenhurst and shoved his arms in it. "What am I supposed to tell Madelaine?"

"You've got me. But you'll have plenty of time to think of a believable lie by tomorrow."

Gravenhurst had already started down the corridor. Grey caught him on the stairs. "I can't allow her to go to my aunt's apartments, wait for me, and then I never show up. I've got to give her some explanation before we leave."

"No time." Gravenhurst didn't pause in his descent. "Pearson has just arrived, and if you haven't figured it out already here is how the chain of command goes—the king commands us all."

"You're enlightening as usual."

Gravenhurst flashed a smug smile. "The king has commanded Pearson to test you in two hours at the Merry Tavern. It's my job to ensure you pass the test. From here to the tavern I'm going to tell you every trick of our trade I know for getting information out of someone."

Grey was mad as hell. He had to excel to make his father proud. To be the best, he needed to know important information in advance. He had to be able to rely on

Gravenhurst. "You're just now teaching me this? Did it not cross your mind to impart some of this information sooner?"

Gravenhurst shrugged. "You're a fast learner, and as you so rightly pointed out, you're already rather deceptive."

He pressed his lips together. He couldn't argue with his own words. "What am I supposed to do?"

"You're to get information out of Constance."

"The chambermaid you've been bedding?"

"I only bedded her once. I found out she's bedding some scar-faced blacksmith from the village who pays handsomely for her favors, and the thought of plundering a woman who just dallied with another man doesn't sit well with me."

"Your standards are impressive."

"Much the same as yours were not long ago."

Grey didn't like that Gravenhurst saw that he wanted to change for Madelaine. It didn't matter that it was true. Nor did it matter he would have eventually told his friend. He needed time. Having Gravenhurst recognize his turnaround made Grey feel weak and vulnerable, much the same as he had before he'd decided he didn't need his father's love. "I never paid a woman for favors." Old habits of self-preservation were hard to quit. He was an ass.

"You should have. No doubt you would have encountered a lot less problems if you had. When a woman is paid for services rendered, she understands perfectly not to expect anything from you but her money."

Grey could've pointed out that the women he had bedded understood not to expect anything more from him than pleasure, but Gravenhurst would argue the point and he'd been an ass enough for one night. Hell, maybe two. The conversation could go on all night. "Let's forget it."

Gravenhurst nodded. "Done."

"Isn't it rather risky to involve a chambermaid or any outsider in our training?"

"There's no risk at all. Constance thinks she's trying to win a bet with me. She has no idea you're attempting to get information from her or about anything else."

The amusement in Gravenhurst's voice didn't sit well with Grey. He trusted his friend with his life, but Gravenhurst had a sense of humor that had led Grey to more trouble than he cared to remember. "Just what sort of bet have you made?"

"I bet her she couldn't seduce you."

"You bloody jackanapes." Grey itched to punch Gravenhurst in the jaw.

"What?"

"I can't let some woman try to seduce me in a public tavern. What if it somehow got back to Madelaine?"

"Don't be ridiculous. It's not as if Lady Madelaine is going to have a conversation with the chambermaid."

That was true enough, but it wasn't the damned point. "I no longer welcome another woman's touch."

Gravenhurst scowled. "What's your bloody point?"

"I don't want Lady Madelaine to think I've lied to her or that I won't be loyal." His ears burned with exposing himself.

"There's no choice."

Bloody, blasted hell. Gravenhurst was right. Grey clenched his jaw. "If it gets back to Lady Madelaine I'm telling her you were trying to seduce Constance."

"Fine."

Grey had to forget Madelaine and what could happen and concentrate on what was about to occur. "What am I trying to learn about Constance?"

"Where she's from and how old she is."

"Simple." Grey smiled grimly into the darkness.

"Not as simple as you might think. She's unusually tight-lipped. It took me these last few days to find out where Constance is from and how old she is. If you fail to tell Pearson the answer when he arrives at the tavern, then it's back to training for the both of us. With *Pearson* as our trainer." Gravenhurst abruptly stopped and pulled up his jacket and shirt sleeve. "See this?"

Grey squinted in the dark night. "No."

Gravenhurst grabbed Grey's hand and shoved it against his arm. "Do you feel that scar?"

Running his fingers down the length of a raised, knotty line, Grey nodded. "What happened?"

"Pearson happened. The man is worse than both of us at not making dangerous contact with his dagger during training. He damn near killed me when he trained me. So, make sure your head is clear of *all* distractions."

"I'm focused."

"You're sure?"

He was still worried about not making an appearance in his aunt's apartments, but Gravenhurst was right. He had to block out all of the distractions. He closed his eyes and took several deep breaths. "I'm ready."

"Not to drag your thought back to Lady Madelaine, but have you carefully thought about what pursuing her means? Do you realize of six of us only one—your father—is married?"

He'd realized it. But he hadn't thought much about it until now. "Madelaine's father was married as well."

"True enough. But he felt he had to marry for the sake of an heir. From what I've been told anyway. Her parents' marriage wasn't a love match. It was convenience and mutual respect. I don't think the woman was ever a weakness for him."

"Your point makes no sense. His enemies could have still gotten to him because of her."

"True," Gravenhurst agreed. "But it's easier to think logically if love isn't involved. He didn't love his wife. But his daughter…"

Grey understood without Gravenhurst finishing. "Madelaine is his weakness."

"I think so." Gravenhurst bounded across the grass toward the stables. "He's acted strange lately, and my theory is it's her. He wants to marry her off, so if something should happen to him, she's taken care of."

Grey paused. What if something should happen to him, and he and Madelaine were married. She'd be left alone. Vulnerable to his enemies. No. He frowned. She'd be surrounded by his family. They'd protect her. Was it fair to drag her into this life he had chosen? Was this the cost of being a spy—living with guilt and fear for those you loved or living with loneliness? He'd just have to get used to constant guilt and fear. He didn't think he could let her go to another, unless she didn't want him. "If things should work out between the lady and me, I'm Stratmore's perfect solution."

After Grey and Gravenhurst mounted the horses the stable master had readied for them, Gravenhurst led them into the dark night. He turned in his saddle to look at Grey. "I don't think Stratmore will consider you a solution. In fact, he might consider your interest in Lady Madelaine a problem. I know I would if I had a daughter."

Grey gripped his reins. He thought he knew what Gravenhurst meant, but he had to know for certain. "What do you mean?"

"I wouldn't want any daughter of mine marrying a man I knew to be a spy. I wouldn't want her bound to someone engaged in life-threatening work, who would be forced to lie to her the rest of their lives. Would you?"

He tensed in his saddle, his fingers curling around his reins so tight, the leather of his gloves bit into his skin. No, he wouldn't like or want a daughter of his to be married to a man who lied to her. But it was too late. He wanted Madelaine. He suspected he was beginning to truly care for her. And his father had made marriage work, so he could too.

He pushed the unwelcome doubts away and signaled his horse into a gallop. If they made excellent time, and he completed this latest assignment quickly, he could get back to catch Madelaine before she left his aunt's apartments. The only problem he foresaw was coming up with a believable explanation for what had detained him. But if he ended up married to Madelaine, he would probably have to lie to her many times, so he needed to welcome the challenge, even if the idea of lying to her sat like a ball of lead in the pit of his stomach.

The more Grey's aunt and sister carried on about how unpardonably rude Grey was, the more Madelaine's embarrassment grew. She pressed a gloved hand to her warm cheek. She had to get out of Helen's apartments and escape to the privacy of her own bedchamber where she could wallow in self-pity. She would have inhaled a deep, calming breath, but her stays prohibited it. The minute she was alone she was going to rip them off and burn them in the fire. It was too bad she couldn't get rid of Grey with the same efficiency. To think she'd dressed with extra care tonight to impress him. She hated stays. And never wore the dratted things, but she'd wanted to show her figure in the most pleasing light. What a silly fool she was.

Elizabeth touched Madelaine's arm. "Maybe Grey's equerry training detained him again. I didn't see him at dinner."

"No, it wasn't that." Madelaine forced herself to look up and prayed her misery didn't show on her face. Helen and Elizabeth exchanged a quick look. So much for disguising her unhappiness. Her throat and nose burned with the unshed tears of humiliation. "When the queen switched the dinner seating tonight, I ended up by Lord Pearson. And when I didn't see Grey at dinner, I inquired whether his equerry training was over. Lord Pearson said it better be because the last he'd seen Lord Grey and Lord Gravenhurst, they were headed to the Merry Tavern."

Her throat felt too thick to continue talking, but she swallowed and stood. "He said nothing else to me, of course. But Lord Thorton, the wretched man, spoke so loudly to Lord Pearson I heard him say the Merry Tavern will indeed make a man merry with its abundance of mead and willing wenches."

"Oh, dear." Helen rose and wrapped her arm around Madelaine's shoulder.

Madelaine's nose tickled unmercifully. She wouldn't cry. She refused to be a blithering child. She'd opened her heart to a known rake and he had trod on it. "I wish I didn't have such excellent hearing. I heard every word."

"It's better to know than to be ignorant, dear. I am sorry." Helen squeezed Madelaine's shoulder. "I'd thought Grey seemed as if he was finally settling down, but I see now I was wrong. Small comfort this may be, but I guarantee you one day Grey will see you at Court, finely dressed with a brood of children and a handsome husband, and he'll sorely regret having botched his chance with you."

"I don't know why I'm so upset." She dabbed at her eyes. "I barely know him, but he made me feel hopeful. I know I'm an oddity, but he seemed to like that." Gads. She'd not meant to expose herself so.

Helen's eyes swam with pity. "Dear, oddballs often turn out to be what we refer to in the *ton* as an Incomparable."

"I'll never be an Incomparable. Mother always said I'd be lucky to find a man who would put up with my oddities."

Helen's eyes narrowed. "I was an oddball, you know. Too educated and too opinionated by half. And then I became fashionable because of my oddity."

"That won't happen for me. Mother warned I'd be my own downfall unless I changed."

"Please don't take this the wrong way, but I knew your mother very well from childhood to our time at Court together. She had a good heart, but tolerance for anyone who did not fit into a perfect mold was not her specialty."

"You didn't understand her," Madelaine protested. It was one thing for her to have been irritated with her mother in life, but she was dead. And she'd not stand here and let anyone disparage her mother.

"You're wrong," Helen said. "You see, I knew her before she was the perfect model of feminine accomplishments. Once, she loved to write, and I remember her saying that she wanted to be a writer someday."

"I never knew she loved to write."

"I daresay you wouldn't have. Her mother was very strict and whipped your mother many times with a cane to rid her of her foolish notions. By the time we came to Court your mother scoffed at anyone who hadn't perfected drawing, knitting, the pianoforte et cetera."

"She wouldn't have been so cruel!" Yet an inner voice whispered memories of all the times her mother had sneered at Madelaine for the things she enjoyed.

Helen offered a gentle smile. "Don't get riled, dear. She didn't mean to be cruel. But if you beat someone enough, they'll gladly conform to the expectations of those around them. And in my experience someone changed from fear often becomes the loudest proponent of what they rebelled against in the first place."

"I feel worse now." Madelaine set down her cup. "I was terribly disobedient and willful. We weren't close, you know. I imagine she hated who I was."

Helen shook her head. "*Who you are*. And I imagine she was envious that you were strong enough not to be cowed."

"She never beat me with a cane." Madelaine didn't want Helen to think her mother could have been that cruel. Her mother had spanked her with her hand and on occasion a belt, but only when she'd deserved it.

Helen arched a thin eyebrow. "Never with a cane you say?"

"No, never."

"How fortunate for you. Though I daresay a hand and other things such as a leather strap could cause their own fair amount of pain."

Madelaine's pulse beat a furious tempo. She wanted to move away from this topic. "I wonder if Father knows about her past."

"I doubt it. I only knew because we grew up together."

It was all so much to take in. The desire to be alone grew stronger until she was fairly itching to flee. "I'd better be going. I received word my father would be here early in the morning, and I've not seen him in months."

"I'll walk with you," Elizabeth said.

Madelaine had almost forgotten her friend's presence because of her unusual quietness. When she looked at Elizabeth, she blinked in shock. Her friend's normally bright eyes appeared dull and tinged yellow. But worse was Elizabeth's complexion. A sheen of sweat covered her forehead and left her usually rosy skin looking pasty. Madelaine grabbed Elizabeth's arm as her friend swayed. "Are you unwell?"

"I must have eaten something bad. Perhaps the fish?" Elizabeth clutched Madelaine's hand, and she had to force herself not to recoil at the clammy touch.

Helen swooped toward them and took Elizabeth's other arm. "You need to get to bed. Louisa!"

Louisa came rushing into the room and bobbed a curtsy. "Milady?"

"Help Madelaine get Elizabeth to her bedchamber. Then hurry back. I'll send a note to my doctor and one to the queen imploring that Elizabeth be excused from service tomorrow."

Not long after, Madelaine and Louisa had Elizabeth tucked into her bed. Madelaine sat beside her friend and pressed a cool rag to her head. "Do you want me to stay?"

"No." Elizabeth shook her head, the damp ringlets clinging to her skin didn't move. "I'll be fine in the morning. I'm sure of it."

Madelaine hesitated a moment. She hated to leave Elizabeth alone but perhaps her friend would rest easier undisturbed. "I'll check on you in the morning before I go to see my father."

"Thank you." Elizabeth's eyes were closed but a small

smile came to her lips.

Madelaine crept toward the door and opened it slowly, not wanting to disturb the slumber that seemed to already be taking hold of Elizabeth.

"Madelaine," came Elizabeth's soft voice from within the darkened room.

She rushed back to her friend's bed and leaned down. "What is it? Do you need something?"

Elizabeth's eyes slowly opened as if the task was a difficult one. "Talk to Grey."

"Shh," Madelaine said instead of certainly not. She'd been humiliated quite enough. "Don't worry about that right now. Just get some rest."

By the time Madelaine climbed into her own bed she felt certain she was so exhausted she'd fall promptly asleep and not have to think about Grey. But sleep evaded her. Worry, on the other hand, kept her close company and caused her to toss and turn in bed for some time.

Had she been a challenge for Grey because she hadn't fallen into his bed as many women must? Clearly, whatever she'd been, he'd tired quickly enough of her. She squeezed her eyes closed, determined not to think of him any longer. Dwelling on Grey wouldn't change the fact that instead of coming to his aunt's apartments to see her, he'd gone off with his friend to a tavern known for its willing wenches. A dull ache strummed in her chest.

Was she judging him too quickly? After all, the ladies of the Court and the queen had judged her and never given her a chance. What if he had a logical explanation? She snorted. She doubted he did. She was just indulging in wishful thinking. *If* on the slightest chance he did *and* he approached her and begged to speak with her, she would possibly listen.

But until she heard his explanation and judged for herself whether it was true she would proceed as if he was a rake after all. Her heart twisted. This was the way it had to be no matter how it hurt. She needed to put him in her past and focus on her future. Her most pressing concern now was really her father. No doubt in the morning he'd want an accounting of how her husband hunting was coming. He was going to be disappointed with her, and the notion of disappointing him made her chest tighten. Starting tomorrow, she'd force herself to master all respectable feminine accomplishments, *and* do her best to be the daughter her father deserved.

The next morning Madelaine went to check in on Elizabeth. She looked worse rather than better, but the doctor was on his way, so Madelaine regretfully left to hurry to the king's Audience Chamber to greet her father before she had to tend to the queen. Halfway up the stairs, her step faltered and her heartbeat raced. Grey stood at the top of the steps. Was he looking for her to explain? She needed to be detached, unless he gave her a reason to be otherwise. She straightened her back and lifted her chin.

"Madelaine!" He bounded down the steps to meet her.

"Good day, Lord Grey." She forced her leaden feet to climb the steps. Her treacherous heart skipped when he fell into step beside her. She glanced at him and wished she hadn't. There'd probably never been a man who looked as fine as Grey did in a deep, blue coat. The color matched the stormy hue of his eyes. Forgiving him would be so easy, but she couldn't be foolish, unless he had a sound, solid explanation.

He nudged her arm. "You're cross."

"Why ever would I be angry?" Did he expect her to do all the work for him? He needed to grovel and beg and explain. "My father is here for a visit, so my heart is light."

"Your heart may be light, but your eyes are heavy with daggers."

She snorted. "Such a witty tongue you have. Did the women last night find you clever?" Blast. She was a miserable failure at pretending she didn't care.

"See—" He grabbed her hand and tugged her into an alcove at the top of the stairs. "You are upset. I'm pleased I'm already learning to read your moods."

She snatched her hand away. Gads! If only she'd not let her emotions overcome her, she would have chosen her words more carefully. His fingers grazed the sleeve of her dress and curled around her elbow. An involuntary shiver went through her at the warmth of his hand seeping through her silk to singe her skin.

"Please, Madelaine. Give me a moment."

Was this more seduction or the accounting she longed for? "I used all my spare moments last night waiting on you. I've none left. Now if you'll excuse me." She looked pointedly at her elbow. If he had nothing to say to defend himself, she had to make herself go.

Dropping his hand, he sighed. "You've every right to be angry, but I can explain."

Her heart skipped a beat. Now they were getting somewhere. "Let me guess, more equerry training?"

"Yes!" He raked a hand through his hair. The motion drew her notice to the utterly disheveled mess. Frowning, she swept her gaze over the rest of him. His clothes were fresh and pressed, but his hair hadn't been combed, a hint of dark stubble graced his face, and—she discreetly sniffed.

"You smell of whiskey, smoke and—" She sniffed again. The unmistakable spicy scent of a woman's perfume lingered on him. Anger swelled inside of her. He dared seek her out to continue his game after spending the night with another woman. Did he think her dull-witted? Expect her to believe his pathetic excuse of more equerry training? She tilted her head back. "Did you just get in?"

"Not long ago, but—"

She held up a palm, glad for the anger that pushed her sadness away. "Did you spend the night with a woman from the Merry Tavern?"

"Certainly not. I spent the night passed out on the floor of the tavern."

She arched her brow. "I feel so much better knowing that."

"You confound me." He cleared his throat. "For once I'm trying to properly court a woman, and what do I find?"

He looked so forlorn that she couldn't help but ask, "What?"

"It's much more bloody difficult than I ever imagined."

"Then quit bothering. You're doing an awful job of wooing me anyway."

He leaned away. "I feared as much. I'll just have to try harder."

"Don't." Her heart lurched at his pronouncement. If he tried harder, she might succumb again. He'd not given a good enough explanation. He wasn't to be counted on.

"I'm afraid I'm rather mule-headed when set on a course. I know you don't believe me, but I was forced to go to the tavern against my will."

"You're right," she snapped. "I don't believe you." Not wanting to listen to anymore of his lies, she bounded away from the alcove and ran smack into an oncoming person.

The collision took her breath away, but she managed to maintain her footing. Constance was not so lucky. The chambermaid fell backwards onto her bottom, the laden silver tray she'd been carrying clanked to the floor with enough noise to make Madelaine wince.

"I'm so sorry, milady."

"I'm the one who should apologize." Madelaine reached to help Constance up, but before the woman clasped onto Madelaine's hand, Grey appeared and kneeling, helped Constance to her feet. Madelaine scowled at his interference, but she couldn't very well be cross with him for lending a helping hand. She bent to pick up the chambermaid's forgotten tray and when she rose, Grey and Constance were staring at each other rather peculiarly. Neither of them spoke a word. A funny, queasiness assaulted Madelaine, worsened by Constance's strong, spicy perfume.

Madelaine looked from Grey to Constance, her stomach plummeting. The sudden dryness of her mouth forced her to swallow repeatedly. "Constance, do you ever get a night off?"

"Rarely. But the queen was in a generous mood yesterday and excused myself and another chambermaid for the night." Constance's gaze lingered on Grey.

"I hope you enjoyed yourself." A dull ache pressed behind Madelaine's right eye. She lifted her unusually heavy arm to rub her temple. The best thing for her heart would be to forget Grey and let her suspicions lay unconfirmed. But she couldn't do it. She had to know if he'd been at the Merry Tavern with Constance. "Did you get to leave the castle and enjoy yourself or were you trapped here?"

Grey shifted from foot to foot, his gaze darting from Madelaine to Constance. Her queasiness intensified. The chambermaid looked at her oddly, and no wonder. Ladies-in-waiting didn't converse with chambermaids let alone inquire as to how they spent their free time.

"Lady Madelaine." Grey touched her elbow, and she instinctively pulled away. He'd hurt her once, she was not about to let him hurt her again. Worry creased his brow. "Your father is walking this way."

Blinking, she glanced down the corridor, lifted her hand and waved. It was as if she was in a dream. Another person going through the motions, but *her* body was moving. Her heart pounded in her ear. She had seconds to secure an answer. "Where did you go?"

When Constance's gaze flew back to Grey's, and his shoulders sagged as he dipped his head as if to give her permission, Madelaine ground her teeth. She didn't need the chambermaid's words to confirm what she now knew. "Never mind," she said, barely above a whisper and turned to meet her father before he reached her. As Madelaine scurried down the hall, Constance's words, "Too bad for you she's a clever one," echoed to her.

Clever indeed. She pasted a smile on her face for her father's benefit. Not astute enough was more like it. A shrewd woman would have heeded the rumors about Grey and stayed as far away from the rake as possible.

Thirteen

The happy smile that lit Madelaine's face when she embraced her father warmed Grey's heart and helped him decide what to do. He couldn't just walk away. Even if she wanted him to. He'd soothe her feelings and make things right. But first—he eyed the chambermaid, Constance. "You might have guessed..." his words trailed off at a glance at Madelaine. Her brow was furrowed and her father's face was set into stern lines.

"Lady Madelaine is the woman you spoke of last night." Constance finished his forgotten sentence for him.

"The very one."

"She's very pretty. But I doubt she'll be willing to please you the way I offered to last night."

"I feel certain you're correct, but she's intrigued me all the same." Constance huffed beside him. "Not to say you're not intriguing," he amended. She was. And not long ago, he would have gladly accepted the offer to share her bed the previous evening, but the time had passed where all he wanted was a good romp. He wanted more. And he only had eyes for Madelaine.

"You're sweet the way you try to appease me. A gold coin would go further though. You're the first man to ever turn down my offer."

He produced a gold coin and held it out. "If Lady Madelaine should question you…"

"She won't. She's a prideful one, she is."

Grey's gaze strayed to Madelaine. Why was she shaking her head? With any luck, it wasn't in answer to being questioned as to whether she'd met anyone she had a tender for. He didn't want to interrupt them, yet he didn't want Madelaine to get away before he gained her forgiveness, and he wanted to greet her father. He refocused on Constance. "But if she should…"

"I'll tell her the truth. You and I spoke for several hours and that was all. When I left, you were all merrily drinking."

Damnation. The truth wouldn't do at all. He didn't want to lie to Madelaine, but the truth made him look like an ass. "Perhaps you could leave off the part about how long we spoke, and just say you talked with me for a moment." He could explain the drinking away by saying they'd been celebrating finishing equerry training. Men would be men, after all.

"Your lady is leaving you," Constance said.

Blast. She and her father were indeed walking away. "Good day," he called over his shoulder. By the time he caught up with Madelaine and Lord Stratmore, his head was not only foggy from last night's drinks, it was pounding. Curse Gravenhurst and Pearson.

"Lady Madelaine."

She faced him, her gaze frigid as a frozen lake. "Lord Grey. What a pleasant surprise. I'd thought you'd gone along with your friend."

There was a lot he could say to that, but not in front of her father. Instead, he smiled, his face tight with the effort. "As you can see, I haven't gone anywhere." He waited, hoping she would give in and introduce him to her father, but from her mutinous airs, he suspected death would come quicker than Madelaine's caving in would.

Her father coughed and when that failed to bring her to snuff on proper etiquette, the duke said, "Who might we have here?"

"Oh very well." Madelaine scowled at Grey. She looked so kissable with her lips pressed together and her eyes sparkling with irritation. "Father, this is Lord Grey, the Duke of Ashdon's son. And, Lord Grey—" Her eyebrows drew up into a haughty arch. "—this is my father, the Duke of Stratmore."

"A pleasure to see you again, Duke."

"Likewise, Lord Grey. I didn't recognize you. You've at least doubled your height since last I met you. And a growth of beard as well."

"I'm afraid I don't recall the last meeting."

"I should think not. It's been a good fifteen years. Have you and Madelaine become friends at Court?"

"I'd like to think so." Grey looked to Madelaine for some slight give in her anger. She glared in return.

"We've only just recently sp—sp—spo." She gave her head a little shake. "*Spoken*."

"Madelaine." Her father narrowed his eyes. "What is it?"

Grey wanted to intervene on her behalf, but if Madelaine was anything like he was interference would only make her discomfort worse.

"N—noth—nothing, Father."

"You're stuttering, and we both know what that means."

Grey didn't know what it meant. He hoped she didn't stutter when distraught because he'd definitely feel to blame. It was hard to imagine he could feel worse than he already did.

"Please, Father. Not now. It's—" she audibly swallowed. "It. Is. Nothing."

Stratmore's gaze flicked to Grey. "Since my daughter refuses to tell me the truth, maybe you will? What is the meaning of her stuttering lies? What have you done to her?"

Stuttering lies? So Madelaine stuttered when she lied? This was a totally different matter. Grey almost smiled in relief. This could be a true blessing if their courtship proceeded to marriage. "I'm afraid I've attempted to begin a courtship of your daughter, but I rather botched it."

A dark look swept across Stratmore's face. Grey stiffened. The man thought Grey meant something debauched. "Nothing untoward, sir, I assure you. I was to meet her in my aunt's apartment last night, with my aunt and sister as chaperone, but I was detained. She's quite understandably vexed with me."

Grey was going to take a large chance. He prayed it paid off. He stared into Madelaine's eyes. "I beg your forgiveness. It wasn't as it seemed. After I passed my training, I was made to join in celebratory drinks that went on for hours. There was no gentlemanly way to excuse myself without causing offense. You must believe I would have very much rather been with you than sit and watch Lord Gravenhurst and the chambermaid flirt with each other."

She wrinkled her nose. "Lord Gravenhurst likes Constance?"

Finally, a break in her anger. "I'd say he more than likes her. Ask him about last night if you wish to confirm what I've said." Gravenhurst could damn well claim he adored Constance to help soothe Madelaine.

She cleared her throat and smiled. "I'm sorry I jumped to conclusions."

"Don't be. I deserve your wariness." He'd never been so

happy for a woman's smile than in this moment.

Stratmore slapped Grey on the back. "Her mother always jumped to conclusions as well. Maddie, you should have said something about this earlier. I'm sorry for being cross with you."

"It's fine, Father." It didn't sound fine. Her voice sounded strained, and she'd shifted away from her father. "I'm pleased you're happy."

"Of course I'm happy. Lord Grey is from a fine family. Tell me, Lord Grey, what do you plan to do in the future? Will you take a commission as the youngest son?"

"Nothing as exciting as that, I'm afraid." Grey wasn't sure how to proceed. Did Stratmore already know Grey was now a spy? Even if he did, Madelaine could never know. Stratmore seemed happy to hear about the courtship. With luck the next bit of news would please the man more and not anger him, if he wasn't already aware of Grey's status. "I've just finished my equerry training."

"Splendid. That's a fine, noble thing to do."

"I think so."

"Who are you serving?"

"Lord Grey is an equerry to your friend Lord Pearson, Father."

Grey smiled at Madelaine's proud tone.

"Well," Stratmore said. "That's most interesting news." The duke fumbled with a button on his coat. Stratmore didn't seem a man to fumble. When he slowly looked up, his blue eyes were intent, and Grey felt a cold draft of displeasure through the layers of his clothes.

He straightened and met the man's gaze which had turned unnaturally bright. "I'd love to discuss my duties with you." What he really wanted to do was assure Stratmore that he had every intention, if his courtship should come to that, of one day being a good husband to Madelaine. Just because she couldn't know he was a spy didn't mean she would be unhappy.

"Madelaine, is the queen not expecting you?" her father asked.

"She is." Madelaine bit her lip and glanced uneasily between Grey and her father. "I do have to go. Father, how long will you be staying? We can visit tonight at dinner and tomorrow—"

"I have to leave after I see the king."

Grey's heart squeezed for the way Madelaine's face fell.

"Take heart, my girl. I'll be back within the month to collect you."

"Collect me?" She shuffled backward, nearly tripping over Grey's boot. He reached out to steady her, though he felt rather unsteady himself. Her father didn't seem to welcome the courtship now that he knew Grey was a spy like himself. His throat tightened with the need to argue his case, but he held his words. No sense trying to convince the duke with Madelaine standing here.

"But, Father—"

Stratmore turned away with a gesture of frustration. "Don't question me. We'll discuss the matter on my return."

Madelaine's gaze met Grey's. Her face had gone pale, but she nodded.

Grey wanted to assure her everything would sort out. He stood still, the blood pounding thickly in his ears.

"Until next month then," she finally said to her father. Her pulse thumped wildly in the open throat of her dress. "Lord Grey."

"Lady Madelaine." His words came out thick with emotion, but she passed by him without another word.

The moment she was out of sight, he addressed Stratmore. "I believe I understand your concerns."

"You don't."

Grey felt certain he did. "Sir, you were married."

"Which is precisely why I know how difficult the lying is. We'll talk no more of it. My decision is made, and the king is expecting me."

"The king expects me too. Madelaine likes me."

Stratmore squinted at Grey. "She likes shooting arrows too. But I ended that folly."

"Sir."

Stratmore jerked his head. "You've been an *equerry* how long?"

"One day."

"Exactly. You know nothing of the job. The dangers. I was married before I became what I am. I'd never have married afterwards, but it was too late. I didn't know better."

"My father makes it work."

An inscrutable look came to Stratmore's face. "Your father lives in a fantasy. He always has."

"Are you denying my courtship?" He hated to ask the question because the answer was almost certainly not in his favor. Yet he had to know what he was up against. Too long he'd lived with assumptions that had been wrong. He'd not make that same mistake ever again.

"I've never denied my daughter anything. Which is part of her problem." The duke glanced toward the stained glass window for a moment then finally back. "You belong to the king in body and soul now, which means you'll never be the man for my daughter. So yes, I'm denying the courtship. Stay away from her; it will be the best for both of you."

Stratmore spun and walked away.

Grey followed silently behind into the king's chambers. There was no way in hell he would simply obey Stratmore and not see Madelaine, but what would she do? He could see the enormous desire to please her father on her face. Pushing the problem aside, he focused on the king.

"Good morning, Your Majesty," he said after Stratmore and the king had greeted one another. "Shall I wait in the outer chamber for you to conclude your business with Lord Stratmore?"

"No. Stay. My business with Stratmore concerns you as well."

Grey settled into a chair near a window and opposite the men. The three faced each other, the sound of rain pounding against the window echoed a continuous tap throughout the silent room. Tension knotted Grey's shoulders, made worse by the wait and the thunder that accompanied the rain. The groan of the heavy door being pulled partially shut seemed to snap the king out of his daze. He ordered all the servants to leave the inner and outer chamber, and the guards were ordered to stand guard at the door to the outer chamber.

Once everyone cleared out, the king leaned forward in his chair, his eyes almost feverish in appearance. "Did you bring it?"

Stratmore glared at Grey then swiftly looked away, nodded and reached inside his coat. He withdrew a rolled up piece of parchment. "It's complete." His gaze flicked once again to Grey before returning to the king. "Perhaps we should go over it *alone*?"

Grey ground his teeth. Not only did Stratmore not want Grey to pursue Madelaine, her father didn't trust him.

"Lord Grey stays." With that pronouncement, the king sat back, his face abstract in thought. Grey barely contained his triumphant smile.

After a few moments, the king focused on Grey. "The code we use to send strategic plans to our armies has been compromised. One of the French has figured the thing out. We know because the last mission your father undertook was sabotaged."

Grey tried not to flinch at the news. To think his father could have been killed was bad enough, but Grey's guilt for the way he'd treated his parents these many years caused a physical ache inside. He wanted to make things right as soon as possible.

The king sighed heavily. "Stratmore has created a new code which will ensure we will once again outsmart Napoleon. He's here today to teach it to me. Forgive him, Lord Grey, he's edgy, as always, and wants you to leave. But distrust of everyone is what makes Stratmore an excellent spy."

"Thank you," Stratmore murmured, looking more murderous than grateful.

"You're entirely welcome," the king said a bit too jovial. Something seemed off about the king's demeanor today, but Grey couldn't figure out what.

"Grey needs to stay," the king continued. "He'll have to learn the code as well."

Stratmore nodded, and the king smacked his hands against his knees, his enthusiasm evident in his gesture. "Show me how it works, and then I'll practice."

Madelaine's father unrolled the parchment and laid it on the table in front of them. Excitement quickened Grey's pulse as he leaned forward. The king traced over the raised letters "QOTM" and "AKUWMK". "What does it spell?"

"Might I suggest you decode it? I think perhaps it's the best way to learn."

The king nodded. "A very sound idea. Tell me how."

"Well." Stratmore sidled closer to the table. "Each letter is represented by the sixth letter after it, created thus to stand for the Circle of Six. For example the 'O—'" Stratmore tapped a finger against the paper "—would be decoded as an 'I.' The exception to the six letter rule is the capitol 'G,' which is always represented by the first letter of the alphabet, created thus to stand as symbolism of your Christian name 'George' who as our leader is always first."

Digesting what he'd learned, Grey studied the letters to the first word. "QOTM" would actually be the word king. He had to clench his teeth to keep from crying out the answer like an eager child. But he *was* eager, by God. He'd not felt this excited about anything in his life.

Grey and Stratmore sat back at the same moment, their gazes locking. Stratmore scowled at him before turning back to the king. Deep in consideration, the king hunched over the scroll, rubbing the bridge of his nose. The time it took for him to decode the word ticked by. Grey's patience strained along with each passing minute, the wait made worse by Stratmore strumming his fingers against the table and the wind howling against the castle windows. Grey felt as if he were being stretched on a rack and at any minute he might snap.

Finally, the king looked up, his eyes disconcerting in their blackness. Grey blinked. The king's eye color seemed washed away by an endless, glassy darkness. The king gazed sightlessly at Grey. A terrible feeling about the king and the whispers Grey had heard, but never credited, rose to almost choke off his air. He shook it off, as he'd discarded many ill feelings. He was the king's man now, for better or worse, he'd protect and serve His Majesty until his death.

"I've got it," the king's voice lowered to a whisper as if

there were someone in the room besides Grey and Stratmore who might hear. "The first word is "king". The king smiled a disturbingly wide smile which looked more like a jester's comedic grin than a king's. The hairs on the back of Grey's neck stood on end at the same time thunder boomed outside.

"Very good, Your Majesty."

Grey scrutinized Stratmore. Was it his imagination or was the man talking to the king in a soothing tone?

"Can you decode the second word?"

The king's brows pulled together in a deep furrow. What took Grey less than a few seconds to decode took the king another long expanse of soundless, painful minutes. Something was not right with His Majesty, and it wasn't Grey's imagination. Lines of worry creased Stratmore's forehead, and his gaze darted continuously from the king to Grey. Damn him to hell if Madelaine's father wasn't assessing him to see if he'd figured out there was a problem with the king.

"The next word is my name." The king's voice held surprising asperity. Grey rubbed at the back of his neck to rid himself of the prickly sensation assaulting him.

Stratmore reached a hand toward the paper on the table. "Perhaps we should continue another day, Your Grace."

The king slammed a hand down on top of Stratmore's. Grey held still as stone, unsure what to do or say. "Don't. Touch. The. Scroll." Each word was a harsh, clipped command. "We'll finish now."

Stratmore slid his hand away from the paper. Wise choice, considering the king fairly foamed at the mouth. His wild gaze locked on Grey. Grey's first instinct was to put distance between himself and his suddenly unpredictable sovereign, but that would be cowardly and unworthy of his station. "Your Majesty?"

With confusion apparent in his eyes, the king shook his head. "I feel a spell coming on. It's muddling my thinking, but I'll manage."

"Of course, Your Majesty." A spell? The whispers were of sudden spells of madness. The prickling sensation was back, but now the tingling covered Grey's entire body.

"Bring me the quill from my desk," the king demanded.

Grey glanced at Stratmore who nodded agreement. The outer chamber was deserted as the king had earlier commanded, yet a whisper of air moved through the room. Had someone just been here? The king's guards stood some ten feet away at the outside of the door. They wouldn't foolishly disobey the king and trespass where they'd been expressly told not to, yet the feeling someone was here, watching and listening enveloped Grey. He glanced around him as he moved toward the king's desk but noted nothing unusual. The fire burned in the grate casting twisted shadows on the wall, but they were just shadows. Still, his heartbeat picked up speed.

Making quick work of it, he retrieved the quill and brought it to the king. When he sat, he positioned himself so he could see into the outer chamber. If someone was there he'd catch them. As the king worked, Grey stared, unmoving, into the other room and counted each noisy inhalation of Stratmore's impatient breathing. Finally, the king set his pen down and wiped a distracted hand across his brow. "I've mastered it. I'm sure of it. Check my work, Stratmore."

Madelaine's father hunched over the list silently, but after a minute a hiss of breath filled the room. When he looked up, his protruding eyes worried Grey. What the hell had the king written down to make Stratmore look ill? A sheen of sweat covered Stratmore's forehead. The man pulled out a handkerchief and wiped his skin with a shaking hand. "You do have it, Your Grace." His Adam's apple bobbed as he spoke. "But let's destroy this immediately."

"Not yet." The king turned his glassy gaze on Grey. Grey's fingers convulsed spasmodically against his leg. He didn't like this strange situation, but he was good and trussed to his vow. "Decode what I've written. I'll see that you can do it as well."

At once, Grey scanned the first sentence the king had written.

An angel of the lord came to me with eyes like stars and clothed in fire. The angel revealed to me a plot of the most insidious nature. My appointed Administration is trying to overthrow me and must therefore all be executed.

Grey swallowed, but his mouth was too dry. Now he knew what had taken the king so long. Before he'd decoded what Stratmore had written, the king had written this message, his own message. Despite himself, Grey glanced around the room. No angels. The king was bloody mad. Or he had been for the minutes the spell had taken him. Sweat broke out on Grey's forehead. He wiped it away with the back of his sleeve. Stratmore was right to want to destroy this immediately.

"Get on with it man," the king barked.

Grey's cheek ticked rapidly. He cleared his throat. "An angel of the lord—"

The king slammed his hand on the arm of his chair. "I've heard of your humor, Lord Grey. But I'm not amused. Read only what's on the paper."

Grey's darted his gaze to Stratmore. The man looked like he was on the verge of a fit. His face was pasty and his eyes were bulging. Stratmore nodded. "Yes, Lord Grey. Simply do as your told."

Grey lowered his voice, wary to read any of the contents aloud but aware if he didn't comply, the king might very well lose his temper and read the translation in a voice loud enough to be overheard by someone besides Grey and Stratmore. "Here," Grey said, pointing to the first line after the mad accusations the king had written, "you've written that my father is to deliver a message to Nelson regarding the movement of Napoleon's fleet across the Atlantic. And each proceeding line regards a new mission and who is to carry it out. Except I'm not on this list."

The king smiled. "Very good. I need to add you."

A distinctive clanking noise came the outer chamber. Grey sprang out of his chair at the same moment Stratmore grabbed for the paper.

Behind him, the king exclaimed, but Grey didn't pause to look back. Instead, he moved into the outer chamber. The chambermaid Constance leaned over the fire with a poker raised high in the air.

"Who let you in here?"

She whirled around and dropped the poker to the ground with a clatter. "The guard. It's time to stoke the fire. The king requires it special every two hours, so he doesn't take chill. The guard said I could enter as long as I was quiet and hurried."

Grey curled his hands into fists. He'd bloody well kill the idiotic guard. The swollen redness of the wench's lips and her half-unlaced bodice told Grey exactly why the guard had made such a foolish choice. "Get out."

He held still as she scrambled out the door, but the minute she was gone he stormed out of the room and jerked the guard toward him. "If you ever disobey the king's orders again I'll see you hung before I eat my evening meal. Understood?"

"Yes, milord," the young guard sputtered without questioning who Grey was or what authority he had over him.

Disgusted, Grey released the man and strode back toward the king's room. He paused at the voices of Stratmore and the king raised in argument inside the chamber. No doubt Stratmore was arguing to destroy the paper immediately. Grey was in hearty agreement, but the thought of disagreeing with the king did not sit well. Still, if he was to protect the king, disagreement was necessary.

Decision made, he started toward the men, but the creak of a door behind him stopped his pursuit. He swung around prepared to bark out another order to stay out, but blinked in surprise at Gravenhurst's drawn face. "Grey, come quick."

A streak of fear went through him at his friend's grave tone. "What is it?"

"It's your sister. She's ill."

Grey glanced back toward the king. He needed to explain his sudden departure.

"I'll explain to the king," Gravenhurst said. "Go now. The physician says Lady Elizabeth doesn't have long."

The dire pronunciation knifed across his heart with more pain than any cut Gravenhurst had given him in training. Grey flew out of the king's chambers without another word.

Fourteen

By the time Grey found the isolated apartment where his sister had been removed, fear had dampened his palms. When he tried to grasp the brass handle to her bedchamber door, his fingers slipped. Cursing, he wiped his hands on his trousers, then tried again. Inside, the room smelled of incense, rosewater and medicine, and the curtains over the window were pushed wide, allowing sunlight to flood it. His shoulders relaxed a little. He'd expected darkness and the sickly stench of death. Maybe Liz wasn't as bad off as Gravenhurst thought.

But as he approached the bed, his stomach pitched. Liz was asleep, her mouth half open and a line of drool running down her cheek. Her skin looked strange, almost like the wax he sealed his letters with. With a shaking hand, he touched her cheek. By God, she was on fire. Glancing behind him, he swept his gaze over the washstand for the pitcher of water, but the stand was empty. Perhaps his aunt had gone for water, for surely his aunt was caring for Liz.

He knelt down beside his sister and picked up her limp hand. Grief tore through him when she didn't stir. Grey studied her. What could be wrong? Fever, for certain, but what was causing it? Her thick black hair clung in wet tendrils to her forehead and neck. Beside her pillow was a wet, crumpled cloth she must have thrown off her head in a fit. She needed to be cooled. He picked up the cloth and growled. The damnable thing was hot. Where was the physician and his aunt?

Anger filled his belly and sent him surging to his feet to prowl the room. Liz wouldn't die. He'd not allow it. She was too young and healthy. And he needed her. She was his confidant, his twin. She understood the loneliness he'd felt most his life because she too had felt like an outcast in their family. Father and Edward had always had a special bond, and Mother and Marianne had been thick as thieves to the exclusion of Liz. When their oldest sister had died, their mother died in spirit right along with her, which was one of the reasons he'd suggested Liz come to Court. Here, she could spread her wings and quit trying to become Marianne to please Mother. If Liz had contracted some vile disease here that killed her, he would never forgive himself.

He paced around the room. He felt helpless and caged. He wanted to flee, saddle up his stallion and ride until numbness took hold. This fear falling over him was unacceptable. Weakness was not an option.

He had to do something. He strode back and forth some more. No good. He was going to go mad. Liz muttered and stirred in her bed. He raced over to her side and fell to his knees. "Liz." He smoothed the damp hair off her forehead. "It's Grey. I'm here, poppet." A crooked, cracked smile wobbled on her lips. Leaning over her, he pressed a kiss to her burning forehead and started to lay his head beside her as they had done as children, but her hand came to his chest to push him away.

"Don't get too close." Her eyes opened into slits, and her hand fell to her side.

"Whatever you have, I'm too strong to succumb."

Liz shook her head. After an interminable moment, she

focused her watery eyes on him. "No. You're not. You're—"
A cough rumbled in her throat becoming so loud and
violent that it curled her body into itself. Grey grasped her
around the shoulders as her body shook with each cough
and ran a hand gently through her hair. "Handkerchief," she
gasped between coughs.

He searched around her bed and found a pile of crumpled handkerchiefs. Frowning at the mess, he handed one to
her and grabbed another one to inspect. The red stains on
the white linen made his blood run cold. His fingers curled
around Liz's shoulder.

Was she thinner than she had been a week ago? A
month? When the last cough died, she flopped back against
the bed covers and lay with her eyes drooping and the
handkerchief balled in her fist. He uncurled her fingers
without her protesting.

Bringing the handkerchief closer, his heart squeezed
painfully at the sight of more blood.

"Consumption," she wheezed. "The doctor thinks I
have consumption."

A strangled sound escaped his throat before he could
control himself. His insides knotted into fear. Consumption
had taken Marianne from them and might as well have
taken their mother. Consumption was horrible. God
couldn't be that bloody cruel to allow two of his sisters to
be taken by the same disease. "Has everyone run off then?"
Bitterness flowed through his veins. He remembered how
some of the servants, including Marianne's lady's maid, had
fled their house when the physician had pronounced she
had consumption.

Liz's eyes opened just a bit. "Not everyone. Aunt Helen
won't go."

"That's my girl." Grey's heart filled with gratitude and

love.

Liz chuckled almost too soft to hear but the act caused another coughing spree to commence. After the attack ended, he pressed a glass of water to her lips. "Drink."

She obeyed, though he wasn't sure how much water actually made it into her mouth. It seemed more ended up on her night rail than down her throat. Once he found a towel and patted her dry, he settled beside her on the bed again. "Where is the physician?"

"Gone to get his bleeding kit." Liz shuddered. She grasped for his hand and when he took up her hand, she curled hers gently into his as she used to do when they were children and would walk hand in hand around the lake. He blinked at the moisture in his eyes. Damned dry room. "Don't let him bleed me." Panic and fear edged her words.

He pictured Marianne, skeletal with blood dripping down her arms from the hundreds of puncture wounds administered by the physician's spring blade. Liz didn't need to plead her case. No way in hell would another well-meaning physician drain too much blood and send another one of his sisters to an early grave. He squeezed Liz's hands. "I'll kill him if he tries."

"Good," she murmured. "Make her go."

"Who, poppet?"

"Madelaine. She won't leave me alone either." Liz coughed again, but this time there was no blood. He swallowed against the consuming dryness in his mouth. Liz smiled wanly. "She's stubborn like Helen. But she must leave, so she will live."

"Don't worry about Madelaine living." The thought of losing Madelaine *and* his sister hollowed out his stomach.

"For you," Liz said. "Silly fool. She's perfect for you. Can't have her dying. Convinced yourself you don't need love." Liz sighed, her eyes fluttering closed. "But you do. You need her. She'll never hurt you as Father has."

"Shh." He tried to soothe her. With a sigh, she settled into the blanket, and he pulled the cover up under her chin. As he watched her fall into a light sleep and then the deeper one of dreams, he moved from the bed so as not to disturb her and pulled a chair beside the bed. He tugged off his jacket and cravat and leaned back to wait. If the physician, his aunt and Madelaine were returning, there was no sense in him going in search of them. He'd likely miss them anyway. He couldn't stomach the thought of leaving Liz alone. He slumped in the chair and rubbed his aching neck. Liz's words rang through his head.

His sister was partially right, he had convinced himself he didn't need love, but finding out the real reason his father and Edward had always seemed to exclude him and not want him around had released some unknown constraint within him. He'd felt it these last few days. A lessening of whatever invisible force had driven him from one scandalous pursuit to the next. Knowing Madelaine and chancing his heart was something he desperately wanted.

What he wasn't entirely certain of was whether she'd welcome his pursuit after he told her that her father had denied his courtship. And a deuced irritating voice kept whispering that he might be selfish in pursuing her. She'd have to go against her father's wishes, *and* didn't she deserve more than a husband who would lie to her? Still, he wasn't selfless enough to let her simply fade out of his life. There was something special about her, some kindred longing in her eyes that moved him.

The door creaked open, and as if summoned by his thoughts of her, Madelaine drifted into the room, her lilac skirts swishing around her ankles. She had a mound of cloths under one elbow and a pitcher of water in her hand. As she moved further into the room, her eyes lit up and a relieved smile came to her face. "You're here!"

Without a word, he stood and went to her. Taking the pitcher of water he set it on the washstand, then moved close to her so their talking would not disturb Liz. "Did you doubt I'd come? Liz is my sister."

"Well, no." Madelaine bit her lip. "But after the doctor said it may be consumption and the queen had Elizabeth moved to these quarters, some of the other ladies-in-waiting said how awful it would be to die as Elizabeth was going to—all alone with no one but the physician to keep her company."

He clenched his jaw, a string of blistering words on the tip of his tongue. He settled on a rather mild statement in case Liz could somehow hear him. "Those women are vain nitwits who know nothing of me and the love I hold for my sister. Death does not scare me, Madelaine, if it means my presence comforts Liz."

"Me, either."

The pull of a real smile tugged at his lips. "I was afraid you might say that."

Madelaine's eyes grew big. "Well, then. I suspect you now see the real, stubborn me. If you'd like to change your mind about courting me, I understand."

"On the contrary. The real you I'm glimpsing makes me want you even more."

A smile played at her lips, though the dark smudges under her eyes and the wisps of disheveled hair framing her face so beautifully reminded him of the gravity of his sister's situation.

Needing for one second to feel the comfort touching Madelaine would offer, he pulled her to him and brushed a quick, light kiss across her warm lips. The contact moved like lightning through his veins. The last thing he wanted to do was release her, especially when a low moan escaped her. But he did before anyone had the chance to pass by the open door, and she was compromised. He may well indeed end up marrying her, but he'd not have her name be-smirched to see the deed accomplished.

Fifteen

Madelaine's sleep had been far from restful this past week. Worry over Elizabeth's worsening condition awoke her as it had all week like clockwork. She dressed and trudged groggily down the five corridors and two flights of stairs toward the isolated hall where Elizabeth had been moved. If Grey was in the room, she wouldn't go in, just as she hadn't the last three nights.

She had to limit the time she was alone with him. It wasn't proper. Not to mention Grey had told her Father had denied his courtship. Until she could speak with her father and ascertain what his objection was and perhaps persuade him differently, she didn't want to go against his wishes. She'd hurt her mother by being so stubborn, and it was too late to make amends, but she was determined never to hurt her father. She would be a model daughter, even if it killed her. *What if Grey finds someone else?* Madelaine clenched her teeth. She hated the voice of doubt inside her head.

She pushed the thought away. There was no sense worrying over something she felt confident could be changed. Likely, someone had whispered in her father's ear of Grey's reputation as a rake. She'd simply explain to Father that he was wrong and tell him how Grey was with his sister. Father would have to change his mind. He'd always been a very reasonable man. Well, except for when he'd insisted she had to find a husband at Court. Still, a part of her understood he was only trying to secure the best future for her.

Coming close to Elizabeth's door, Madelaine took extra care not to make a sound. She just wanted to reassure herself that Elizabeth was still alive. She prayed Helen was there and not Grey. Every time she saw him, she had to fight the compulsion to talk to him, and after the dream she'd just had about him, her need to be close to him was like a consuming hunger.

She cracked open Elizabeth's door. Her pulse skittered at the sight of Grey by his sister's side, his head bent and his hands clasped together in front of him. His deep murmur floated to Madelaine, and her mouth dropped open. Grey was a praying man? She listened closer, her eyes bugging. Not only was Grey praying, he was begging God to spare his sister's life and take him instead. No, no, no, foolish man! Tears filled her eyes. She couldn't live without him. She quickly said a prayer for Elizabeth's recovery and Grey's continuing health.

She pulled the door quietly closed and sagged against the wall. She was a fool to think she'd put up some barrier between herself and Grey. Seeing him now begging for his sister's life was like a bucket of cold water thrown on her head. There were not enough barriers in the world to guard her heart from Grey.

The way he'd helped care for his sister had shown him to be loving and honorable and everything she had ever dreamed of in a man. When had she started to lose her heart to him? She laughed at that. Most likely the moment she'd met him in Golden Square.

She moaned and pressed her hand over her mouth to hush herself. Even if she'd been sensible enough not to melt like a schoolgirl at his touch, no warm-blooded woman could keep herself fortified against a man who brushed his sister's hair, patiently gave her sips of water and broth, and threatened bodily harm to the physician that had come to bleed Elizabeth.

Madelaine's heart pounded in her ears. The wisest thing she could do was avoid him completely until she could speak with her father. That way she would ensure not losing her senses. Pressing away from the wall, she straightened and made her way back to her room. She couldn't wait a whole month to speak with Grey again. It was more than she could stand.

But what could she do? As she undressed, she considered her prospects. There was only one thing to bring her father back sooner. She sat down and dipped her quill in ink. How should she word her letter to Father? If she was careful with her words, she'd not be lying and Father would come quickly. Smiling at her cleverness, she wrote one line. *Come with haste. Something dreadful has happened.*

That should do it, and she'd not lied. Elizabeth's sickness was dreadful. Hopefully, by the time Father got here, Elizabeth would be well, and Madelaine, Elizabeth and Helen could explain to her father how Grey was truly an honorable man. Then Grey could court her, and she could fall guiltlessly in love.

Avoiding Grey was much harder than Madelaine imagined. She was partly thrilled and dismayed that he went to such efforts to see her. Wherever she seemed to go, she would catch glimpses of him, but she managed to keep her distance. The hardest times were when she was in Elizabeth's room, and he would come to care for his sister. Madelaine always fled, offering some stuttering, flimsy excuse. Yesterday's had been especially bad. Grey had raised one eyebrow, and she'd known he didn't believe her. She'd entertained the idea of telling him the truth. Yet the thought of sitting before him and explaining that she was staying away because when she was near him she didn't trust herself not to go against her father's wishes, made her stomach pitch precariously.

With that in mind, she rose early. She had to visit Elizabeth before Grey even considered coming. If he kept to the same routine of the last two weeks, he would tend to his equerry duties first and then come to his sister's room around noon. When Madelaine finished translating a letter for the queen, she begged to be excused to go check on Elizabeth. The queen was surprisingly kind and gracious. No doubt the kindness had everything to do with her good feelings toward Elizabeth and Grey and nothing to do with Madelaine personally, but whatever the reason, she welcomed the reprieve from the scolding and glares.

When she reached Elizabeth's apartment around ten, she took several deep breaths before entering. All her composure left her and she squealed as she ran into the room.

"You're awake!"

Elizabeth was propped against a mound of pillows. Her cheeks looked rosy, but with the light glow of health and not the burn of fever. Her blue eyes sparkled without the glassiness that had worried Madelaine so this past week. Dark smudges still lay under her eyes, and her face had a new hollowness around the cheekbones, but she looked vastly improved. "You look wonderful!"

Elizabeth smiled wanly. "Liar."

"Oh, no." Madelaine shook her head as she and Helen exchanged smiles of greeting. "I stammer when I lie, so rest assured I'm telling the truth."

"Come." Elizabeth chuckled and patted the bed. "Sit by me and tell me of you and Grey. I'm not sure how much longer I can stay awake."

Madelaine pulled up the chair, but the last thing she wanted to do was talk about her and Grey. "Does your brother know you're better?"

"He knows," Helen answered, coming to sit by Elizabeth on the bed. "He was here last night when her fever broke, and he was here this morning when the doctor saw her. I've never seen a man as close to crying with relief as Grey was."

"Aunt," Elizabeth scolded. "Grey wouldn't like you saying such things."

"Pish-posh. As if I give a fig what Grey or any man likes. Except the king." She winked. "The freedom to be outrageously blunt comes with having buried my husband." She smiled wickedly. "And being wealthier than most helps."

Elizabeth shook her head then glanced at Madelaine. "Ignore her."

Secretly, Madelaine hoped she would someday be as confident as Helen was. "What did the doctor say?"

"That I've made a miraculous recovery." Elizabeth promptly yawned.

"And that she doesn't need to tire herself," Helen added. "She's to rest, which is precisely what I've been trying to get her to do."

"I don't want to rest," Elizabeth protested, but she yawned again.

"If you don't rest you won't get better and then who

will be on my side against Grace?"

"Has she been awful? Tell me what she's done."

"I will, but only if you lay down and close your eyes."

"This is splendid," Elizabeth said. "It's like being put to sleep with my own special fairy tale. My nanny used to tell the best stories."

"Sit up," Madelaine commanded. She quickly rearranged Elizabeth's pillows and then gently helped her to lie down. "Now close your eyes and listen."

She spent the next hour regaling Elizabeth with tales of Grace's wicked ways. When she was finished, Helen sang Elizabeth a song, until her eyes drifted shut, her breathing became even and her chest rose and fell with deep sleep.

Helen clucked her tongue as she looked at the clock. "I've got to go," she said in a whisper. "But Grey will be here soon."

"I need to go too." Madelaine pushed back her chair to stand.

"Madelaine, are you still angry with Grey because of the night he didn't show up to my apartments?" Her voice had risen. Madelaine darted a glance at Elizabeth. Still sleeping. Good. Helen took Madelaine by the elbow and led her closer to the door. "If you're still angry, I think it's quite unforgiving, given what you've seen of his character these past two weeks."

"I'm not still angry." Madelaine flushed with embarrassment. How could she explain to Helen that she was afraid to be alone with Grey because she was fearful of breaking her promise to herself?

"Then why not stay and sit with him? I know he wants you to. And Louisa can stay here. I'll be fine without her, and she's hard of hearing so you may speak freely to Grey."

Madelaine glanced at Louisa, who sat quietly knitting in

a corner. Could she stay with Grey and Helen's lady's maid? She felt herself wavering, and then Grey's deep laughter filled the hallway. Her stomach fluttered, and she shook her head while scrambling around the room to gather the remainder of her things. "I can't. I must go, now." She could hear Grey talking to someone outside the door, and longing to be near him pierced her heart.

Helen stomped her slipper. "I don't understand you," she said in a low tone. "I don't mean to be overly bold but you do like him, don't you?"

"Yes, of course I do."

"Well then, my dear, if you don't want to lose him, you'd better act as if you like him before another lady steals his heart."

"Don't put ridiculous notions in Madelaine's head, Aunt Helen." Grey's deep voice made Madelaine jump. Her gaze flew to the doorway where he stood and a tremor filled her. He was perfectly shaven, his thick wavy hair wet and combed back from his face. He wore a dark blue coat that enhanced the golden color of his skin beautifully, and his tan breeches clung to his lean, muscular thighs. He looked the impeccable gentleman of Court except for the bloody gash on his face.

Her resolve not to say more than a polite greeting to him was forgotten on a rush of words. "What happened to you?" She was not conscious she'd moved until she stood right before him, and his heady masculine scent invaded her, but she could not will herself to move away.

He raised a gloved hand to his right cheek. "Is the damned thing bleeding again?"

She nodded. "What happened?"

"More training. But I was distracted with other thoughts." His gaze locked on her, smoky blue and intense.

"You'll be the death of him," his aunt murmured as she gave him a kiss and swept out of the room with her lady's maid behind her. From the hall came Helen's impatient voice. "Come, Lady Madelaine, *if* you still are departing."

A sense of vital desperation clung to Grey as a faint, sardonic smile curved his lips. "You don't have to avoid me. You've made clear your wishes."

It had been on the tip of her tongue to say goodbye, but his words changed everything. He'd completely misinterpreted why she was avoiding him, and his misunderstanding was entirely her fault. She needed to be truthful with him. Her stomach rolled and heat crept up her chest and face. She had to be brave. She *had* to tell him, or risk losing him to another woman, as his aunt had so bluntly pointed out. "Lady Helen, I'll be staying if your lady's maid can still act as chaperone."

Helen's silent answer was to send her maid scurrying back into the room. Louisa bobbed a curtsy to them. "Where would you like me?"

"Yorkshire," Grey responded with a scowl toward the door where Helen's laughter trickled back to them from the hall.

Madelaine pressed her lips together on her amusement. "Why don't you take the settee? It's the most comfortable chair in the room and you can spread out your knitting." Not to mention it was the only place she and Grey would have been able to sit close together. Putting Louisa there took care of the problem of her and Grey possibly touching. Even an inadvertent caress could crumble her defenses.

As Louisa shuffled over to the settee, a faint smile curved Grey's lips. "Why do you need another chaperone? My sister is here. And she's on the mend." Grey swept his hand toward the bed where Elizabeth slept so soundly that her snoring filled the room.

Madelaine arched an eyebrow. "Yes, a fine chaperone she'd make."

Grey grinned lazily, his gaze sweeping down the length of Madelaine's body. "She seems the perfect chaperone to me."

"You mustn't say such things."

"What did I say?" He looked utterly innocent and handsome.

She laughed as she recounted his words. "You said nothing. But it's the *way* you say nothing."

"I promise to say everything in the most monotone voice I can muster the entire time we're together." He motioned toward two chairs under the window that faced Elizabeth's bed. "We can sit there, talk and keep an eye on Liz at the same time."

Madelaine nodded and started toward the chairs, startling when Grey took her hand. "Lord Grey," she chided, addressing him formally because of Louisa's presence. She tried to pull her hand away, but he held tight.

"Just leading you safely to your seat," he said in a voice so lacking intonation that she chuckled.

"How very kind of you, Lord Grey. I've been walking on my own two legs for twenty years now. I'm quite the expert."

"Yes, but this floor is treacherously bumpy." He made a show of tapping his foot on the floor.

Once seated, he released her hand, but not without trailing his fingers along the inside of her palm. Delicious tingling sensations ran from her palm, up the length of her arm and sent her heart into a faster beat. Tongue tied with how he made her feel *and* nervous over how to start her confession, she settled on an obvious task. "Shall I clean your cut for you?"

"If you're not afraid to touch me." A provocative challenge rang in his words.

Madelaine narrowed her eyes in warning even as her body responded to the subtle change of his tone. She rose, wet a rag, and came to sit beside him. "You've forgotten yourself." She dabbed at his cut.

"I'm terribly sorry." He grinned sheepishly, and she could just imagine him young, full of mischief, and grinning precisely that way to his nanny.

After she wiped the last traces of blood away, she returned the rag to the wash stand and settled back beside Grey. "I bet you were never spanked as a child, were you?"

"Of course not."

She suddenly recalled the last spanking her mother had given her. A neighbor had come to call and Madelaine had tromped through the house in a pair of breeches she'd stolen from one of the servant boy's rooms. Later, after the neighbor had left, her mother had come to Madelaine's room, shut the door, and whipped her until welts covered Madelaine's bottom. She'd forgotten the moment until just now.

"Madelaine," Grey said lowly, his voice so razor-sharp that it snapped her from her recollection, and she glanced automatically to Elizabeth's bed to see what was the matter. But Elizabeth lay still, her snoring filling the room.

"What's the matter?" The dark look on his face puzzled her.

He reached for her suddenly, and with the memory of her mother's last spanking fresh in her mind, she shoved her chair backwards out of his reach.

"*Madelaine.*" He dropped his hand and sat very still. "Goddamn," he whispered. "Did your father beat you as a child?"

"No." She was very glad he'd not asked about her mother. She'd never told a soul about the spankings she'd received from her mother every time she'd been a disappointment, but now that she was remembering them, she was shocked to realize just how many she could recall, and the pain of what her mother called "a simple spanking".

He studied her intently for a moment before speaking. "Who beat you?"

Heat flooded her cheeks, and she swallowed convulsively against the feeling that her tongue was tied. "N-n-no one."

His eyes glittered as he stared. "Madelaine, you're lying to me." His voice was low and fierce. "Tell me. I'll keep your secret."

His scent of freshly washed male surrounded her. When had he moved his chair closer? Their arms touched and their legs brushed. She glanced worriedly at Louisa, but the woman's eyes were closed and her mouth was hanging open. Wonderful, her chaperone, her lone defense against her own desire for Grey, was fast asleep. Discomfited, she pressed her fingers to her temple and took a deep, calming breath. "My mother didn't beat me," she said without stuttering, so it had to be true. "She s-sp—" She clenched her teeth and took another deep breath. "She spanked me when I deserved it, which was quite a lot given how disobedient I was."

He slid his arm around the back of her chair to rest on her shoulders, while he smoothed her hair in a repeated, calming fashion with his free hand. "What sort of spankings?"

She sighed at the relaxing feeling his touch brought her. Closing her eyes, she leaned her head against his arm. "The typical sort with her hand and sometimes a leather strap."

"And did it hurt very much?"

"I don't know." But her bottom screamed now in re-membrance.

"*Madelaine.*"

She opened her eyes and looked at him. His face was inches from hers. She tried to draw back, but he slid his hand to the base of her skull and held her locked in place. "Did it hurt?"

He'd not relent until he had his answer. She could see it in the dark glint of his stormy gaze. "Yes, it hurt. Terribly. I usually couldn't sit the next day. Are you satisfied?"

She tried to turn her face from his, but his other hand came up and captured her chin. "No, I'm angry as hell. Did your father hit you too? Because if he did—"

"No," she said as sharply as she dared with two people sleeping so near. "As far as I know, he never had an inkling Mother hit me. He was gone often to see the king and on various trips, and when he came home Mother would always be upset with him for having been gone as long as he was. I think they were too busy arguing over how much he was gone to talk much about me other than for Mother to bemoan what a failure I was as a proper lady."

Grey looked at her as if he was struggling with some great emotion. He stroked her bottom lip with his finger, igniting that familiar fire he'd lit before deep in her belly. "I'll never hurt you, or let anyone else hurt you again."

The shock of his lips on hers silenced anything she was about to say and allowed him complete access to her mouth. His tongue slipped inside like silk, but burning hot. He explored her mouth gently with erotic strokes until the fire in her belly started to spread up her body, and a low moan escaped her. Then just as suddenly as he'd started the kiss, he pulled away but captured her hand as he did so and brought it to his face. "I wish we were alone." His voice was raw and gravelly.

She traced down the slope of his jawline, and then made herself pull away. "I wish it too, but I know it's very good we are not."

"Why's that?" His hand was again around her shoulder, his fingers brushing lightly back and forth over the skin exposed at the base of her neck.

"Because you scare me."

"I scare you?" He stopped brushing her lip.

"No, no." She shook her head. "The way you make me feel when I'm around you scares me."

"Ah." He smiled, two dimples appearing in either side of his cheeks. "That's different. That kind of fear I like. You should release yourself to your fears. A little bit, that is."

God, the man was impossible. His every word sounded like an invitation to sin, and she very much wanted to respond "yes", but she couldn't. Yet she could offer him the truth of her heart. "I've avoided you since you told me what my father said because I was afraid if I was alone with you too much, I would break my vow to be an obedient daughter."

"I see." He fiddled with one of the flowers embroidered on her dress. "So you do want me to continue to court you?"

"Very much," she whispered, suddenly feeling shy.

A crease lined his forehead. "And if your father won't relent and give his permission?"

She refused to consider the possibility. "He won't refuse me. He's very reasonable, and I'm sure his worry has to do with your reputation at Court. But once he hears how honorable you really are, and I tell him how you cared for your sister, I know he'll change his mind."

"What if your father is refusing my courtship because of other reasons?"

She frowned. "What else could there be?"

Grey shrugged, not meeting her gaze. "Nothing." His tone was harsh. "There's nothing." He looked up and smiled. "Together we'll change his mind."

She nodded. They had to change his mind. She didn't think she could defy her father. His disappointment would be so great, and there was part of her that wondered whether it was her mother's disappointment with her that had led to her parents' last argument that had sent her mother tearing off on her stallion into a snowstorm and her death. "So you don't mind waiting to court me?"

"I'm courting you now." He grinned. "And I mind very much waiting for you, but I suspect you're worth the wait. Will you consider something for me?"

"What?"

"Will you see me if someone is always present, and I vow not to touch you again until we have your Father's agreement that I may court you?"

"Yes." Her husky tone made her wince. She had to get a little control. It was hard. She wanted more than anything to spend more time with him. "I'll see you as long as someone is always present." After all no harm could come if he kept his vow.

Sixteen

Madelaine crumpled the paper in her hand, plopped onto her bed, and stared into the crackling fire. She was utterly disgruntled. Why hadn't Grey kissed her when they'd strolled in the garden tonight? It wasn't as if there hadn't been ample opportunity. His aunt had left them for a moment to speak with an old acquaintance. Madelaine had been so sure she'd get a kiss or at the very least he'd try to hold her hand. He'd pointed out stars. She kicked her slippers onto the floor. Stars were perfectly lovely, but she'd wanted his lips on hers not his knowledge.

She was being unreasonable, but she didn't care. This week had been horrid. Grey had kept to his vow not to touch her like a saint. She wanted to kick herself for agreeing to his suggestion. The letter she'd just received from her father didn't improve her mood.

She'd not been prepared for him to refuse to come back to the castle. Let alone under *any circumstances, barring imminent danger to herself or the return of the Prince of Wales from his trip abroad.* His words made it next to impossible to obey his wishes. If Grey didn't touch her soon she'd go insane.

She closed her eyes and listened to the wood pop in the fire grate. There were two choices. She and Grey could keep on as they had been or they could allow small harmless touches, such as a brush of the hand or even a chaste kiss. Butterflies danced in her stomach.

She felt trapped between desire and duty. What to do? She plucked at her coverlet. Her heart told her Grey was honorable. Father *would* see reason. Eventually. Setting her worries aside long enough to dress for bed, she donned her night rail and looked out at the moon. Was Grey somewhere gazing at the same sky? Would she see him tomorrow and have to endure more sweet torture?

She closed the shutters of the small window. She longed to be alone with Grey and feel his hand cup her face and his lips crush against hers as they had before. She yanked back her covers and settled into her cool sheets.

She was sick of the yearning gnawing at her every waking moment. If she was sure she could convince her father to agree to Grey's suit, there was nothing really forcing her to endure this torture one more moment. She smiled. That was an easy decision. Why on earth had it taken her so long to make it? Tomorrow, she'd somehow show Grey that he needed to break his vow. She wrinkled her nose. However could she do that without embarrassing herself? She could brush his hand when no one was looking, or maybe they'd even find themselves alone again for a moment and *she'd* kiss *him*. The scandalizing thought made her grin. She was looking forward to getting him to break his vow.

When she woke the next morning and learned the queen had unexpectedly departed for Kew with a small, select entourage of the king's men, two of the king's physicians and all the ladies-in-waiting except for her and Elizabeth, Madelaine was thrilled. This was perfect. Now, all she needed to do was find Grey.

Perhaps Elizabeth could somehow help her come up with a plan to be alone with him for a few minutes.

Madelaine raced through the halls as quickly as she could and arrived breathless at Elizabeth's room. She burst through the door and stopped at the sight. Grey kneeled by his sister's bed, a crumpled letter in his hand and an amused smile on his face. Elizabeth's face held deep lines of worry. The only noise in the room was the loud snoring of Louisa, who sat slumped on the settee.

Madelaine inched open the door and winced at the loud creak of the hinges. Grey rose and motioned her over. When she was close to the bed, he drew her near his side. His unexpected touch sent her pulse soaring. His hand lingered on hers for the briefest second but even after he released her, her skin tingled with awareness. "Lady Madelaine, I'm glad you're here. Maybe you can convince my sister there's nothing to worry about. Nothing I've said seems to be doing the trick."

Madelaine sat and took Elizabeth's hand. "Worrying is bad for your recovery. Stop immediately."

Elizabeth frowned. "Grey said almost the exact same thing, but I can't help but worry when he's been called home so cryptically."

Madelaine's heart lurched. "Home?"

Elizabeth nodded. "Foxhaven, my oldest brother, has summoned Grey home immediately with no explanation. It's unlike him to be enigmatic."

Grey laughed, but it sounded forced. "Edward is highhanded, Liz. Surely you've not forgotten that. He's probably taken it in his head that I've done something unpardonable and doesn't want to write it in the letter because he fears I'll avoid him. I'll go home, soothe his worries, and then I'll return."

Grey's gaze had locked on Madelaine. His promise to return made her stomach somersault. "When will you be departing?"

"Now."

"Now?" She cursed the bad timing. "How long will you be gone?"

He gazed down. "Possibly a sennight or two."

Two weeks? Why didn't he appear as upset as she felt? As he leaned down, hugged his sister and said his goodbye, Madelaine tried desperately to breathe normally, but catching a proper breath was difficult. Her chest felt compressed, her throat tight. When he stood and faced her, so near she could smell the scent of pine lingering on his skin and see the flecks of grey in his blue eyes, she willed him to touch her.

He reached for her hand, and her pulse leapt. But then he withdrew, his hands clenching at his sides. He wanted to touch her! She would have thrown herself into his arms and lavished him with kisses if not for his sister. "Goodbye, Lady Madelaine." His voice sounded strained. "I hope to see you very soon."

She swallowed against her dry throat. "Sooner I hope rather than later, Lord Grey. Safe travels."

He dipped his head to her and walked out the door. When the door shut, her shoulders sagged. She wanted to run after him and assure him she'd wait for him, but how would she explain herself to his sister? She glanced at Elizabeth. Elizabeth stared back with a small smile. "If you go quickly down the garden path by Frogmore, you'll catch him at the edge of the woods. He must go that way to get to our home. No one would see you there. But mind you, if you're not back in fifteen minutes, I'll wake Louisa and send her after you."

Madelaine's heart soared. "Thank you, Elizabeth! I vow I'll pay you back this kindness."

Elizabeth laughed. "You've no need to pay me back for anything. You've sat as nursemaid to me for weeks and helped bring me back from the dead. Grey told me he wants to court you, and he told me of your father's refusal. Take heart, Madelaine. I've never known Grey not to get what he wants. I don't know how he'll do it, but I've no doubt he'll bring your father around. Go now and wear my cloak, in case someone should see you."

Madelaine threw on Elizabeth's cloak and pulled the hood around her face. "I'll return soon." She raced out of the castle, taking care to avoid being seen by anyone. The brisk morning air burned her lungs. Ignoring the burn, she ran down the garden path, past Frogmore and toward the edge of the woods. Her slippers pounded against the hard dirt. She had to catch Grey before he was too far out of her reach. As she rounded the bend in the trail, she gasped as Grey disappeared into the thick woods.

"Grey!" she shouted, hoping if anyone happened to be near they would think it was his sister running after him. He whipped around in the saddle, a smile spreading across his face. Flying down the slope of the trail, the toe of her slipper hit a gnarled root that rose above the dirt. She almost tripped, but Grey was before her and pulled her into his strong embrace and into the cover of the woods.

"Madelaine." His husky voice slid over her and made a deep ache bloom in the pit of her belly. He pushed her hood off her head. "It was foolish of you to come after me.

"Do you want me to go back?"

"The devil you say. I'm supremely glad you're foolish." He delved one gloved hand into her hair, twining around the strands and bringing her head close to his. Her heavy breathing filled her ears as he pulled off his other glove with his teeth and spit it to the ground. He slid his bare hand reverently over her cheek, sending sparks of desire through her entire body.

"I'm sorry." He trailed his fingers gently down the exposed skin of her neck, then back up to her lips, her cheeks, her eyelids. He placed a kiss on each lid before his warm lips found hers and plundered her mouth. She was going to die from wanting him.

She slid her hands up his arms and trailed her fingers over the swell of muscle not even his heavy overcoat could disguise before resting her hand on the curve of his broad shoulder. She wanted to feel more of him. As their tongues met and receded, she ran her hands over the stubble of his beard and into his thick hair.

After a moment, he pulled back and stared at her. "I'm sorry I broke my vow."

The fact that he didn't look a bit sorry made her grin. "I'm not."

He brushed a kiss across her lips before pulling her against his chest. Her head rested under his chin, the strong beat of his heart echoing in her ear. "I had made up my mind to demand you kiss me today."

"Really?" He tipped her chin back, so she had to meet his eyes.

She nodded shyly.

"Thank God. I've ached to touch you. Damned stupid of me to promise not to."

She grinned. "I wish one of us would have bent a little sooner."

"What of your father?" Worry creased Grey's brow.

Madelaine sighed. That was an excellent question. Guilt prickled at her. "He wrote me this morning and refused to come back to Court until the prince returns from abroad or if I'm in danger."

Grey frowned, a look of consternation making the crease on his brow deepen. "It's odd that he speaks of danger and waits to come back when Prinny does."

Madelaine shrugged. It was odd. Father had done many strange things lately, but she had no answers, and he wasn't forthcoming. Yet odd as it was, some of his actions did follow with his personality. "Father has always been overly concerned with my safety. It's one of the reasons he taught me how to defend myself. He wanted to teach Mother as well, but she refused to learn. Besides that, who knows my father's mind? Perhaps the king commands he speak with the prince on a sensitive matter."

Grey's frown deepened. "Perhaps. Is your father's letter what changed your mind about my vow to you?"

She held his searching gaze. There had to be nothing but truth between them. She'd have none of the secrets her mother had always claimed her father kept from her. "His letter, my desire." Her honest words brought a hot blush to her cheeks. Grey bent his head to kiss her again, but she stopped him. "And coming to know you better. You are honorable. He will have to see that and relent." She expected her words to wipe away the creases of worry on his face, but if anything, his body grew rigid. "What is it?" she asked, her heartbeat skipping.

"What if he won't grant me permission to wed you? What then? Would you elope with me?" Grey's tone vibrated with worry.

A hiss of breath escaped her. Forget the worry. He'd just said wed her. Did he know he wanted to marry her? Could she disobey her father and elope with Grey? The scandal and heartbreak would hurt him terribly, and she'd already caused him so much pain by driving a wedge between him and Mother. Yet she was falling in love with

Grey. She couldn't imagine marrying anyone else. She had to be honest with him. "Grey, I—"

He pressed his fingers to her lips. "Don't answer. I see what you intend to say in your sad eyes, and I admire you for your loyalty. It won't come to a choice for you. I vow it. Your father will grant his blessing, one way or another." Grey grasped her face in his hands and gave her a long, lingering kiss. "I'll be back for you. I swear it."

Her heart beat furiously as she let him go. She prayed her loyalty to her father didn't cause her to lose Grey. He knew she was odd, and he didn't care. In fact, he liked it. It seemed like a miracle. She couldn't speak for fear that she'd beg him to come back soon. Be loyal. Not forget her. She had to be dignified. Didn't she?

After he mounted his horse, he turned and waved. She watched him ride away, feeling as if he took a part of her with him. When he was out of sight, she forced herself to hurry back to the castle so Elizabeth wouldn't come looking for her. Had he really said he'd come back for her and ask her if she would elope with him, if it came to that? His words made her smile, but something niggled at her. She went through their conversation again, analyzing their exchange. What on earth had Grey meant when he said her father would grant his blessing one way or the other? She'd have to ask him about his words next time she saw him.

Seventeen

$\mathcal{G}$rey was exhausted, so when he rode up to his family home, he blinked with confusion. Why was black material hanging in every window? Surely that wasn't mourning cloth. A terrible premonition twisted his gut. He'd lied to Liz and Madelaine when he'd said he wasn't worried about his brother summoning him home. He'd been concerned. But his unease had been because he didn't want to leave for France until he had things settled with Madelaine and her father.

His unease shifted. He rode toward the stables, intending to hand over his horse to the stable master, but the stables were unusually empty of help. His wariness grew. Everything seemed in order, right down to the horses in their stalls, *except* his father's favorite horses were missing. Had his father taken one of the carriages out or ridden the horses somewhere with his brother? His instincts told him differently.

After putting Cypress in a stall, he hurried toward the house. Carriage wheels turning on the long drive alerted him to someone's approach. He stopped, half-expecting his father, but it was his brother's carriage. Dread propelled him down the drive. The driver pulled to a halt beside Grey. His brother descended the stairs and looked at him with sunken eyes and a face haunted by a nightmare. The air rushed from Grey's lungs.

"What's happened?" His heart thudded.

Edward shook his head and drew him into a hug. Grey flinched at the unusual show of affection and pulled out of his brother's grip. "Is it Mother or Father?"

Edward ran a hand through his hair. "Come with me inside. I'll tell you in there." His voice was toneless.

Grey had to swallow repeatedly before he could speak. "You can give me bad news outside just as well as inside. Get on with it."

Edward's face went dead white. "Father and Mother are dead. Killed four days ago in a horrific carriage accident. I called you home to see them buried—" His voice cracked and he cleared his throat.

Grey's own throat closed up at the tears in Edward's eyes. His mind shrank from his brother's words, but he forced himself to speak. "Go on." His voice cracked.

Edward nodded. "The bodies couldn't wait any longer. I'd hoped perhaps Elizabeth could travel with you, but your letter reached me of her illness, before I sent my summons to you." He gestured over his shoulder. "They're buried in the orchard."

Grey swallowed the bile rising in his throat. His chance to make amends was gone. He wanted to crumble to his knees but he stood. Like the dutiful second son. "They can't be dead."

Edward closed his eyes and inhaled a long breath. "They are."

Grey shook his head, his mind refusing to accept what his brother said. "No."

Edward's eyes snapped open and he swiped at them with his coat sleeve. "Damn it, Grey." His trembling tone was like a gut punch. "You're going to have to snap out of it. I'm sorry to be cold and rush you, but this is just the way it is." Edward turned on his heel and started walking toward the house. "I've not slept more than two hours in four days. *Four days.*" He spun around, his eyes wild. "That's a long time to go without proper sleep. I'm seeing things and hearing things everywhere I go. I know their death was an accident, but—" He stopped abruptly and looked at the driver standing by the carriage. "Leave us," he commanded harshly.

Once the coachman was out of sight, Edward took a deep breath, his chest rising in a puff. He darted his gaze around them then finally settled back on Grey. "I'm hearing things. Seeing things. I need sleep. I've a mound of papers to go through, I need to speak with you about your assignment to find De La Touche, and I need to track down Pearson who failed to send me details of your training as he was supposed to do."

"He was at the castle," Grey mumbled, his mind heavy with a thick fog, pierced only by his sharp regret. "I intended to apologize. To tell Father how sorry I was. To tell Mother I'd come to see her more." Grey heard the way his voice shook, but he was helpless to stop it. "I didn't know what he was. Or what you were. If only I'd known I would have understood so much more."

Edward clasped Grey's shoulder. "I know. And I'm sorry. I don't mean to be harsh. It's the grief."

"I understand." The words were for Edward's benefit. He didn't understand. Why had he had to spend so many years feeling unloved? Unwanted. The second son Father could've easily done without. Self-pity and yearning had cost him years. He'd meant to change it all. He clenched his hands into fist. He'd get no second chance now.

"Grey." Edward's word was a wary sigh. "Father and

you were so much alike. He didn't want to tell you about us until he was certain you were suited for the life of a spy. It seemed obvious to me years ago, but Father wouldn't hear of telling you until you'd had a proper chance to meet a woman, get married and settle down. Once you proved you'd never do that, he sent you to the king to be told what we were. Not the way I would have done it, but I had no say in the matter."

No one had ever had any say but Father, and he'd not said enough. Anger coursed through him. "Why the hell would it matter if I were married?" Grey asked, thinking suddenly of Madelaine.

"Because Father knew, as we all do, that a wife makes you vulnerable. A wife is something that can be used to bring you down, and it's wiser not to give the enemy one more weapon to use against you." Edward watched Grey with a steady gaze. "Is there something I should know?"

Grey shook his head. He couldn't think about all of this right now.

After a moment, his brother turned away, shoulders slumping, and walked toward the house once more.

The butler scrambled out of the way as Grey followed Edward through the front door to Father's study. Grey paused just inside the door. He would never come home to see his mother and father sitting in here again. Impossible. He walked over to his mother's favorite chair, picked up the shawl draped over the back of the dark leather, and inhaled deeply of the lingering flowery scent.

She'd rocked him as a toddler wearing this shawl, nursed him when he was sick, unlike many ladies of the *ton* who let the nannies do all the caretaking. Hell, she'd probably prayed he'd return her love by taking care of her, doting on her. His heart lurched. He was a bastard. He'd failed his mother and his father. His pathetic, wrong reasons didn't change the facts. When Edward thrust a full glass of whiskey toward him, he set the shawl down and took the drink.

The dark amber liquid sloshed as he swirled it under his nose, savoring the calming musk before tipping the glass and taking a long drink. Along with the whisky, mild warmth settled in the pit of his belly to partially fill the hollow space Edward's news had left.

Edward downed his drink then set the glass on the side table. "I'm going to bed. Don't wake me unless the house is burning down round my ears. We'll talk tomorrow about how to tell Liz."

Grey nodded his agreement. Left alone in the study with nothing but his guilt and thoughts, he stared outside at the falling snow. He felt like he was falling. How could it be that he'd been so sure of things a few hours ago? He replayed the last angry conversation he'd had with his father, until the guilt sent him to his feet to pace the room.

He stalked to the sideboard to pour another drink, but his hands shook and the whiskey kept sloshing over the rim of the glass. Giving up, he set the glass down and strode out of the study, down the corridors and out the front door into the dark, cold night.

He didn't know where he intended to go until he was halfway up the hill to the orchard where Edward had buried their parents. He stopped in front of the fresh graves, the dark dirt dusted with white snow. His lungs burned with each ragged inhalation of breath. He dropped to his knees in front of the graves, the snow instantly seeping through the wool of his trousers. After a moment, the lower half of his body was numb.

He wanted to be numb and forget his parents were

dead. He'd not been close to Mother in years. His father never. The weight of his fault sunk him all the way to the ground. A violent trembling shook his body, and his teeth chattered, until he clamped his jaw shut. He'd missed the chance to tell his parents he was sorry for the pain and worry he'd caused them. He'd missed the chance to show his father that his trust had not been misplaced.

What could he do now? He let out a breath he hadn't realized he was holding, a white ring against the dark night. The thoughts he'd pushed away earlier when speaking with Edward came to the surface. He winced, reality setting in. He had to give up the one thing he had come to want more than anything in his life. *Madelaine.* He didn't want to endanger her, and he could never turn his back on what his father had expected him to do. It seemed what he wanted and what life gave him would forever be at cross purposes. Leaning over, he lay his hand first on his mother's cold headstone and then on his father's. "I'll make you proud."

Once Grey returned to the house, he grabbed a bottle of whiskey and headed up the stairs to his old room. He tugged off his coat and cravat then sank into a deep chair. In one day he'd lost his mother, his father, and the woman he was coming to love. He tilted the bottle and drank deeply, searching for the same numbness for his mind that the snow had offered his body.

For the next couple of weeks, Grey worked by Edward's side to set their parent's affairs in order and to make sure their death was indeed an accident. Once the accident site had been combed and surveyed and every piece of broken carriage had been sifted through and studied, the misfortune of their parent's tragic deaths couldn't be denied. Once they found the shattered wheel, which Edward belatedly remembered Father had put off repairing, and they studied the snow-slick road which still showed signs of the tracks that had sent the carriage over the embankment, they both agreed it wasn't murder.

After working so closely with Edward, Grey now felt more a part of the household than he ever had before. How bloody ironic. Bitterness filled him. The bitterness ebbed after a few days, and thoughts of Madelaine replaced it. The last thing he wanted to do was think about Madelaine and having to face her, or his parents' death, or having to go back to Court and break the news to Liz. He fought back reality by doggedly filling his hours with a thousand tasks followed by hours of training in weapons with Edward at the end of each day.

His barrier against reality would have been perfect if it wasn't for the thoughts that slipped into his dreams. Waking night after night drenched in sweat, recalling some way or another he had purposely hurt his father or remembering his promise to Madelaine to return for her was going to be the death of him.

He took to drinking several glasses of whiskey a night in an effort to have a dreamless sleep, but when he realized how much whiskey he'd consumed after only two weeks, he ceased drinking all together. The dreams returned in violent force, so when he woke now, he'd stalk to the ballroom and spend the silent hours between dark to dawn practicing with weapons, until he felt sure he was just as good as his father would have expected.

Some nights, he saw Edward prowling the halls, or walking aimlessly outside in the gardens in the snow. They didn't acknowledge each other. To do so would have been to acknowledge their demons. Edward's glazed-eyed look told Grey his brother welcomed avoiding reality just as much as he did. It was easy to keep putting off the inevitable confrontation with Madelaine and Liz, because the thought of it made him ache deep inside where he'd not known he was capable of hurting.

In the third week, Gravenhurst sent a letter informing them the king was still in Kew recovering from a sudden bout with madness, but that His Majesty was on the mend. The news reinforced, in Grey's mind, his decision to stay at his brother's home until the king was fully recovered. Only the king could give word for Grey and Gravenhurst to leave for France, and the last thing Grey wanted to do was go back to Court and have to stay and wait for the king to give the order.

Once at Court he'd want to deliver the news to Liz, speak with Madelaine, and then need to leave immediately for France. Seeing Madelaine day after day, while knowing she would one day soon lie in another man's arms, become another man's wife would be like a knife in the gut. Reality waited like an obedient dog. On the morning of the fourth week, Gravenhurst arrived before dawn waking Grey from a troubled sleep.

Grey dressed hastily and met Edward and Gravenhurst in the library.

Gravenhurst was never one for niceties, but this morning he didn't even offer a greeting before he thrust a letter at Grey and one at Edward. Both men read in silence for a moment. Grey's heart roared in his ears. After a moment, he met Gravenhurst's steady gaze. "Do you know what this letter says?"

"Of course. I'm to go with you to Lancashire."

"Lancashire?" Edward glanced at both men. "Why does

the king send you there?"

"His letter to you doesn't explain?" Grey asked.

"He expressed his sincere sorrow for our parents' deaths and bade me to find Pearson immediately. What does your letter say?"

Grey handed the letter to Edward. His brother's face soon mirrored the skepticism Grey felt. "I don't believe Stratmore is a traitor to the king."

Grey let out the breath he'd been holding. "Neither do I," he agreed, glad his brother had voiced the same opinion about Madelaine's father. Grey glanced at Gravenhurst, the most cynical man he knew. "What about you?"

"When my uncle murdered my father, I learned no man is above treachery if the circumstances are right."

Edward waved the king's letter in front of Grey and Gravenhurst. "What paper is the king talking about that has gone missing?"

Grey raised a questioning eyebrow at Gravenhurst. "Did he tell you?"

"He did. But you may do the honors, since you were there."

Grey quickly explained about the new code Stratmore had created and about the meeting where the duke had shown the king and Grey the code. Then haltingly, he told Edward of the king's spell that day and the madness he'd written about with the angels telling him things and needing to execute his administrators.

By the time Grey was finished, Edward's complexion was pasty. He walked over to the study door, shut it, and turned back to Grey. "That was damned foolhardy of the king to write down some of the missions he planned to assign us. Even if he was simply practicing the code."

Grey nodded. The rest of what the king wrote hung

between them like a deadly snake. Was Edward going to ignore the king's other words? Grey couldn't do that. "We have to find that paper and destroy it. It could be used to prove the king is mad."

Edward's eyes narrowed. "Was temporarily confused. Under a spell."

"Alright. Temporary madness. That could do grave harm if not monitored."

"We've been monitoring him, Grey. That's part of your job as one of us."

Grey's jaw went slack. "I had no idea."

A sardonic smile tugged on Edward's lips. "It's not something I think the king wished to tell you, unless the need arose. He'd hoped his spells were over."

"Yet they're not. So where do we go from here?" He wasn't sure what Edward wanted from him, but he wanted to do what his brother expected. His father would have wanted no less.

Edward let out a long sigh. "We keep watch as we've done. Guard him closer. And when he's fully recovered we gently approach him about the possibility of putting further measures into place if the time should ever come that the spell occur too often and pose too much of a danger."

That sounded reasonable. "The king claims to have put the paper in his nightstand that night. Perhaps Stratmore took it and burned it because he knew it could harm the king? We all agree it should be destroyed."

Edward hit his open hand with his fist. "Yes, we all agree, but none of us would take the paper and destroy it without the king's permission. It is *his* paper. He gives the orders. If Stratmore stole the paper then he committed an act of theft and deliberately disobeyed the king we all vowed to protect always and serve forever. Let us hope the king destroyed the paper and forgot when he was overcome by the next dark spell. He fell ill right after Stratmore's visit, did he not?"

"He did."

"Did you notice any tension between them when you were with them?"

"Only the tension brought on by what the king wrote." Grey shrugged. "They argued, but if it was over the paper, I couldn't say." The dire implications for Madelaine's future if her father was named a traitor to the king made Grey's gut twist. "If Stratmore did take the paper, do you think the king would forgive him if the duke assured him he was simply trying to protect His Majesty from himself?"

"It's hard to say. They've been lifelong friends. Yet I don't know any man, let alone a king, who'd be happy to think he needs to be protected from himself. And as I've already said, it's our sworn duty to obey the king's orders." Edward made a guttural sound in his throat. "What a mess. The king *could* forgive Stratmore or he could just as soon hang him for treason. Let's pray the king remembers he burned the paper or finds it before a choice of the duke's life or death must be made. Is there anything else you remember about that meeting? *Anything* unusual?"

Grey thought for a moment and almost felt foolish to mention Constance, but surely Edward would want to know every detail. "There was a chambermaid in the room. Constance. She bribed one of the guards to let her in to finish her work."

Edward waved a hand. "That's normal. I'm forever running into maids here in places they shouldn't be. They sleep too late or work too slow and then have to find a way to sneak and catch up because they're afraid they'll get in trouble. Forget her. She's trivial."

Grey's face burned with embarrassment. He'd have to do better. "She's forgotten. But I must say I had no idea you understood the minds of the staff so well."

Edward scowled. "There's a great deal you don't know about me, Grey."

Grey clenched his jaw on harsh retort. Fighting would do no good. "So we proceed as if he's committed treason, even though we don't think it so?"

"Yes. We may not think it's so, but until we're certain it's not, he's an enemy of the Crown. Proceed as if he's a thief or worse."

Grey frowned. "What do you mean, '"or worse?"'"

Edward held himself stiff as he answered. "I mean we must consider all possibilities. Even the worst ones such as Stratmore is not only a thief, but perhaps a traitor who is working to overthrow the king."

Grey grimaced. "That's absurd."

The corner of Edward's mouth jerked with a tick. "You're wrong. It's not absurd. It's being cautious. And caution will keep you alive. Don't forget that."

Grey nodded. Perhaps Edward was right. He'd been a spy far longer than Grey. "I won't forget."

Edward's shoulders slumped. Had his brother been expecting a fight? Grey was heartily glad he'd listened for once in his life. Edward waved toward the door. "You two better get going. The sooner this nasty business is behind us the better."

Grey couldn't agree more. Madelaine would have enough reason to hate him, but if she learned he was responsible for taking her father to the tower on charges of treason, she'd hate him even more. He wanted things settled, preferably in the duke's favor.

"Are you ready," he asked Gravenhurst. "We've a hard

ride ahead of us, and an even harder confrontation. There's no doubt in my mind Stratmore won't like being hauled to the tower by us under suspicion of treason, and the duke already has a mild dislike of me."

His brother blinked at him. "Why's that?" Edward asked as he sat down.

"It doesn't matter. The situation he disliked is no longer." Grey narrowed his eyes at Gravenhurst, a silent warning to keep what he knew to himself. Gravenhurst gave a barely perceptible inclination.

"You're sure?" Edward prodded.

"Yes," Grey said in a tone he hoped Edward would recognize as final.

"All right then. You two be sure to keep Stratmore's imprisonment in the tower a secret. No one is to know but the three of us, until I or the king say otherwise."

Grey didn't like the way Edward was barking orders at him as if he were dull-witted. "I read the letter, Edward, and Gravenhurst did too. We know the king's wishes."

"Sorry," Edward said. "It will take me a while to be used to being in charge without being overbearing."

"In charge?" Grey repeated.

"With Father dead, Stratmore imprisoned, and Pearson missing for the moment, I'm, by default, the leader of our little circle."

"So you are," Grey agreed, trying not to think about his father or Madelaine, or anything but the job ahead of him. "What if Stratmore's servants question us?"

"They won't. Stratmore will know what's at stake if anyone should find out about his imprisonment. Even if he's not found guilty and hung, his daughter's future would be jeopardized, if word got out. He won't want that. I've no worry he won't cooperate."

"I disagree," Gravenhurst said. "You assume he's innocent, though you just told us to proceed as if he's not only a thief but a conspirator in a plot to overthrow the king. If he's guilty, he may very well run. His life will probably mean more to him in that case than his daughter making a good match."

Edward steepled his hands in front of his face, his brow furrowing. Grey was finding it hard focusing on anything but his worry for Madelaine. He struggled to push thoughts of her from his mind.

"You're right." Edward moved to stand. "Lure Stratmore away from his house, secure him, and then send the servants away so you can search the house for the king's paper or any clues. Do not leave any space unturned. If it's there, if it still exists, you need to find it and destroy it. And if you find anything else of importance, bring it to me."

"And if we find nothing?"

"Then treat him as if he's guilty, until the king decides otherwise."

Within the hour, Grey and Gravenhurst were on the road to Lancashire. They didn't speak for a while, until they stopped to water the horses then Gravenhurst said, "Do you expect me to believe you've forgotten the lady and you can be impartial?"

Grey gritted his teeth together, releasing them after he felt under control. "I do. I know my duty, and duty will always be first to me."

"Bah," Gravenhurst mumbled as he dismounted. "Then you're a daft fool who mistakenly believes himself indestructible. That woman's your deadly weakness, no matter how strong you think you are. Stay away from her."

Eighteen

$\mathcal{E}$ven in the tower the social classes were evident, *if* you had enough money to purchase comfortable quarters, but there were some crimes, such as the ones Madelaine's father stood accused of, that prohibited the prisoner being allowed to pay for acceptable quarters. For the worst criminals the tower was an abominably dreary place crawling with bugs and rats and filled with the constant nerve-grating moans of those who'd been condemned to wait there until trial or death, whichever fate or the king served them.

Grey had walked through the noisy halls three days prior, his body recoiling at the sights and sounds within the dingy walls. Yet he managed to do his duty and force one foot after the other to take Stratmore to the dungeon where he was to be kept in secret, while he and Gravenhurst tried to get him to confess his guilt and await Edward's arrival.

In order to lessen the chance of the guards or anyone who might see Gravenhurst or Grey coming or going from the dungeon, they both agreed to stay there until Edward arrived and Stratmore's fate was decided. After one night in the shadowy darkness of the dungeon, Grey understood why the tower dungeon was referred to as the pit of Hell. Dampness permeated the walls, the floors, the air, and worst of all, the bug-infested cot Grey had to sleep on. And

though the pitiful pleas for release were barely distinguisha-
ble down here, the muffled moans did carry through the air,
down the winding stone steps, and seep under the locked,
dark wooden door. The constant hint of noise was like an
annoying whisper in Grey's ear. He'd taken to humming to
himself to block out the sounds of misery.

But it was neither the dampness nor the noise that kept
him up at night. His worry for Madelaine did that. If
Stratmore was guilty, what would become of her? So far the
man had maintained his innocence, but his shifty eyes hid
something. By the third day of being locked in the tower,
trying unsuccessfully to get Stratmore to admit his guilt,
Grey was relieved when Edward arrived, but his relief was
short lived.

"What do you mean, Stratmore murdered Pearson?"
Grey asked, facing Edward in the small confines of the
entranceway to the room they had Stratmore locked in.

Gravenhurst, who'd been preoccupied shoving the
bread and cheese Edward had brought them into his mouth,
audibly swallowed his food before speaking. "Let me get
this straight." He stood from where he'd been sitting at a
filthy table. "You're telling us Stratmore murdered
Pearson—a brother in arms?" Gravenhurst's voice had
dropped to a low whisper.

"I'm telling you that I found Pearson dead." Anger
vibrated Edward's fierce whisper. "Stabbed repeatedly in the
gut. Beside his body the word 'honor' had been drawn in
the dirt with an X through it. The conclusion is obvious."

"How does that prove Stratmore's guilt?" Grey demanded.

"*Honor* is the word engraved on the inside of Stratmore's ring that the king gave him," Edward said patiently.

Grey shook his head. "I don't believe for a second the

man would be so stupid as to kill a fellow spy, and then engrave his name in the dirt as a calling card to lead us straight to him. Besides, what would be his motive for killing Pearson?"

"Money." Gravenhurst's voice was toneless. "It's well known his coffers are extremely low, and he and the king have fought much of late. Maybe Stratmore's turned traitor, and he's being paid by the Frenchies to gather information. Mayhap Pearson found out, or maybe Stratmore's been paid to kill us one by one so Napoleon, the rutting bastard, will win the war."

"You've been a spy too long," Grey said, not liking how Edward appeared to be considering Gravenhurst's ludicrous suggestions. It was one thing to proceed with caution, but it was quite another to proceed on a mad conjecture. "The man is not so stupid as to trace the word 'honor' in the dirt for everyone to see."

"But he didn't write it," Edward said. "Pearson did."

"His dead corpse told you so, did it?" Grey demanded.

Edward flushed at this, but met Grey's gaze with sharp green eyes. "I checked Pearson's fingertips. They were caked with dirt. The word had been written in blood. His blood. I know because I forced myself to bend his stiff arm and hand and write another word in the dirt to see if the width of his fingertip and the markings on his skin would match what was in the dirt. It did. Perfectly. There's no doubt in my mind Pearson wrote the word *honor* and then crossed it out."

Grey focused on breathing through his clenched teeth and fought the desire to punch his brother in the nose. "If Pearson wanted everyone to know who murdered him why the hell wouldn't he have just written Stratmore's name?"

"I can't say, *Grey*. I've not got access to the dead man's

thoughts, so all I can do is speculate."

Grey jerked his gaze away from the insect climbing the wall that he'd been focusing on to try to calm himself and met his brother's gaze. "I don't see what this has to do with the king's paper. If Stratmore is selling secrets to the French or killing spies for money, what would he need the damned paper for?"

"Nothing." Edward pulled out a chair to sprawl in it. "I don't have the answers yet, but I plan to get them."

Gravenhurst drummed his fingers on the table. "If Stratmore is guilty then we've stopped him. He's locked up here, and our secrets, as well as our lives, are safe."

Edward shook his head. "It's not so simple. Someone tried to shoot me when I was leaving Pearson's house. I tracked them to the woods, but I couldn't find them."

Fatigue crashed into Grey, and he reluctantly pulled out the last chair and sank into it. "So you really think Stratmore was working with someone who is still out there?"

Edward nodded. "And if I'm right, that person will be coming for us."

Grey rolled his shoulders to combat his mounting tension. Evidence was piling up against Madelaine's father. Evidence that seemed hard to deny.

Gravenhurst leaned forward. "Keep the faith, Grey. Edward isn't always right. Only usually."

Edward took a drink from his flask, then wiped the back of his hand across his mouth, eyeing Grey with what appeared to be amusement mingled with respect. "No, I'm not always right. But I've never been wrong when it comes to my work."

Grey glanced at Gravenhurst who nodded in confirmation.

"Then what do you propose we do? Stratmore isn't

confessing, and I'd venture to say the threat of death won't even break the man."

"I'd have to agree," Edward said thoughtfully. "So we won't threaten *him*. We'll strike at the one person he cares about."

"You can't mean to use..." Gravenhurst began, but got no more than that out before Grey's fist crashed into this brother's nose, sending him sprawling backward onto the floor with blood gushing down his face.

White fury consumed Grey as he towered over his brother. "You'll use Madelaine to break her father over my dead body."

Edward glowered up at Grey while searching for a linen square. Growling when he found his pockets empty, he snatched the rumpled cravat that Gravenhurst shoved at him. After the bleeding of his nose was stopped, he lowered the blood-soaked cravat, his eyes narrowing into dark, green slits. "Am I to take it," he said, in a voice muffled by his blood-clogged nose, "that you care for the lady?"

"Take it any damn way you please," Grey snarled, unable to bring his temper down. "You won't use her. I won't stand for it."

Shrugging off Gravenhurst's help, Edward stood and dusted himself off. "Need I remind you that you vowed to serve the king over all others?"

"You need not," Grey said. His father would be damned disappointed if Grey failed at being a spy on his very first assignment. His stomach burned with the poison of what he had to do. He could not fail the king, *and* he had to somehow protect Madelaine. "Whatever you have in mind for Lady Madelaine, I'll be the one to do it."

"You're sure?" Edward's eyes lost their hard edge, softening now with sympathy. "Wouldn't it be easier for you to let Gravenhurst or myself handle the lady? If what I have in mind doesn't work, then we'll have to use her, deceive her, and maybe even put her life in danger."

He recoiled at his brother's suggestion. "I'll do it," he said, determined to protect Madelaine from his brother, her father, and whoever else might be lurking out there. He'd promised to protect her, and that was one promise he'd keep, no matter what he had to do not to break it. He may have given the king his vow, but he'd given Madelaine his heart.

With the queen gone from the castle for the last month life should have been perfect for Madelaine. Yet despite, her solid friendship with Elizabeth and having as much time to slip away and practice archery as one could hope for, unhappiness shrouded each day that Grey failed to return. The least he could have done, *if* he had a sensitive bone in his body, was to write a letter and let them know he'd arrived home safely.

Maybe he was not writing because he'd decided that courting her was more trouble than she was worth, but he should be kind enough to send word to his sister. Elizabeth had almost died for goodness sake. Didn't the man know worry could put a person back in their sick bed? Convincing herself she had to write Grey for Elizabeth's sake, Madelaine put pen to paper and demanded he write to his sister immediately if he wasn't planning on coming back before they were all old and gray.

She reread the letter when she was done. It was good. Commanding without being harsh, *and* she'd managed to resist mentioning how much she missed him nor had she reminded him of his promise to come back for her. She folded the letter to seal it, but her backbone dissolved as she thought of never seeing Grey again.

What good would being stoic do her if he married another? Carefully, she opened the letter, dipped her quill in ink and penned one last line. *I do miss you terribly, in case you doubt my feelings.* She sealed the letter and took it to be sent before she could reconsider how desperate the last line probably made her seem.

She didn't expect the letter to make Grey magically appear, though she half hoped it would, so several days later when Elizabeth confided that her eldest brother Edward was coming to collect her and take her home—as it had been decided by the family that Court life might be too stressful on someone recovering from near death—Madelaine had to hurry from the room before Elizabeth saw the tears threatening to spill over.

Once in the safety of her room, Madelaine dashed the tears away as she paced back and forth. Just because Grey wasn't coming did not mean he didn't still want to court her. Perhaps, something had arisen at home that required his attention or maybe Elizabeth's eldest brother simply wanted to be the one to collect Elizabeth since he'd not seen her in so long.

There was no point in believing the worst, until the worst was confirmed. And if it was? She flopped down on her bed with a groan. If Grey had changed his mind about her, she would simply have to carry on. Exactly how, escaped her at the moment, since she was quite certain she had fallen in love with him.

Two days later, Madelaine was helping Elizabeth pack her last few things when a knock resounded at the door followed by a gruff, "Elizabeth. Might I enter?"

A broad smile spread across Elizabeth's face. She dropped the shawl she'd been folding and gripped Madelaine's arm. "That's Edward. Perhaps Grey has come as well!"

Despite Madelaine's best intentions not to get her hopes up, the emotion swelled inside her. Elizabeth swung open the door, and Madelaine barely managed to gulp back her cry of joy. Instinctually, she moved toward Grey, but stopped when his gaze locked on her. She'd seen that frigid look before when he'd sized up Lord Thorton, but this was worse than Grey's murderous gaze of anger. He stared at her as if he'd never seen her before, as if she were a stranger.

"What's happened?" She didn't care that it wasn't her place to demand any answers. Grey blinked, his expression changing from cold to warm, as he seemed to so easily do. He didn't fool her. A haggardness of body and spirit clung to him. It wasn't just the beard and blood-shot eyes that made her think so. He was different. There was a hardness to his eyes that he'd not possessed a month ago.

"Let's all go into the chamber," Elizabeth's eldest brother suggested.

Elizabeth pulled Madelaine back inside with her, and they settled on the bed. The men didn't sit, but loomed over them, until finally Elizabeth's eldest brother offered Madelaine a cursory nod. "I'm the Duke—" Grey's brother abruptly stopped his introduction, his face whitening. "You must be Lady Madelaine?"

Madelaine nodded, but before she could say anything else, Elizabeth scrambled from the bed and stood toe-to-toe with her eldest brother. "What do you mean introducing yourself as a duke?"

"You bloody clod," Grey snarled at his brother as he

took Elizabeth by the arm. It almost seemed he intended to hold her up. Madelaine furrowed her brow. "Liz," Grey said in a soft voice. "Mother and Father are dead."

"What?" Elizabeth whispered. The confusion clouding her face mirrored Madelaine's feelings.

"Dead," Grey tried again with such heartbreaking gentleness that Madelaine's nose and throat burned with the sudden need to cry.

"I don't believe you." Elizabeth's voice was raspy.

When her declaration was met by silence, she repeated herself louder. "I don't believe you," she screeched, her eyes turning wild, her fingers clawing at her brother's arms for release.

Madelaine couldn't move. The scene transfixed her in horror to the bed. Politeness demanded she quietly exit, but she could not make her legs work nor bring herself to abandon Elizabeth and Grey for the sake of politeness.

"They are dead," Grey reiterated.

"You're lying," Elizabeth accused, even as tears streamed down her face. "Why are you lying?" Her voice rose to a higher pitch. Grey gazed at Madelaine. The helplessness in his eyes broke her heart. She stood, intent on taking Elizabeth from him and holding her friend gently to try to make her hear the truth, but Elizabeth's brother, The Duke of Ashdon, stepped forward and took Elizabeth from Grey.

Madelaine watched in mute horror while His Grace tried for several minutes to rationalize with Elizabeth, but her protests grew in volume until she was screaming. Finally, he shook her. She could have sworn Elizabeth's teeth rattled together with each violent shake of her body.

"Stop it." Madelaine gripped the duke's arm. "You'll hurt her. Please." She tugged at the man's thick, corded arms until he released his sister.

Elizabeth moaned incoherently as Madelaine struggled to get her to the bed. In an instant, Grey was at Elizabeth's other side and helped Madelaine to guide her to sit. "What happened?" she asked over Elizabeth's wracking sobs.

Either her imagination was running wild, or Grey was really assessing her as he appeared to be doing. But for what purpose? Were his parents' deaths horrific? Did he think she too might lose control? Finally, he spoke, his words coming out as if each had been ripped from his throat. "A carriage accident. They had a bad wheel. It broke and the carriage tumbled down an embankment and killed them both."

At his pronouncement, Elizabeth's head lulled backward and her eyes fluttered closed. The sudden silence of the room seemed strange after the deafening noise of Elizabeth's crying. With Grey's help, Madelaine laid Elizabeth on the bed. Once Madelaine had Elizabeth situated, she turned and caught Grey staring at her. The unveiled pain and anguish in his eyes tore at her. She reached toward him to soothe him, but he flinched away, as if he could not bear her touch.

She understood the pain of losing a parent, better than most, but he seemed more than pained, seething with an anger that was directed at her. Maybe, it was simply the shock of everything, yet she felt very out of place, very much an intruder. She wrung her hands together. She didn't want to leave Grey or Elizabeth, but she didn't feel welcome here. "Maybe I had better go to my own room," she said, moving to leave.

In a flash, Grey stood between her and the door. "There's something I have to tell you."

She would have been relieved that he'd stopped her, but his foreboding tone scared her, and sent shivers of wariness over her skin. "What is it?"

Nineteen

Grey shot his brother a warning look to remind him to keep to their agreement. If the price of protecting Madelaine was that she might later hate him, he'd gladly pay the ransom. He did not want to lie to her, to use her as a pawn, but he'd given his word to protect the king, and he'd keep it. He glanced at his sister who was stirring on the bed. "We cannot speak here."

Madelaine followed his gaze. "Where then?"

"The tower. Your father is being kept there."

"What?" All color leeched from her face, making her appear frail and frightened. He hated that he was causing her fear, but there was simply no choice.

"Come." He took her by the elbow to lead her out the door. She opened her mouth to ask him a question, but he shook his head and handed her cape to her. "Keep your questions for now and put this on." She seemed as if she would argue, but after a moment, she took the cape and shrugged it on.

His heart lurched. Even in drab wool, she was beautiful. "Raise the hood," he commanded as he closed the door to his sister's bedroom without a backward glance. Edward would be waiting to hear a report, giving Grey just enough time to play the sympathetic suitor, take Madelaine to her father, and peer through the peephole in the room where they kept him to listen and see if Stratmore let anything slip or made a confession. Gravenhurst would see Liz safely home, far away from any possible taint of scandal.

Grey was still angry with his brother and Gravenhurst, though they only did what they must to protect the king as well as themselves. And so would he. He would protect the king, but God help him, he would protect Madelaine as well, if it were possible.

He glanced at her as they walked silently through the halls. She turned her head enough that he could see her face drawn with worry. Did she sense his stare? He grasped her arm to stop her and fought back the fear that someone else would see her and then question what she was doing. At this late hour, his fear was no doubt unfounded, yet it choked off his air just the same.

He pulled her hood tighter around her face so that if anyone was still lurking in the halls they'd mistake her for a lady of the night. Reaching down, he clasped her cold, clammy hands and blew on them to warm them. "Keep your face hidden."

She nodded, her hand going to the closure of her cape and holding it tight under her chin. His gut twisted as he pressed a hand to her back to lead her out of the castle. Since the moment his brother had told him of Pearson's death and his belief that Stratmore had killed him, Grey had gone through every possible way this could end. There was no good way, unless Stratmore was innocent of everything, and Grey's gut told him otherwise. The worst ending would be Stratmore being hung, and Madelaine being thrown on the mercy of the Court. Likely they'd toss her from Court and take her father's property. Or what if they decided she'd helped her father? Would they go so far as to hang her right beside him, unless she was protected by someone? Fear made his heart pound faster.

She was an only child with no other living relatives. She had no one. No one but him. If the worst came to pass, he would marry her to give her the protection of his name, but then who would protect her from the dangers his life would likely present them both? That was a worry for much later. One concern at a time.

At the river, he helped her into the boat Edward had arranged to take them to the tower. The boat rocked gently as he led her to the bow. They sat, and he pulled her to his side, and slid his arm around her upper back to rest his hand on the gentle, sloping curve of her shoulder. The boatman was one of their paid employees, yet Edward had warned Grey to take no chances with anyone overhearing anything.

As the boat started to swish through the water, Grey took her hand in his, compelled to offer what comfort he could. Since he was supposed to be gaining her trust, he told himself his intimacy was acceptable, though he was aware of just how much he enjoyed touching her, no matter the reason. She turned her face, so that in the light of the lantern he saw she'd not relaxed in the slightest, not that he blamed her.

"Your father is being held under suspicion of treason and murder." He kept his tone low.

She jerked under his arm, but to his surprise, she didn't cry out or jump to her feet in outrage. Her eyes narrowed, her only show of anger. "Tell me." Her voice emotionless and steely like he'd expect from a man. Then again, given what he knew about her, he should have guessed she'd react with the same calm calculation it took to shoot a target perfectly.

In a low voice, Grey told her of the missing paper of the king's, but not what was on it. He then told her of Pearson being killed, but avoided the specifics of what indicated her father had a hand in it. He tensed, expecting her to demand the particulars; she did not.

"Why are you here?" Her face was fierce and expectant. Her question caught him off guard, though he'd rehearsed what he would say if she did ask it. "What role could an equerry possibly play in the politics of the king?"

"My role is one of support for you."

"That's no answer." She tugged her hand out of his grasp.

He sighed inwardly. He'd hoped to avoid too many lies, but she left him little choice. "I've the ear of the king as my father's son, and my brother more so than I, as the new Duke of Ashford. The king will listen to my brother's council on this matter."

"And what will your brother advise the king? Will he tell him my father is innocent, because surely he is?" Passion laced her words, her eyes burned bright and her face flushed.

Grey chose his words carefully before answering. "What my brother says depends on you."

"On me?" Her brow furrowed.

"Yes. Edward has asked that you speak with your father. He thinks Stratmore will tell you of his guilt or innocence. Edward already spoke with him at the king's bequest but he feels your father is holding something back."

Her mouth turned down. "But why would the king involve your brother? Why does the king not speak to my father himself?"

"He's recovering from an illness at Kew, and as I told you, Edward is now the Duke of Ashford, a powerful landholder and one of the wealthiest men in England. The king always seeks the council of his wealthiest landholders, as they have almost as much at stake at keeping the peace in England as the king does."

"Your brother can't think my father would steal from His Majesty. My father loves the king! They're lifelong friends. Father has served His Majesty well all my life." Her voice had risen as her words picked up tempo. Grey gripped her hand to remind her to keep her voice low.

"I'm sorry." When she wiped an errant tear running down her cheek, his heart constricted in sympathy. "And murder…" She shuddered, her words trailing off. "He'll be hung if he's found guilty. Grey please—" She rested her other hand on top of his while she searched his eyes. "You must help me prove my father's innocence."

Sour bile rose in the back of his throat for his deception, however necessary for her protection. "Of course I'll help you. Whatever you need me to do, I will."

If his prayers were answered, she would need no help from him because her father would somehow be proven innocent, though Grey could not see how.

Madelaine tried to control her trembling as the boat passed through the entrance of Traitor's Gate, but a quiver ran through her despite her best efforts. Her mind scrambled frantically over what she had just learned. How could it have come to be that her father was being held on suspicion of murder and treason?

Her throat clenched with the need to cry out. Her poor, poor father. How angry and worried he must be! At the very least, if word of this got out, his good name would be tarnished, and at the worst—She turned her thoughts away from the possibility, unable to face such a thing. She'd not lose her father, and she'd somehow help him set this all to rights.

Anger made her shaking commence again. Grey squeezed her hand. She was incredibly grateful to have him at her side and to know he would do everything in his power to help her prove her father's innocence. She hadn't been sure what response to expect from Grey since he'd acted so oddly in his sister's room.

As the boat neared the dock, the boatman jumped up to grab the rope being thrown to him and pull the boat to dock. Grey helped her from the boat, but even when her feet were on solid ground, she still felt as if she were swaying so that when she took a step, she tilted. Grey's hand came around her waist while he kept a firm grip on her other hand. "Come," he said in a gentle tone. "Your father is this way."

She hadn't known what to expect inside the tower, so when they first entered and passed by the guards and into brightly lit halls that appeared rather clean for a prison, she sagged in relief against Grey. Thank God her father was not being kept in squalor. "Are the prisoners' rooms on this floor?"

"Some." Grey maneuvered her past the first door which was cracked open enough that with a glance inside, she saw a man sitting at a desk with an opulent meal spread out before him and a decanter of wine in his hand. "Is he a prisoner?"

Grey nodded.

"Is my father on this floor?"

The muscles of his arm tensed. "No, he's farther down."

"What is it?" she demanded, taking care to keep her tone hushed. "Is he harmed?"

"No." Grey didn't stop to look at her. He led her

through a door to a narrow passageway of stairs. They spiraled sharply down, and with a glance, she stared into what appeared to be an endless pit of darkness illuminated every few feet by glowing torches. Her palms grew sweaty with her unease.

She swallowed the fear that had suddenly risen inside of her. "How far down?" Her voice sounded wobbly to her own ears.

"Far. Prepare yourself. And don't let go of the railing." Grey stopped and looked up at her. "Your father's crimes are grave. In accordance, he's being held in the dungeon." The darkness obscured his face, his ominous tone raised the hairs on the back of her neck.

"His purported crimes," she said.

"Of course." Grey continued down the stairs.

She didn't want to follow into the darkness, but what choice did she have? As they descended, the temperature dropped, the air became damp, and the steps narrowed and shortened. She clung to the railing for life and sanity. The overwhelming sense that she was marching willingly to her own doom filled her. The disgusting, sticky cobwebs clinging to her arms didn't help calm her. She wanted to rub at her skin to get rid of the cobwebs, but she was afraid to let go of the rail. She gritted her teeth and kept her hand on the rail.

When they reached the end of the stairs, she gasped and rubbed at her arms.

"What's wrong?" Grey's tone vibrated with worry.

"Cobwebs." She couldn't keep the revulsion out of her voice.

"Maybe you're more like the average woman than I thought."

She glared at him in the darkness. "I'm not like the

average woman. Cobwebs are disgusting."

He chuckled. "Come."

She followed him through a creaky door and stopped in a room where mold and dirt swirled in the air and filled her nostrils. Coughing, she eyed the door she assumed led to her father's room and tried to ignore the despair rising in her chest and threatening to spill over.

Bitter laughter escaped her. "I'm surprised they don't have a guard down here."

Grey held up a key. "There's no need. There's no way out except the way we just came from, and there's no way into this room except this key." With a click of the lock, the door creaked open. Madelaine stepped inside, not sure what to expect. Her father stood in the middle of the room facing her. His clean-shaven appearance took her by surprise. She'd been expecting him to be ragged.

"Madelaine." Her father opened his arms, and she rushed into his warm, loving embrace. Tears immediately sprang to her eyes and leaked down her cheeks. Behind her, the door clicked shut. Later, she would have to thank Grey for giving her time alone with her father. She pulled out of her father's embrace and studied him, looking for signs of abuse. "Have they been kind to you?"

A smile twisted his lips. "As kind as you'd expect men bent on proving my guilt to be."

"But I see no bruises or cuts. It appears they've not raised a hand to you."

Her father scrubbed a hand across his face. "No, Maddie. They've not beaten me. You can be sure they have other ways of trying to gain a confession from me."

She wrinkled her brow, considering what her father had said. "What ways?"

"Come." He led her to the table in the corner of his

room. "Let's not waste our time together on how they mean to coerce me. There's no preventing it anyway, and we've important matters to discuss." Her father's gaze danced around the room and settled on a crack in the brick. He stared overly long at the crack, then turned his gaze away and stared at his hands mumbling about "not being sure" while his fingers clutched and unclutched hers.

"Father." She gripped his fingers in order to get him to stop his rhythmic motion. For a moment, it seemed he hadn't heard her. His mumbling continued and his fingers moved spasmodically under hers, and then suddenly it stopped and his blood-shot gaze rose to her face.

"Father, I know you're not guilty!"

His expression was vacant. "It matters not. I'll likely die in here."

"Don't say that." She moved her chair until she sat beside him. "You're innocent, and we'll prove it. I'll prove it."

His cloudy gaze became alert and clear, his hands clutching her arms in a grip that made her wince. "Listen to me, Madelaine." His voice reverberated off the stone walls. "Stay out of this. You're but a mere woman. God help me, your mother was right and I was wrong. Act like a woman, not the creature I was raising you to be. Forget everything I ever taught you and leave this place as quickly as you can before they hang me, despite my innocence, and then perhaps turn an eye to punishing you for the crimes they've decided I committed."

Madelaine scrambled to her feet wanting to escape the horror of what her father was saying, but her legs barely held her up from their trembling. She stumbled and then righted herself by pressing a hand against the slick wall. "Don't speak as if you're already dead. We will prove your innocence. I know you wouldn't steal from the king and murder a man. You're good."

Her father rose and made his way to stand in front of her. He wrapped his arms around her, led her to his cot and sat them both down on the mattress. He pressed his mouth near her ear, his warm breath tickling her. "I'm not guilty of all they say, but I am guilty of some of it." His words filled her head and poisoned her heart. She bit her lower lip on her cry, but she could not stop her sharp intake of breath. "Make your way home. I've hidden money in the wine cellar and the king's paper in a green bottle on the fourth shelf. Get the paper to the prince. He's the only one who can save me."

The door slammed open, causing her to jump. She jerked away from her father. Grey's face flickered in shadows. As he came closer, she could see the concern in his eyes. Grey clutched her arm and pulled her away from her father. "That's all the time they'll allow us, Madelaine."

She didn't have time to protest as she was tugged toward the door.

"Don't trust anyone," her father called to her back. She looked over her shoulder, and her father pointed at Grey. "Don't forget. Trust no one. Least of all him."

Before she could respond, she was yanked through the door, and Grey slammed it shut. With a soft click, he locked the door, and led them both away and toward the stairs. She trembled violently with shock. Her father was not guilty of murder, but he was guilty of treason. Why? Why would he do such a thing? And did it even matter? He was her father. She couldn't let him hang if there was a chance to save him.

Grey pressed her against the damp, stone wall of the staircase. He trapped her legs between his thighs, and then he moved his arms to either side of her shoulders. His gaze searched hers. "What did he say? How can I help?"

She looked into his eyes and read yearning mixed with concern. Could she trust him? Her heart told her yes, but what if it was just because that's what she wanted to believe? She couldn't stake her father's life on it. "He said he's not guilty. He said to go home before they hang him because the truth matters little if he can't prove it."

Her low voice hitched on her partial lie. Warm tears filled her eyes. She didn't hold them back, as she'd always done with her mother. She allowed them to flow down her face just as she allowed Grey to take her in his strong embrace. The knowledge that she was lying to him, that this would likely be the last time he ever held her made her tears come harder, until she was hiccupping as she cried. If she'd had any doubt she loved Grey, she was sure she did now, which made her betrayal and lies all the harder to bear.

Twenty

When the clock in the servant's hall struck ten, the upstairs chambermaids' voices filled the halls as they made their way toward their sleeping quarters to end another long day serving in the castle. Madelaine hovered in an alcove—well aware she was taking a great risk of raising suspicion if the wrong person saw her. She couldn't flee for home yet. She had to see her father first, and in order to do that she needed some help.

Grey's brother had given her some shifty looks. He didn't seem the type to trust or take chances. Likely, someone was watching her, thanks to him. With Elizabeth gone, Madelaine didn't have a single friend to turn to, not that she could have been able to turn to Elizabeth anyway. Her chest ached with loneliness, her throat with unshed tears. Alone again. Would she forever be the outsider, the outcast?

Madelaine clenched the material of her dress and fought back the fears that threatened to render her helpless. Father was an admitted traitor, therefore soon he would either be dead or disgraced, and soon she would be disgraced too. And a traitor to the king. The thought sent icy tingles down her spine.

Her friendship with Elizabeth had to be over for Elizabeth's sake, just as Madelaine's hope for a future with Grey was over. She had no choice but to help her father, but that didn't mean she'd let Grey put his own neck in danger for her.

She rubbed the back of her hand over her tickling nose. Her stomach turned and knotted as she went over her plan once again. Where the blazes was Constance? With her flaming red hair, she should be easy to spot among the other chambermaids. Madelaine had heard enough castle gossip to know Constance would do anything for a bit of coin, so hopefully she would be so glad not to have to earn her extra money on her back that she'd ask no questions.

Madelaine pressed further into the dark shadows as the maids passed by her. Finally, a woman with red hair walked down the passageway. And alone! Finally, a blessing. Madelaine stepped from the shadows. "Constance."

The chambermaid's eyes narrowed and then her mouth dropped open. "Lady Madelaine, whatever are you doing below stairs?"

"Where's your room?"

Constance pointed down the hall.

Madelaine pulled up her hood and motioned forward. "Take me there, please. I need your help."

"My lady—"

Before the chambermaid could finish her sentence Madelaine pulled out the heavy bag of coins under her cloak. "Consider this the first installment for your troubles." She handed the jingling pouch to the maid and watched Constance's mouth turn up with a slight smile. "There'll be more of this to come if you keep your silence."

"This way," Constance said and rushed toward her room.

Once the door was softly shut and Madelaine spared a glance for the barren room to ensure no one else was in there, she focused on Constance. "I need you to help me with something."

Grey leaned against the cold, stone wall of the alleyway by the river Thames with his eyes shut and tried to sleep, but sleep would not come. Deep tiredness settled into his bones. The town could burn around him and he'd not be able to move a muscle, but still sleep evaded him. It wasn't the cold or the draft off the water keeping him awake, nor was it Edward who kept annoyingly tapping his foot as he watched for Madelaine. It was worry for Madelaine.

She was settled safely in her room. He'd stayed outside her door for well over an hour listening to her soft crying. When she had fallen silent, he'd crept away. His worry wasn't for her safety at this moment, but for her safety tomorrow, and the next day and a year from now. If her father was going to be hung, Grey would marry her to protect her from those at Court who would harm her, but he could not get past his growing fear that he would be endangering her by marrying her.

What else could he do? He could find someone else to marry her. Surely with enough gold—he shoved the thought away as he envisioned the sort of unworthy man who would marry a woman tainted by a treasonous father. Madelaine's life could very well end up a living hell married to such a greedy bastard.

She could give her life to the Church, but somehow he didn't think she'd willingly do that, and deep within himself he wouldn't want her to. He was scum. No, he was greedy scum. He wanted to marry her. He loved her. There was no sense denying it. He wasn't happy with her father's predicament. Far from it. Grey hated it. But he couldn't deny there was a part of him relieved that the only choice seemed marriage. And since that's the way it was, he wished the damned guilt would go away.

But it gnawed at him. She was innocent and good and pure, and he was none of those things. She deserved better than him, but fate had dealt her a bad turn. He stood and vowed to do everything in his power to protect her always from his enemies. Protecting her started now. He'd not indulge his brother for one more minute. Madelaine was not an accomplice as Edward suggested. She would not be fleeing in the middle of the night to meet the French spy Edward believed her father must be working with. "I'm going upstairs to my warm, soft bed." Grey bent to retrieve his satchel. "Madelaine won't be sneaking out because she's innocent."

"Don't be fooled," Edward said.

Grey flung his satchel on his back and walked toward his brother. "You're the fool to waste your time out here."

Edward pointed toward the river. "Who's the fool? Look there, brother. And never forget this moment in case you foolishly let your heart rule your head again. Our little pigeon has flown her coop, exactly as I predicted."

Grey pushed Edward out of the way to get a good view of the river embankment where the boatman they'd employed was docked. There was no denying that a slight woman, with Madelaine's exact build, slipped into the boat. And even if Grey wanted to deny it was her, when her brown cloak parted and revealed the same blue dress she'd been wearing earlier, the truth was undeniable. "Goddamn it." He couldn't say more. He watched her pay their man and the boat headed down the river and away from the castle. His mind reeled with disbelief. This was Madelaine, his sweet, innocent Madelaine. He shoved the doubts away. "There has to be an explanation."

Edward tugged Grey toward the river where they had another boat waiting. "Oh, to be sure," he said snidely. "The word traitor explains it all, if you ask me. Now, untie the boat," Edward demanded as he got on.

Grey undid the rope as fast as he could and climbed aboard. The boat dipped as he stepped on and glared at Edward.

"She's no traitor." His steely tone dared his brother to argue.

"I'll not stand here arguing with you, Grey. We'll follow her and see which one of us is right." Edward stared at him across the space. "But mark my words, she's hiding something."

Grey shook off his initial shock. "Shut up. She might just be afraid. I'd be, if I were her. Think of it. Her father could be hung as soon as tomorrow if the king appears and says it's to be so. She thinks she has no one. Maybe she's trying to get home where at least she may have a loyal friend."

Edward shook his head. "I don't agree. Why not leave in the morning instead of like a conspirator stealing away in the night? Besides, you can't be trusted when it comes to her. She's gotten under your skin."

Grey gritted his teeth. He'd not deny the statement, but Edward was wrong on one account. "My first loyalty is to the king. If Madelaine is guilty of helping her father, I'll stop her. Mark my words."

"I need no words, just actions."

Up ahead, Madelaine stood at the helm of the boat. Where the hell was she going? For a good quarter of an hour, they followed her, until the boat maneuvered to the side of the river bank and Madelaine got out with the boatman's help. As she started walking toward the dark woods, Grey spoke. "That's the way to her home." He didn't bother to hide a triumphant smile. When Edward didn't answer, but pulled their boat beside the other, Grey spoke again. "I told you."

"We'll see," Edward said. "Granger," he called to the boatman of Madelaine's boat. "Who was the lady and where's she going?"

Grey didn't bother to wait for an answer. He scrambled out of the boat; his boots crunching twigs and leaves as he landed on dry ground. Without a backward glance, he raced toward Madelaine's departing figure. At the moment, he didn't care about anything but being with her and protecting her. If she wanted to go home, he'd take her there, let her have a few days to mourn her loss and then he'd marry her. He wanted to make her his wife before her father was dead. That way no one could stop them and no one would dare to publicly lay any blame or suspicion at her feet since she would be part of his family.

He strode forward and when he was within range where he thought she'd hear, he called out, "Madelaine!" She kept walking into the woods. He frowned. Had she not heard him? "Madelaine!" He doubled his steps. Her steps quickened in time with his, each crunch of her boot against the dry leaves coming faster than before until she was running.

"Madelaine, for God's sake! Stop!" He broke out into a run, shoving branches out of the path as he did. Dry limbs snagged on his coat and scraped his face as he ran. He raced forward, determined to reach her. Within a few strides, he grabbed her arm.

He whipped her around to face him, whatever soothing

words he thought to say died. Constance glared back at him. His mind reeled and then fear for Madelaine surged through his veins. He gripped Constance's arms harder than he'd normally ever handle any lady. "Why the devil do you have on Lady Madelaine's dress? Where is she? What have you done?"

Constance wrenched her arm from his grip. "The lady paid me to pretend I was her. As to where she is, I couldn't say. As to what I've done—" Constance shrugged. "—no more than any other dirt poor servant. I took good money offered for a job that harmed no one. You'd do the same if you had as many mouths to feed and bodies to keep warm as I do." Constance leveled him with a scathing look of hatred. "Then again, I doubt you understand how hunger can gnaw at the belly, and how you can be so cold you doubt you'll ever feel warm again."

He didn't know, and he felt the fool standing there harassing a woman who was only trying to keep her family from starving and freezing to death.

Panicked determination swept across Constance's face as shoved her hands on her hips. "Can I go now? I do believe my job's finished."

He nodded mutely. Madelaine's possible betrayal cut like a sharp knife across his heart. He stood, listening to the departing sounds of the woman's footsteps, and then a burning anger with himself started deep in his belly and boiled to the surface propelling him into motion. He swung around and almost ran smack into Edward. "So help me God, if you say a word I'll lay you low with a single blow."

Edward's eyes narrowed to slits. "Have it your way. But you'll see soon that I'm right."

"I refuse to believe the worst of her unless I have definite proof the worst is true."

"Grey—"

"No," Grey interrupted. He'd not spill his guts here and tell his brother how alone he'd always felt because he'd chosen to believe his own father didn't love him. He'd not spin a sorry tale about how he'd learned the truth about Father, and until Madelaine had come into his life he'd thought he was unworthy of being loved, even though the tale was true. All Edward need know was that Grey would not abandon Madelaine unless he had absolute proof of her guilt. "I'll stand her protector until I'm certain of her guilt."

Edward nodded. "Fine. Then let us hurry and catch her yet and get to the bottom of everything. But when we do catch her, brother, you need to be prepared. If I'm right and you're wrong, you will still need her to think you love her if she's to confide in you."

Grey nodded. It wouldn't be hard to play the part of the besotted fool. He *was* besotted. He loved her with an ache that stunned him. What would be hard would be to trap her if and when he learned she was betraying the king. He wasn't sure how he would separate duty from love, but if she was guilty he would have to.

Twenty-One

Madelaine rapped softly on the door to her father's cell. "Father," she whispered. Nerves were making her jumpy. She glanced over her shoulder to ensure she didn't see the flickering light of a torch guiding the guard downstairs. She doubted she had more than ten minutes before he returned to his post with the blanket she'd demanded and realized he'd been duped. And then what? Would he immediately check the dungeon?

She knocked a little harder as cold sweat trickled down her back and dampened her underarms. "Father!" She was more worried now the guard would return before she was back than being overheard.

The sound of shuffling feet reached her from under the door. She slumped against the wood. Inhaling a deep breath, she forced herself to straighten and clutched tightly around the dagger she'd stolen.

"Madelaine?" Her father's face appeared at the small, barred window. His dark eyes locked on her. I told you to make your way home, girl."

"Why did you betray the king?" She blinked at the useless tears filling her eyes. "I'll gladly give my life to save you, Father, but I deserve to know *why* I might die."

"Silly, girl." His voice was low and soothing. "Come closer."

She pressed her cheek to the bar where he stretched his fingers between the iron railings. He traced softly over her cheek before cupping her chin. "You're not going to die and neither am I, as long as you do what I say. Do you believe me?"

"I wouldn't be here if I didn't."

"Good. Have you heard any whispers at Court about the king?"

Despite knowing they were alone, she scanned the shadows and dark corners. "I've heard he has dark spells where he forgets himself, who he is. Some say he's going mad. Just gossip."

Her father curled his fingers tighter around her chin.

She jerked away. "You hurt me," she accused, rubbing at her skin.

"I'm sorry." He gripped the bars. "It's not gossip. The king *is* going mad."

"You've seen it?" She couldn't repress the shiver that raced across her skin.

"Several times. The paper the king accused me of stealing was one where not only did he write that an angel came to him and told him he needed to execute his cabinet because they're trying to overthrow him, but he also wrote things he planned for the army to do against Napoleon. If that paper ever fell into the wrong hands it could be England's downfall. England's enemies are constantly sending people into our midst to steal our secrets. The king is sick. He's a danger to England. I stole his paper when he refused to burn it. I knew then someone had to stop him, and none of the other fools who surround him are willing to risk his wrath."

"You risk your life."

"Yes, I do. For England, I risk it all."

Reluctant relief filled her. He'd done what he had because he wanted to protect England. He wanted only to help the king.

"Maddie, with the king's madness he wrote about angels and executions; that paper is the proof the prince needs to become regent. Once the king is proven a danger to England, they'll have to let the prince rule. Get the paper and take it to the prince. I would have done it right away, but the prince was abroad. He'll recognize the king's writing and know that his father cannot be trusted with England's secrets. The prince should be back from his travels any day. Give it to him. Only to him. Do you understand?"

She frowned. "I do, but is he so mad then? Are you and the prince not trying to put him off his throne?"

Her father rattled the bar. "To protect him. To protect England. Will you help me?"

Her heartbeat strummed in her ears. "Why did you say earlier to trust no one? Surely—"

The pounding of footsteps cut off her question. She jerked toward the stairs. Light flooded the entrance to the small room. *Too late.* It was too late to flee. She scanned the small room. On shaking legs, she raced over to the dark corner and ran her hands over the cold stone. There was no space wide enough to wedge herself in. Hysteria made her heart thump painfully and her skin tingle as if needles stuck her at once all over.

Light illuminated the shadowy room and obscured the face of the man holding the torch. Digging her nails into the stone and pressing herself as flat as she could, she held her breath. Maybe the guard wouldn't notice her in the corner. She'd been lucky not to stutter earlier when lying. She'd never been lucky twice. Her father babbled words at the man, but fear made it impossible for Madelaine to concentrate.

For one breathless second, hope filled her. The guard had been easy to dupe into thinking she was a whore who offered herself to him for coin. Maybe her father could get him to leave. The torch lowered, and her hope disappeared. Grey's older brother Lord Ashford stared at her with cold eyes. His lips thinned as he advanced toward her. Her heart hammered to a deafening roar and without consideration, she raised her dagger and flung it at him.

He jerked to the left, but not fast enough. Her dagger stuck in his left shoulder. With a roar, he bent his head to rip out the dagger. She sprang for the stairs. He caught her on the fifth step, jerked her hard against his chest and locked his arm around her waist. He hefted her off the ground. She flailed, her feet dangling in front of her.

Above her, the pounding of frantic footsteps on stone rushed toward them. She refused to give up. Rearing her head back, she connected with Lord Ashford's nose. A sickening crunch followed. He dropped her and she scrambled on the slimy steps.

Could she reach the next level before Lord Ashford caught her? She had to find a way out. The light came toward her quicker than her trembling legs would go. Five seconds until she was captured maybe.

The light robbed her of the ability to see. Blinded, she reached forward, when hands grasped her. Terror seized her voice.

"I've got you," Grey whispered as he flung her over his broad shoulder. "Where do you need to go? How can I help?"

"My home," she mumbled, wilting against him, too exhausted to explain and too desperate to refuse.

Grey held Madelaine tightly against him as he drove them deep into the woods. Doubt tore through him, making him numb. Was she traitor or victim? A picture of her frantic face illuminated by the eerie glow of the torches in the tower filled his head. She was running, that much was for certain. But from what? Was she running to save her own life because she was guilty of treason or was she running because she was innocent and her father had told her to go? Grey refused to believe she was guilty. Not yet. Running didn't prove culpability.

"Stop at once," she demanded, the back of her head coming away from its resting position on his chest and her bottom scooting forward in the saddle to put a slight distance between their bodies.

He pulled up on Cypress's reins until the horse came to a panting halt. Grey prayed his brother was not right. He jumped down then helped Madelaine from the saddle. One look at her, with her hair tumbling invitingly over her shoulders and across her ample bosom, stirred his groin. God, he was warped for his lust to awaken at a time like this. But her dress was revealing and inviting and—Why the hell was she dressed like that? Jealously and anger stirred.

"Do you care to explain the dress?" He wrapped his hands around her waist while trying to tear his eyes from her creamy breasts.

Her slow slide down the length of his body did nothing to dampen his raging desire. Her feet hit the ground and she stepped away from him, her rounded eyes meeting his. "After rescuing me from trying to escape your brother do you really want me to explain my attire? Surely there are other more pressing questions on your mind."

There were a thousand more relevant questions, but he wasn't sure he wanted the answers or if he got answers would they be honest? "Were you trying to free your father?"

She jerked her head. "As if I could."

"That's not an answer."

"No, I was not trying to free him." Her shoulders slumped, and he fought the urge to fold her into his arms. She had gone there for a reason. He had to know why. "Why were you there?"

"Why do you think?" she asked faintly.

Ah. Here was the tricky part. He knew what he wanted to believe, but was he fooling himself? Was Edward right? Would he not be able to read the truth in her eyes because he didn't want to see the truth? "I think you were desperate to see your father one last time." Her eyes widened at his statement. "Am I right?"

"Yes." Her voice trembled. "I had to say goodbye." She sniffed and wiped at her face. "He's all I have in this world, Grey. I—I cannot stay to see him hanged. I just want to go home. I don't want to be here when he's killed."

Grey enfolded her into his arms, relief pouring through him. He didn't give a damn what Edward thought, Madelaine was innocent. She needed him.

He stroked a hand through her hair, aware of a stirring of his blood and a pounding of his pulse. He was helpless to stop his reaction to her. The best he could do was try to control himself. "I'll take you home. And I'll send a note to my brother explaining everything, so he won't pursue punishing you."

She pulled away. "No. Don't do that. You shouldn't involve yourself in my troubles or place me between you and your brother."

"Nonsense." He pulled her to him. When he saw her mouth part as if to protest, he kissed her. He meant only to silence her while he thought how to convince her to allow him to take her home. He'd never let her out of his sight now. Not only was he worried for her safety, but it was imperative to prove her innocence to Edward. When his mouth met hers, and her warm lips parted, he tasted her sweetness and lost control. He kissed her hungrily, their tongues swirling and touching then retreating and coming together once again.

He wanted more. He wanted to shelter her and ravish her at the same time. The dueling desires drove his kiss to a frenzied level. He ravaged her mouth with kiss after kiss, and she responded by pressing her mouth harder against his. Their hands worked frantically over each other. He slid his hands over her smooth skin, pushing her dress off her shoulder, tugging open her bodice, and slipping a finger under her dress to release her taut nipple. He wrenched his mouth away from hers only to lower it to her nipple where he swirled his tongue around the peak. A shudder of desire coursed through him when a strangled moan escaped her. Whatever control he'd had left fled with the knowledge that she wanted him with the same desperation. He cupped her breast to gain better access, and he grasped her bottom in his other hand to haul her firmly against his hard body.

He wanted her with an intensity that blinded him to all else. Before he could make his muddled mind decide what to do, she jerked away, and even in the dark of the forest, he sensed her embarrassment by her frantic breathing and the rustling of her clothes as she hastily drew her dress up to cover herself. "I'm sorry," he quickly said. God, he was a wretched bastard. He'd almost taken his future wife's innocence with the cold dirt and dry leaves as their bed.

"Please, Grey." Her boots crunched on twigs and leaves as she retreated. "You must leave me. I'll make my way home on my own."

His mouth fell open. Damned, foolish woman. This was exactly why he loved her. She thought to protect him from her predicament. But she'd not considered that she'd be raped or murdered before she ever got out of the forest. "How do you plan to get home alone? Will you walk?"

"I—I'd n—n—not thought how to get there."

"That's obvious," he said flatly. "This forest is teeming with thieves, murderers and rapists. You'll be lucky to make it out with your virginity *and* your clothes intact." He heard her swallow. Good. She needed to understand how vulnerable she was without him. He suspected she'd fight his proposal, but he'd prevail.

"Maybe I cou—could hire someone to take me home."

"Have you any money?"

"No." Her voice was high, strained. "Could you loan me some?"

"Hell no. I'll see you there myself, Madelaine."

"You don't owe me anything."

"But I do. I love you, and I intend to marry you."

"Oh, Grey!" She fell against his chest, clutching his arms.

His heart lurched at her touch.

"This was much easier than I thought," he murmured in her hair as he caressed the silken strands.

She jerked away. "No. You misunderstand! I can't fathom you'd still want to marry me now. I—" Her words cut off as she slid her hand to his head and tugged him toward her. He met her mouth in a sweet kiss that took his breath and infused him with another rush of lust. "You can't marry me now, Grey. I'd never let you align yourself with me and the taint my father's dishonor will bring."

"This is more like how I thought you'd react," he said wryly.

"It has to be this way. You must know that."

"I know no such thing. All I know is I'll be the one to see you home safely or you won't go home at all." Let her think the battle was over. He had many other weapons he could use if she pushed him and he didn't mind one bit the idea of seducing her in order to secure her hand in marriage. The foolish woman loved him just as much as he loved her. For the first time ever, he was completely and utterly happy.

His throat constricted. He wasn't alone. Unloved. Unwanted. She loved him. He would make her see she needed him. Couldn't live without him. The idea of going back to a life of loneliness made him shudder. No amount of denying his feelings would work this time.

Twenty-Two

Once Grey secured another horse for Madelaine, they set out toward Lancashire. Their relentless pace made conversation impossible, a reprieve Madelaine welcomed. She had no idea what to say. The idea of lying to Grey after he had said he still wanted to marry her, and was risking his life to help her, made her sick to her stomach. She wanted nothing more than to be able to tell him the truth, but she couldn't betray her father that way nor endanger Grey's future.

Besides, what if Grey was horrified when he learned what her father had done, and he took the paper to prove her father's guilt? The possibility wasn't out of the realm of possibilities, given his brother was so close with the king. Grey would feel loyalty to his brother and the king, and rightly so. Madelaine's own tug of loyalty to the king filled her with conflict and uncertainty.

She wasn't sure she agreed with what her father was doing, but he did what he thought best for the country, and he was counting on her to save him. He had told her exactly what to do, and for once in her life she was going to be obedient. She owed her father this much and so much more.

By the time they stopped at daybreak to water, feed, and rest the horses, tiredness seeped into her bones, making her eyes flinty and her limbs heavy. She eagerly slid from her horse toward Grey's outstretched hands and didn't pull away when her body pressed down the length of his. The courtyard of the inn was deserted, and no one came to take their horses as she expected.

Once she felt steady, she pushed away from Grey and glanced at the inn. Layer upon layer of white paint peeled from the wood, and broken shutters framed the dilapidated windows. Discarded paper and glass littered the ground, and the smell of rotten fish filled the air. Madelaine sniffed. The stench of years of garbage filled her nose, gagging her. Her head pounded from lack of sleep and food. She swallowed, her tongue thick with thirst, her throat dry as kindling. "Where are we?"

"The Navigation Inn. It's not fit for a proper lady, which is exactly why we're here. We won't run into anyone we know, so your reputation will be safe." Grey stared at her, unblinking.

She nearly laughed. He was utterly serious. "I hardly think my reputation will matter in a few days." If she was successful at retrieving her father's paper and getting it to the prince, her father would live. But either way, success or failure, his betrayal of the king would become public, and whatever slim chance she'd ever had at making a successful marriage would disappear. Yet she didn't care about that. The only man she would ever want was the man standing in front of her, and she could never have him now. Once he knew what she had done, he would hate her.

He scowled. "As my wife your reputation will matter to *me*, Madelaine."

The fact he still wanted to marry her, even though he thought her father was about to hang for treason, filled her with an aching, longing love. She'd never betray her father, but she could take one thing for herself. She grasped Grey's hand. "Let's get a room."

His eyebrows raised at her suggestion. He grasped her hand. "One room?"

"One," she confirmed.

He smiled. "Does this mean you're agreeing to marry me?"

"Really, Grey." She batted her eyes flirtatiously, hoping to move his thoughts from marriage. "For a man who is supposed to be a notorious rake, I'd think you'd jump at the chance to share my bed."

He brushed his hand slowly down her cheek, his eyes darkening to a deep blue. "My love, I tremor in anticipation of sharing your bed, yet I find myself in the strange position of wanting to make sure you will be mine forever."

His hard thighs and center pressed against her hips and belly as his gaze locked with hers. She brushed back a lock of hair that had fallen over his forehead. "I will be yours forever. I vow this to you." And it wasn't a lie, so she didn't even stutter. In her heart she would be Grey's wife, though it could never be so on paper.

He flashed a wicked grin. "Then by all means, let's secure a room immediately."

Strangely enough, as she followed him, her knees did not shake with fear at the innocence she was about to freely give away. Once she lay with Grey, it was doubtful another lord would want her. Her heart pounded in anticipation, not anxiety. Her only regret was that her father would be disappointed. Then again, she doubted her father now held any expectations or hopes of her making a decent match, so maybe she would not be disappointing him on that count.

She followed Grey through the door of the tavern. Ale and sweat swirled in the air, and haggard faces glanced their way, dismissing them in the same breath. Grey had been right. This place was disgusting and a perfect place to go unnoticed.

As Grey spoke with the innkeeper and secured them a room, Madelaine stood silently in a corner of the shabby lobby, if you could call the small room outside of the tavern a lobby. Once Grey was finished, he held out his hand. She slipped her hand into his as he led her up a narrow set of stairs. They did not speak, which was a good thing because she did not think she could find any words to say besides *I want you*. At the top of the stairs, he took a right, passed two doors then stopped in front of the third. "This is us."

She nodded and smiled. She didn't want him to think she was nervous, but suddenly she was. Her mother had never spoken to her about the marriage act. She wished they'd been closer, and she had an inkling of what to expect.

Grey led her into the small room, dismal with its faded green coverlet, threadbare carpet and dented dresser. The surroundings mattered little to her, as long as Grey was with her, but the room smelled of mold, and that she couldn't stand. She strode to the small window, but could not get it open. Behind her, she smelled a burning wick and light flickered against the wall creating dancing shadows. Grey came up behind her, his arms sliding beside hers, his hands covering her smaller ones. "Together?"

She nodded, her heart beat increasing with each breath. The window lock snapped open and Grey pushed open the shutters, a cool breeze hitting her face. She inhaled deeply of the fresh air heavy with moisture of an oncoming rain.

"Madelaine," Grey whispered against her neck as he stroked her hair. She pressed her back against his length. She savored the strength of the man behind her and the warmth of his arms as they circled her waist and turned her toward him.

He raised her chin until she stared into his eyes. "Tell me you want me."

"I want you." There was no need to play coy or hesitate. Tonight would represent the thousands of moments they would never share again. There was no time for fear or anything else. She pressed her mouth to his, willing her problems to the darkest recesses of her mind. Their tongues intertwined and touched gently, then greedily.

He roamed his hands up and down her back in a rhythmic, almost frenzied pattern. Then he delved his fingers beneath the material of her dress, pulling the cotton gently off one shoulder. The warmth of his fingers against her bare skin sent a shudder through her body.

The material slid lower until her breast was exposed, and he licked and teased the peak. Sensations exploded through her and caused her to gasp. She curled her fingers into his arms, afraid her legs would simply give out. He tugged her dress over her shoulder, her hips and down her legs, somehow expertly managing to find access to the juncture between her thighs.

She pressed her hands against his back to draw him closer, while he pulled her tighter, suckling harder as his fingertips found the place throbbing between her legs. A sob escaped her as she gave up any fight and gloried in the movement of his fingers. They massaged her, her need building until she was sure she would die. "Please," she cried, not at all sure what she was begging for.

His fingers moved at a more rapid pace. "Let yourself go."

Hadn't she already? Yet even as she questioned it, a crescendo built within her, her pulse pounding a fierce beat through her veins as a hot, searing liquid exploded within her. She sank into his arms, panting with the release of the throbbing in her loins and buried her face against his chest as she ran her fingers over coiled, warm arms.

How would it feel to have Grey inside of her? New longing sprang within her.

"Madelaine," he whispered into her ear as he gently tilted her head back.

Raw need filled his voice, but when she looked into his eyes, she gasped. His eyes shimmered with longing. It was hard to believe she had thought at one time that he needed nothing and no one. She could not deny what she saw. Tonight, she'd give him what he desired, and she would try to forget that soon she would betray his trust.

Cupping his face with her hands, she kissed his neck, the stubble of his chin, and his lips. A craving to touch every part of him filled her. She twined her fingers through his hair as he lifted her off the ground and carried her to the bed. He settled her and stood over her looking down at her.

Outside, a storm brewed which matched the tempest within her. Rain beat against the inn and gusts of wind smacked against the wooden shutters making them rattle. "A storm's coming," she said.

Grey kneeled before her and took her hand in his. "In here too."

She nodded.

"This will be different than moments ago."

Good God. Was he trying to prepare her? Her heart tugged at his thoughtfulness. "I'm aware." Though only slightly, but he didn't need to know how utterly naïve she was.

"Are you sure you know what you're doing?"

"I know exactly what I'm doing." For tonight she did anyway.

His gaze burned her. "This makes you mine. There's no turning back."

She wanted to be his forever. Even if only like this. "I know."

He slid a gold ring off his finger and held it toward her. "I don't have a ring for you yet, but soon you'll wear one—mine. For now, I pledge my loyalty to you and swear it on this ring, which holds great meaning to me." He kissed the ring, and she swallowed back thick tears. God, how much would he hate her tomorrow? Was this wrong? She was too selfish to change her mind now. He cupped her chin. "Will you pledge your loyalty to me?"

She could. She would always be loyal only to him, but he may not see it that way. Still, she had no choice. Shaking, she leaned forward and pressed her lips to the cool metal. "You have my undying loyalty." She took the ring from him, kissed it and handed it back to him.

He slid the ring on, cupped her neck and drew her face close to his. A deep ache coiled through her when his lips brushed her tender mouth.

"You are so damn beautiful." His voice hitched.

That she made him vulnerable made her tremble anew. She shook her head.

"Don't do that." His tone was sharp, insistent. "You *are* beautiful. I know your mother made you feel ugly because you were different, but it's that difference that makes you so beautiful, so special to me."

His words unlocked a part of her she hadn't realized had been barred against people. Inside, she felt as if she shattered. Moaning, she pulled his head closer still, needing more of him. His mouth crushed down on hers in a plundering kiss that robbed her of coherent thought. Blood surged through her veins; the rush of heat through her body was extraordinary. His hands were underneath her, scooping her up and laying her back against the soft pillows. As she reached for him, he rolled off the bed and stood beside her. His eyes held hers while he stripped the clothing from his body.

She meant to protest the loss of his heat, but as he revealed himself, she sighed. His skin glowed in the candlelight. She caught her breath as she drank in his appearance. He was hard and sculpted, just as she had always imagined her knight would be. There was nothing soft or relenting about the rippling muscles of his flat abdomen or the rising curves of his arms. His broad shoulders appeared strong enough to withstand many blows from an enemy, and based on the angry red zigzagging scars on his right shoulder, she realized he'd already withstood some sort of wounds.

She scrambled off the bed and licked his shoulder, and then she kissed the scar once, twice, three times. "How did you get this?"

"Equerry training." He sounded guarded. Maybe training had not gone well.

"You should choose a less dangerous profession."

He laughed. "I wish I could. Too late for that, my love."

My love. The sound of the endearment from his lips made her smile. She trailed her fingers down the smooth skin of his chest, grinning when he shuddered beneath her fingertips. "Is that because of my touch?"

"It's because I want you too much." He cupped her breasts, causing her nipples to harden.

Her newfound power made her dizzy with excitement. "How much do you want me?"

Laughter rumbled from his chest. "I ache all over."

She nodded, understanding his need because her body

burned as well. His mouth slanted then, trailed kisses down her neck, over her collarbone, and back up to her lips.

Now she was the one shivering from desire. Heat singed her skin every place his warm mouth touched her. Madness and need consumed her, overriding any doubts. She wanted to rub her lips against every part of his body. She kissed his shoulder, his neck, his chest.

The length of his body covered her for a moment, wiry hair to smooth skin. Once again, his mouth found her breast, sucking greedily until she moaned and writhed beneath him. Her loins pulsed, and she ground her pelvis against him, gasping at the sparks of pleasure that shot through her. "What happens now?"

He smiled slowly. "Now I bring you pleasure again." He caressed her belly before moving to the juncture between her thighs.

"No!" Laughing, she tried to scramble out of his reach, but his hands locked down on her legs like two steel manacles. "Oh yes, my love. The more pleasure now, the less pain in a moment."

"But you already brought me pleasure," she protested.

"And I intend to keep bringing you pleasure the rest of your life. It's my most sacred duty as your husband."

Her heart slammed against her chest at his revealing words. "You are not my husband."

His brow puckered. "Not yet. But I will be soon."

There was no point arguing. What could she say anyway? *Tomorrow I'm intending to flee you and betray your trust?* She nodded and forced herself to relax. His fingers massaged across the sensitive place between her legs, but this time light as a feather until she was pushing against him in silent demand that he move faster and harder. He acquiesced without a word.

Need coiled once again within her, driving her to clench the sheets as her body quivered with wanting. Her longing slowly grew stronger like the heat of the sun from morning to afternoon, until she burned within. "Please," she moaned. This time she knew exactly what she begged for. That same release, but not from his hands. She wanted to feel him sheathed inside her. She pushed his hands away and dug her nails into his sides. "Take me."

He hovered above her, sweat covering his brow. His ragged breathing told her just how difficult prolonging his own pleasure had become. One strong hand slid below her pelvis and lifted her toward him before he drove into her. She tensed with a twinge of pain, but he was hot, hard and pulsing. He stroked once, twice, three times. The pain disappeared, and she lost count, desperate to meet him stroke for stroke. She clutched his back, moaning.

He nipped at the sensitive skin of her ear. "Let go, my love."

She pulled him to her, wanting to bury herself within him, until they were one. Every muscle in her body clenched as wave after wave of pleasure rolled through her. Her back arched as her head fell back. He groaned and drove faster, harder until his muscles shook beneath her fingertips. With a final stroke, his body shuddered, tightened and trembled with his release.

He sagged against her, slick with sweat. They lay for a moment panting with exhaustion, until he moved off her onto his back then tugged her against his side. She snuggled up to him and laid her head on his chest to count the beats of his heart. "I love you." The thought had been flooding her mind. She'd not intended to say it, because it would seem a lie tomorrow, but she couldn't hold back.

He pressed a kiss to her forehead. "And I love you."

Doubts about her decisions crept into her head. Maybe she could trust him? The errant thought horrified her. Not only was it breaking her vow, it would be putting Grey in danger, if things should go badly. No. She had to leave him. To protect him.

The candle in the room burned itself out. Madelaine lay very still and pretended to be asleep. Grey's chest rose shallowly at first and then deeply and his heartbeat against her ear slowed as well. She rose until she could see his face, but could not make out his expression in the dark. Yet his moans indicated he dreamed.

With care, she rolled slowly away from him and swung her legs over the bed. Her feet touched the material of her dress, and she silently bent, retrieved it and quickly put on her clothes. Her body was sore all over, but she welcomed every precious ache that had come from giving herself to him. Within a few minutes, she was at the stables, where the boy who was paid to keep the horses was only too glad to hand over Grey's stallion for a handful of coins. She started to walk away, but then thought perhaps she better take the other horse as well. She gulped as she handed the last of her coins over. That was the last of two years' worth of pin money.

Yet, she had to spend it. She could not afford Grey reaching her before she met the prince. After another exchange of coins, she got on Grey's stallion and led the other horse deep into the woods where she swatted it in the opposite direction of the inn. When she was certain the horse ran away, she turned the stallion and galloped toward home and a future filled with only one certainty—she would always love Grey and he'd likely hate her until his dying day.

Twenty-Three

Madelaine wept for the first hour of her ride. In all her fantasies of her first time with Grey, she never imagined fleeing. His undying love. Yes. Marriage. Absolutely. Betraying him? No. The possibility hadn't crossed her mind. It didn't matter she was doing what she had to. Knowing she had no choice did nothing to obliterate the queasiness of betraying Grey nor the certainty that a future with him was lost to her forever. Moreover, she was terrified about what her future *would* bring. What would happen once she found the king's paper and took it to the prince? What sort of battle lines would be drawn then between the king and the prince as they fought for control of the throne?

The nagging feeling that she and her father would be standing on the wrong side of the battle plagued her. Even if Father was correct and the king was going mad, to go behind the king's back and strip away his power without consulting him or trying to come up with some sort of alternative seemed morally wrong. She wished there was some other course, but she couldn't think of one nor would anyone listen to her, even if she could.

She struggled to push the thoughts of the king and Grey out of her head and concentrate on the road. As she neared her home and made her way down the long drive, she gripped the reins and her heart pounded in trepidation. She gasped as the estate came into view. This was not the home she had left over a year ago.

There was no welcoming light, no smell of fresh baked bread or apple tarts, no servants bustling about or even the whinny of the horses from the stables. Hope and life had deserted this dark, silent place. She had thought she'd been prepared for what she would find, since Grey had told her his brother had forced her father to dismiss all the servants with some cockamamie tale about financial woes, but she shook as she viewed her home so different than her memories. Though Lord Ashford had done her father a favor, by removing the very people who would spread gossip about him being arrested for treason, she couldn't squelch the anger running through her veins when she opened the front door and saw the shambles her childhood home had been left in.

Overturned furniture and paper littered the floors. After pushing a chair out of her way, she stalked from the entrance hall to the library, then through the ballroom and drawing room. Disorder reigned in every room. Drawers lay half open or pulled all the way out and left on the floor. The books in the library had been removed from the shelves. Chairs were overturned, no doubt in the men's haste to try to locate the paper that would prove her father's guilt. But Father was clever. Thank God! If he'd not hidden the paper he would be dead already. Neither Lord Ashford nor the king was likely to give a whit that her father meant only to protect England. Men and their games. They were all arrogant and self-serving, except for Grey.

Ugly treacherous thoughts reared as she picked her way through the disorder and toward the kitchen and the door that led to the cellar. Every step on the marble floor echoed in the eerie silence. She passed a ball of ribbon lying on the floor. Abby's ribbon! She bent, picked up the ribbon and fingered the silken thread. "*Abby*. Where are you?"

Madelaine gulped back the sadness threatening to over-come her. She'd not given one thought to her childhood friend or any of the servants, for that matter. And blast Father, neither had he! His betrayal of the king had put them all in a precarious position.

She prayed Abby and her mother had found someone to take them in or even new employment. If they hadn't, maybe when things settled she could find Abby and bring her and her mother back here, or if not here wherever fate forced them to settle. God! She clenched the ribbon in her hand. It may do Abby more harm than good if she worked for Madelaine and her father, assuming they'd be in any sort of position to employ a servant.

She squeezed her eyes shut and breathed deeply. She had to quit thinking about the future and secure the list for the prince. Opening her eyes, she strode down the hall and made her way to the back and through the door to the kitchen. Here everything was perfectly in its place. They'd never thought to look in the kitchen, let alone the wine cellar. With her lips pressed together, she quickly found a candle and then made her way down the dark cellar stairs.

She'd always hated the damp, dark cellar. Her heart raced and her palms sweated. She shuffled past the barrels to the back where the wine bottles were. The endless rows filled her with dread. Dusty containers lined the walls eight rows deep. Dirt and dust filled her lungs and made her cough.

Something creaked in the room, and she darted a look around seeing nothing but glass and wood. Trying to ignore the despair the rows conjured, she eyed the towering racks and hurried to the fourth row. In the middle of a sea of white bottles was a green one. The relief that poured through her made her tremble so that she had to set her taper on the shelf. It was just as well. She needed her hands free. She closed her fingers around the green bottle, and after a moment she managed to open it and turn it upside down. Inside the empty bottle the smooth edge of a rolled up piece of paper protruded.

Grabbing the edge of the scroll, she tugged it out. For a moment, she eyed the paper, suspended between duty and curiosity. If she was going to risk her life and betray her king, she wanted to see exactly what he had written. After unrolling the paper, it shook as she brought it close to read. The first lines were the king's mad statement about the angel visiting him, just as her father had said. Her scalp tingled as she read the king's disturbing words. She moved her gaze down the paper. The distinctive slanted scrawl of her father's handwriting leapt out at her and made her gasp. Trembling, she moved her finger along the first line. *Primary Code of the Network Language.*

She traced the second entry. *"QOTM" and "AKUXMK."* The code made no sense to her, but after reading further, she thought she had it. Her father had always made her solve elaborate puzzles he'd created and for the first time ever she was glad for it. This was not a complicated puzzle. The English word was written below the coded word which represented it. The coded word was her father's handwriting, but the decoded word was not.

She rubbed the paper between her fingers as she thought. Why had Father created ciphers for the king? Not enough sleep and lack of food sent a wave of exhaustion rolling through her that left her dizzy. For one bleak second, she thought she might swoon, but after a moment the spinning stopped, and she once again composed herself to study the paper.

Blast her father.

Her belly clenched in denial but the truth was in swirly dark ink before her eyes. Father had not told her the whole truth. He'd not said a word about being involved in creating a code for the king. Dizziness overwhelmed her again. She squeezed her eyes shut, breathed deeply and reached a steadying hand toward the shelf. Gripping the wood so tight her fingers ached, she swayed as wave after wave of nausea consumed her. Sweat, damp and sticky, trickled down her sides and covered her brow.

If Father had omitted part of the truth, what else might he have lied about? Her mother's voice, bitter and accusing, filled Madelaine's head. How many times had her father returned from a long trip only for her mother to scream that he was lying about where he'd been, what he'd been doing. For years, her parents had scurried off to the garden to argue in private, only they were never alone.

Madelaine's secret hiding place had been in the garden. By the age of ten, she knew Mother thought Father was in love with someone else and that he secretly went to meet her time and again. And Madelaine would never forget the awful day her Mother had begged him not to go on the trip he had planned. She promised to be sweeter, more loving and make Madelaine a better, more dutiful daughter.

Her mother's pleas had fallen on deaf ears. He'd left, not to return for two months, and the beatings while he was gone had been the worst Madelaine had ever received. But the beatings paled in comparison to the guilt that ate at her. She vowed to be a better daughter, one that would not cause her mother heartache and make her so angry that she fought with Father. She vowed to be the kind of daughter

Father would want to come back to. *Then* he would stay with them. *Then* he would love them.

But when he came back from his trip, he'd sought her out instead of Mother. That had been the best and worst day ever. He'd taught her a new way he'd learned to shoot his bow, and she'd eagerly gone with him for the better part of a day into the woods to hunt and shoot. Abby and her mother had even joined them for a time, which had never happened before and never happened again. When they'd all returned to the house, her mother had been livid beyond reason and had smacked Madelaine across the face with a hairbrush.

Madelaine opened her eyes and rubbed her cheek, which throbbed as if just freshly hit. She could see her parents standing before her as if time had not moved forward a single second, minute, hour or day. Father grabbing Mother's arm as she raised it to strike again, and Mother's stricken face before she fled the room—those memories never faded. Abby and her mother had scurried off to the kitchen when Father had commanded them to go. Madelaine had crawled into bed early that night and prayed things would be better on the morrow, but the next day her parents barely spoke, and her mother made sure she knew it was all her fault.

Madelaine kneaded her fingers into her aching head. In her heart, she didn't believe her father betrayed her mother, nor was she sure he had really loved her. What was he doing all those times he was gone? Was a glimmer of the truth here in this paper?

Her pulse raced as she read the next two lines written by the king's hand. "King George III's personal spies and missions," she muttered aloud. Disbelief caused her to laugh nervously. *Head of circle of six – Fifth Duke of Ashdon–*

mission — deliver message to Nelson regarding the movement of Napoleon's fleet across the Atlantic.

Dear God! Grey's brother was a spy, or did this note refer to Grey's father? It must have been written before Grey's father's death. Madelaine pressed a hand to her head as her thoughts spun. The circle of six held no meaning for her, but if Grey's father had been a spy that could explain why Grey had been held at arm's length all his life. She became excited thinking of how happy Grey would be to know his father really had loved him and had only tried to protect him, but then she remembered she had to avoid Grey, and even if she did see him at Court, it wasn't as if she could tell him what she knew.

Unless—All the air in her lungs swooshed out in a rush. Did he already know? *Was he a spy as well?* The paper crumpled as she curled her fingers into a fist. Her blood rushed to her temples. Had Grey lied to her?

Flashes of his injuries skimmed through her thoughts. Cuts, scrapes, and fresh scars that seemed too harsh for a mere equerry filled her with doubt. She couldn't consider that he might have lied. Because if he was the king's man, then did that mean he had used her to get to her father? Ruthlessly, she shoved the doubt away and hugged herself.

Yet the doubt was relentless, like a driving rain that wouldn't let up. It bore into her, chilling her skin and froze her all the way through. Gulping, she forced herself to look at the paper once again. Her heart pounded as she read each line while holding her breath and praying she'd not see Grey's name, yet praying she'd find answers.

Her hopes rose as she read through the names and the missions—Lord Gravenhurst and Grey's brother were on the list with missions by their names, but Grey was not mentioned. The next name caused her to bite down hard on her lip, her stomach pitching.

She blinked, yet the name was still there. Her father was a spy for the king. Had he always been? It explained his long absences and why he could never tell Mother where he was or what he was doing. How horrible for Mother and him. Madelaine groaned.

Her parents had barely stood a chance at happiness with this secret between them. Maybe her willful ways had been one thing too many between her parents. She had to make amends for her part in driving her parents apart. She had to do her Father's bidding and trust him. Didn't she? Doubt warred within her. The king believed he could depend on her father, and her father was betraying the king. Instinct made her want to know more, but what would she do if what she learned made her think her father was wrong? Could she still do what he demanded? It was better to never know, to not have to decide.

A scratching noise behind her made her jump. Whirling around, she grabbed the taper off the shelf. Light flickered in front of her, illuminating the distance from her to the stairs. There was no one there, yet her skin prickled. How long before Grey caught up with her, or worse his brother or Lord Gravenhurst? She might be able to convince Grey of her innocence, but his brother and Lord Gravenhurst wouldn't listen to a word she said, especially since she'd wounded Grey's brother. And then another thought struck. Somewhere out there was a murderer and it wasn't her father. Fear stilled her breathing altogether. She listened to the silence.

A clanking, as if a bottle had been tipped over, resounded. Every instinct she possessed urged her to flee but first she needed the money her father had hidden. She snatched the bottle up, expecting to find money in it, but the bottle was empty.

Her hands flew from bottle to bottle in search of the money as her heart slammed painfully, making her chest ache. She tried to calm herself, to order her thoughts, but it was impossible as fear clawed its way up her insides and choked her. Her hands shook. She could hardly grasp the bottles. In the blackness, she could have sworn she heard a man's voice.

Wildly, she gazed around at the shadows, the walls, the hundreds of bottles. Were the walls closer, the shadows darker, the bottles multiplying? She jerked away from the shelf desperate to run upstairs to the open space and light.

Her shoulder bumped a bottle on the edge of the shelf as she turned. The bottle teetered before toppling to the ground. Shards flew and crackled on impact with the hard floor. To her left, the distinct sound of feet shuffling pierced through her fear. An icy chill coursed down her spine. Automatically, she lifted her boot to get the dagger she'd stolen. She felt around for where she'd made a slit on the outside of her boot for it, and then froze. Her heart plunged. Damnation. She'd left the dagger buried in Grey's brother's shoulder.

Twenty-Four

*D*isbelief held Grey immobilized in the shadowy corner of Stratmore's cellar. His blood rushed violently through his veins. He'd risked his career as a spy, his relationship with his brother and his honor by placing Madelaine above the king, and he'd judged her wrongly. He'd risked his heart, a foolishness he'd sworn never to do after a lifetime of building defenses around it. And what had he exposed himself for? Not the angel he'd imagined but a clever viper.

She stood with the wide-eyed stare he imagined most traitors would have when caught red-handed. Except she was the most beautiful traitor he would probably ever come up against. Her gaze swept over the darkness as her hand moved and her skirts fell back down around her ankles. His fingers tingled in remembrance of just how silky her skin was. He gritted his teeth.

She hadn't seen him yet. He saw the king's paper. She'd known exactly where to find it. Invisible bands wrapped around his heart and squeezed what was left of the useless thing. She'd played him for a fool with her innocent smiles and clear brown eyes, and he'd nearly killed himself to get here and protect her, even after she'd stolen away like a guilty person would. He hadn't wanted to believe it possible.

White hot fury rose inside him, but even in the midst of his anger the idea of harm coming to her sat like a lead ball in the pit of his stomach. Foolish as hell considering he was going to have to deliver her to the tower to await punishment for treason, which would likely be her death. Jesus God. He'd not really considered it until now. Could he do it? He thought instantly of his vow to the king and to her. *Damn her.* Her actions left him no choice.

"Who's there?" Her voice was strong and clear and reminded him why he'd fallen for her. Her bravery when she sensed danger made pride swell up in him. Misplaced pride he couldn't afford to have.

He stepped from the shadows and into the soft glow of light from her taper. "It's Grey. Not who you were expecting, I suppose."

He tensed, thinking she might try to run, or gasp, or even play the fool and try to hide the list and convince him she had no idea what he was talking about. Stark relief lit her face. His mind reeled. Was this a game she played or genuine?

Damn it. He curled his hands into fists. It didn't matter whether she was glad to see him or not. He could not allow himself to be stupid. He stepped toward her to grab her in case she tried to run, but before he touched her, she flung herself into his arms.

Calling on a will he wasn't sure he possessed, he stood like stone as she ran her hands over his face, neck and chest then clutched his arms. The paper fluttered in the clutch of her fingers.

"Grey," she cried out before kissing him. He tried not to respond, but her taste and her tongue mingling with his sent lust and want surging through him. The desire to ravish her and forget that she was just as likely to bury a nice sharp dagger in his back as rake her nails in her pleasure down his sensitive skin consumed him. He pulled away from the kiss, but she pressed close to him, laying her head against his chest.

His blood rushed thickly in his ears, and he turned his head away from hers, so that every time he inhaled he would not get a whiff of her delectable scent. His stomach turned. Now he had to do what he had never wanted, had fought against.

"Grey, I'm so sorry I left you like I did." She pressed her lips to his chest, his heart lurching despite his best efforts to remain unmoved by whatever she might say. The rustle of the king's paper in her hand was the thing he needed to make him rein in his galloping heart.

He eyed the paper with contempt, but when he met her gaze he smiled, careful not to show how he truly felt. "What do you have there?"

She quickly folded the paper and slipped it into her boot. "A goodbye letter from my father."

"Hidden in a bottle?" He couldn't help the sarcasm in his tone.

"He d—didn't want your brother or another of the k— king's men to take it if they found it, so he hid it."

He clenched his jaw. Had she forgotten her stutter gave her lying away? "How very deceptive of him."

"Deceptive?" She bit her lip. "I suppose you could see it that way, but he felt he had to do what he did. Grey, I'm so happy to see you."

He raised his eyebrows. "You'll understand if I find that hard to believe since you fled without waking me, stole my horse—"

"Borrowed," she interrupted.

"Fine. Borrowed my horse and made sure the other

horse ran off."

She dropped her hands from his arms and stepped away. "It was for your own good. I'm a sinking ship."

"I'm an expert swimmer, my sweet."

"Please." Her voice hitched. "You have to let me go. I— I don't want you to be hurt by me."

"Too late for that." Damnation. He ground his teeth. He'd meant to never let her know she'd hurt him.

"Grey." His name was a strangled word from her lips. "I didn't mean to hurt you. Lying with you was selfish. But I wanted a memory of you. A memory to last me. But now I want you to let me go."

"Why the hurry?" He snapped the question out harsher than he'd intended, but his damned aching heart made him surly.

She let out a shaky sigh. "I've somewhere I need to go."

Like the tower. His nostrils flared as he struggled to control himself. "Then I'll take you."

"No."

He'd had enough of this back and forth banter. Time was ticking away and taking his control of his temper with it. "You don't want to marry me. All right. I'm a grown man. I can take rejection. But what I can't take is the thought of you being accosted, raped or worse because you stupidly traveled without a chaperone."

"I can't let you come. It's t—too d—d—dangerous for y—you." Her face reddened with the effort to choke out her lies. He wanted to shake her silly. She'd be dead before the next dawn if she tried to lie to anyone who had half a brain.

His head pounded. He didn't want to be her punisher. He wanted to be her protector, but what he wanted didn't matter one damn bit. "I'm afraid we are at an impasse. I won't let you go anywhere without me. I will deliver you safely to someone who I deem trustworthy." The lies left him feeling as if he'd swallowed a mouthful of ashes. "Where is it you need to go?"

Her shoulders slumped and the breath rushed out of her lungs in an exasperated sigh. He hated to see her look so defeated. Yet knowing how determined she was she might see his stipulation as a temporary setback; try to run again the first chance she got. Or would she try to kill him? He had to make certain she didn't get her hands on a weapon. His patience snapped under the long, silent moment. "Either tell me now where you want me to take you or I'm going to deliver you back to the castle."

"No!" The word was swift and strident. "I need to go to the prince."

"The prince?" Grey couldn't fathom what the prince had to do with any of this, unless Madelaine's father had fallen into the camp of men who believed the prince should be regent. Fury, like he'd never known coursed through him as he struggled to fit all the pieces together. But the damned pieces didn't fit. The prince wouldn't kill the king's spies to gain the throne, would he?

"If your father is innocent surely he would want you to go to the king."

She inhaled as if to speak, but then said nothing. Likely she had no idea what to say. It would have been a perverted pleasure to point out what a lousy traitor she was making, but instead he clamped his teeth together. Leading someone to her own doom was not nearly as fun as he'd presumed when he'd imagined what being a spy would be like. But then again, he'd never considered he'd be leading the only woman he'd ever loved to her death.

His brother had been very specific with his orders. If Grey found proof of Madelaine's guilt he was to first try to

learn who she and her father were working with, and once
he had the information, he was to destroy the king's paper if
it was in her possession and bring her to the tower. The
king didn't want the paper kept, even as proof of Stratmore's guilt, since it also confirmed the king fell into spells
of madness.

He itched to snatch off the boot she'd stuffed the paper
in. Hell. Really he wanted to take off all her clothes, ravish
her and then burn the paper in front of her. Part of him
wanted to show her he could be just as cold and calculating
as she could, and part of him wanted to shelter her from her
own folly, convince her to pretend she knew nothing about
what her father had done, and cover up her part in this
whole sordid mess. Common sense and duty barely won
out. Grey swallowed convulsively, his mouth dry as paper.
"Why do you want to go to the prince?"

She was trapped. In order to get to the prince, she was
going to have to allow Grey to take her there, or take her
most of the way. Without any money for traveling with and
based on Grey's steely-eyed look of determination, there
didn't seem to be another choice but to capitulate.

Guilt immediately ate at her. Grey was risking his reputation, possibly his life for her, and she was repaying him by
lying to him and leading him straight into the mess her
father had created. This is exactly what she hadn't wanted.
Grey's loyalty to the king would come under question by
his association with her. She'd simply have to escape him
once they were close enough to the prince for her to reach
him on her own.

"Madelaine." Grey's voice vibrated with impatience.

Not that she blamed him. She prayed she'd manage to lie without stuttering. "With the king in one of his dark spells, the prince is my father's best hope for a pardon."

"How do you know about the king's dark spells?" Grey demanded.

"Same as you, I imagine. The whispers in the Court are rampant, and when he left so suddenly for Kew…" she shrugged. "People talked, and I couldn't help but overhear."

He scrutinized her with flinty eyes. "What makes you think the prince will pardon your father for stealing the king's paper and for killing a man?"

Anger flared in her breast. "Because there is no proof! My father i—i—is—" Damnation! She could not choke out the words "—is loyal to the king." She took a deep breath. "My father is loyal to England. The prince will know he would never do anything to harm the king." Father did think he was doing what was best, after all. "And I vow on my honor Father did not kill anyone."

"If you say so." Grey reached across the space that had widened between them. "Come to me."

She shouldn't. She should keep her distance. But it was impossible. She walked to him, and he folded her in his arms. The linen of his shirt tickled her cheek, and his smell of woods, horse and sweat filled her nose. She pressed her head to his chest, listening to his strong heartbeat as his hand stroked gently through her hair. A rattling sigh escaped her. His gentle touch made her want to spill the whole truth to him about his father, his brother, and her father. But if she did, she had no doubt he'd promptly drag her back to his brother and the tower, and then there'd be no one to save her father.

She couldn't expect Grey to understand why her father had done what he had because she wasn't sure she understood herself. But he was her father. And she owed him her loyalty. *Even if he's wrong about the king?* A voice whispered in her head. She squeezed her eyes shut, willing the voice away. She'd made terrible choices that had driven her mother and father to argue over her, but Father had stood by her side and it had cost him his wife. Besides, how could she ever learn if her father was wrong about the king? It wasn't as if she could seek an audience with His Majesty and study his condition to determine just how much these spells affected him.

Grey pressed a kiss to the top of her head. "We'd better get going."

She pulled back enough to see his expression. Was that disgust flickering in his eyes? She blinked, and whatever she'd seen was gone. She rubbed her burning eyes. "I'm exhausted."

"You can sleep while I drive the coach to Kew."

"Kew?" Her throat constricted with fear. Had he changed his mind? "I need to see the prince, not the king."

"I know." Grey took her hand and led her toward the stairs. "The prince is in Kew."

That couldn't be right. Her father had said the prince was on a trip. "How do you know?"

Grey paused at the top of the stairs and looked down at her. "My brother told me at Court."

Her heart raced at his words. Now was a perfect opportunity to try to ease some of his suffering over thinking his father never cared for him. "Your brother knows a great deal about politics. I imagine your father knew a great deal as well."

An odd expression crossed Grey's face. "As I've said, he had the king's ear as a wealthy landowner. Why do you ask?"

She followed him through the cellar door and into the kitchen. "I just wonder if perhaps your father might have been so busy with the king's business that it caused him to neglect you."

Grey wheeled around. "What are you trying to tell me, Madelaine?"

Behind Grey a pot flashed in a sliver of moonlight above his head. Madelaine blinked, sure she was seeing things. But when the pot flashed again and came down with a resounding thump on the back of Grey's head, Madelaine screamed as he crumpled to his knees with a groan.

Twenty-Five

"Grey," Madelaine exclaimed and bent to help him stand.

Grey waved her off. "I'll live. Luckily for your friend, I've a hard head."

Madelaine rose and glared at Abby. "Abigail Langley! What on earth are you doing here? And what were you thinking?"

Abby lifted her hem, gave Grey a narrow-eyed look, and scrambled around him before coming to stand in front of Madelaine and embrace her in a hug. "I'm here because someone in the village said they saw a woman riding hell-bent toward your home. I knew right away it had to be you. You're the only woman I know who rides a horse as a man does."

Madelaine frowned. "I'm sure there has to be at least one other woman who doesn't like riding sidesaddle."

Grey rose to his feet, rubbing his head. "Why on earth did you hit me?"

"I thought Madelaine needed saving from you." Abby gave Grey a cool look that made Madelaine smile.

She'd never known a servant quite as confident or proud as Abby. Madelaine was so glad to see her and know she was all right.

"Where are you staying? Are you safe? Did you find employment?"

Abby cleared her throat. "I'm in town at the local inn. Mother went to Uncle Jake's. He was only willing to take one of us in."

Madelaine's jaw dropped. The local inn was no place for any young woman who wanted to keep her innocence or a decent future. She grasped Abby by the arm. "Oh, Abby! I swear when Father gets out of this mess, he'll come for you. And your mother," Madelaine added as an afterthought.

"I'm not worried. Especially since you're here now. You are here to stay, aren't you?"

Madelaine glanced at Grey. Abby was the one person Madelaine could confide in and Abby had a good head for figuring things out. But she couldn't tell her friend the truth of what was happening in front of Grey. But if Abby came with them, surely there would be a moment when they were alone, or when Grey fell asleep that they could talk. The man had to sleep, after all. An idea struck Madelaine, and she turned to Grey. "Do you think your aunt or sister would take Abby on as a servant?"

He yawned as if bored with the conversation. "If I ask them to."

Madelaine wet her lips, embarrassed to be asking him for anything in light of what she'd done and what she was planning to do. What choice was there, though? If Grey promised to find Abby employment, he'd keep his word no matter what occurred. "Abby is an excellent hairdresser and seamstress."

Abby nodded. "Truly I am, Lord Drivel."

Grey smiled. "You recognize me?"

"Yes." Her tone held amusement.

Grey's eyes narrowed. "Was this before or after you hit me?"

Her lips pressed together, but her smile was evident.

"Before."

"Then why on earth did you hit me?" He sounded irritable with his clipped words.

"Because, Lord Drivel," Abby replied, her tone uncharacteristically tart. "I recognized you from the day Lady Madelaine and I met you in Golden Square, but I *also* recognize you from the day you and your men dragged Lord Stratmore from this house."

"What's she talking about?" Madelaine's stomach twisted into knots.

Grey shot her a wary glance. "I'm Lord Pearson's equerry."

"And?" Did he expect her to be satisfied with that one line?

"And Lord Pearson was required by the king to come question your father, so I was required as well."

Anger and disbelief curled inside her belly. "You lied to me."

"I didn't. You didn't ask me if I came here, so I didn't lie. Frankly, I didn't relish the idea of telling you I was in the company of men who took your father to the tower for treason and murder."

"What!" Abby's face turned pale.

Madelaine ignored her friend and kept her gaze firmly on Grey. She could understand why he might be worried about telling her, but he *had* lied, and she suspected he was lying to her now. But about what? The only thing she could think of was that Grey knew exactly what his brother and father were. Maybe Grey was a spy for the king as well. But if he was, then did he truly love her or was he using her to trap her father? Her father's words about not trusting anyone, especially Grey, flooded her mind. A tremor ran through her. She'd been a fool, made dull-witted by love.

She pasted what she prayed was an understanding smile on her face. "I can see why you would have been reluctant to tell me you helped drag my father to the tower. I would have felt the same way had the situations been reversed."

"I'm glad you understand." He held his arm out to her. "We need to get going. I don't like traveling in the dark, but I don't think we have time to wait for daybreak."

She hesitated before taking his arm. "Will you recommend Abby to your aunt?" She didn't want to drag Abby into this mess, but leaving her here alone would be worse.

"I vow my aunt will give Abby a position, no matter what."

No matter what? Madelaine's lips trembled as she tried to offer a gracious smile. Did he mean no matter if I'm lying to you, or if I'll betray you and see you hung beside your father? She didn't like this game she was being forced to play. If Grey didn't love her, she would be heartbroken. And if he did, she would also be heartbroken when he realized she had betrayed him. There was no way to win. And no way out. At this point, she just prayed she could keep herself and her father alive.

After Grey secured the horses to Madelaine's father's carriage, they left for Kew. Madelaine wanted to spill her heart out to Abby and see if she had any other ideas, but Abby prevented that scenario when she insisted on riding on the driver's bench with Grey. Grey refused to let anyone drive the carriage but him. Stupid man. They'd end up dead with him at the reins. Red streaked the whites of his eyes and he yawned every few minutes. He had to be exhausted. Abby obviously could see it as well or she wouldn't have insisted on riding beside him. Maybe Abby thought she could grab the reins if he fell asleep?

There was no point in arguing. All three of them were

stubborn people, and they could stand around all day fighting about who should drive and who should sleep and never get anywhere. There was not a minute to waste if she was going to save her father. Madelaine resigned herself to talk to Abby later and then climbed into the carriage and settled herself on the soft cushion. She stared out of the window into the passing darkness as the carriage bumped along the road at a fast-paced clip. Was Grey eager to get her to Kew to help her or was everything that he'd told her a lie?

Dear God! If she and Grey *had* married, and he was a spy, she would have been unknowingly married to a spy, just as her mother had been. The idea of almost living her mother's same fate made her gulp. She didn't want a life of secrets and lies that led to anger and unhappiness. All she'd ever wanted was to be accepted and loved for who she really was. She'd thought she'd found that with Grey.

A warm trail of tears slid down her face. She brushed them away impatiently. She had no time for tears or a broken heart. Later, once her father was released, she'd attend to her heart. Methodically, she thought of and discarded ways to escape Grey. It would be easier now that Abby was with her. Between the two of them, they should be able to overcome him if they could get their hands on his pistol. When he slept, possibly?

She leaned her head against the side of the carriage as despair overwhelmed her, constricting her throat and her heart. When she'd given her heart to Grey she'd never imagined ending up here. Maybe it was her due penance. Punishment for contributing to the problems between her parents that had driven them apart. She squeezed her eyes shut wanting to sleep for a while and forget everything. The rocking of the carriage calmed her like a drug and after a bit, her body grew heavy and her mind began to drift.

Madelaine awoke when her head smacked against the side of the carriage. When the vehicle jerked hard to the left, she gripped her seat to avoid flying out of it then attempted to move toward the window. What was happening? She was halfway across the seat when the carriage hit a bump forcing her to cling to the cushion. Outside, a loud noise boomed through the air. Was that a pistol being fired? Her heart took off in a gallop that matched the pace of the horses.

The carriage slowed and came to a shuddering stop. Momentum threw her off the seat and to her knees. Pain sliced into her bones and vibrated up the length of her body. Before she could rise, the door whipped open, and a strong hand gripped her arm. Grey pulled her out of the carriage and plopped her onto her feet. Her skin tingled with fear. When she didn't see Abby, Madelaine scanned the perimeter of the forest. "Where is she?"

Grey pointed toward the dense woods. "I sent her that way. Someone's been following us." Behind them in the pitch-black dark the hard clopping of horses' hooves rang in the mostly silent woods, then suddenly stopped.

"Damn it." Grey glanced behind him into the darkness. "Follow Abby," he whispered. "And keep running until you reach Cheshire if I don't catch up with you. It's close. Go to the King's Inn and ask for Charlie."

Grey suddenly ducked and yanked Madelaine to the ground with him. She hit the dirt with a thud, the hard, unforgiving ground knocking the air out of her lungs. Bright stars shone in her eyes and a dull ache exploded across her temples.

"We're being shot at," Grey hissed, dragging her belly-first through the dry leaves over hard ground.

"I got that," she murmured. Another shot exploded, the sound making her instinctively cover her head with her free hand.

"Help me," Grey demanded. She pushed with her feet against the dirt to slide toward the tree she made out in the darkness. The pistol exploded again, the noise of the shot amplified by the increasing nearness. A scream wrenched from her throat as bark from the tree beside her hit her in the right cheek. A sharp sting slashed across her skin followed immediately by warm, sticky blood.

"Goddamn it," Grey growled. "I'll kill whoever's trying to kill us."

"Perfectly reasonable." She wiped at her cheek while pushing with her feet and shimmying over the dirt and rough roots of the tree to take shelter behind the large trunk. Just as they settled behind the trunk, Grey slammed his hand over her head and pressed her face, mouth first, into the dirt. For a moment panic clawed at her throat. He was going to suffocate her. Wait. She sniffed. She could breathe. She took a ragged breath and pushed his hand away. "Grey?"

"Stay down." She didn't need to be told twice. Bullets flew nearby, the loud pop of each shot resounding in her ears. The smell of smoke filled the air. She jumped at the cocking click of Grey's pistol. His hand settled briefly on her back as if to calm her. "It's too late for you to run. I'm sorry."

The anguish that filled his voice made her heart jerk but there was no time to respond. She locked her gaze on a lone figure emerging on the path in a sliver of moonlight. Blazes.

She couldn't see his face. He came a step closer, and she clutched at the ground. He had two pistols aimed directly at them.

Grey scrambled to his knees, raised his own pistol and fired.

The man disappeared off the trail leaving only the harrowing sound of a deranged cackle. Madelaine breathed in as all the sounds of the forest crashed around her sensitive ears. Twigs snapped, animals scampered, and somewhere to the right of them a terrible voice rose out of the dark shadows.

"You'll die tonight, Lord Grey."

She trembled.

"Who are you?" Grey demanded as he worked to reload his pistol.

"I'm the man who is going to destroy you."

Madelaine's breath caught in her throat. Instinctively, she grasped the back of Grey's coat. He pushed her away, the hard bark from the tree scraping her legs through the thin material of her dress. He moved directly in front of her. "Let the lady go. She's innocent."

"Innocent?" the man called back. "No one's innocent, young lord. Best for you to understand that right now. If you've turned your back on the fair Lady Madelaine, I suggest you turn round. The biggest threat always comes from those you trust most."

Madelaine's breast swelled with a silent protest. She couldn't see Grey's face and how the man's words affected him, but the muscles of his back tensed under her grasping fingertips. To their left a horse came charging out of the woods without a rider. A distraction. Her mind registered the fact. She turned to the right, Grey did the same. But it was too late. The hesitation had cost them. The stranger stood on the path directly in front of them. She smelled his sweat and the gunpowder that had discharged from his pistols. He stepped closer, his face blanketed by the dark. "Hand over Lady Madelaine," the man growled.

Grey stood and moved out from behind the tree with his pistol aimed at the man.

"I wouldn't shoot if I were you, Lord Grey. I've two pistols. Even if you manage to hit me, I could still shoot her. I don't want to. But to save myself, I will. Don't make me."

Though she thought the tree would protect her, Madelaine shrank further behind the oak and away from the man. Something about his voice struck greater fear in her than the two pistols he aimed at them. Frantically, she searched the ground for a stick to use to throw at the man to distract him and give Grey a fighting chance.

"Move and you're dead," Grey snarled.

"An impasse?" the man taunted.

Madelaine closed her fingers over dirt, twigs and leaves. None of that could help her. Her throat constricted with despair. She couldn't just let Grey die. She pushed herself off the ground to charge at the man. A strong arm clamped around her waist and a rough hand over her mouth.

She was propelled backward through the air by whoever had her. Not more than ten feet away, her feet touched the ground, and she was jerked roughly around. Lord Gravenhurst glared at her. "Don't move a goddamn inch." He withdrew a pistol and crawled silently back toward the oak tree and Grey. Relief threatened to buckle her knees, but there was no time for respite or indecision. Grey would be fine now.

This was her chance to flee. She waivered for a second, caught by wanting to make sure Grey emerged alive and knowing if she didn't go she might not get another chance.

A stick broke beside her, and her heart jumped and then plunged as a figure emerged from the woods.

"It's Abby," Abby whispered.

Madelaine released a rush of breath, all her nerves tingling. "We need to escape."

Abby didn't hesitate or question. She yanked Madelaine toward her and pulled her up an incline. As they climbed the small slope and deeper into the dark woods, branches scratched Madelaine's arms and face and tore at her clothing. Sharp pains pricked her sides as she ran and her breath came in short gasps. At the top of the hill, they stopped by a large tree.

"One minute," she choked out, doubling over. She put her hand out to keep from falling, but her legs gave way. With a thump, she sagged to her knees, her hands splayed atop gnarled roots meandering in all directions.

Abby fell beside her with a huff. They sat for a moment, their ragged breathing the only noise Madelaine could hear until a bang rent the night. She jerked and shoved at the leafy ground to gain purchase. Her heartbeat roared in her ears. Was Grey wounded? Should she go back or forward? Another pistol fired into the silent night. Her heart pumped furiously, indecision making her sick. If she went back, she could be killed or captured. If she went forward, she'd save her father.

"Let's go," she said, her voice raw with pain and sorrow. "We've got to get to Kew and the prince." They barreled through the woods away from the stranger and Grey. The muscles in her legs burned as she climbed the hill, but she pushed herself to keep going. Through the thinning trees, a steep drop opened to her right.

Tears burned her eyes, and her throat ached with the need to cry. She shoved branches out of her path as she ran, the tears breaking through her determination and blurring her vision. Unable to see properly, she wiped furiously at her eyes. A branch caught her in the chest. It knocked the wind out of her and she stumbled on a root.

She teetered at the edge of the cliff, her arms flailing for purchase through the air. Abby's scream of horror followed Madelaine over the side. Jutting trees jabbed into her sensitive flesh as she fell. Her body rolled and bounced off the brush, tumbling until she hit the bottom and struck her head with a thud. Streaks of pain shot through her skull and blackness swept across her vision.

Twenty-Six

"Wake up, Madelaine."

Madelaine batted the noise away and tried to turn from the hot breath tickling her face. Her neck ached and her legs would not move to turn her body. Dear God, she was crippled. Her eyes flew open. The fog of sleep lifted and Grey's concerned face loomed in front of her. Bright stars and moonlight twinkled behind him making him look for a moment like her personal angel. "How do you feel?" His voice shook.

How did she feel? Her body throbbed. Her head pounded, stars danced in her vision, and her throat was so dry she might choke. "Water," she croaked.

Grey pressed a leather pouch to her mouth, his movements stiff and awkward.

Her eyes widened at the bloody bandage wrapped around his arm. "You were shot."

He nodded. "Surface wound. The bullet scraped my arm."

"The stranger?"

All the concern that had filled Grey's eyes drained away. He stared at her with contempt. "Your accomplice escaped."

"My what?" She struggled to sit up, but her hands... her hands were bound. Her gaze flew to her feet. Bound as well.

At least she wasn't crippled. She rolled onto her side and awkwardly made her way up.

Grey watched her with raised eyebrows.

Her head swam and bile threatened to make her lose what little food was in her belly. She started to fall back over, but Grey yanked her all the way into a sitting position and leaned her against a tree. For a moment, she closed her eyes and concentrated on not being sick.

"Leave her alone," Abby demanded from somewhere nearby.

Madelaine inched open her eyes and searched out her friend. Abby sat with her ankles and wrists bound directly across from Madelaine not more than five strides away. "Are you unharmed?"

Abby nodded. "My wrists and ankles ache, *of course*."

Madelaine shifted her attention back to Grey and blinked at the unexpected sight of Lord Gravenhurst as well. "You move with disconcerting silence," she snapped at Lord Gravenhurst.

His teeth flashed with a gleaming smile. "It's a gift. I'm going to comb the woods one more time. You'll be all right here until I get back?" he said to Grey.

Without looking at Lord Gravenhurst, Grey nodded and waved him away. "Go. I won't be foolish again."

Lord Gravenhurst rose and disappeared into the woods before she addressed Grey. "Why have you bound Abby and me?"

He rocked off his haunches and loomed in front of her. "Because, my sweet, you tried to escape me while your friend tried to shoot me."

Madelaine snapped her gaze to Abby, but Grey jerked her head back to him. "Not that friend, my consummate little actress." His hands had come to her arms as he crouched in front of her.

She licked her dry, cracked lips. What Grey said made no sense. "I don't know that man. He was a stranger to me."

Grey reached into his coat and withdrew a paper. "And I suppose you don't know what this is either?"

Her heart sank with recognition. "It's not as it seems."

"It never is, in my experience." The loathing and pain in his voice sliced at her. "You lied to me. You said this was a goodbye letter from your father, yet this is the king's paper. The very one your father was accused of stealing. So what's not as it seems? Are you not a liar or is your father not a thief? Not a traitor? Or are you saying you're not a traitor? A liar? An expert deceiver?"

She swallowed convulsively. She was a liar and now a traitor. "I lied to save my father. He stole that paper to protect England." The words sounded foolish, but she pushed on. "The king's going mad and Father wanted to get the paper to the prince, so he may have proof of the king's unstable mind. Then the prince will be able to rule in the king's stead."

"Your father's the mad one." Grey shoved the paper back into his coat.

"Grey." Desperation made her voice come out high and brittle. "You promised to help me."

He jerked away from her and stood. "That was before your friend tried to kill me. I'd be stupid to deny your part now. You're helping your father and whoever he's working with try to kill the king's men."

Her mouth dropped open at his accusation. "I vow I'm not."

"Don't lie to me anymore, Madelaine." His tone was savage and unrelenting as the hardest steel.

Anger flared in her chest. "You seem to know an awful lot for a mere equerry." Without replying, he twisted and stomped into the woods. Hot tears coursed down her cheeks. She was all the things he accused her of, but what was he? Who was he? He was no mere equerry with all he knew. Doubt and betrayal gnawed at her. Had he used her simply to try to prove her father's guilt? If so, it had worked beautifully.

"Madelaine?"

She shifted to face Abby.

"Tell me what's going on."

Not about to shout all her secrets, Madelaine scooted on her bottom across the ground. Once she was beside Abby, she took a deep breath. "My father was a spy for the king."

Abby responded with a sharp intake of breath, followed by, "And?"

"And he has betrayed the king. Father thinks it's for the good of the kingdom, but I don't know." She hung her head low. "I just don't know," she whispered. "Now I'm a traitor too. And Lord Grey thinks I'm helping Father and some other accomplice kill the king's men."

Abby nudged Madelaine's shoulder with her own until Madelaine reluctantly looked up. "Did you know that man on the trail?" Abby asked, barely above a whisper.

"No." Madelaine shook her head. "I swear I didn't. And Father may be a traitor, but he's no killer."

"I know," Abby soothed. "What are we going to do now?"

Madelaine shook her head but didn't answer. Footsteps crunched through the woods toward them. Grey and Lord Gravenhurst appeared side by side. Grey bent down in front of her. "We will untie you to eat, drink and have a moment of privacy, but then you'll be bound again so we can sleep. Understand?"

She nodded. She wasn't about to argue and cause him to change his mind. He yanked her ropes off her wrists and ankles and pointed to a log. "Sit there. And don't say a word." She sniffed at his command but held her silence.

A few moments later Abby was dumped unceremoniously beside her. Madelaine opened her mouth to thank Grey, but he cut her off. "Don't speak, Madelaine. I've my temper under control for the moment, but one wrong word from you might make me lose it, and I'll not be responsible for what I do to you after that."

She clamped her mouth closed at his ominous words and then ate and drank without speaking. She was almost positive that he'd lied to her too, but blast the brutish man, without proof she dare not risk what he might do.

Madelaine awoke to darkness like she'd never seen. She blinked, confused about where she was. Grey's voice floated to her. She froze as the memories flooded her and made her shake. Cold air licked her bare face and hands but something heavy covered her body, offering a little warmth. She ran her fingertips over the fine material and when she got to the hard buttons, she stilled, a lump forming in her throat. When had Grey covered her with his coat? The small gesture of kindness filled her with hope that perhaps he really did care about her, and made her cringe that she should care at all.

Immediately, she moved to sit up and realized she could. She glanced at her hands and feet. Grey or Lord Gravenhurst had untied her while she slept. But which man had taken pity on her? Her foolish heart wanted to think it was Grey.

Glancing around, she located Abby asleep on the other side of the clearing. Clever. Even if Madelaine wanted to escape, they knew she'd never leave Abby and to get to her friend, she'd have to cross right in front of Grey. She was as good as stuck, unless she wanted to add Abby to the list of people she had betrayed. If she couldn't escape, then she planned to learn as much as she could. She strained to hear what the men were saying but only caught snatches of the conversation.

Inching her body along the dirt, she moved a bit closer and froze when Lord Gravenhurst stood. She squeezed her eyes shut and feigned sleep taking care to breathe deeply.

"So you didn't recognize the man either?" Grey asked.

"No. The woods were thick where we were. The trees and underbrush blocked most light. But even in the shadow of darkness, I could tell his face was not right."

"Yes." Grey's voice held a note of curiosity. "The outline of his jaw and cheek was a misshapen mess."

"I'll tell you one thing for sure," Lord Gravenhurst said. "The man isn't French. Whoever they're working with, it's not the French."

Grey spoke like a man who knew all about the king's spies. Her throat constricted as she waited for them to speak again.

"I got that much from his accent," Grey replied. "Why the hell are you here?"

Madelaine slowly opened her eyes and stared into the dark. She wished she could see their faces.

"You're damn lucky I am," Lord Gravenhurst said. "If it wasn't for me, you'd be dead."

Grey scoffed. "By the time you came to help me, I already had the man on the run."

"Ah, yes. He was running to get into better position to shoot you again."

"Did my brother send you to check up on me and make sure I was doing my job?"

Madelaine dug her fingers into the dirt. Every word Grey spoke crushed her anew. He was a spy. He had to be. What was his job? Seduce and destroy? Her heart thumped heavily.

"I've lost contact with your brother," Lord Gravenhurst said. "That's why I came to you. To see if he'd changed his mind and followed you."

"When did you lose contact?" Concern filled Grey's tone.

"I sent a carrier pigeon to tell Ashdon my lead had come up empty, and when I got no response back as to what to do next, I went back to the castle and tower. He was neither place, so I thought he might have come to find you."

"I haven't heard from him either. Maybe he's waiting for me in Kew. I sent a message to him before I left the inn telling him I was going to Lancashire to get Madelaine and bring her to Kew to stand before the king."

A cry threatened to escape her. She bit down on her cheek and pressed her face into the dirt with horror. He'd never intended to help her. He'd used her and lied to her. He was no better than she was. He was worse.

And to think guilt had been her constant companion since the moment she'd decided to help her father. A big part of that guilt had been because she was betraying Grey. Blast him. He'd never loved her. Her mind shrank away from the truth. She'd thought she'd met a man who really loved her for who she was, or had been, but it was a lie. Her breathing picked up speed, until fear of alerting the men that she was awake forced her to bite her lip. She bit hard until the blood came, and she was able to control her breathing once again.

"Shall I go with you to Kew?" Lord Gravenhurst asked.

"No. Go to my parents' home—that is…I mean Edward's, now. If he's not there, meet me at the tower. I suspect once the king speaks with Madelaine, that's where he'll send her. I'll take her there and then we can either search together for my brother, or if we've heard from him, we'll set out to find whoever it is they're working with."

"Do you think she'll tell you?"

"I mean to try to get the information out of her." Grey sounded tired and reluctant. Or maybe she just wished that was the way he sounded. She didn't know what was real and what was false anymore.

"Seduction again, is it?" Lord Gravenhurst's voice was with filled restrained laughter.

She couldn't decide who disgusted her more—Lord Gravenhurst or Grey. Grey won since he'd broken her heart.

"Shut up," Grey snapped. "And get going. I'm worried about Edward."

"All right." Shuffling feet alerted Madelaine that Lord Gravenhurst was indeed departing. Something was dragged across the dirt before whistling through the air and smacking with a thud against what sounded like flesh. Then a horse's neigh filled the heavy air, followed by the clopping of horseshoes.

Madelaine stood and waited for Grey to face her. No point even trying to run. His outline was close in a sliver of moonlight. She'd never make it farther than to Abby before he caught her and tied her up again.

After what seemed an eternity, he wheeled around and

stared. After a moment, he walked toward her, his boots crushing leaves and breaking twigs as he came near. He stopped before her, his scent flooding her, his heat invading her space. "How long have you been awake?"

A dam of hurt inside her broke. She pulled her hand back and slapped him. In a flash, he slid his hand around her neck. He flipped her onto her back with a thud. He loomed over her, the weight of his body crushing her, his heartbeat drilling into her chest.

"You never loved me," she said on a half-broken sob.

He cupped her face and squeezed. "Don't you dare say that." His voice shook. "I loved you. I risked everything wanting to believe you. I would've broken my Goddamn vow to the king for you. Forsaken my honor and my family to protect you." He released her chin and dragged her up by the arms. When they were both standing he shook her until her teeth rattled in her head. "I offered you my heart and you offer me lies."

"You speak of lies!" She wrenched free, shaking from head to toe. "You lied to me, *spy!*" She flung the accusation at him, too hurt to say anything else.

A guttural cry came from him. He yanked her to him. He dove a hand into her hair and pulled her head back. "That's right. I'm a spy. Now you know my secret. I work to serve our king while you work to bring him low."

Despite her determination to stay brave, tears stung her eyes. "I work to save my father. That's all I strive for."

"And what of the man who tried to kill me? The same man who no doubt you and your father conspired with to help kill Lord Pearson. What was the plan? Kill all the king's spies one by one, until there was none of us left to fight against your father's plan to overthrow the king?"

Madelaine's shoulders sagged with weariness. "I do not

know the man who shot you."

"Lies," Grey spat with bitterness.

"I know nothing of any plan. All I know is my father believes the king is going mad, and he did what he thought best when he took the list the king made. Father intended to give it to no one but the prince, and only for the prince to use it for England's good."

"Since when is a son stealing a throne from a father good? Tell me, my sweet, what good can come of that?"

"I don't know." She pressed her fingers against her throbbing temples. She was so tired, too tired to fight, almost too tired to carry on. "I did what my father bid me. What choice do I have? He's my father, and I owe him fidelity."

Grey clamped a hand around her arm like a vise. "Not at the sake of your own integrity."

She tried to wiggle her arm out of his grasp, but he held tight. His blunt words drove into her heart and stirred thoughts she'd had herself, but it wasn't so simple. "He stood by me for years when my mother tore me down with cruel words and treatment." She used her free hand to wipe away the inconvenient tears. "If it wasn't for me, they'd have never had their last fight, and my mother would be alive. So you see, I owe him fidelity as my father *and* as payment for the wrong I've done."

Grey released her arm at the same time he shoved her away. "Every time you speak, I wish my damned heart would stop speeding up for you, but it speeds and it speeds. Maybe only death will cure me of you."

Her heart wrenched at the pain in his voice. She reached for him with an unsteady hand.

He pulled back as if her touch was poison and stared at her. "I welcome an early death if that's my only release from you." He spun on his heel, his shoulders hunching forward. "No more talking to me unless I ask you a direct question. You're an excellent actress, and I no longer wish to be a gullible fool." He pivoted toward her. "Now wake your friend. We're leaving for Kew."

Unnerved by the fierce anger vibrating in Grey's voice, Madelaine rushed over to Abby. She kneeled down to shake her, but Abby was already awake. "No need. Your voices woke me."

Madelaine pressed her hands to her cheeks, an embarrassed flush heating her. "How much did you hear?" she whispered.

"Nearly every word, I suspect. Enough to know he still loves you and enough to know you are a fool. Your father is not the bloody saint you've built in your mind."

"No plotting," Grey thundered and stormed toward them. Before Madelaine could utter a protest, he shoved her onto the front seat of the carriage and within seconds he deposited Abby into the carriage.

He took the seat beside Madelaine and clicked his tongue at the horses. As they started to move, the sun crested over the trees and shone the first rays of light down upon them. The first thing Madelaine noticed was that Grey held the reins so tight his knuckles were white. She turned her gaze to his face where the muscle in his jaw ticked steadily. She didn't know what to say, but she felt she had to say something for her deception, though he'd deceived her as well. "Grey, I—"

"Not. A. Word," he said, cutting her off. "One word and I'll pull over and stuff my handkerchief in your mouth and bind it closed. Understand?"

She nodded and clamped her mouth shut.

Twenty-Seven

A chant ran through Grey's mind as he drove the horses and gripped the reins so hard the leather bit into his skin through his gloves. *Damn. Damn. Damn.* He kept the litany going, afraid if he stopped the doubt would creep in again. Doubt about Madelaine's guilt would make him weak. Doubt about her part in this disaster would make him break. Doubt that he could take her to the tower knowing it would mean her death would make him let her go.

Damn. Damn. Damn. If he focused on the chant and the steady, fast clop of the horses' hooves, he could keep his uncertainty away. His ploy worked for the better part of three hours, but then she fell asleep and slumped against him, soft, trusting and beautiful. Her flowery smell invaded first his nose, then his mind and finally his heart. He stared alternately between the road and her beautiful lips. Then the road and the long, slender slope of her neck. Road and black eyelashes against creamy skin.

Blast! He jerked the reins hard to the right as he almost drove them off the road. Madelaine moaned and stirred beside him, but she did not wake. No indeed. She snuggled into him, and then she flopped onto her side, her head landing in his lap and her slender fingers curling around his thigh. A sigh escaped her.

He tensed every muscle. Longing and need shot

through him. He'd never allowed himself to need anyone after he'd failed to gain his father's love, and then Madelaine had come along. She'd stolen his heart with her uniqueness and her goodness. Anger stirred. What goodness? It was a lie.

Or was it?

Was she merely a pawn in her father's game? When he recalled her kisses, the way she looked naked, and the love he thought they'd shared, he wanted to believe in her. What would doubt do? Give her a fighting chance to escape? Would she abandon her father if she saw the king and understood what was at stake?

She moved again, her hair falling like a thick blanket over her face to hide it. He resisted the twitching urge to push the tresses behind her ears. Pain tore him apart from the inside out. Maybe this pain was his punishment.

He'd given a vow to the king and then he'd turned around and been prepared to abandon his vow. What sort of man was he? Grey laughed bitterly. He'd set out to prove himself worthy of his father's trust and he'd proven just the opposite. Old, familiar self-pity poured through him, but he ruthlessly reined it in.

"Grey," Madelaine whimpered in her sleep.

"Hell." He was too weak to deny himself one more touch. Reaching down, he stroked her hair, then gently pushed it away from her face. Even scratched and dirty she was beautiful. No chant would help him now. Thoughts pounded him from every direction. He glanced down at her again. This was the last time he would allow himself to touch her. "You break my heart," he whispered and then looked up to drive them toward Kew.

The palace at Kew sprawled across a bright green lawn with rows of lush trees surrounding the palace on either side. Any other time, Madelaine would have longed to sit in the grass occupied with nothing more than memorizing every detail of the beautiful building. Holding herself stiff on the carriage bench careful not to brush her leg against Grey's, she dismissed the beauty around her. She needed to concentrate, but fear made it hard.

The sun cast fading rays on the lawn to join the developing shadows and cool breeze. Night was fast approaching. The darkness would certainly suit her mood better than the sunshine of the day had. It had been humiliating to wake with her head on Grey's lap, but when he never said a word, nor spoke to her the entire trip here, her humiliation had grown.

The carriage rumbled down the stone drive toward the entrance. Once Grey pulled it to a stop, stable hands emerged to hold the horses. Grey dismounted, then held his hand out to Madelaine to help her down the three steps.

She blinked. It was hard to believe he was willing to touch her. With hesitation, she grasped his hand. He curled his fingers around hers, and his heated touch seeped through the material of her gloves. Her heart swelled. She nearly blurted out the love that was still inside of her. She looked down, afraid one glimpse of her face would reveal to Grey how she still foolishly felt about him. To be fair though, love would take time to kill if it could even be obliterated at all. Of course, the noose they intended to put around her neck would take care of her feelings soon enough. She gulped at the thought.

Grey helped Abby out of the carriage and then led them both up the steps to the front entrance. To Madelaine's utter astonishment, the door swung open to reveal a butler and Grey's Aunt Helen, dressed resplendently in gold.

Grey's mouth dropped half-open. Obviously, he'd not expected his aunt to be here. "Aunt Helen?" Grey swooped through the door and dragged Madelaine behind him. Did he think she would try to escape even now?

Once they were inside and the door was shut, the angry voices somewhere close were impossible to ignore. Madelaine studied Grey's aunt. She looked composed except for her furrowed brow.

"What are you doing here, Aunt Helen?"

"The queen requested I come to be with her, but I'm to leave today. The king wished all but family members and the doctors to leave."

Grey nodded, his gaze straying from his aunt to the sitting room down the hall where the arguing voices appeared to be coming from.

Helen gestured to the bags sitting against the wall. "I was just about to depart. My driver is pulling my carriage around now." Helen smiled at Madelaine. "It's good to see you, my dear. I was worried about your abrupt departure from Court. No one seemed to really know where you had gone. Is all well?"

Grey pushed Abby toward his aunt, which saved Madelaine from having to lie. "This is Abby," Grey said. "She needs employment and comes highly recommended. Can you take her with you as a personal favor to me and employ her?"

Helen raised her eyebrows but nodded. "It just so happens I need another lady's maid. My current one has gotten so old she sleeps all the time. This will be perfect. Louisa can train you and eventually you can take her place. We can discuss the particulars in the carriage, if this suits you?"

Abby nodded then bit her lip as she focused on Madelaine.

Tears constricted Madelaine's throat. Was Grey sending Abby away now so she would not be with her when they took her to the tower? She was grateful. She loved Abby and if she could save her from harm then she would. "Go, Abby." Madelaine's voice hitched. "There's nothing you can do for me."

"But, Madelaine—"

"I insist. Besides, I don't think Lord Grey will allow you to stay. Will you, my lord?"

He shook his head, settling his gaze, cold as ice, on her. "I'm afraid not."

She sucked in a choked breath but said nothing. Whatever he'd felt for her was gone, if it had ever been truth. Loneliness swallowed her.

Abby flung herself at Madelaine with a sob. "My lady," she moaned.

"Grey," Helen said, her tone halting. "Might they have a private moment to say goodbye?"

"I suppose it can do no harm."

Madelaine gave Helen a grateful smile as the woman put her arm around Madelaine and led her and Abby out the door. Helen's carriage was already in front, her coachman waiting. He rushed past them and came out carrying the first of many bags.

Abby squeezed Madelaine's hand before addressing Grey. "Might we have our moment now, my lord?"

"Certainly. I'll just help with the bags."

The notion was absurd, but Madelaine held her comment. Helen kissed Madelaine's cheek. "I'll see you soon, dear."

Madelaine doubted that, unless Helen attended hangings or by some miracle, it didn't come to that. "Thank you for your kindness," she said, barely managing to hold in the sob threatening to escape.

"Nonsense. We ladies of the Court must stick together," Helen said, before sweeping into her carriage and shutting the door.

Abby immediately grabbed Madelaine by the arms. "You must listen."

Madelaine nodded.

"I know you think you were the wedge that drove your parents apart, but it's not true."

"Don't try to make me feel better," Madelaine said.

"I'm not." Abby released her and unclamped the gold locket around her neck. She handed it to Madelaine. "Open it."

Madelaine frowned but complied. A picture of her father was on one side of the locket beside a picture of Abby's mother. "Oh, Abby. I'm sure he thought of you as a daughter as well."

"No, Madelaine." Abby's voice was pained. "He didn't, though he knew he was my father."

"What?" She had to be misunderstanding.

"You didn't drive a wedge between your parents. My mother did. And then I did. Your father and my mother had an affair, and I was the product, born three months before you."

"I don't believe you." Madelaine's stomach clenched.

"It's true. Your mother didn't hate you. I think she hated the life she was stuck in. Ma told me when your mother found out about their affair, your father promised her she could leave." Abby snorted. "Men and their promises. He said they would live apart as if they were not married, but she could reap the benefits of his money and title. Then your mother found out she was pregnant, and he wouldn't let her go until he was sure she wasn't having a son."

Bitterness filled Madelaine's mouth like the tartest of candies. She sucked her cheeks in. She'd thought her father had adored her from the day she was born. He'd been the one person who'd loved her unconditionally, until her mother had died and he'd wanted her to change. She'd been wrong. He'd not loved her from her birth. He'd wanted a son. Hoped for a son. Was there nothing about her life that had been as she thought? "Why didn't he leave after I was born?"

"Your father had left on a trip. He was gone for near a year, and Ma told me when he returned you were coming up to your first birthday. You were already reckless like a boy. He instantly loved you and refused to let you go. He told your mother to leave, but she stayed because she loved you too. She didn't hate *you*. She hated *him* and the fact that you loved him."

Tears blurred Madelaine's eyes. Her mother had stayed for her. Yet she'd taken her anger with Father out on her. Father had wanted a son, gotten a girl and did really love her. She'd been born an oddity, but Father had loved that. It suited him because he'd wanted a son. In a way it made sense. She dashed a shaking hand over her eyes. If only she'd known her mother had loved her a little, life would have been so much easier. If she'd known her mother had stayed for her, she would have done everything in her power to be the daughter she wanted. Behind her, footsteps clomped down the stairs.

"Time to go, miss," the coachman said.

Abby gripped Madelaine in a fierce hug. "I love you," she whispered in Madelaine's ear. "Save yourself. Your father has lost his way, but he wouldn't want you to go down with him."

Madelaine watched the carriage drive away and take the only person she could really trust out of her life, probably for good. Her knees felt like cream, but she managed to stay upright. Grey stood silently beside her; close enough so she couldn't run yet not so close they might accidentally brush against one another. Thoughts swirled in her head. She couldn't save her father, but could she save herself?

Twenty-Eight

Madelaine bit her lip with uncertainty. Even if she could bring herself to abandon her father, would Grey let her escape? She harbored no illusions that she could get away from him unless he willingly let her go. If he had really loved her he might, but if he'd been using her, she didn't stand a chance. How to ferret out which was the truth. Before she could decide, he faced her and stared for a long moment like he might stare at a snake set to strike.

"Come." He took her hand and pulled her toward the door.

She didn't resist. What was the point? His look of disgust said everything. He'd never let her escape. As they entered the house, angry voices drifted toward them. Grey paused midway down the hall as if trying to decide whether to take her with him or leave her here. Making up his mind, he tugged her down the hall and stopped in front of a door that led into what appeared to be the king's audience room.

Madelaine gasped as she peered into the room. His Majesty's hair stuck out in spiky patches from his head. He seemed nothing like the orderly king she was used to seeing. His clothing was a wrinkled mess and a shadow of stubble covered his normally rosy cheeks. And his eyes... She shivered at the sight of his wild eyes. He looked angry enough to kill someone. He struck out at one of his pages while the other one advanced toward the king.

"You deceived me," the king said to the room full of men. His voice was barely above a whisper, but the dark, unyielding tone held the promise of retribution. The king's sudden change of demeanor made the hairs at the back of her neck rise.

She tensed, expecting someone to demand she and Grey leave at once, but no one spared them notice. She tried to capture Grey's attention, but his focus was riveted to the scene before him.

The king advanced once again on the servant. "You cannot keep me here."

In answer, the taller of the two pages reached out to restrain His Majesty.

The king slapped the man's hand away. "You dare to touch your king!"

The page's eyes widened as if he was at a loss for what to do. A man with a shock of white hair moved cautiously toward the king, a needle gripped in his hand. "Your Majesty," he implored.

The king jerked toward the man. "You cannot make me eat! You cannot make me sleep!" The king pounded his fist against the chair he stood in front of. "Where is my queen? Where are my daughters?"

"Please, Your Majesty." The physician, because surely he was one, tried to inch toward the king once more.

"Stay back," the king hissed. "I don't trust you. You lured me from my home with lies."

Madelaine's blood ran colder than the wintery waters of the river by her house. Beside her, Grey tensed. Was the king now insane? Was this what her father feared would come to pass and why he'd betrayed his liege? She swayed with the emotions of relief and pity.

"Your Majesty," the physician tried again, his tone dropping close to a whisper. "No one wants your throne."

A strangled laugh escaped the king. "Everyone wants my throne, right down to my eldest son."

Madelaine nearly gasped. How right he was. She didn't think the king was insane. He was sick, and he was angry because he knew many of those he needed to trust most were untrustworthy. Would turn on him. As her father had.

The king swung toward the door, and Madelaine hurried to scurry out of his way and the fury blazing from his eyes. He stopped in his tracks, his gaze widening for a moment as he assessed her, and then he inclined his head, once again every bit the strong leader, the noble king.

Her heart squeezed for him and what he must be enduring. To be unsure of your own mind and then to think you could not count on those around you to stand by you, her father included. She swallowed the lump in her throat.

"Lady Madelaine, to what do we owe this honor?"

She dropped to a curtsy, unsure what to say. When she stood, it was as if the tension of the room had drained away. "Your Majesty, I'm being escorted back to the castle by Lord Grey." She regarded Grey. Let him tell the king she was a traitor, she'd not name herself so, even if it was now true. She loved the king, and if the decision had been hers alone to make—the truth struck her. By God, she would have never made the decision her father had.

"Lord Grey? I thought not to see you for some time. Do you not have business elsewhere?"

"Yes, Your Majesty, but Lord Pearson charged me with seeing Lady Madelaine to her home and then back to Windsor first."

The king's mouth turned downward. "Come to my chambers. It seems we need to talk." Command given, he exited the room, his gold-threaded robe flying out behind him. Grey grabbed Madelaine's hand and pulled her behind him, and within a few moments she sat in a room and wrapped her hands around her waist to hide their shaking.

The king swept his gaze over her. "You have your mother's eyes, rich amber like the finest tea in the kingdom."

"You remember my mother?" Madelaine asked in surprise.

The king smiled, the act transforming his haggard face and making him appear almost healthy for a moment.

"But of course. I remember all beautiful women, but especially one who served my queen with such graciousness."

Madelaine caught her breath. Thank goodness the king didn't know how her mother had really felt about the queen. That would not help Madelaine to plead her case now. "My mother was very pleased to serve you," Madelaine said, glad she could craft an answer that was not a lie.

The king leaned back in his chair. "I know. I admired your mother. It's why I married her to your father. I thought to do her a service, but I fear I dealt them both a disservice."

"I never knew you suggested my father marry my mother."

The king chuckled. "I didn't suggest it, Lady Madelaine. I commanded it, which is what kings do. Yet sometimes, even kings make a mistake, which is why I surround myself with wise men to counsel me." The king focused on Grey. "Lord Grey, see Lady Madelaine to the library and then you and I shall speak."

Madelaine stood and curtsied. Her eyes watered with emotion. His Majesty was obviously very astute when he

was in his right mind. Anger flared in her. Her father was
wrong. The king could rule, if strong men would help him
as her father should have kept doing. Had he tried? Had he
tried and the king refused? If not, she couldn't fathom what
had turned her father against the man he'd served his entire
life.

❦

Madelaine stayed in the seat where Grey had deposited her
with instructions not to move a muscle. But the more she
thought things over the more she decided she had every
right to know what her fate was going to be. She eyed the
closed library door and then the closed door that led to the
king's private chambers adjacent to the room she sat in.

One thing she'd grown good at over the years was
eavesdropping to learn if her parents were fighting. That
way she knew when to try to avoid her mother. She could
hear secrets outside the thickest door so long as there was a
crack at the bottom. The ornate door to the king's private
chamber with the sun filtering into the library from the
bottom was no different than the less expensive door in her
home.

She rose, careful not to make a sound, and crept over to
the library door where she turned the lock to ensure she
would not be discovered. Then, with a thudding heart, she
tiptoed to the adjacent door and sinking to her knees,
pressed close to the ground and the space where the sun
shone in. She couldn't see anything but that hardly
mattered, she knew the king's voice.

"Terrible business," he said, paper crinkling on the
other side of the door. Had Grey given the king back his
paper? Was her father now condemned? Was she con-

demned?

"Sire, what do you wish me to do?" Grey asked.

Drumming—fingers on a table perhaps—came from the room. "I don't know. I cannot ignore my own culpability. I knew Stratmore was angry when I forced him to leave France. He was sure Sutton was alive, and he could save him. I was sure I'd lose one more good and loyal spy if Stratmore stayed to try to find Sutton. Even after we found Sutton's ring, I could see the anger toward me in Stratmore's eyes. I think he blamed me for Sutton's death. He thinks I made the wrong decision, but damn it—"

The bang on the other side of the room was followed by the sound of something—glass—which fell and shattered. Madelaine inhaled a steadying breath and pressed closer to the floor.

"I didn't make the decision alone. I sought your father's advice as I will now seek your brother's. I know my limitations with my malady."

"Of course, Your Majesty."

A chair squeaked, and suddenly the shadow of shoes fell by the door. Madelaine rested her hands against the floor, held her breath and prepared to jump and run to her chair if the door started to open.

"I want you to vow something to me, Lord Grey, as I made your brother vow and your father before him."

"Of course."

"If you see that my mind is too addled to rule, and your brother agrees, I have written my express wishes that my son rule as regent. The paper is locked in the gold box in my room at Windsor. Your brother knows the box. Take the paper, get it to the prince, and I've no doubt he'll be happy to take my throne from me. Vow this to me."

"I vow it," Grey swore, his voice trembling.

Madelaine rose on shaking legs and made her way to the chair. She sunk down and buried her face in her hands, struggling to contain her sobs for her king, her father and herself. Father was a fool. He'd betrayed his king when there was no need, and she'd willingly gone down with him. Maybe she was a fool too.

What had driven Father's choices? Had he done it because of an old anger about being forced to marry Mother? Or maybe the king forcing Father to leave a comrade he didn't know for certain was dead? Had that been the thing that turned Father? It didn't matter. The deed was done. Even now, Grey was probably telling the king of her part. Soon she'd be locked in the tower.

Twenty-Nine

*G*rey picked up the paper and walked to the fireplace. He threw it into the flames, watching as it curled inward, flames blackening the paper into ash. It was gone, but what he had to do lingered heavy in his mind. He turned his ring, examining his thoughts.

Damn, Madelaine. He hated her, yet he still loved her. He could slightly understand if it was only a matter of her compulsion to help her father if he was attempting to protect England, but he couldn't understand her helping her father or anyone else to kill another spy…Had she known of that? Would she continue her father's plan—whatever the hell it was—if Grey kept her part secret? Even now, was she plotting a way to escape and meet up with the man who had tried to kill him in the woods?

"Grey?" The king's voice startled him out of his musings.

He swung around and tensed at the sight of Gravenhurst standing by the king's side, the king's pallor shockingly white. Grey clenched his jaw. He couldn't afford to become so distracted by Madelaine that he didn't notice when someone entered a room, or that the king needed him.

"Ring for my doctor," the king commanded.

Gravenhurst immediately rang the bell on the table by

the king's chair and within seconds, the king's physician swept into the room. "My lord?"

"I feel dizzy." The king's voice rasped through the room.

The physician gestured to Gravenhurst. "Fetch the pages. Your Majesty, the bloodletting is making you dizzy. You need broth and rest."

Two pages rushed into the room and took the king by either arm to lead him toward the door. The king turned at the threshold and looked at Grey and Gravenhurst. "I leave matters in your capable hands for now. Keep me updated."

Grey bowed and when the door shut, he spoke. "Did you find Edward?"

Gravenhurst shook his head, his face paling until the scar on his forehead stood out like a beacon. "What's wrong?" Grey demanded, fear making his tone sharper and louder than he'd intended.

Gravenhurst slid a hand into the pouch at his side and withdrew a soiled, crumpled piece of paper. Gravenhurst unfolded the note. Fear inched along Grey's skin. The missive was the size they used to send messages between each other by carrier pigeons. Gravenhurst looked up, his eyes burning bright. "I never made it to your home. I stopped halfway to water the horses and check in with one of our contacts who maintains a pigeon house for us. A bird had just arrived with this note and a small package."

Grey took the note from Gravenhurst and scanned the scrawl. *Lords Grey and Gravenhurst, I have Ashford. I'll trade his life for that of the lovely Lady Madelaine. Meet me on the 8th at the Dockside Warehouse. Come alone or Ashford dies.*

Today was the eighth. Grey frowned, trying to order his thoughts. "How do we know whoever this is, really has Edward?" There was much more he cared to ask, but all he could focus on right now was that one question. Later, he'd ask questions with his pistol pointed at the person he was questioning.

Gravenhurst thrust a ring toward Grey. Even before looking at the word "allegiance" engraved on the inside, he knew it was Edward's. Ice thickened his blood as he stormed toward the door Madelaine was sitting behind. He plowed through the entrance, a loud bang announcing his arrival.

She scrambled to her feet, her eyes wide with fear. Gripping her by the arms, Grey wanted to shake her until her teeth rattled in her head. Instead, he forced himself to release her, wincing at the sight of her reddened flesh where he'd held her too tightly. Blood roared in his ears as he tried to find a calm he didn't feel. How could she be part of this folly? Had he been so wrong about her? Could she really be plotting to kill the king's spies? All the evidence suggested so. His jaw ticked uncontrollably, until he had to press a finger against the tick to try to stop it.

He stood on legs that felt shamefully weak, unable to look away from her. Anger curdled in his belly. He moved a hand toward her, and she flinched away then spoke in a rush of words. "Grey, I'm sorry. I know how upset you must be."

"You cannot begin to fathom." He was drowning in her amber eyes. "I'm looking at you, but I don't know you. And I realize now I never did." Just like he'd never known his father. There was too much pain inside of him. He had to once again find a way to convince himself he needed no one.

Madelaine struggled to stay awake, but the dark night and the clopping of the horse's hooves worked as a sleeping draft on her exhausted body. She felt herself slumping forward, too tired to hold herself upright any longer. Her head rested against Gravenhurst's back, her foggy mind cruelly reminding her that Grey hated her so much he couldn't even bring himself to touch her. With a sigh, she closed her eyes and drifted.

A crack of thunder in the sky awoke her sometime later. She sat up and stretched her aching muscles, blinking at the sight of large ships around her. Water clapped rhythmically against the side of the docks as the horses walked down the cobblestone road and a ship's horn blew from somewhere on the sea. "Why are we at the docks?" she demanded, not that she was in any rush to join her father in the tower.

She didn't expect Grey to answer. He'd not spoken to her since asking who she was. Her heart ached at the memory of his words. "Lord Gravenhurst, are you now ignoring me as well?"

He pulled up on the reins and stopped the horse. Grey came to a halt beside them so that he faced her. "We're here to meet your friend. He wants you, in exchange for my brother's life, and I intend to deliver you."

"What—?" she choked out in astonishment.

Grey's lips curled back over his teeth. "As if you weren't expecting something like this. Don't worry, sweet Madelaine. I'll hunt the two of you down once my brother is secure, and bring you and your accomplice back to the tower to join your father in death."

Her belly twisted into knots of dread. "I don't know this man. I don't have an accomplice, and if you deliver me to whoever this is, you need not bother to come looking for me. I'm certain I'll be dead."

"Stop lying." Grey's voice was flat, as if he couldn't be bothered with what she'd just said.

Something in Madelaine snapped. She shoved back from Gravenhurst, threw her leg over the horse and jumped. She was running the second her feet hit ground. Maybe before. Behind her, shouts commenced followed by the urgent pounding of feet against the stones. She didn't know where she was going, but she'd not allow Grey to deliver her to a lunatic. Her breathing came hard as fear and the blood pumping through her veins drove her around the corner of the main street and into an alley.

Up ahead, music poured into the alley from an open door and the raucous voices of sailors almost made her cry. If she could make it into that tavern maybe she could lose Grey. *And then what?* She didn't know. But what choice did she have?

"Madelaine!" Grey roared as she dodged through the open door of the tavern and stopped short at the sea of faces pressed into the small room. This was perfect! She maneuvered around small tables crowded with drunken men while frantically searching for another way out. Tankards of ale clanked against tables to mix with the rumble of voices.

"Look, mates, an angel's floatin' by," a deep voice slurred before a hand grabbed her bottom and squeezed. With a yelp, she tried to bat the man's hand away, but he only squeezed harder. A chorus of raucous laughter erupted from the table, and a new fear, a fear of unspeakable horrors crawled up her flesh. She scanned the faces around the table, her heart hammering painfully and her gaze landed on the only man not smiling. He was dressed as every other man here, but his hair, pale like the moon, was secured neatly back at the nape of his neck. His cheekbones were high, his nose patrician, and his full lips pressed together distastefully. He was her best hope. Pleading with her eyes, she prayed he would help her.

His fist slammed into the face of the man groping her, the man's hand dropping with a howl as he fell out of his chair gripping his nose. Madelaine squeezed her eyes to make sure she'd not imagined things. She'd not seen the blond man move until he'd thrown the punch. The table grew silent, but the noise continued around them.

She stiffened as her savior rose and towered over her. He placed an arm around Madelaine's waist while glowering at the men around the table. "Don't any of the rotted lot of you have sisters back home?"

Madelaine blinked in surprise at the man's impeccable, lordly accent.

He glanced down at her. "Can I buy you a drink?"

She darted a gaze toward the door. "No, but you could tell me if there's another way out of here."

The man pointed toward the back of the tavern. "Leads into an alley that will take you straight to the main road."

She nearly fainted with relief, started to thank him, then saw the gleam of a knife blade on the table. That was just what she needed if she should come face to face with any more ruffians. Or if she had to threaten Grey to escape him. "Is that your knife?"

"It is now." He flashed a smile. "I won it in a game of cards."

She tugged at the large ruby ring on her finger, the only jewelry she wore. "I'll trade you this ring for that knife."

The man eyed the ring for a moment then grabbed the knife and discretely handed it to her hilt first. "Seems like a good trade." He leaned in close. "You better sheath it in front of this lot. They get jumpy when they see a woman with a weapon."

She slipped the knife into her boot and let her skirts drop. "Thank you." As she started to move away, he grabbed her arm, her heart lurching.

"Do you need help?"

Expelling a sigh of relief, she shook her head and forced a smile she didn't feel. She'd not drag one more person into this mess. Besides, she didn't know this man. "I just need to go." She stared pointedly at her arm.

Once released, she wound through the crowd and made her way to the back door. Her heart thumped, all her nerves tingling. When the door easily opened, she stepped into the dark night and pressed a trembling hand to her forehead. She glanced left to right and saw no one. She needed to flee right now and get as far away from the docks as possible. Once she was hidden, she would figure out the rest.

Quickening her steps, she ran toward the street that led to the main road and raced around the corner. She needed to find a horse or carriage to steal. Let them add theft to her other crimes. Did it really matter? Laughing bitterly, she swiped at the tears leaking out of her eyes then stopped to pull out her weapon. As she bent to retrieve her dagger, an arm swooped around her waist jerking her off her feet. The unmistakable cold, hard metal of a pistol pressed into her forehead. "Got you."

Thirty

Madelaine bucked her body, trying to break the hold on her.

"Don't make me hurt you, Madelaine," Grey whispered in her ear. She stilled, fear clogging her throat. Immediately, he set her on her feet. Gravenhurst eyed her piteously. Warmth spread up her neck and over her face. Gads! What a time to be embarrassed. But she was. Grey's hatred of her was palpable in his voice, his stance, the way he flinched when he touched her.

He pointed the pistol ahead of him. "Will you kindly move that way?"

As if she had a choice? She started to walk but picked up pace when the pistol nudged her in the back. "Faster, sweet. I wouldn't want your dragging feet to get my brother killed."

By faster, Grey meant run. They raced down the street, pains jabbing in her side. A large building loomed at the end of the lane. Grey stopped and jerked her to the side of the road behind some crates.

He shoved her to the ground, her palms scraping against gravel. An involuntary hiss of pain escaped her, and she automatically cradled her hands to her body.

Grey dropped down beside her, his thigh brushing hers, his tense, bulging muscles pressed hard against her leg. He turned to Gravenhurst who crouched at her other side. "You approach from the left, and we'll come from the right. I expect he'll be shooting at us."

Gravenhurst nodded. "One of us should make it."

"I'll wait here," Madelaine offered with a nervous laugh.

Both men eyed her without a smile.

Grey grabbed her by the arm and hauled her up. "Stay behind me unless you want your friend to accidentally shoot you when he's aiming for me."

She nodded, too afraid to point out, once again, that whoever this man was, he was no friend of hers. They crept through the darkness, darting around trees and winding their way toward the right side of the warehouse. As they reached a door, a shot rang out in the night seeming to come from somewhere above them in the building.

"Damn it." Grey gripped her arm once again. "You better hope Gravenhurst is all right, Madelaine."

She tried to wrench free, but he tightened his fingers like bands of steel. "I do hope he lives, and if you want to live you need to release me and concentrate on killing whoever wants to kill you."

He frowned. "I suppose of the two of you, your accomplice is the bigger threat since you're not armed." He gripped her chin. "One false move and I'll shoot you."

She nodded. Finally, he was going to concentrate on protecting himself. Later, she'd allow herself to wallow in the fact that he had no qualms about shooting her. She sniffed.

"Stay by my side," he whispered and moved up the dark stairs. As a board creaked under his weight, Grey bit back a curse and threw his arm out in front of her. He touched the next step with the tip of his boot. When no noise followed, he motioned her forward. At the top, they rounded the corner and followed the glow of light coming from the end of the hall.

As they crept along, gooseflesh rose on Madelaine's arms. Without a sound, Grey stopped in front of the door and raised his pistol.

She gulped back a cry of fear. A man, his face so hideously burned that she recoiled at the sight of the mangled flesh, stood facing the door with one pistol pointed at Grey and another pointed at Grey's brother's head. Lord Ashford was bound by rope to a chair, a rag stuffed in his mouth and secured with more rope tied over his parted lips. He immediately bucked in his chair when he saw them. The wood scraped against the hardwood floor, but Lord Ashford's efforts did him no good. Angry sounds poured from him, impossible to understand because of the gag.

"You took long enough, Lord Grey."

The muscle at the side of Grey's jaw ticked furiously, but he simply inclined his head. "My apologies. I'm here now to make the trade."

"Send Lady Madelaine to me, and then I'll send you Ashford."

A scream of protest rose in Madelaine's throat. God, how he must hate her.

"I think not," Grey replied.

She had to lock her knees not to crumble with relief.

The scarred man responded by shoving his pistol hard into Lord Ashford's temple. Grey's brother groaned in response. "I'm afraid I'll have to shoot your brother unless you do what I say."

Madelaine watched Grey. His lips move in a silent swear. Why wasn't he sending her over? Did he truly not want to? Did he still care for her despite what he believed about her?

He glanced between her and his brother, the tick in his jaw becoming so pronounced she counted ten beats. He loved her still, or at least he didn't want her to die! Her heart squeezed with happiness at the same time fear rose up and nearly gagged her. If Grey didn't make the trade, he would surely die trying to save his brother. And maybe his brother would die too. Maybe they'd all die anyway, unless she did something. She could save Grey and his brother if she was brave enough and cunning. She'd rather risk everything than nothing as she'd done her entire life.

Praying she didn't end up shot in the back, she bolted across the room, her muscles tensing and her eyes seeking an opening.

Betrayed yet again. Grey locked gazes with Edward as Madelaine flew across the room. Edward leaned his chair far to the right. As it started to topple, Grey pulled the trigger of his pistol, blood roaring in his ears. Something sharp skimmed across his shoulder and caused his pistol to jerk to the right. Pain, like the quick slice of a knife, yet different, flared across the path of the wound and coursed down his arms. His finger numbed instantly. He dropped his pistol by his feet.

He stared in horror as the stranger aimed one of his pistols at the floor where Edward lay. Grey's legs propelled him forward to charge the man. Madelaine's scream tore through the hum in his head, but a deafening explosion drowned the sound of her fear and all else out.

Madelaine and the man crumpled like puppets whose strings had been abruptly cut. Grey reached them as her head hit the ground with a sickening thud, lolling back, her eyes fluttering shut. He focused on the man. He lay perfectly still, face up and eyes open wide with death. A dagger, jeweled at the hilt, protruded from the man's neck. Good. The bastard.

Grey swayed on his feet, disbelief making the room swim. Madelaine hadn't betrayed him. She'd saved him. He scrambled to his brother and jerked off the gag.

"Forget me," Edward barked. "Help her. Help Lady Madelaine."

Rushing back to Madelaine, Grey ripped off his cravat and pressed it to her side where he thought the blood was coming from. From outside the door, noise reached him—a tap followed by a drag. Someone approached. He laid Madelaine against the ground, lunged toward the dead man and yanked the dagger out of his neck.

Grey was on his feet when Gravenhurst appeared at the door, pistol aimed forward and dragging his right leg behind him. Gravenhurst stopped in the doorway, his pistol falling to his thigh and his mouth dropping open. "What happened?"

"Madelaine saved us. Do you know of a physician around here?" Grey demanded, releasing the dagger by his brother's head and scooping Madelaine into his arms. Her head lulled back like one of his sister's childhood dolls. A chill swept over him. She couldn't die. He'd been wrong. So wrong.

He pressed her close as he strode toward the door. Her coldness made his chill feel like a fever. He stopped in front of Gravenhurst. "Is there a physician near?" he asked again.

"Milsford Street. One block over and turn right. He's in the white house. Tell him Gravenhurst sent you. We'll be there shortly."

Grey wrapped his arms tighter around her body as he

ran down the stairs and out into the night. "Don't die on me, Madelaine." But with each step, the coldness of her skin increased, making his throat tighten with fear of losing her.

He could see the white house at the end of the street, yet the harder he ran, the greater the distance to the house seemed. Driving himself forward like a man possessed, he reached the house, and kicked open the door instead of slowing down to knock.

A man, dressed in his retiring robe, barreled into the entranceway with a brass candleholder gripped in his hand. "Who the bloody hell are you?" the man demanded, his gaze sweeping over Grey but settling on Madelaine.

"Gravenhurst sent me."

"Not again!" the man growled and set the candleholder on a side table. Grey didn't have time to sort out what the man meant. He hoisted Madelaine up so the physician could see her blood-soaked side. "Will you help her? She's been shot."

"I can see that." The man pushed Grey down the hall toward an open door. "My office," he murmured to Grey's raised eyebrows.

"Put her there." The physician nodded toward a table. "And then move out of the way if you want me to work."

Grey laid her gently down, his stomach clenching at her pasty skin and her blood covering his hands as he brought them away from her. He stared at her, unable to make his legs carry him away. He loved her. And he'd almost handed her over to death. She must have seen it. Known it. And had sacrificed herself to save him. Shame and disgust rolled in his belly.

"Get out of the way!" The physician shoved him aside.

He stumbled backward as the man frantically ripped her dress from her body. Grey trembled so violently he had to lean against the wall for support.

Soft fingers curling around his arm startled him. He looked down into the concerned face of a pretty brunette. Her blue eyes blinked at him. "The best way to help her is by allowing my husband to work," the physician's wife said.

Grey tried to comprehend where the woman might have come from, but his mind felt fuzzy as if he'd drank too much. God! He wished he were sloshed and this were a bad dream. Seeming to understand his shock, the woman took him by the arm and guided him out of the room, talking to him in low tones as she led him down the hall and into a study.

He fell, more so than sat, into the chair she offered, and when she poured a full glass of whiskey and pushed the glass toward him, he didn't hesitate to drink. The woman hurried from the room, and he dropped his head into his hands. He loved Madelaine, probably since the day he'd met her in Golden Square. He was an idiot. He should have listened to her. She wasn't conspiring to murder them. She'd saved them.

He rubbed his stinging eyes and sat back in the chair. He'd failed her. He should have married her the minute he'd found out her father was in trouble. He should have protected her. Was he to forever be wrong about those he loved, losing them one by one as punishment for being an idiot?

Without her, he was nothing. He turned the ring on his finger, duty warring against love, desire against honor. Without hesitation, he yanked the ring off his finger and threw it against the window. It smacked the glass then clattered to the ground. His father had probably just flipped over in his grave. Grey loathed himself for his betrayal, but he'd live with the guilt. What he could not live without was

Madelaine. And now, he'd do everything in his power to protect her.

He sat that way, unable to move, unwilling to think about anything but willing her to stay alive, until the creak of the door alerted him to someone entering the room. Edward dragged into the room and slumped into the chair opposite Grey. With his lip cut and swollen, his eye blackened and a nasty gash on his forehead, it appeared he had put up a fight before being captured by the man in the warehouse. Edward's eyebrows puckered together, a deep crease appearing between his eyes. He glanced around the room, got up and came back toward Grey holding a towel.

"Your shoulder is bleeding."

Grey looked in surprise at his shoulder. He'd forgotten a bullet had skimmed him there. He slipped off his shirt and surveyed the wound. Not bad. Not nearly as dangerous as Madelaine's wound. Pouring some of the whiskey from the crystal decanter onto the towel, he blotted the towel against his shoulder and clenched his teeth against the pain. Once he felt the wound numb, and decided it was clean enough, he shrugged his shirt back on and regarded Edward. "Did you know that man?"

"I used to." Edward reached for the decanter with a trembling hand and sloshed whiskey into Grey's glass. Edward pulled the glass toward him, picked it up and downed the liquid. "How is Lady Madelaine?"

Grey struggled to control his emotions. "The physician is working on her."

"The physician is called Plumbe."

Grey didn't give a damn what the man's name was as long as Madelaine lived. "Tell me about the man in the warehouse."

Edward's gaze fell to the desk. "His name was Sutton."

"I thought he was dead?"

"Apparently not." Edward leaned forward. "It seems Sutton didn't appreciate being left for dead in France."

"He told you that?"

Edward nodded. "That and more. He told me how he planned to kill me. I was to be burned. Since Father had been our leader, Sutton felt I deserved the most painful death as his heir."

Grey couldn't suppress the shudder that took hold of him. "And Madelaine?" Grey wanted to kill the man with his bare hands. It was too bad he was already dead. "What did he want Madelaine for?"

"He wanted to kill her in front of her father, so Stratmore would die twice as he deserved." Edward shrugged. "Sutton's words not mine. According to him, Stratmore would suffer watching his daughter die, suffer knowing his name was disgraced, and then get what he deserved by being hung."

Grey gripped the desk, his knuckles turning white. "How the hell did he plan to get Madelaine into the tower, kill her, and then take her body back out so no one would know she was dead before Stratmore was killed?"

"I don't know." Edward scrubbed a hand across his face then winced when his fingers brushed his bruises. "Sutton was deranged. Broken mentally. And God help me, Grey, I can't help but wonder if the king hadn't commanded Father to pull Stratmore out of France if we could have saved Sutton, *and* Stratmore, *and* Pearson."

"Pearson? Did Sutton kill Pearson?"

Edward reached into his coat and threw something on the desk. The gold ring rolled for a moment before it stilled. Grey didn't have to pick it up to know it was Pearson's. "Sutton set Stratmore up." Grey's mind whirred with the realization.

"Yes."

"But how did he know what Stratmore had done in taking the king's list? How did Sutton know his plan had a chance in hell of working?"

"That's a good question. The obvious answer is he had someone on the inside of the castle working for him. Someone in a position to hear things. Any ideas?"

"Not a bloody one." Grey rubbed his throbbing temples. "I'm having a hard time thinking on this right now."

"It's all right. I sent Gravenhurst back to Windsor to try to ferret out who Sutton had working for him."

"What about Gravenhurst's leg? And getting the bullet out?"

"There's no bullet. He twisted his ankle when he dodged the bullet meant to kill him. He'll be like new in a few days. What about you?"

"What about me?" Grey would never be the same again if Madelaine died. There would be no "like new." He would rather be dead too.

"What are you going to do? What do you plan to tell the king about Lady Madelaine?"

Grey's heart thudded so hard he had to resist the urge not to rub at his chest. "What did Gravenhurst say?"

Edward's eyes narrowed into slits. "He said to ask *you*. That he had no knowledge of what Lady Madelaine did or did not know in regard to her father and his stealing of the king's paper."

Grey would kiss Gravenhurst the next time he saw him. Well, maybe not kiss him, but drinks and thanks were certainly in order. True, he'd not told Gravenhurst in words what Madelaine had tried to do to help her father, but surely his friend had judged her by Grey's actions toward her. Yet, Gravenhurst was allowing Grey to decide for himself what should be done. It was akin to giving his blessing and promising silence.

"Lady Madelaine had no knowledge that her father stole the paper from the king. She's innocent. And I plan to tell the king exactly that."

Edward's eyebrows rose. "You're sure?"

Grey nodded.

Suddenly, Edward reached across the desk and clasped Grey by the hand. "Father would be proud of the man you've become."

Grey pulled his hand free. "Father would not be proud. I misjudged Madelaine, and my error may yet mean her death." He glanced toward the door, willing Plumbe or his wife to come with news.

"You love her." It was a statement rather than a question.

"I do. And if she lives and will have me, I intend to marry her. Yet one more reason I would have given Father to be disappointed in me."

"He wouldn't have been disappointed."

Grey scoffed with disbelief. "You said yourself Father thought wives were weakness for spies."

"He did. But he also took a wife and loved Mother very much." Edward smiled. "As I said before, the two of you are more alike than either of you ever saw. It's why you didn't rub along well."

Grey stood and moved to the door to peer down the hall. Impatience clawed at him. If he didn't have some news soon, he'd go mad. "I always thought you were more like Father." He stared out the window into the street shining with the first rays of daylight.

Edward came up behind Grey and grasped him on the

shoulder. "Not in matters of the heart. Where that's concerned, I am practical where you two are romantic. If I ever take a wife, it will simply be because I must produce an heir. But only if you don't produce one for me."

It was on the tip of Grey's tongue to reply, but Plumbe appeared in the hall, and Grey raced toward the man. "How is she?"

The man's eyes cast downward and Grey's heart plunged. The physician wiped his hands on his bloody apron before raising his gaze to Grey's. "She's alive for now. I can't say what tomorrow will bring."

Thirty-One

$\mathcal{G}$rey's hand shook as he reached out to caress Madelaine's cheek. Behind him, he heard footsteps and glanced back to see the physician.

Plumbe came to stand by Grey. "The bullet passed cleanly through her side."

Grey nodded as he stared down at her and watched the rise and fall of her chest. The motion, though ragged, gave him hope. "What's the danger?"

"Infection. I sewed her up as best as I could. Now we wait and hope fever doesn't kill her. I'll leave you alone for a bit. But I'll be down the hall if you need me."

Grey pulled a chair close, sat, and took her hand. It was clammy and warm. He lay his head on the edge of her bed and pressed his cheek into her palm, remembering what it felt like when she'd caressed him with tenderness. Emotion clogged his throat. Christ! If she died and left him, he'd never bloody well forgive himself, not that he was sure he could anyway.

He lay there for hours, listening to her breathe, glad to know she still was with him. Sometime after the shadows had shifted in the room, the door creaked open. Grey lifted his head to find Edward standing by the bed. "How is she?"

"No change."

Edward shifted from foot to foot then cleared his throat.

"I should probably depart for Kew, but if you need me to stay with you…"

"No." Grey sat up fully. She'd live or die without Edward here, and if she died, Grey would rather not have an audience when he fell apart. "The king will want to hear a report. You should go. When she's better, I'll bring her to Windsor to marry her, if she'll have me."

Edward squeezed Grey's shoulder. "I'll pray for her."

"I thought you didn't believe in God anymore."

Edward shrugged. "I don't. But I could be wrong, so just in case, I'll pray for Madelaine."

"Thank you," Grey choked out.

As Edward slipped out the door, Plumbe's wife slipped in carrying a tray laden with bread, cheese, wine and some cuts of meat. Grey's stomach rolled in protest. "Thank you, but I'm not hungry."

She tisked. "Your woman will need your strength when she awakens. It won't do for you to be too sick to care for her. You need food and sleep."

"What's your name, madame?"

"Rose. Call me Rose."

Grey smiled. "Rose, I'll eat, but I won't sleep."

She thrust the tray at him. "We shall see. You've dark circles under your blood-shot eyes. Once your belly is full, you'll sleep."

He'd never be able to sleep until Madelaine was out of danger, but he didn't bother to argue further with Rose. She was being kind, and he would not repay her kindness with ungraciousness. As he ate, he half-heartedly listened to Rose talk. Her voice grew low, and he was unable to keep up with her words. Her lips moved, but he heard no sound. His head bobbed to the side, and several times he jerked upright.

He awoke confused. The room was dark, except for a splash of moonlight streaming through the window. The bed was soft enough, but small and he needed more blanket. He tugged on the scratchy wool tucked under his chin, and when he did, his shoulder screamed in protest and his awareness came back like a gut punch.

Jolting from the bed, he raced out the door and into the dark hall of the house. Which room was Madelaine's? Everything appeared different at night. He threw open several doors before he found her room, almost stumbling in his eagerness to see her. She moaned, and he fell to her side and laid a hand on her brow, only to draw back in horror at the fiery heat of her skin. Fever! "Plumbe!"

Within seconds, Plumbe barreled through the door with Rose on his heels.

"She's on fire," Grey said as he stroked her forehead.

The physician placed his hand on Madelaine's forehead, his lips pressing together. "Fever's taken hold."

"Please do something."

"Rose, bring the water basin and sponge."

His wife hurried out of the room and came back within moments with a basin sloshing with water. She dipped a sponge into the water.

"Let me," Grey said, his voice a desperate thread-bare plea.

Rose handed the sponge to him. "Start at her head and work down."

He nodded, rolled up his sleeves, and gently brought the sponge to her forehead. She moaned and thrashed about, making him have to grit his teeth together on a string of curses.

He wiped her face, then her long slender arms and legs. "Stay with me," he whispered, not caring that Plumbe and his wife could hear him. Grey continued to sponge her until his arm burned from the motion. Pausing, he placed a hand against her forehead. "God damn it. It's not working."

Rose came toward him and took the sponge. She dropped it in the basin and eyed him with sympathy. "No more for now."

"What then?" He tried to focus with his blurry vision.

"Pray," Rose said simply. "Ask God to be merciful and bring your woman back to you."

As Plumbe and Rose shuffled out of the room, Grey dropped to his knees and prayed. "Please," he whispered. "Nothing matters but her. *I love her.*" He squeezed his eyes shut, and swallowed, lest the tears overcome him. But what the bloody hell did it matter if they did? He opened his eyes. Tears trickled down his face. Tears he'd never allowed himself to shed as a boy, or a young man, or even as a man when he'd felt alone. It felt bloody foreign but he cried. For her, he cried. "Take me. Me."

The litany continued until his throat was raw, and he couldn't speak another word. Exhausted, he rose and pressed his head against her chest to hear the steady thump of her heart. Whatever barriers he had once erected, Madelaine had destroyed. He wanted only to love her for the rest of his life.

Heat rolled across Madelaine's body like a raging fire, burning her face, neck, arms, legs, destroying her from the inside out. The merciless heat would not let up. It engulfed her, making her want to scream and come out of her skin.

Was she asleep or awake? Was this a nightmare or her reality? She could see nothing but rolling waves of brilliant red. The flame called to her, beckoned her to come closer. She tried to resist, but the flames slithered toward her like a stealthy snake and coiled its heat around her ankles to drag her, screaming and thrashing, into the turbulent flames.

Fire crackled around her, the smell of smoke infusing her nose and lungs. She coughed and her eyes watered but strangely now that she stood in the heat, peace came over her.

When next she was aware, her skin felt odd, not burning and melting off her bones as it had before, nor mildly warm as it had most recently. She looked around, really looked into the flames, and they parted before her. Eagerly, she walked through the towering wall of red that danced on either side of her some twenty feet up. When she came to the end of the burning tunnel the flames gave way to lush green grass, a brilliant blue sky and the edge of a river bank.

She knew this river. Scurrying to her knees and then her belly, she leaned over the edge of the embankment and dipped her fingers in the cold water. The coolness made her throat ache. She cupped her hands and drank greedily, handful after handful, of the water, until it dribbled down her chin and she almost choked on her last mouthful. God that felt good! She splashed the water all over her body, crying out at the momentary release from the pain. After a while, she no longer felt the burning, and the thirst in her throat was quenched.

She flipped onto her back and slid her hands behind her head to stare at the huge, fluffy clouds above her. A bird flew in circles high up in the sky, and if she strained very hard, she could hear the flapping of its powerful wings as it soared. She wanted to fly free like that bird. She squeezed her eyes shut and wished with all her heart, and when she opened them she was hovering in the air, not flying, but looking down at herself lying in a bed with rumpled sheets half over her bare legs.

She gazed at herself in wonder. She didn't remember her legs being so pretty. Her skin appeared almost translucent, and if she stared long enough she thought she could make out her bones underneath her skin. *Impossible.* Her eyes wandered to her face, skin bloodless and shimmering with sweat, her cheekbones protruding. She reached down to run a finger over a sharp cheekbone and smooth back her tangled, matted hair when her eyes suddenly opened.

Her amber eyes stared back at her with all the understanding of a mother's love. She reached out, her hand touching the hand of her other self that lay in the bed. "Come," her other self whispered. "Time to go."

She turned hand in hand with the other her to fly away, but a man standing at the foot of the bed caught her attention. His eyes, blue like the sky before a winter storm, looked straight into her soul. She knew him, but couldn't recall his name, yet her heart squeezed at the sight of him.

She loved him.

He squeezed his eyes shut as she stared, his shoulders shaking with a tremor that vibrated the air she floated in. A dark-haired woman moved to stand beside him and put her hand on his shoulder. He opened his eyes, and the shimmering tears made Madelaine want to cry.

She didn't want him to be so sad, so broken. She glanced up at the bright sky calling her then to her right to tell the mirror her to go, but her other self was no longer there. "Stay," a voice—her mother's voice—said to her. "I'm proud of you. I love you."

Cool tears trailed down Madelaine's cheek. She glanced once more at the sky, took a deep breath and locked her gaze on the man. She'd stay. He needed her.

Thirty-Two

Madelaine slept for long periods, waking briefly when someone would press a drink or broth to her lips or a cold sponge to her body. She hated that sponge! She tried to draw away from it, but hands always gripped her and kept her locked in place.

Sometimes she would float out of her body, but she didn't fly again, nor did she see her other self. Mumbling voices spoke near her, but she couldn't make out what they said. One voice, deep and melodic, started to become clear word by word. *Need you.* Was the first thing she made out. Then sometime later, a day? A week? One minute ago? *Love you. Stay with me.* She nodded, her head as heavy as her grandfather's old steel sword she once tried to lift off the wall where it hung.

That voice stayed with her all the time, speaking soft words. Sometimes it almost felt as if the words caressed her hands, cheeks and brushed across her lips. There it was again! A brush across her lips. She shivered in response and forced her eyes open.

Stormy blue eyes stared back at her, widening then filling with tears.

"Grey?" she croaked, thinking that was his name.

"Madelaine?" His voice cracked, and his head dropped beside hers. His heavy breathing filled her ear and his warm breath tickled her lobe. "Thank you, God." His face came back into view and he pressed his lips against hers. This time she knew exactly what that feather-light brush was and her blood stirred to life once again.

The first couple of days it was all she could do to stay awake long enough to put a string of words together to form a sentence. She would fall asleep in the middle of her comments or listening to someone talk, but whenever she woke, Grey was always there, whispering he loved her and telling her that everything would be all right and asking for forgiveness.

She wanted to believe everything would be all right, but as her memories returned, fear trickled in and tears began to flow down her face.

"What's wrong?" Grey clutched her hand. "Do you feel unwell? Shall I fetch Plumbe?"

"No." She shook her head. "You keep saying it's going to be all right, but the last thing I remember is that you hated me and wanted to trade me for your brother's life. Then I thought..." she averted her eyes, embarrassed, but she had to know. "Then I thought perhaps you really did care, and I couldn't let you or your brother die to save me."

He pressed his head to her chest, his hands coming to either shoulder. "I love you. I was wrong to ever believe you could be part of a plot to kill the king's spies. I'm so sorry."

She shook her head, dismayed at the pain in his voice. "You weren't wrong to distrust me. I was trying to help my father get the list to the prince. I didn't see what else I could do. I should have told you. Trusted in you."

"I understand why you didn't. I've had time to think about it while you've been sick. If my father needed my help to save his life, I would have done everything in my power to save him." Grey brushed a hand over her hair. "Your loyalty is but one of the reasons I love you, Madelaine. Can you ever forgive me?"

Forgive him? She reached out and traced her fingers over the stubble on his jaw. He wanted her forgiveness? Her heart exploded with joy. She'd been too afraid to hope. She forced herself to hold his gaze. "Do you love me?"

His gaze opened wide. "Don't you know?"

She shook her head. Call her obtuse, but she wanted no misunderstanding between them. He ran his fingers over her collarbone then moved slowly to her lips where he rubbed his thumb back and forth, her heart racing with each delicious sweep of his finger. His hand moved to her neck and gently grasped her there. "So beautiful," he murmured and pressed a kiss to her neck then trailed kisses back up to her lips. "I love you," he whispered, before kissing her.

Her lips parted immediately, their tongues mingling to stroke, explore and reignite the spark that had never died. Heat kindled low in her belly and spread through her limbs until she was panting.

Grey broke the kiss off slowly and pulled back. He tucked a bit of her hair behind her ear. "I won't have you getting too worked up until you regain all your strength." The wicked smile of promise that curled his lips made her heart hammer. She wished nothing else was pressing on her mind, and that she could stare into his eyes the rest of the day, but she had to ask the questions she needed answers to. "What about the king and my father and me? And who was the man in the warehouse? Why did he want to kill you? And me? And—"

Grey pressed a finger to her lips, his eyes crinkling in a smile. "I'll answer every question you have but one at a time and while you eat."

"Eat?" She wrinkled her brow. She didn't care about eating at this moment.

Grey motioned to the doorway and Rose—she recognized the woman from an earlier lucid moment—scurried in with a tray laden with a bowl of steaming soup and a glass of clear water. Madelaine's stomach growled.

"Your stomach agrees with me, even if your head doesn't," Grey said, taking the tray from Rose and dipping the spoon into the soup. "Open."

She complied, but only because she was suddenly famished. As she ate, he spoke about the spy Sutton, and how he'd come to be at the warehouse and wanted to kill the other spies as well as her.

The truth was horrible. She pressed her lips together. The man had done wicked things but look what had happened to him. He'd been abandoned. She couldn't help but feel sorry for him.

"Madelaine?" Grey sounded concerned.

"Sorry." She shook her head. "I was just thinking how sad it was." She took the napkin Grey offered her and patted her mouth.

"Only you would find a deranged man's tale sad. Need I remind you, he tried to kill you?"

"You need not. I bet you feel sorry for him too. You just don't want to admit it."

Grey held her gaze. "I wanted to kill him. But you already had. I hate him for what he did, yet I do feel sorry for him."

Madelaine sighed. "Thank you for being honest."

"You're welcome. Anything else?"

She didn't particularly want to address the "anything else," but they couldn't ignore it. "So now you know for certain neither my father or I were plotting to kill anyone, yet my father stealing the king's list remains a fact. And it remains a fact that I tried to help him."

Grey set the tray on the table beside her bed. "The king knows nothing of your part."

She frowned. "Are you not sworn to tell him?"

Grey nodded. "I am. And I vowed to put him above all else and everyone else as long as I served him as a spy, which is why I can no longer serve him."

"What?"

He took her hands in his. "When you're well enough, we'll make our way to Windsor and marry, if you'll have me?"

She wanted to nod, but what was his condition? "What is the sacrifice?"

"Sacrifice?" His brow wrinkled as if she spoke in a foreign tongue.

She glared at him. "Don't act as if you don't know what I'm speaking of. At what price will our marriage take place?"

He squeezed her hand. "A price I am more than glad to pay."

She averted her gaze to their intertwined hands, suddenly fearful of what he was going to do. Something was missing. "Where is your ring?"

"I no longer wear it." He held her gaze without blinking.

"You would turn against your vow for me?" Her body shook with her question.

"I already have." Passion laced his words. "I love you. You mean more to me than my honor or my life."

"Grey." She leaned forward and pressed her lips to his. "I cannot allow that. We'll tell the king what I've done and beg his mercy for myself and my father. It can be no other way."

He shook his head. "I've already told the king you had no knowledge of what your father did. And I told my brother the same thing. I swore you were innocent. If you say otherwise now, you risk my life for lying to the king."

Her breath caught in her throat. "You've trapped me."

"Yes." He did not look the least bit ashamed or repentant. He cupped her face. "I had to. I'm sorry." He didn't sound sorry. "I love you, and I couldn't risk your demanding to save my honor by risking your own neck."

Warm tears slid down her face. No one, not even her father, had ever put her first above all else. She loved Grey with a fierceness that scared her. "What will you do if you're no longer a spy?"

He kissed her on the head and then rose. "Perhaps I'll really try my hand at being an *equerry*. Or maybe I'll just spend the rest of my life making sure you're happy."

"Won't you miss serving the king?"

"I will." His tone was grave. "But how can I serve him when I've broken my vow to put his concerns above all else?"

She twisted her hands together at the look of sorrow on Grey's face. "You did it for me. You won't break your vow again. I know you won't. You're the most honorable man I know."

"My sweet, Madelaine." Grey brushed a hand against her cheek. "I would break my vow again if it meant saving you. And if we are blessed with children, I would break my vow to protect them first as well. No. I can no longer trust myself to keep the vow I gave."

She rose up to her knees, her head spinning with the sudden movement. Grey caught her behind her waist and held her against him. Her fingers curled into his side. "Your father surely felt the same way. Surely, he put you and your brother, sister and mother before the king."

Grey's brow furrowed. "I don't know. I don't know if he ever had to make a choice between us and the king."

Desperate to make things right for him, Madelaine's words came out in a rush. "I want to marry you, but I vow I won't unless you promise me you'll speak with your brother before you tell the king you no longer wish to be a spy. You don't have to tell your brother about what I've done, though I wish you would. Simply ask him if your father ever had to make hard choices, learn what your father did and then decide your path."

After a moment, Grey nodded. "All right. Once we get to Windsor, I'll speak with my brother. Now rest, if you feel up to it we'll travel back tomorrow. I don't want to delay any longer. *And* I've an idea for how we can perhaps convince the king to be lenient toward your father."

"Tell me!" Madelaine's heart thumped wildly against her breast.

"After you sleep. And not before."

Two days later Madelaine's stomach churned as Grey led her through the corridors of Windsor castle and to his aunt's apartments. She was to wait with Helen while he went and talked to his brother. She'd been the one to prod him into this action, but now that they were on the course, she was worried. What if Grey's father had never been in a situation where he had to put his family over his vow?

She pressed a hand to her queasy stomach. That was silly. Surely he had and Grey would soon learn he could serve the king and be the husband he wanted to be at the same time. Still, she worried now that she'd convinced Grey to talk to his brother, the possibility was there that he could change his mind about marrying her.

She struggled to silence the annoying voice of doubt as Grey knocked on his Aunt Helen's door. When the door opened and Abby stood smiling on the other side, Madelaine stepped into the room and grasped Abby to her. She pressed close to Abby's ear. "Are you being treated well?"

Abby nodded. "Lady Helen is wonderfully witty and has been very gracious to me."

"Thank you, dear," Helen chimed coming through the short hall that led to the sitting room.

Madelaine regarded Helen with an amused smile. "I can see how it is you've come by so many castle secrets."

Helen patted her hair, which was swept up into a flattering updo. "I do have excellent hearing. And it so happens I've recently heard a new bit of salacious gossip."

"Are you going to share it?" Madelaine was all too glad for the happy moment. Today may yet end in tragedy if the king refused to listen to Grey's suggestion regarding her father, so she'd linger in bliss as long as she could.

Helen grabbed Madelaine by the hands. She blinked at the unexpected contact. "Grey wrote that the two of you are to be married tonight!"

Madelaine's jaw dropped open. She forced herself to close it. "Tonight?" Her pulse raced ahead. She wanted to marry Grey, but *tonight*? She said the first thing that popped into her mind. "We've no priest."

Grey smiled indulgently at her. "We do. My brother has arranged it *and* called in a favor to get us a special license."

"But you haven't even spoken to your brother yet," she said, all too aware that Abby and Helen were looking between her and Grey as they spoke. "What if you change your mind, depending on what he says?"

"I'll not change my mind, Madelaine." He turned to his aunt. "Might I have a private moment?"

"Hmm?" His aunt looked riveted to her spot.

Grey sighed, his exasperation unmistakable. "I'd like a moment alone with Madelaine, Aunt. Don't you and Abby have something you need to do?"

"Of course," Helen exclaimed, a blush staining her cheeks. "We can get Madelaine's flowers and gown ready."

"My what?" Madelaine exclaimed.

Helen's answer was an airy wave of her hand as she and Abby departed the room.

Grey slipped an arm around Madelaine's waist and drew her near. His heat and warmth instantly calmed her racing heart. "Nothing Edward says will change the fact that I want to marry you tonight. Whether I leave my brother and feel I can continue as an *equerry* or seek a new profession, I will do it with you as my wife. And I refuse to wait to marry you and chance you concocting some scheme to save me from myself."

"Bravo!" Helen cried from the other room.

Grey grinned, and Madelaine couldn't help but smile back. He loved her just as she loved him, heart and soul. No matter what came next, they had each other. He pressed his lips to her ear. "Besides, the king might be more amenable to pretending to pardon your father in a fit of madness if he understands that I will personally ensure my father-in-law stays away from Court and behaves."

She pressed her head against his chest and curled her fingers around his arms. "I've no right to ask this of you."

"You did not ask." He pulled back and kissed her full on the mouth. She returned the kiss with abandonment, not caring that Helen and Abby might be watching from the other room. The way he kissed her stole her breath and left her body feeling as if she floated. Heat crept over her and thoughts of the two of them entwined in each other's arms as they had been before filled her head. It was a good thing they'd be married tonight. She refused to sleep in any bed but his, though propriety would demand otherwise if they were unwed. When a throat cleared in the other room, Grey laughed and brushed his finger over her swollen, throbbing lips. "Get ready for our wedding while I'm gone."

She nodded, pressing her fingers to her lips. "Hurry back."

"Always, for you," he said before leaving.

She traced a finger over her lips. She was loved by a man who adored her for her oddness. How surprising and wonderful. She wished her mother was still alive. For the first time ever, she felt something she was doing—marrying Grey—would have made her mother proud, and she was doing it in her own unique way.

Grey had been so sure Edward would tell him Father had always put the king first. When his brother told him otherwise, Grey could do no more than stare, while trying to comprehend that he had truly not known his father and deal with the sadness and regret that swelled within him.

Edward leaned back in his chair with a smile. "Why the astonished look? Did you expect to hear otherwise?"

"I counted on it. I'm uncertain what to do. I'd planned on telling the king today that I'm retiring from the circle."

Edward's eyebrows furrowed. "Why the hell would you do that? We need you more than ever now, after losing Pearson and Stratmore. The king may let Stratmore live, after hearing what you've told me, but you know the man will never serve with us again."

"I know it." Grey circled his shoulders around and tried to ease some of the tension that mounted every time he thought about Stratmore's life being in his hands. Would Madelaine forgive him if he failed to convince His Majesty to allow her father to keep his life? The thought of her enduring such pain because he had not succeeded sat like a lead ball in the pit of his stomach.

"Grey, you've not answered me."

"What did you ask?"

Edward leaned forward and placed his palms on the table. "I asked why you would think it necessary to quit the circle."

"I was worried that if the choice came to the king or Madelaine, I would choose Madelaine." No sense in burdening Edward with the knowledge of what Grey had already done.

Edward nodded. "I won't pretend to understand. I'm not like you and Father. I've never met a woman who's made me doubt the king should be first in my life. Yet Father managed to serve both the king *and* be a good husband. I've no doubt you'll manage it as well."

Grey sagged in his chair at Edward's unrealized blessing. Marrying Madelaine would not have changed no matter what Edward said, but knowing he was treading the same path his father had managed made Grey feel more secure. He rose and glanced down at his brother. "I want to speak with the king before my wedding tonight. What of his mind? How was he when last you saw him?"

"Completely well and reasonable. I say we go to him now and beg Stratmore's case. The king's consent to let Stratmore live would probably make your bride very happy."

"We?" Grey raised an eyebrow. "You'll go with me? I would not have thought you could stomach asking the king to pardon Stratmore when the man was going to try to help put the prince on the throne."

"I do it for you." Edward's voice was low. "You are my brother, and I'll always stand by you. I believe you lost this." Edward held Grey's ring to him.

Grey took it and grasped Edward. To hear his brother say he would always stand by him was like hearing words he'd always longed for. He'd wanted to hear them from his father, but his father *had* cared, and now Edward and he had the kind of relationship he'd longed for but could never quite grasp because of his hurt. Father had to be smiling on them. Today was full of surprises. Pray God, they were all good.

Thirty-Three

Madelaine ran a finger over the gown she wore. It was beautiful with the encrusted pearls in a pattern of leaves. It fit a bit too tight, but the lush robe of silver brocade that billowed from her shoulders would help disguise that.

"Thank you for allowing me to borrow your wedding gown, Helen."

Helen clasped Madelaine to her. "I always hoped for a daughter to wear my dress. Oh, my dear." She sniffed. "You look exquisite."

Butterflies fluttered in Madelaine's stomach. She had delayed putting on her wedding gown when Grey had sent word pushing the ceremony time back, but now that the gown was on, if someone dared to knock on that door and give her another note, she'd storm the castle and drag Grey to the altar.

Helen patted Madelaine's arm. "Everyone in my family is always late. Wipe the furrow from your brow and remember that. Tardiness doesn't mean Grey has changed his mind."

"I'm not worried. I trust in Grey's love." The truth made her smile.

"It's good to see you so sure and happy. I'm off to the chapel," Helen said. "Abby will see you safely there."

Madelaine nodded, wishing her father would be with her as she got married, yet knowing the futility of the wish.

Once she and Abby were alone in the room, Madelaine faced Abby. "I vow to you that if Father is pardoned, I will do everything in my power to ensure he treats you like a daughter, but I want you to know I always wished you were my sister, and no matter the history, I'm glad you are."

The two of them clung together for a moment, hugging, laughing and alternately sniffing, but Abby scolded Madelaine when a tear slipped down her cheek. "Don't you dare cry and ruin how beautiful you look. Things will work out. I firmly believe it. No doubt Lord Grey has already set everything to rights."

Madelaine nibbled her lip. "I hope so. I wish I could have gone with him to speak with the king."

"Well, you couldn't." Abby placed a wreath of flowers on Madelaine's head. "He thinks only to protect you, and you need to let him."

A few minutes later, they entered the courtyard before the chapel, and Abby paused by the fountain. "I'm so happy for you. And I know your father—"

"Our father," Madelaine corrected in a very low voice.

Abby frowned, but jerked her head in a nod. "He'll be happy for you too, once he hears about your wedding, of course."

Madelaine blinked back tears at the reminder that while she was dressed in finery and about to marry the man she loved, her father had counted on her to save him and she had failed. It didn't seem right to marry Grey today when her father might hang tomorrow or the next day, yet marrying Grey would not change her father's fate.

"Ready?" Abby asked.

Madelaine nodded and drew in a deep breath as she

followed Abby to the chapel door.

Shifting from foot to foot, Grey stood at the front of the chapel beside his brother and tried to quell his impatience. Getting the king to agree to pardon Stratmore had been much easier than Grey had expected. No one outside of their small circle, and the two guards assigned to watch Stratmore at the tower, knew of his incarceration, and Grey suspected that fact, along with the king's guilt over Sutton, helped decide the king's mind. Those who had known Stratmore was in the tower now thought he'd been cleared and was free to go home. Of course, Grey was now responsible for making sure Stratmore never attempted to come back to Court, but he had no worries about that.

He would do anything for Madelaine, and when he'd told Stratmore that he was not going to hang, the man had alternated between relief and fear the king would make another bad decision that would cost another man his life. Stratmore's fears had calmed when Grey told him the king had put cautionary measures in place in case his mind became muddled again. Then Madelaine's father had become angry when Grey had given him the news of his impending marriage. Stratmore was a smart man. He'd agreed to come rather quickly when Grey told him he could either give his blessing to the wedding, or Grey would pretend he had and not release the man until after the wedding was over.

Stratmore glared at Grey from the back of the church. Grey didn't mind the duke's anger. The most important thing was how happy Madelaine would be to see her father when she entered the church and to have him walk with her down the aisle, even if the man did have to leave Court immediately after with Edward as his escort.

Edward tapped Grey on the shoulder. "You can quit fidgeting now. Your bride's here."

The first person Madelaine saw when she entered the church was her father. He stood by the door, his hair freshly cut, clothes pressed to perfection, but dark shadows under his eyes. "Father!" Her voice caught in her throat, and she dashed at the tears streaming down her face.

He embraced her and pressed a kiss to her head. "I'm sorry," he whispered. "I should have never asked for your help. I set you an impossible task against formidable opponents."

"Do you regret the choice you made?"

"I made it out of love for the king and England, but I fear I was wrong, that I went about trying to protect the king in the wrong way. I was angry, confused and desperate, but none of it excuses my betrayal. I've sat in the grime, and I've realized my betrayal of the king was worse than anything I blamed on him."

His voice broke on the last word and dropped even lower. "I cannot change what I've done, and I've been thrown from Court, but I've been told by Lord Grey, I'll keep my life and my properties. If you can find it in your heart to forgive me, I beg you to try."

"I do forgive you." She kissed his cheek and then his hands. "And I need to ask forgiveness of you."

His eyebrows furrowed together. "For what?"

"For refusing to be a dutiful daughter. For putting strife between you and Mother when there was already so much tension between you. I cannot change that I took her from you." Madelaine's throat clenched on admitting aloud her greatest shame.

"You didn't take her."

"Your last fight was over me, was it not?"

"No, my dear, it was not. Our last fight was over my own flaws and desires."

"I think I may know something of what you speak," Madelaine said.

Her father's eyes rounded in surprise. "If you do, then surely you understand now why your mother was angry so often. It was anger toward me. Not you. Unfortunately, she took it out on you. But she did love you. And she would have wanted you to be happy. You are sure Lord Grey will make you happy?"

"I'm sure."

"Do you really know him?"

Madelaine met her father's seeking gaze. "He's told me everything. I know about the circle."

Her father's lips parted in surprise before curling in a faint smile. "Lord Grey is wise, indeed. I wish I'd only been so sage."

"He's also impatient," Madelaine gently said, aware they'd been standing here for several long minutes.

"Yes, yes. Come. Let us get you married."

She took the elbow her father proffered and walked into the main chapel. Her eyes widened at the beauty of the room. Candlelight fluttered everywhere, illuminating the tall oak choir stalls, ornately carved with fretted canopies over them. When the music commenced, Madelaine took a deep breath and walked slowly down the aisle.

A short, rotund priest stood in front of the altar with Grey and Ashford to his left. Grey turned fully toward her.

She missed a step and would have tripped, but her father gripped her arm and kept her upright. Grey looked devastatingly handsome and slightly dangerous, dressed head to toe in black, except for his snowy white linen shirt and cravat.

His breeches clung indecently to his legs and conjured memories of his hard body pressed against hers. A slight smile pulled at his lips, causing a lovely crinkle around his eyes. She trembled in response.

At the altar, her father released her and she took Grey's hand.

"Enchanting," he whispered.

"So are you." She tried to concentrate as the priest spoke, but her heart drummed against her ribs, and each time Grey rubbed his thumb over the back of her hand, she forgot to listen. Disbelieving she was actually about to be married to the man who had her whole heart, she kept looking at him until the priest cleared his throat with a pointed look at her.

As Grey repeated his vows, she listened to the words of commitment, honor and trust, understanding with a deep instinct he would never break a single oath. He slid a heavy gold band on her finger and pledged his love.

At the end of her vows, Madelaine placed Grey's wedding band on his finger before the priest pronounced them husband and wife. Grey enfolded her in his arms and he gave her a passionate kiss that ended only when cheering and clapping broke out around them. A blush heated her cheeks and neck, but she didn't care. She no longer cared about anything but loving Grey.

Madelaine was shocked to see the queen stand from the pews, all the ladies-in-waiting rising behind her. When the queen and Grace smiled at Madelaine at the same time, all she could do was stare in wonder. Grey pressed his lips close to her ear. "Aunt Helen spoke with the queen and was able to convince her of the error of her ways in her treatment of you. And as you know, the ladies-in-waiting follow the queen's lead."

Madelaine didn't have time to do more than nod at the astonishing revelations before the queen was before her. "Congratulations." She extended her hand for Madelaine and Grey to kiss. "I would like to offer you a wedding gift. I had one of my personal chambers made into a wedding chamber for you."

That was likely as close to an apology as Madelaine would ever receive. "Thank you, Your Majesty. I hope we can return such a generous offer someday."

"There is no need." The queen beamed. "Go and enjoy being young, healthy and in love. I took it upon myself to have all your belongings transferred into the bedchamber. So off with you both." The queen waved them away.

"Slow down." Madelaine giggled as Grey nearly ran with her down the aisle and scooped her up to deposit her into the carriage. He clambered in and gave a clipped order to go.

She looked out the window with a grin at the frowning guests filing out of the chapel with rice bags in hand, and then she turned her gaze to her husband. "That was unpardonably rude of us."

He yanked off his cravat with one hand while he grasped her arm with his other and pulled her nearer to him. His powerful thigh brushed her, and his masculine scent surrounded her. He licked his lips, his eyes sparkling. "I'll tell the coachman to turn around and head back to the chapel, if you wish it."

"Don't you dare." She pressed her hand against his chest

then slid it down to rest on his leg near the top of his thigh. His muscles jerked under her touch. "All I want," she said, kissing his neck and then lower at his open collar where hair peeked from his shirt, "is to have you take me in your arms and love me forever."

"Oh, I'll take you," he promised, nipping at her ear until she moaned. "And I'll love you forever and beyond."

Grey studied Madelaine's face as they entered the bed-chamber and she took in the rich red and gold silk of the heavy bedding with the mounds of soft inviting pillows. For him it invoked images of the two of them intertwined and naked. Was it the same for her? "What do you think?"

A smile curved the corners of her mouth, and her eyes grew slumberous. "It's too wicked to say, so I shall say this—I think the king should use your aunt in future negotiations. She obviously has a talent for convincing people of things that would have never entered their mind."

He chuckled as he slid his arms around Madelaine's waist and closed the door with the toe of his shoe. "I would have liked to have seen how Helen persuaded the queen she'd been wrong while somehow managing not to rile the queen's temper."

"Me too." Madelaine leaned her head back against his chest. "That particular talent would be helpful when it comes to you."

He inhaled the scent of fresh flowers that wafted from her hair and tightened his grip around the soft curve of her waist. "I'll tell you a secret." He swept her hair off her neck and kissed the long, elegant slope. His blood went straight to his groin.

Her answer was a moan followed by a ragged, "What?"

He trailed his fingers over her collarbone, then slid them lower to rub gently over one hard nipple that strained against the material of her wedding dress before lavishing the same attention on the other. She twisted to face him, her face flushed pink with desire. When she licked her lips, his blood strummed in his ears to join the throbbing in his groin.

"What's your secret?" Her husky question made him want to forget talking, rip off all her clothes, and show her how weak with need she made him just by simply being near.

He slid his hands around her back to the exquisite curve of her delectable bottom and squeezed the inviting flesh. Her eyes rounded, but she did not lean away as he pulled her against his hard groin. "If ever you want to convince me of something, just appear naked, and I vow my temper will not be roused, no matter the request."

She cocked her head to the side, her pink tongue darting out to wet her lips once more. "That's good to know, but that may spark some interesting talk among our household staff."

"True." He massaged her bottom while enjoying watching her pupils dilate. The ache in his groin had grown painful, but he would take things slow with her tonight. He'd promised himself tonight was about pleasing her, giving all to her. "I suppose if you want to convince me of something without my temper coming to play then make sure to do it in the bedroom."

"Or lock the door of the room we're in." She grinned wickedly. "I believe I would start like this." Her hand slid down his chest, leaving gooseflesh in its wake, coming to rest on his shaft. She squeezed with slight pressure that tore a ragged groan from his throat.

"God, I crave you." He swooped one arm beneath her legs and picked her up. A growl escaped his lips as her soft body pushed harder against his aching staff. When she touched his face with her fingertips, a shudder coursed through him.

She pressed a velvet kiss against his lips. "I crave you too."

That was all the invitation he needed. His mouth came down upon hers, the fierceness of his need to be inside his wife stunning him. She met each stroke of his tongue with her own as her hands slid up to his neck and delved into his hair. When her nails raked over his scalp, desire shot from his head, down his body and propelled him toward the bed. He set her on the edge and kneeled in front of her. His hands shook with need as he attempted to undue the rows of buttons that fastened her dress. "Damnation," he swore, frustrated with all the fasteners.

"Let me." Her strained voice revealed the urgency she felt.

Coming to her knees, she unhooked her dress, and as she worked, he kissed her neck, massaging the tender skin with his lips until she moaned low. The shimmering material slid off her shoulders, down her arms and fell at her knees. He laid her back gently and ran his fingers up the smooth skin of her legs before bringing his hands back down again and slipping the dress off her feet to deposit it in a heap on the floor.

With nothing covering her but her stays, which thrust her breasts upward, she lay before him. "Beautiful temptress." He glided a finger down her taut belly, her sharp intake of breath music to fuel his desire. "You're flawless. Amazing."

"You're rather amazing yourself, but entirely too clothed," she said with breathiness.

"Let me remedy that immediately." He shed his clothes and came down to trail kisses on her creamy flesh. Her body strained toward his mouth, and when he pressed his lips to her chest her heart pounded against his lips. "You're mine," he vowed, unlacing the stays, which bound her breasts. When they thrust forward with the release of the garment, he brought his mouth over her inviting, rosy nipple and suckled for a moment before flicking his tongue back and forth.

Desire struck him like a merciless wave, but he refused to give in to his own need before he had brought her pleasure. She moaned then clenched his hair in her fists. He wanted nothing more than to part her milky thighs and thrust himself into her repeatedly, but he clenched his teeth and bent to slowly remove her silk stockings and ribbon garters. He rolled the material of her stockings down her long legs then trailed his tongue over her skin. "You have the most beautiful legs."

"And you have the most beautiful mouth."

He slipped his hands onto her thighs, spread them wide, and lowered himself between them. "Let me show you exactly what I can do with my mouth."

"Hmm?" was her dazed reply.

In answer, he touched his tongue to the most sensitive part of her body and licked, slowly and deliberately.

Madelaine's eyes flew wide open, and even as jolts of unspeakable pleasure vibrated from her center to every part of her body, her hands tugged at Grey's hair in a desperate attempt to get him to raise his head. When he finally relented in his mind-numbing assault of her flesh, he rose up and met her gaze.

"This cannot be decent." She attempted to scoot back from him, but his fingers under her bottom held her in place.

"Probably not." He lowered his mouth to the soft flesh between her thighs again.

A thousand sparks arched her entire body as his tongue circled her flesh repeatedly. Heat jolted through her. She no longer cared if it was decent. All she cared about was drawing his mouth closer to her. With that thought, she thrust her hips upward, toward his tongue which moved faster, circling relentlessly until a sharp yearning pulsated within her. "Oh, my God," she moaned and dug her nails into his back. "Please."

His tongue flicked, and sucked, pulled and circled. She bucked, consumed by fiery heat and desire. Her belly clenched, then deep within her all her muscles clenched as she rode with the spasms and drowned in the waves of pleasure that followed.

Yet, even then, her desire was not sated. "Take me now," she demanded, not caring how she sounded.

Grey didn't hesitate. He rose and plunged deep within her, filling her, with his hard, throbbing shaft that promised to be the answer to her greatest need. She wrapped her legs around his sides as he slid slowly in and out, his pace increasing while the tide within her built once again. Her mind spun as he whispered, "Hold on to me."

Circling her arms around his back she clung to him, until she could not hold back any longer and pushed her hips upward to meet him as he thrust deep within her once again. Tremor after tremor racked her body, leaving her floating, spent, and breathless. Yet, Grey was not done. A thrill coursed through her as he slid her legs over his shoulders, his body glistening with sweat, the muscles of his arms straining with his effort. He delved into her hard and fast. Madelaine welcomed every thrust. She rose with him in wild pleasure once again as his own release found him and took him over the edge then dropped him down to her where he rolled off of her and brought her with him to lay against his side.

One of his arms draped around her shoulder, while his other hand came to her hair and stroked it. Their heavy breathing filled the room, slowly growing into the barest hiss. Grey's hand stilled and then came to her chin. He turned her to look at him. "Feel free to come to me at any time no matter who I'm with if you want to try to persuade me of something without riling my temper. I vow to drop everything for you."

Madelaine's answer was a sleepy, sated chuckle.

The next day before departing for their new home where Madelaine would settle in while Grey was on his mission, they decided to take one last ride around the castle grounds. As they neared the lake, Madelaine pulled up on her reins. "I do believe Constance is having another rendezvous," she said, watching as the maid adjusted her cape, tidied her hair and then started trudging in their general direction.

"Do you want to go back the way we came, so we don't embarrass her?" Grey asked.

Madelaine smiled at her husband's consideration, but kept her gaze trained on the cave. "I don't think it's necessary. Whoever she was with is not following her."

"Maybe the man already departed." Amusement laced Grey's tone.

"Likely. Go ahead for the castle. I never got the chance to thank Constance for helping me, so I could see my father."

"I'll not leave you alone anywhere until I know who helped Sutton get his information."

Madelaine scowled, though secretly pleased Grey was protective of her. "All right. Wait around the bend where you can see us, but we cannot see you. That way I can thank Constance, without making her worried that someone else knows she helped me to leave the castle, besides she and I."

"Agreed." Grey kissed her on the cheek and rode toward the turn in the path.

Some minutes later, Constance crested the hill and Madelaine rode toward her, waving. "Constance!"

The maid's face drained of color and the small pouch she held in her hands slipped to the ground.

Madelaine frowned as she scrambled from her horse and strode toward Constance. Was it embarrassment or something else that held the woman still as a stone? Maybe the man she'd met was still in the cave after all. Madelaine scooped up the pouch and held it toward the maid. "You dropped this." The pouch held coins if the weight and noise were any indication.

Constance did not reach for her money. "You're alive."

The whispered words, reverberating with accusation, sent tendrils of fear racing down Madelaine's spine. She shuffled backwards, her gaze darting to the bend in the road where Grey awaited. Blast! Her dagger was by her bedside. She forced a smile. "Of course. Did you think otherwise?"

The maid blinked as if a trance had been lifted. A shaky

smile pulled at her lips. "I was worried for you when you never returned from seeing your father."

The hair on the back of Madelaine's neck stood on end. She'd never told Constance that she was going to see her father. She'd just offered money for the maid's clothes and help and let Constance assume a lover was waiting for her. Madelaine stepped back again, but this time Constance moved forward, her lips pressing together and her hand darting down toward her boot.

Madelaine lunged past her, but Constance caught her by the arm, whirled her around, slapped a hand over her mouth and pressed the sharp point of her dagger into Madelaine's neck. "That was a stupid slip of the tongue," Constance said.

Madelaine didn't dare move. The point of the blade was digging into her pulsing vein.

"Can't say I'm sorry for it, though. If you're alive, it means Sutton is dead, and my lord had promised to take me and my siblings away from here once you and your man were dead. Lord Sutton was nothing to look at, but he was generous and put food in my baby brother's and sister's bellies. I would have been a proper lady married to him."

Madelaine scanned the path for Grey, but it was empty. Cold sweat broke out on her skin, and her stomach rolled. After everything to die here, with Grey so near yet too far to help her. Her heartbeat roared in her ears. "Goodbye, Lady Madelaine."

The words pushed Madelaine into a frenzy. She bit down on Constance's hand while reaching for the dagger and tugging the hilt. The blade scraped across her neck as she struggled with Constance, but with a scream of fury, she ripped the blade out of the maid's hands and swung Constance around while pushing the dagger's tip into the woman's back. "If you move, I'll plunge this dagger through your back and pierce your heart. You'll die instantly. Understand?"

"Yes," Constance replied, her tone stiff.

From behind Madelaine, hooves pounded down the path, and her name was a ferocious cry that filled the air. Grey was beside her before she could question Constance. He dropped down from his horse, pistol in hand and pointed at Constance's back. He brushed Madelaine's neck where blood trickled down. "Are you all right?"

"A small cut," Madelaine replied, her voice steady but her legs trembling with relief that she would live another day to be Grey's wife. "Darling?"

"Yes, dearest," Grey replied as if it were every day the two of them stood with dagger and pistol in hand and an enemy before them.

A high keening came from Constance, her hand's clenching at her sides.

"I've discovered who helped Sutton," Madelaine said, over Constance's loud noise.

"Indeed," Grey replied. "I cannot believe I ever thought you a weakness to avoid."

Madelaine flashed a loving smile at her husband. "You've much to learn about me, Lord Drivel."

Epilogue

Three months later

Madelaine made her way through the sunny halls of her home, humming as she strolled. She came to stand in front of Grey's closed study door, a smile pulling at her lips and a hand resting for a brief moment on her belly. Anticipation swelled within her, but as angry voices rose on the other side of the door, she frowned. Then, as she had been doing for years, she pressed her ear to the door.

Geraldine, the housekeeper, came around the corner with a silver tray in hand, her eyes widening when she saw Madelaine. Madelaine suppressed a giggle and held her hand toward Geraldine. "Give me the tray."

"My lady?"

"The tray," Madelaine said impatiently. "I'll take it in to my husband." It was the perfect excuse to interrupt him.

"But, my lady," Geraldine started to protest. Madelaine patted the elderly woman. "It's perfectly fine. He knows I have a mind of my own. He won't hold you responsible. Now, give me the tray."

Geraldine's eyebrows furrowed, but she handed over the tray and with a shake of her head, and murmuring, scurried down the hall.

Madelaine opened the door and swept into the study. Grey and Gravenhurst faced each other with stormy looks.

Her heart gave a little lurch. Was this about a mission? The timing would be awful, but she refused to let anything dampen her spirits. "Good afternoon, my dear." She set the tray on the side table and went to stand by Grey.

"Lord Gravenhurst, to what do we owe this pleasure? A mission?"

Lord Gravenhurst's gaze flicked to Grey and back to her. The man was disconcerting as always. "Not exactly," he said, pulling at his cravat.

Madelaine frowned. She'd never seen Lord Gravenhurst uncomfortable or at a loss for words. What in the world could be the matter? Something grave surely, or a matter of the heart. "Is it a lady?"

His throat clearing and him shifting from foot to foot told her she'd hit her target, though she'd shot the arrow blindly. "I see. Anyone I know?"

The guttural throat sounds coming from Grey surprised her.

"Who is it?" she demanded.

"Madelaine." Grey's one word warned of his raised temper. Whoever this conversation was about, Grey was not happy. Madelaine's curiosity was definitely piqued, but right now she had much more important things on her mind. She shelved the mystery.

"Grey, I need to speak with you in private for a few minutes." Would a few minutes be enough? Well, if they hurried, though, Grey was not one to hurry, which she adored.

"Now?" His eyebrows shot upward.

"Yes, please." She slipped her hand through his arm. "In the bedroom."

His eyes widened at her pronouncement, and the frown that had tugged at his lips turned into a smile. "Gravenhurst, I'll be back shortly."

Grey glanced at Madelaine, and she shook her head. He led her toward the door and called over his shoulder, "Make that in a little while."

Madelaine had to double her footsteps to keep up with Grey as he raced them up the stairs and to their bedroom. He shut the door and faced her. "What is it you need, my dear? I'm all ears and ready to be convinced."

Grey's voice was thick with desire that Madelaine's body instantly responded to. But her desire would have to wait for a minute. "I'm getting fat."

"What?" Grey looked confused. "Is this a woman's worry? You're perfect."

"Hmm..." She licked her lips. "I've gained some weight." Her heart thudded heavily in her ears.

Grey brushed his hand down her arm. "You are more beautiful than ever. Where have you gained weight? I don't see it."

She took his warm hand and placed it on her belly. "Here, my darling. I've gained weight here. And soon, you will see it when the baby really starts to grow."

"Truly?" He placed his hand on her belly, his fingers curling ever so slightly.

Warm tingles of happiness danced through her body.

"Truly, dearest. You are going to be a father."

"I don't think I can get any happier," Grey said.

Madelaine grasped his lapels and tugged him closer. "I'm sure I can make you happier."

He regarded her curiously.

"What is it, dearest?" She squeezed his hand to encourage him to tell her.

"When I was young I sought to feel loved, and then I sought to avoid it when I grew older. When I least expected love, there you were, the answer to what I didn't even realize I was still searching for. Thank you for your love and our precious child." He leaned down and gave her a kiss that curled her toes and made her feel at once desired, protected and cherished.

Dear Readers,

I hope you enjoyed the book. I invite you to leave a review for it, and to try the first chapter of My Fair Duchess, A Once Upon a Rogue novel, Book 1.

Prologue

The Year of Our Lord 1795
St. Ives, Cambridgeshire, England

The day Colin Sinclair, the Marquess of Nortingham and the future Duke of Aversley, entered the world, he brought nothing but havoc with him.

The Duchess of Aversley's birthing screams filled Waverly House, accompanied by the relentless pattering of rain that beat against the large glass window of Alexander Sinclair's study. The current Duke of Aversley gripped the edge of his desk, the wood digging into his palms. He did not know how much more he could take or how much longer he could acquiesce to his wife's refusal of his request to be present in the birthing room. He knew his wish was unusual and that she feared what he saw would dampen his desire for her, but nothing would ever do that.

Camilla's hoarse voice sliced through the silence again and fed the festering fear that filled him. She might die from this.

The possibility made him tremble. Why hadn't he controlled his lust? After six failed attempts to give him a child, Camilla's body was weak. He'd known the truth but had chosen to ignore it. Moisture dampened his silk shirt, and Camilla screeched once more. He shook his head, trying to ward off the sound.

He reached across his desk, and with a pounding heart and trembling hand, he slid the crystal decanter toward him. If he did not do something to calm his nerves, he would bolt straight out of this room and barge into their bedchamber. The last thing he wanted to do was cause Camilla undue anxiety. The Scotch lapped over the edge of the tumbler as he poured it, dripping small droplets of liquor on the contracts he had been blindly staring at for the last four hours.

He did not make a move to rescue the papers as the ink blurred. He did not give a goddamn about the papers. All he cared about was Camilla. The physician's previous words of warning that the duchess should not try for an heir again played repeatedly through Alexander's mind. The words grew in volume as the storm raged outside and his wife's shrieks tore through the mansion.

Alexander could have lived a thousand lifetimes without an heir, but he was a weak fool. He craved Camilla, body and soul. His desire, along with his pompous certainty that everything would eventually turn out all right for them because he was the duke, had caused him to ignore the physician and eagerly yield to his wife's fervent wish to have a child.

As Camilla's high, keening wails vibrated the air around him, he gripped his glass a fraction harder. The crystal cracked, cutting his hand with razor-like precision. He yanked off his cravat and wrapped it around his bleeding hand. Lightning split the shadows in the room with bright, blinding light, followed by his study door crashing open and Camilla's sister, Jane, flying through the entrance. Her red hair streamed out behind her, tears running down her face.

"The physician says come now. Camilla's—" Jane's voice cracked. She dashed a hand across her wet cheeks and moved across the room and around the desk to stand behind his chair. She placed a hand on his shoulder. "Camilla is dying. The doctor needs you to tell him whether to try to save her or the baby."

Pain, the likes of which the duke had never experienced, sliced through his chest and curled in his belly. A fierce cramp immediately seized him. "What sort of choice is that?" he cried as he stood.

Jane nodded sympathetically, then simply turned and motioned him to follow her. With effort, he forced his numb legs to move up the stairs toward his wife's moans. With every step, his heartbeat increased until he was certain it would pound out of his chest. He could not live without her, yet he knew she would not want to live without the babe. If he told the doctor to save her over their child, she would hate him, and misery would continue to plague her and chafe as it had done every time she had lost a babe these past six years.

He could not cause her such pain, but he could not pick the child over her. Outside the bedchamber door, Jane paused and turned to him, her face splotchy. "What are you going to do? I must know to prepare myself."

Alexander had never been a praying man, despite the fact that his mother had been a devout believer and had tried to get him to be one, as well. His father and grandfather had always said Aversley dukes made their own fates and only weak men looked to a higher power to grant them favors and exceptions. Alexander stiffened. He was a stupid fool who had thought himself more powerful than God. The day his mother had died, she had told him that one day, he would have to pay for this sin.

Was today the day? Alexander drew in a long, shuddering breath, mind racing. What could he do? He would renounce every conviction he held dear to keep his wife and child.

Squeezing his eyes shut, he made a vow to God. If He would save Camilla and the babe, he would pray every day and seek God's wisdom in all things. Surely, this penance would suffice.

A blood-curdling scream split the silence. Alexander's heart exploded as he shoved past Jane and threw the door open. The cream-colored sheets of their bed, now soaked crimson, lay scattered on the dark hardwood floor. Camilla, appearing incredibly small, twisted and whimpered in the center of the gigantic four-poster. Her once-white lacy gown was bunched at her waist to expose her slender legs, and Alexander winced at the blood smeared across her normally olive skin.

Moving toward her, his world tilted. His wife, his Camilla, stared at him with glazed eyes and cracked lips. A deathly pallor had replaced the healthy flush her face usually held. Blue veins pulsed along the base of her neck, giving her skin a thin, papery appearance. The sour stench of death filled the heavy air.

Only seconds had passed, yet it seemed like much longer. The physician swung toward Alexander. He appeared aged since coming through the door hours before; deep lines marked his forehead, the sides of his eyes, and around his mouth. Normally an impeccably kept man, his hair dangled over his right eye, and his shirt, stained dark red, hung out from his trousers. Shoving his hair out of his eye, the physician asked, "Who do you want me to try to save, Your Grace?"

Alexander curled his hands into fists by his sides, hissing at the throbbing pain the movement caused his cut palm. His mother's last words echoed in his head: *Great sins require great penance.*

The duke glanced at his wife's face, then slowly slid his gaze to her swollen belly. "Both of them," he responded. Fresh sweat broke out across his forehead as the doctor shook his head.

"The babe is twisted the wrong way. Even if I can get it out, Her Grace will be ripped beyond repair. She'll likely bleed out."

Anger coursed through Alexander's veins. "Both of them," he repeated, his voice shaking.

"If she lives, I'm certain she'll be barren. You are sure?"

"Positive," he snapped, seized by a wave of nausea and a certainty that he had failed to give up enough to save them both. Rushing to Camilla's side, he kneeled and gripped her hand as her back formed a perfect arch and another cry broke past her lips—the loudest scream yet.

Alexander closed his eyes and fervently vowed to God never to touch his wife again if only she and his babe would be allowed to live. He would do this and would keep his sacrifice between God and himself for as long as he drew breath and never tell a living soul of his penance. This time he would heed his mother's warnings. Her threadbare voice filled his head as he murmured her words. "True atonement is between the sinner and God or else it is not true, and the day of reckoning will come more terrible and shattering than imaginable."

Alexander repeated the oath, coldness gripping him and

burrowing into his bones.

Moments later, his throat burned, and he could not stop the tears of happiness and relief that rolled down his face as he cradled his healthy son in his arms.

Then in a faint but happy voice Camilla called out to him. "Alex, come to me," Camilla murmured, gazing at him with shining eyes and raising a willowy arm to beckon him. He froze where he stood and curled his fingers tighter around his swaddled son, desperate to hold on to the joy of seconds ago, and yet the elation slipped away when realizing the promise he had made to God.

That vow had saved his wife and child. As much as he wanted to tell Camilla of it now, as her forehead wrinkled and uncertainty filled her eyes, fear stilled his tongue. What if he told her, and then she died? Or the babe died?

"You've done well, Camilla," he said in a cool tone. The words felt ripped from his gut. Inside, he throbbed, raw and broken.

He handed the babe to Jane and then turned on his heel and quit the room. At the stairs, he gripped the banister for support as he summoned the butler and gave the orders to remove his belongings from the bedchamber he had shared with Camilla since the day they had married.

As he feared, as soon as Camilla was able to, she came to him, desperate and pleading for explanations. Her words seared his heart and branded him with misery. He trembled every time he sent her away from him, and her broken-hearted sobs rang through the halls. The pain that stole her smile and the gleam that had once filled her eyes made him fear for her and for them, but the dreams that dogged him of her death or their son's death should the vow be broken frightened him more. Sleeplessness plagued him, and he took to creeping into his son's nursery, where he would send the nanny away and rock his boy until the wee hours of the morning, pouring all his love into his child.

Days slid into months that turned to the first year and then the second. As his bond with Camilla weakened, his tie to his heir strengthened. Laughter filled Waverly House, but it was only the child's laughter and Alexander's. It seemed to him, the closer he became to his child and the more attention he lavished on him, the larger the wall became between him and Camilla until she reminded him of an angry queen reigning in her mountainous tower of ice. Yet, it was his fault she was there with no hope of rescue.

The night she quit coming to his bedchamber, Alexander thanked God and prayed she would now turn the love he knew was in her to their son, whom she seemed to blame for Alexander's abandonment. He awoke in the morning, and when the nanny brought Colin to Alexander, he decided to carry his son with him to break his fast, in hopes that Camilla would want to hold him. As he entered the room with Colin, she did not smile. Her lips thinned with obvious anger as she excused herself, and he was caught between the wish to cry and the urge to rage at her.

Still, his fingers burned to hold her hand and itched to caress the gentle slope of her cheekbone. Eventually, his skin became cold. His fingers curiously numb. Then one day, sitting across from him at dinner in the silent dining room, Camilla looked at him and he recoiled at the sharp thorns of revenge shining in her eyes.

The following week the Season began, and he dutifully escorted her to the first ball. Knots of tension made his shoulders ache as they walked down the staircase, side by side, so close yet a thousand ballrooms apart. After they were announced, she turned to him and he prepared himself to decline her request to dance.

She raised one eyebrow, her lips curling into a thinly veiled smile of contempt. "Quit cringing, Alexander. You may go to the card room. My dances are all taken, I assure you."

Within moments, she twirled onto the dance floor, first with one gentleman and then another and another until the night faded near to morning. Alexander stood in the shadows, leaning against a column and never moving, aware of the curious looks people cast his way. He was helplessly sure his wife was trying to hurt him, and he silently started to pray she would finally turn all her wrath at how he had changed to him and begin to love the child she had longed for...and for whom she had almost died.

Series by Julie Johnstone

Scottish Medieval Romance Books:

Highlanders Through Time Series
Sinful Scot, Book 1
Sexy Scot, Book 2
Seductive Scot, Book 3
Scandalous Scot, Book 4

Highlander Vows: Entangled Hearts Series
When a Laird Loves a Lady, Book 1
Wicked Highland Wishes, Book 2
Christmas in the Scot's Arms, Book 3
When a Highlander Loses His Heart, Book 4
How a Scot Surrenders to a Lady, Book 5
When a Warrior Woos a Lass, Book 6
When a Scot Gives His Heart, Book 7
When a Highlander Weds a Hellion, Book 8
How to Heal a Highland Heart, Book 9
The Heart of a Highlander, Book 10

Renegade Scots Series
Outlaw King, Book 1
Highland Defender, Book 2
Highland Avenger, Book 3

Regency Romance Books:

A Whisper of Scandal Series
Bargaining with a Rake, Book 1
Conspiring with a Rogue, Book 2

Keep In Touch

Get Julie Johnstone's Newsletter
juliejohnstoneauthor.com

Join her Reading Group
facebook.com/groups/1500294650186536

Like her Facebook Page
facebook.com/authorjuliejohnstone

Stalk her Instagram
instagram.com/authorjuliejohnstone

Hang out with her on Goodreads
goodreads.com/author/show/2354638.Julie_Johnstone

Hear about her sales via Bookbub
bookbub.com/authors/julie-johnstone

Follow her Amazon Page
amazon.com/Julie-Johnstone/e/B0062AW98S

About the Author

Julie Johnstone is a *USA Today* and #1 Amazon bestselling author. Scottish historical romance, Regency historical romance, and historical time travel romance featuring highlanders, aristocrats, and modern-day bad billionaire bad boys are her love, and she enjoys creating both with a hefty dose of twists, plenty of heartstring tugs, and a guaranteed happily ever after.

Her books have been dubbed "fabulously entertaining and engaging," making readers cry, laugh, and swoon. Johnstone lives in Alabama with her very own lowlander husband, her two children – the heir and the spare, her snobby cat, and her perpetually happy dog.

In her spare time she enjoys way too much coffee balanced by hot yoga, reading, and traveling.

www.ingramcontent.com/pod-product-compliance
Lightning Source LLC
Chambersburg PA
CBHW030248270626
47156CB00021B/199